The Summer
of Everything

The Summer of Everything

Picture Perfect

Wish You Were Here

CATHERINE CLARK

HARPER TEEN

An Imprint of HarperCollinsPublishers

HarperTeen is an imprint of HarperCollins Publishers.

The Summer of Everything
Copyright © 2016 by Catherine Clark
All rights reserved. Printed in the United States of America.
No part of this book may be used or reproduced in any manner whatsoever without
written permission except in the case of brief quotations embodied in critical
articles and reviews. For information address HarperCollins Children's Books, a
division of HarperCollins Publishers, 195 Broadway, New York, NY 10007.
www.epicreads.com

ISBN 978-0-06-235922-3

Typography by Ray Shappell
16 17 18 19 20   CG/RRDH   10 9 8 7 6 5 4 3 2 1

❖

Originally published separately as *Picture Perfect* and *Wish You Were Here*
First Edition, 2016

Contents

Picture Perfect

Chapter 1

"I can't wait to see all the guys."

You might have thought that was me talking, as I headed into the town of Kill Devil Hills, North Carolina, my destination for a two-week summer stay on the Outer Banks.

But no. It was my dad, of all people.

And it's not what you might be thinking *now*, either. He was talking about seeing his best friends from college.

We meet up every few years on a big reunion trip with "the guys," their wives, their kids, and other assorted members of their families—dogs, parents, random cousins, nannies, you name it. I think it's Dad's favorite vacation, because he and his buddies play golf, sit around reminiscing, and stay up late talking every night.

Even though that occasionally gets a little boring, I like going on these trips, because I've gotten to be friends with "the guys'" offspring, who have sprung off like me: Heather Olsen, Adam Thompson, and Spencer Flanagan. I couldn't wait to see all of them.

It had been two years since the last vacation reunion for the four of us, which was *almost*, but not quite, long enough to make me forget what an idiot I'd made of myself the last time, when I was fifteen, Spencer had been sixteen, and I'd told him that I thought he was really cool and that we really clicked and that I wished we lived closer because then we could . . . well, you get the gist. *Embarrassing.* With a capital *E*. Maybe three of them, in fact. EEEmbarrassing. Like an extra-wide foot that I'd stuck in my mouth.

But enough about me and my slipup. I basically love these trips because we end up in cool locations like this, a place I'd never seen, or even gotten close to seeing, before now.

Living in the Midwest, we don't get to the coast much. And this was even beyond the coast—if that's possible—on a strip of land that was as far as you could get without becoming an island. Or maybe it was an island. What do I know? We live in "fly-over land." On the plus side, we don't have earthquakes, hurricanes, or tropical storms. On the minus side, we have the occasional nearby tornado and no ocean access.

"This is just *beautiful*," Mom said as we turned off the main four-lane road, and onto a smaller road with giant three- and four-story beach houses on each side of it. "Isn't it, Emily?"

"Those houses are gigantic. Is that where we're staying? In one of those?" I asked.

"Yup. Remember the pictures we checked out online?" Dad asked from the front seat of our rental car. We'd flown into Norfolk, Virginia, and driven south from there.

"Not really," I said. I hadn't paid all that much attention, to be honest. I was too busy finishing up my senior year, getting my college plans set, figuring out how to squeeze a two-week vacation into a summer in which I needed to make as much money as possible.

In July and August, I'd be back home working at Constant Camera full-time, saving money for textbooks and anything else I might need when I got to college. Fortunately, I'd received a few gifts for my graduation that would help out a lot—gift cards, as well as supplies for my hopefully budding career in photography. I planned to take lots of pictures while on this vacation and turn them into something I could give everyone at the end of the two weeks—a calendar. I'd left my new Mac at home because of the hassle of traveling with it—Mom was afraid it would get I-Jacked—and I'd brought my inexpensive camera instead of my digital SLR, so I wasn't working with my usual stuff. But I was still confident I could get plenty of good pictures—after all, it's not necessarily always the equipment, it's whether you have an eye for it or not.

We were getting close to the house number we were looking for when Dad stopped the car as two college-age-looking guys stepped out to cross the street. They had beach towels slung around their necks and bare chests with nice abs, and wore low-riding surf shorts. One of them carried a Frisbee, while another had a volleyball tucked under his arm.

I sat up in the backseat, wondering if that was Adam and Spencer. But no, upon closer inspection, one of them had short, nearly platinum-blond hair, and the other's was brown, shoulder-length—not at all like Spencer and Adam.

Which wasn't a bad thing, because I was looking forward to seeing what guys might be around, too. And I *didn't* mean Dad's college buddies or their sons.

While we were stopped, the guy carrying the volleyball leaned down and peered into the car—I guess he'd caught me staring at him. He smiled at me, then waved with a casual salute.

I smiled and waved back to him. I wanted to take a lot of pictures, so why not start now? I buzzed the window down. "Hold on a second, okay?" I asked. I grabbed my slim, shiny green camera from my bag, and took some quick shots as they played along, grinning and flexing their muscles, showing off a couple of tattoos.

"Emily." My mother peered back at me over the front seat. "What are you doing?"

"Capturing the local flavor," I said as a car behind us honked its horn, and the guys hustled across the street so we could get moving again. "Just trying to blend in with that whole Southern hospitality thing."

"Hmph," my mother said, while my dad laughed.

I turned around and looked out the back window at the guys, wondering if we'd be staying anywhere close by, when Mom shrieked, "Look! There's the house!"

My dad slammed on the brakes, which screeched like the sound of a hundred wailing—and possibly ill—seals. Dad has this awful habit of calling Rent-a-Rustbucket in order to save money. Consequently, we end up driving broken-down automobiles whenever we go on vacation.

Dad backed up and turned into a small parking lot behind the tall, skinny house. I immediately recognized all the *L* bumper stickers and Linden College window-clings on the cars in the lot.

"Look!" Mom pointed at a Linden College banner that was hanging off the third-floor balcony, flapping in the breeze. There was a giant green, leafy linden tree on the dark blue banner background, and in the center, a heart-shaped leaf with a giant *L* in the middle.

Sometimes my dad's Linden school pride got a little ridiculous—for instance, he couldn't possibly get dressed in the morning (at least on weekends and vacations) without donning some piece of Linden College apparel, and he owns about fourteen different ball caps, some faded and tattered and some brand-new—but since I'd actually be going off to school there in the fall, it was kind of a nice feeling to see the banner.

Dad parked the car with a screech of the brakes and we started to climb out. I closed the door, and I swear a piece of the car fell off onto the pavement.

There was a second or two where I was dreading the inevitable hugging and screaming that went along with greeting everyone. Then the back door opened, I saw Adam's dad, and the feeling was over.

"Jay, you could have at least rented a decent car for once in your life," Mr. Thompson said.

"Why change now?" my dad replied as he clapped him on the back.

"Once a cheapskate, always a cheapskate, huh, Emily?" Mr. Thompson gave me a little shoulder hug.

"Don't get me started," I mumbled, looking up at him with a smile.

"Adam just took off on a run down the beach," Mr. Thompson said. "Heather and her mom are off shopping somewhere. I know Adam is psyched to see you."

"Cool." I grinned. Although I hadn't seen Adam for two years, we'd always gotten along pretty well—I figured we still would. Even if we didn't stay in touch very often, we'd known each other so long that it was kind of like being cousins.

Just then the door opened again and Adam's stepmom and his two younger half brothers charged outside. In another minute, it was total chaos, with everyone yelling, hugging, and talking all at once.

Of course, they were talking about how middle-aged and out of shape they'd all gotten, and how many vacation days they got, and whether there was enough beer for the night. What was next? Medicare? Retirement plans?

I had to figure out where the people my actual age had hidden themselves.

As they say on *Grey's Anatomy*: *"Stat."*

Ten minutes later, after dumping my suitcase in my room, I stood on the giant back deck, overlooking the ocean. There were houses up and down the beach, all looking pretty similar. On one side of us there seemed to be a large, extended family, complete with lots of young kids, grandparents, and about a dozen beach balls and other water toys floating in their pool.

The house on the other side of us had beach towels lined up on the deck railing, flapping in the warm breeze, and a couple of lacrosse sticks, a random collection of Frisbees, and badminton racquets strewn on the deck, along with a cooler and some empty cans of Red Bull and bottles of sports drink. Something about it screamed "young guys" to me, which seemed promising, but maybe I was just being overly hopeful—or naive. Maybe it was actually screaming "old guys who don't recycle."

Down by the ocean, some kids were playing in the sand, building sand castles and moats, while others swam and tried to ride waves on boogie boards.

"I've made a list of top ten Outer Banks destinations. I read eight different guidebooks and compiled my own list," my mom was explaining to Mrs. Thompson when I walked over to them. "We'll need to go food shopping tonight, of course, and make a schedule for who cooks which night."

"Oh, relax, you can do the shopping tomorrow. Things are very casual around here," Mrs. Thompson said to her. "Dinner's already on the grill, put your feet up." She turned to me. "You should go say hi to Adam. He's down there, in the water."

"He is?"

She gestured for me to join her at the edge of the deck. "He's right there. Don't you see him?"

All I could see except for young kids was a man with large shoulders doing the crawl, his arms powerfully slicing through the water. "That?" I coughed. "That person is Adam?"

His stepmom nodded. "Of course."

Wow. Really? I wanted to say. When I focused on him again, as he strode out of the surf, I nearly dropped my camera over the railing and into the sand. "You know what? I think I *will* go say hi." *Hi, and who are you, and what have you done with my formerly semi-wimpy friend?*

I walked down the steps to the beach in disbelief. Last time I'd seen Adam, his voice was squeaking, and he was on the scrawny side—a wrestler at one of the lower weights, like 145. Not anymore. He had muscular arms and shoulders, and he looked about a foot taller than he had two years ago. His curly brown hair was cut short.

You look different, I wanted to say, but that would be dumb. *You look different and I sound like an idiot, so really, nothing's changed.*

Why was it that whenever I tried to talk to a guy, I started speaking a completely different language? Stupidese?

"Emily?" he asked.

I nodded, noticing that his voice was slightly deeper than I remembered it. It was sort of like he'd gone into a time machine and come out in the future, whereas I felt exactly the same. "Hi."

He leaned back into the surf to wet his hair. "You look different," he said when he stood up.

"Oh, yeah? I do?" *Different how?* I wanted to ask, but that was potentially embarrassing. Different in the way he did? Like . . . sexy? I waited for him to elaborate, but he didn't. "Well, uh, you do, too," I said.

"Right." He smiled, then picked up his towel and dried his hair. As he had the towel over his head, I took the opportunity to check him out again. Man. What a difference a couple years could make. He used to wear wire-rim glasses, but now, apparently, he had contacts, like me.

There was always this really uncomfortable moment when we first tried to talk after not having seen each other for so long.

"So, how are you?" I asked, patting his shoulder, and then we sort of hugged, very awkwardly, the way you hug someone without actually touching them. Sort of like the Hollywood fake-kiss.

"All right, knock it off, you two!" a voice said.

Funny—that didn't *sound* like my mother, but who else would care if I hugged a suddenly semi-hot Adam?

Chapter 2

I turned to look at who was coming toward us, but the sun was in my eyes.

"You guys!" Heather Olsen cried. "It's *me*." She had on a pair of short shorts and a couple of layered tank tops. She ran up to us, and I gave her a big hug, squeezing her tightly.

"Yay, you're here!" I said. "I haven't seen you in forever."

"I know. Isn't it ridiculous, considering how close we live?" she replied.

I gave her another hug, because the last time we'd gotten together wasn't for a vacation—it was for her dad's memorial service nearly a year ago. We hadn't visited much that time, but we'd stayed in close touch throughout the past year with emails. Adam and Spencer hadn't come to the service, only their parents had, because they now lived pretty far away—Adam and his family lived in Oregon, while Spencer's was in Vermont. Heather and I were the ones still sort of near where everyone started out—Madison, Wisconsin, where they'd all moved and rented a house together *after* college and gone to grad school. We still lived in Madison, while Heather and her mom lived in Chicago, which was only about three hours away. Still, we were usually both so busy we didn't see each other often enough.

"What are you—" Adam asked as Heather jumped on his back, like she wanted a piggy-back ride. "I wasn't sure you were coming," he said when she dropped off his back and gave him a playful shove.

"Why wouldn't I?" Heather stared at him, hands on her hips. "No. Only kidding. I know why. But the other guys put on the major hard sell, or maybe it was a guilt trip. Anyway, Mom finally agreed. I told her I wanted to see you guys."

"I'm really glad you came," I told her. "It wouldn't be the same, you know. Without you." I felt myself tripping over my tongue. "Right, Adam?"

"Definitely." Adam looked up at a few pelicans flying past. "It wouldn't count as a reunion."

"We have traditions," I said. "You know. You and Spencer make fun of me and Heather until you run out of put-downs, then you resort to practical jokes."

"Me?" Adam turned to me, not looking amused. "No, I don't."

"You do," I said.

"It's a good thing I'm here, because Emily couldn't possibly defend herself on her own, right?" Heather said.

"What? I could too defend myself," I said. I put up my fists, which aren't all that impressive, actually, considering my arms have this certain resemblance to sticks. All the muscle tone I'd had from ballet over the years had started to fizzle, like the deflating air mattress I'd been forced to sleep on the night before at my aunt and uncle's, who live close to the airport.

"Yeah, but not *well*." Heather punched Adam lightly on the arm, which was no longer an arm but a massive bicep. She rubbed her knuckles afterward and looked up at him. "Speaking of self-defense. Work out much?"

"Yeah." He shrugged. "I just finished baseball season."

"I thought they banned steroids in baseball," Heather said.

Adam laughed, looking slightly embarrassed. "Shut up."

"Fine. You know what? I'm starved. When do we eat? I think I saw some brats on the grill."

"What else is new?" I asked, rolling my eyes. "Cheddar or beer style?"

"You can take my dad out of Wisconsin, but you can't take his bratwurst away," Adam said.

Heather started to run back up the stairs to the deck, then she stopped and looked over her shoulder. "Well, come on, guys, I'm not going to eat by myself."

"We're coming," I told her.

"I forgot how she is," Adam commented as we walked over to the stairs together, me loving the feeling of digging my toes into the soft, warm sand. "I mean, maybe it's a good thing she hasn't changed, with everything that's happened."

"How is she?" I asked.

"Like, um, a whirling dervish," Adam said. "Those things that spin around and around."

"Whirling dervish? Wow, have you been taking vocab vitamins along with your steroids?" I asked.

"Shut up." He gave me a playful—but still possibly bruising, with his strength—hip check as we headed up to the deck. "I don't take steroids, okay? I mean, I know guys who've done it and it's disgusting. So let's not talk about that anymore," Adam said in a more serious tone.

"Agreed," I said. "I didn't really think that, you know." Although it had kind of crossed my mind, because I didn't understand how he'd transformed himself. If he'd changed that much . . . what would Spencer look like? "Anyway, let's forget we ever said anything, and just eat."

"Deal." Adam picked up a paper plate and started loading it with food. I followed his lead, taking some of almost everything.

Heather and I sat next to each other on the deck. We both sat cross-legged, in a sort of yoga position. She's tiny—about five feet tall—and used to do gymnastics at the same level I danced—we were both a little obsessed. She'd always been amazingly flexible, and I was, too, so we used to spend these vacations trying to out-bend each other doing splits, back bends, handstands, and anything else we could do to be pretzel-esque. Adam and Spencer had dubbed us the tumbling twins—or maybe it was the tumbling twits. I suddenly couldn't remember.

Maybe there were some things about our last get-together that I'd purposely forgotten, like the look on Spencer's face when I'd awkwardly tried to tell him how I felt—or the look of his back, rather, when he turned away, ignoring me, as if I hadn't said anything. A person can forget a lot in two years. But that? No. And if I hadn't forgotten, I worried he hadn't, either.

Maybe the Flanagans won't come, I thought, looking around at everyone else already gathered. Maybe they decided to stay home. Maybe their car broke down and they'd decided to just can it.

Oh, relax, I told myself as I bit into a cob of buttery corn. *Spencer has moved on, and so have you. You've had tons of other guys in your life since then. Sure. There's that tech guy at the Apple store . . . and the guy at the Starbucks drive-through you flirted with—once— and . . . um . . .*

Adam sat down across from us. "What's wrong with chairs, anyway? You guys against chairs? Wait, I know. You have to stretch. Isn't that what you were always doing?"

"Before I quit gymnastics," Heather said. "Actually, I just didn't see enough chairs."

"When did you quit gymnastics?" Adam asked, sounding genuinely surprised.

"After the accident," she said. "I broke a few ribs, and . . . it hurt to breathe, never mind flip. Plus I was just ready to make some changes."

Adam nodded. "Yeah. Sorry about that. I mean . . . about everything. Must have been really hard."

There was a long pause. I looked at Adam, then at Heather, then at my plate, wishing I could say something decent that didn't sound completely clichéd.

"You know what?" Heather suddenly looked up at both of us and smiled. "We have to go out tonight."

"We do?" I asked. I hadn't pictured going out and partying as being in the cards, not with the proportion of parents to us. I mean, it was something I'd hoped to achieve, but only in a fantasy, which is the way most of my daring plans occur.

"We do. I mean, do you really want to sit around and listen to the guys all night? First they'll talk about the place where they all lived, and who never washed the dishes, and who did, and who partied the most, and what girl they tried to date but who wasn't interested in any of them—"

We all laughed, but I also couldn't help but wonder if Heather was feeling a little uncomfortable listening to all the guys reminisce, when her dad wasn't around to join in anymore. As much as hearing my dad's stories over and over again annoyed me, at least I still had the chance to listen to them.

I stood up to get a little more food and took a serving of Mrs. Olsen's famous marshmallow Jell-O salad, which she's been making for every get-together since forever and that I've been eating for about as long.

"When did your mom have time to make this?" I asked Heather, taking a bite.

"This afternoon. We got here earlier today, then went out shopping for new swimsuits," Heather explained. "There are some *amazing* shops around here. Where were you guys when we got here?" she asked Adam.

"Tim and Tyler wanted to go to an amusement park. I think we went on about twelve kiddie pirate rides."

"I can't believe they're already four," I said. "Seems like they were just born, you know?"

"Ha! Maybe to *you*," Adam said.

"I always kind of wanted siblings," I said. "Someone to take the focus off of *me*."

"I hear you," added Heather with a nod.

There was a loud knock on the fence surrounding the pool area. "Anyone here?" a deep voice called through the fence.

"No!" everyone called back at once.

"Thought so. Let's go, Spence," I heard Mr. Flanagan say.

I kind of held my breath. After Adam, I couldn't wait to see what Spencer looked like. Would he have changed that much, too? I was nervous, maybe even dreading it a little bit. What if he'd changed? What if he was even more handsome than he had been at sixteen? Or, potentially worse, even more conceited?

The gate opened—Mrs. Flanagan was towing a large suitcase, while Spencer and his dad carried a kayak over their heads, which they leaned against the fence.

"You kayaked here?" asked Mr. Thompson. "No wonder it took you so long."

"Anything to save gas money," Mrs. Flanagan answered with a smile.

Spencer was wearing an orange UVM T-shirt and long khaki shorts. He was barefoot. I suddenly remembered how he liked to go barefoot all the time, and wondered how that worked out during the winters. I rarely saw him during the winter. Maybe he had a completely different look.

"You're here!" Heather said, throwing her arms around Spencer.

Spencer stepped back with an awkward smile, escaping Heather's grasp. "Hey."

"Hey?" Heather repeated. "Is that all you're going to say?"

He looked at her and lifted his eyebrows, like he was trying to think of something better to say, but he couldn't. "Sorry about your dad," he said.

"Thanks." Heather hugged him again. "I appreciate that." She let him go and looked up at him. "But I didn't mean that." There was an awkward pause. "Well? Are you going to hug Emily or not?"

Good question, I thought. What was the etiquette for this kind of situation? It was like Heather could see that things were awkward, but I'd never told her about my dumb confession of love—or was it *like*?—to Spencer two years ago.

He gazed at me for a second, rubbing his eyes, because clearly he'd just woken up after the extremely long car trip. "Emily. That you?" he asked, scratching the side of his face, which looked a little stubbly. He was turning into a grown-up. He had actual stubble.

I laughed. "Of course it's me. Who else would it be? Hi." I punched his arm a little awkwardly, but hit it harder than I meant to, and we sort of hugged, but sort of almost toppled over at the same time.

"Ouch. You're tall," he said.

"Me? No, I'm the same height I used to be," I said, pulling a sticky strand of my hair off of my face.

"You have something in your hair," Spencer said.

"Still?" I pulled at a few more hairs, then found a clump of mini-marshmallows. I could feel myself blush as I attempted to pull them out. Fortunately, I have thickish hair—but unfortunately, it's black, so every speck of marshmallow showed. This wasn't exactly how I'd wanted my reunion with Spencer to go.

"It's the Mello Jell-O," Heather explained to him.

Spencer rubbed his forehead. "The what?"

"My mom's famous mold dessert thingy."

"Your mom serves mold?"

"No, stupid, it's a mold, as in a shape. And it has fruit and marsh-mallows in it—"

"Oh, yeah. Now I remember. Well, I guess everyone has to be famous for *some*thing."

Heather shoved him. "Are you dissing my mom?"

"No, just gelatin. So what happened? Did you dive into the bowl?" Spencer asked me.

No, I was eating it when you showed up, and I guess I got a little flustered, and my spoon ended up in my hair. "Ha-ha," I said in a deadpan tone. "It's a styling product, okay?"

"Well . . . style away," Spencer said, surveying the deck.

"Same old obnoxious Spencer," Heather muttered under her breath as Spencer left us to get a burger.

It was true that he treated us like we were little kids, even though he was only a year older than us. He usually made a big effort to remind us that he was older. Heather, Adam, and I were just *so* immature. We were like *infants*, compared to him.

The three of us sat down to finish eating dinner, and Spencer joined us. As soon as Heather tossed her paper plate into the trash can, she stood up, looked at the three of us, and said, "What are you guys waiting for? Come on, let's get out of here, go out somewhere fun."

"Go out? But I just got here," Spencer protested. "I don't even know what room I'm in, or where my stuff should go."

"We'll figure it out when we get back. You can unpack later. You've got two weeks to unpack." Heather pulled Spencer to his feet and guided him toward the deck steps.

"Technically, no, because I'll have to unpack in order to change my clothes, like tomorrow," Spencer said. "Anyway, where are we going and what's the rush?"

"I don't know. We'll find a place," said Heather confidently, looping her arm through his.

I interrupted the parents for a second to tell them that the four of us were going for a walk. They barely paused talking long enough to hear what I had to say. Dad mumbled, "That's great, honey," then went back to some story about sophomore year and a football game they lost by one point.

Just before I went to join Spencer, Heather, and Adam, I stopped and took a picture of the three of them as they pushed and shoved each other on the stairs. A lot of things had changed since we first became friends when we were little, but some things hadn't changed at all.

I was starting down the stairs when a Frisbee came sailing over the fence and nearly knocked me in the head. I reached up instinctively to shield my face and the Frisbee hit my hands and fell to the deck.

"Little help?" a guy's voice called over from next door.

"Oh. H-hi," I stammered as he got closer. I wasn't sure, but it looked like the same guy who'd said hi to me earlier in the car—the one with the short, platinum-blond hair.

"Did I see you earlier? You took my picture," he said. "Old car, screechy brakes—that was you, right?"

Thanks, Dad, I thought, *for making such a great impression.* I nodded, feeling flustered.

"You find everything okay?" he asked "Y'all looked a little lost."

Y'all. Was that cute or what? "We were. My dad nearly caused a wreck when he stopped and turned. I think I've got whiplash." *Of course, maybe that was from looking out the back window at you.* "But. Anyway." I laughed. "We made it."

"Cool. Well, ask us if you need to know where to go for stuff. We've already been here a week so we know our way around."

"Great. That'd be, uh, really, uh, helpful," I told him. *Especially if you decided to give me a personal tour of the town.* "Are you, um, here with family, too?" I asked.

"No, friends," he said.

"That sounds fun," I replied. "So, I'm—"

"Emily!" my mom suddenly called over to me. "Don't forget to take your sweater, hon, it might get chilly!"

"I'll be fine!" I called back over my shoulder at my mom. I could have killed her right then. She could be so overprotective that she made me seem a lot younger than I actually was. Half the time, she acted as if I didn't know how to take care of myself.

"Here." He tossed a sweatshirt over the fence. "No need to run for a sweater. Just leave this on the railing here when you get back. Or return it to me tomorrow. Whatever."

"Really? You sure?" *You don't even know me. And I don't know you, though I wouldn't mind.*

"Don't stress. It's yours for the night." He smiled.

"Well, um, thanks. Cool." I was trying to act casual, like this was something that happened to me all the time, when in reality, I'd never worn a guy's clothes before—not any guy I was interested in, anyway. Girls at school were always wearing boyfriends' sweaters and letter jackets and things like that. The closest I'd ever gotten was borrowing Erik Hansen's stocking cap on a biology class field trip when it was ten below. Stocking caps belonging to hockey players weren't exactly sexy. Smelly, yes. "Thanks again. I'm sure I'll be freezing and I'll be, you know, so grateful." I held up the sweatshirt. "So, see you around . . . ?" I paused, waiting for him to tell me his name.

"No doubt. See you tomorrow!"

Promise? I thought as I watched him fling the Frisbee to his friends on the other side of the deck and they all jogged down the steps to the beach. Maybe this vacation had a lot more in store for me than I'd thought. Maybe instead of just taking pictures of my friends and their boyfriends, I'd be *in* the picture, for a change—with what's his name.

"Come on, Emily! We're waiting!" Heather yelled to me from the town-side of the house, yanking me back to reality.

Chapter 3

"You still walk funny," Spencer commented as he followed me into a coffee shop we'd found on the busy main drag, not too far from our rental house.

"Thanks," I said, looking around the place for a table. "Thanks so much."

"So do *you*." Heather jabbed Spencer in the back as we stood at the counter to order.

"It wasn't an insult. I'm just saying she still walks like a ballerina," said Spencer.

"How would you know how a ballerina walks?" asked Heather. "Don't tell me one actually *dated* you."

I didn't give him a chance to answer. "Anyway, it's ballet dancer, not ballerina. Not that I'm particular or anything." I pulled at the light blue sweatshirt I'd wrapped around my waist. *His* light blue sweatshirt. Whoever *he* was. Sigh.

I probably would have worn it no matter what, just because, but the air-conditioning was turned up high—or down low, rather—and I was already freezing, with goose bumps covering my arms. I hate it when my mother turns out to be right, that when she tells me to take another layer, I do turn out to need one. She's spent lots of years being a stage mom, I guess, and she's used to the role even if I've outgrown it.

But if my mother found out I was putting on a sweatshirt that belonged to some guy I didn't even know, she'd have a heart attack—and, at the same time, before she crumpled to the ground, she'd spray me down with extra-strength antibacterial gel.

The cotton sweatshirt material was very soft, like it had been worn and washed a hundred times. I loved how it felt, especially that it was an extra-baggy extra-large. It was like wearing a fleece blanket.

"UNC? Is that where you're going?" Spencer asked, pointing to the initials on the front of the sweatshirt.

"Uh—me? No," I said quickly. I didn't want to tell him that I'd borrowed it from our hot next-door neighbor. For one thing, he wouldn't agree on the "hot" description, and for another, he'd immediately start teasing me about chasing after guys, as if it was something I regularly did. In truth, I only managed to do it on these vacations, with Heather. The rest of my life was usually so over-scheduled that I didn't often have the chance to talk to guys, much less borrow sweatshirts from them. "It's, um, borrowed."

"Borrowed? From who, your dad?" Spencer asked.

"No," I said, not wanting to get into it.

"Oh, my God—it's your boyfriend's, isn't it?" Heather cried. "You finally have a boyfriend and you're holding out on me?" she announced to nearly the entire coffee shop.

Did she have to say "finally"?

I wanted to put up the sweatshirt hood, cover my face with it, draw the strings into a knot, and disappear. "It's not . . . no," I stammered. *At least, not yet.*

Heather peered at me with narrow, suspicious eyes. "Are you sure?"

"Very sure. Let's change the subject," I suggested. I was so embarrassed that I couldn't even look at Adam and Spencer.

"Okay, I'll save you," Spencer volunteered. "So, about that weird walk of yours. Are you still into ballet?"

"I didn't know you cared," Heather teased him.

"I don't. I'm just trying to make conversation that isn't about guys," he said as he stirred a packet of raw sugar into his iced coffee. "So we don't end up discussing all your crushes, like we did on the rest of all our trips."

"Jealous or something? Should we only talk about *you*?" Heather asked, and we all laughed.

"I'm sure we'll be doing that enough," I muttered.

"What's that?" Spencer asked.

"Nothing." I sipped my strawberry smoothie. "Back to ballet. I've really scaled back a lot. I no longer train six hours a day and make my entire schedule around it."

"But you were such a good dancer. Ballerina. Whatever. Weren't you?" asked Adam.

"Thanks, yeah, I was okay. But you know. Things change." I shrugged.

"What happened?" Spencer asked. "I mean, last I knew, you got some big part. That's *all* your parents wrote about in their Christmas letter."

Our parents are all nuts about sending out these long, complicated letters every Christmas to update each other, with embarrassing details about us and our "phases." Heather and I once completely rewrote our parents' letters and sent each other parodies of them. In my version, I'd gone through a brilliant-actor phase and gone on to star on Broadway; in hers, she'd entered a genius phase and become the youngest-ever winner of the Nobel Peace Prize.

"Not this past year—*two* Christmases ago," I corrected him. "I know. And they sent a picture, which I begged them not to do."

Spencer cleared his throat. "It wasn't just one picture. It was a *collage*," he said.

"That wasn't my idea!" I protested, laughing. "Anyway, you know how you can be really into something for a while, and then it's just not your thing anymore."

"Like you and *Sesame Street*," Heather teased Spencer.

"I just realized that it was taking up all my time. You can't do anything else, it's your whole life, which is fine for some people, but it wasn't for me," I said. "I kind of wanted to have a normal life."

"Good luck with *that*," Spencer muttered.

After a while it had been more my mother's dream than my own, to be truthful. I still loved dance and I always would, but there was so much more to me than just ballet. Or at least that's what I thought when I realized I wanted to quit. Other people might see it differently—in fact, *were* seeing it differently. Talk about being typecast.

"So if you're no longer a prima ballerina," said Spencer, "what *are* you into?"

"Photography," I said.

"Oh, really? Just that?" asked Spencer.

"Why, what am I supposed to be into?" I retorted.

"Spencer, somehow you can insult people without trying very hard. Have you noticed?" Heather said. "I mean, good luck making friends at college, with that attitude. Speaking of. Where *are* you two going to college?" she asked. "We never heard. Is the reason we don't already know because you didn't get in anywhere?"

"Yeah, right," Spencer muttered. "Didn't you get the press release? I'm going to Linden."

I nearly choked on the smoothie sip I'd just taken. *Did he just say "Linden"?* I wondered. *Maybe he said Clinton. Or London.*

"Wait a second," I said. "I thought you were at the University of Vermont."

"You're transferring?" asked Heather, not sounding nearly as stunned as I did. "Cool! You'll be a sophomore there, so you can be our cool, older friend. Well, older anyway."

"But I thought you were at UVM," I said again. "I mean, you have the shirt. And everything."

"And you have a UNC sweatshirt and that doesn't mean anything, does it?"

"No, but—"

"Anyway, I won't be a sophomore, because I changed my mind and took the last year off to volunteer. I'll be a freshman like you guys, well, except I have some AP credits, and I'll still be older than you, and therefore more mature, and you'll be lucky if I talk to you at Linden," Spencer said, then he smiled. "Kidding."

"We're going to be so popular, you'll be lucky if we talk to *you*," Heather replied.

I tried not to think of how weird that would be, at a small school with Spencer, the guy I'd made my one and only pass at. Would I have to bribe him to keep it to himself?

Then again, maybe he didn't even really remember. It had been the last night of our trip to the Dells when I blurted out how we should stay in touch and how we were such a good match. I'd still had that electrified feeling—maybe *fried* was a better word for it—when I first saw him today, but who knew what he was up to these days? Maybe he had a serious girlfriend back home. I'd have to find out.

Anyway, I'd had serious changes in my life, too, since then. Serious relationships. Okay, mostly just in my mind, but still.

Linden only had about 1,100 students, but it wasn't that small a campus. It wasn't as if he'd be in all my classes. He'd probably stay away from me—far away.

"So what did you do all last year, then? As a volunteer?" I asked.

"I worked for Habitat for Humanity, building houses—mostly in the local area, but also doing some traveling to help in other spots—"

"Then how come your parents didn't mention *that* in their holiday letter?" Heather teased.

"My parents don't send a holiday letter," he said.

"Oh. So *they're* the normal ones," I observed. Spencer already seemed conceited enough, so I didn't tell him how cool I thought that was, that he took time off to help other people. That was the kind of thing I'd totally wanted to do myself, but I didn't have the guts to just put my life on hold. He did. "So what exactly made you volunteer?" I asked.

"Um, I don't know." He fiddled with the napkin under his coffee cup. He looked a little flustered by the question. "Just, you know. Seemed like I could use a break from school and my local chapter needed help, so . . ."

Heather started to smile. "So let me get this straight. You'll be a freshman, like us. You, who've tortured us and taunted us every year about being so much *older* than us—"

"Which I still am. And I might be a freshman, but I couldn't be like you guys even if I tried."

"Oh, of course not. Never." I rolled my eyes. "Heather, how in the world are we ever going to fit our baby cribs and playpens into our dorm rooms?"

She smiled. "So what about you, Adam?" Heather asked. "Oh, wow. Don't tell me we're all going to Linden. Is it something they put in our drinking water?"

"Um. Speaking of water. Does anyone else besides me need some?" Adam started to get up and head to the counter.

"Dodging the question, huh?" Heather prodded.

"I was trying to," he said with an awkward laugh as he sat back down. "I don't know where I'm going to end up in the fall. Actually I got into Oregon State, but I'm, um, wait-listed at Linden. But I'm sure I'll get in. Totally. Just mailed in my application late, that's all. They're going to give me a hard time about it and make me wait. I'm a legacy—we all are. They always let in legacies." He coughed. "Right?"

My cell started ringing. It was my dad's ring tone—I have it set to the Linden school song. When everyone heard that, they started laughing and accusing me of being obsessed already.

"Where are you?" Dad asked.

"We're having coffee," I said.

"Coffee? You don't drink coffee at night," he said.

Somehow that made him worry that I wasn't telling the truth. "What, do you think I'm making that up? Okay, so the deep dark truth is that I'm having a smoothie. At a coffee *shop*," I said. "And afterward we're going to walk around and check out the area."

"Check out what?" Dad asked.

I swear he's not that old and hard of hearing. I just have a crummy phone. Again, my parents tend to opt for the bargains in life—with the exception of what they'd spent over the years on ballet, for me. The phone had been "refurbished," but apparently its first owner was an octopus, or someone who spent a lot of time in the sea. It had a constant bubbling sound in the background.

Heather grabbed the phone from me and said, "We haven't seen each other in forever, Mr. Matthias. We have a lot to talk about, okay?"

I could hear my dad laughing over the phone as they spoke for a minute, then Heather handed it back to me. "We'll be back soon," I promised.

"Parents still a little overprotective, huh?" asked Adam as I slipped my phone back into my pocket.

"A smidge," I said. Over the past year, my parents had been gradually adjusting to the fact that my social life wasn't entirely about ballet anymore. They were having a hard time with the fact they couldn't always reach me at the studio, where I'd be hanging out with three other dancers. Even if there were guys around—like an occasional partner from time to time—usually they weren't my type, or rather, I wasn't theirs.

"Don't worry, we can always sneak out later." Heather picked up her coffee cup and slid her handbag over her shoulder.

"We can?" I asked.

"Sure. Didn't you see how many *doors* that house had? There's no way they can keep track of us every second." She smiled, then put her arm around my shoulder and we sort of danced out of the coffee shop.

We headed back to the house, and Heather and I caught up some more while Adam and Spencer walked ahead of us, having an in-depth discussion about baseball. I think. I never watch baseball, so I had no idea what they were talking about, actually.

"Okay, so here's the way I see it." Heather smoothed her long blond hair back into a barrette. We'd always been complete opposites: She was blond, I was brunette; she was loud, and I was quiet; she was bold and I was, well, faint. Un-bold.

"We're here for our last real vacation before we head to college, which will be very serious and boring and not fun," Heather continued.

"It will? What about the parties?" I asked. "The football games, the frats—you know, all the things our dads—" I caught myself, feeling horribly insensitive. "The stuff the guys go on and on about, reliving their glory days."

"Just work with me for a second. What I'm trying to say is that we have fourteen days here, so let's find some amazing guys to have summer flings with. Are you in?"

"Uh . . . is that the plan?" I asked. She made it sound so easy.

"Pretty much. I'll help you find a guy, and you'll help me find one, which shouldn't be that hard because it seems like there are tons of them around here on vacation just like us. . . ."

"True," I agreed, thinking of our hot next-door neighbor, whatever his name was.

"And we'll just have one of those painstakingly sad brief summer love affairs—"

I laughed. "You've been watching too many movies," I said. "That doesn't happen in real life."

"What do you know about real life, anyway? You've been stuck in a dance studio the past five years," Heather teased.

"Hm. You might have something there," I agreed.

"You have perfect posture and positions, and like, no dates," Heather said. "Am I right?"

"Well, you don't have to make me sound that pathetic," I replied with a laugh.

She laughed, too. "Hey, I'm only saying that because I know

that's how *I* was with gymnastics. I spent every summer at gymnastics camp, every afternoon training. . . . I loved it, but it puts some serious limits on your social life."

"True." I remembered wishing I didn't have so many commitments, that I had time to just hang out at the mall and boy-shop with my friends.

"Anyway. This will be something short, just a fling. It's not something that you're going to continue, like a relationship or whatever. I mean, I guess if it worked out, and you didn't live completely on other sides of the country—but be realistic. We're going off to college and we're not going to be tied down to some guy who isn't even *there*."

I stopped walking and looked at her. "Wow. You *have* thought about this a lot. Did you map out the whole thing, like what we say and when we say it?" *Because I can use that kind of help,* I thought. A sheet of instructions. No, a booklet. And a website with updates.

"Shut up, it was a long plane ride this morning. I had time," she said. "So. We'll get started first thing tomorrow. What we need to do is meet some guys and—"

"I already met someone," I admitted.

"Are you kidding?" She pushed me. "When?"

"Right when we were leaving tonight! I almost got my head cut off by a Frisbee, but it was worth it, because I met the guy next door. Really nice. He loaned me this sweatshirt."

"So that's where you got it," she said, nodding. "*Really.* Well, this sounds promising! So what was his name?"

"Name? Well, um . . ."

"You didn't get his *name*?" Heather demanded.

"I didn't tell him my name, either, so—"

"And that makes it *right*?"

"He's staying next door to us. We'll see him again."

"Still. You ask a guy's name. It lets them know you're interested. I mean, are you with me, or not?"

"Fine. I'll get his name first thing tomorrow," I promised.

I wasn't planning to tell Heather how clueless I was about dating, but I didn't think I'd need to. She could tell.

To tell the truth, I was starting to think that I'd head to college without ever having had a real boyfriend—and a date at the seventh-grade dance didn't count.

That sounded so, so wrong. And so very, very likely.

But it wasn't as if I'd *tried* to be single. Forever. It just worked out that way. And it wasn't only the Spencer incident where I'd failed miserably.

When I was a junior, there was this one British guy I totally loved named Gavin. He moved. To Arizona. I mean, what were his parents thinking, moving to Arizona, when he's British? For some reason he belonged more in Wisconsin. Because of me, because I was there. Not that I ever managed to talk to him for more than ten minutes, and not that I ever had the nerve to ask him out. But still, I loved him. Deeply.

Then, on a more serious note, there was my friend Terence, who lived down the block and who I used to spend all my time with. At one point senior year I realized that I loved him also. Like, in the way that you shouldn't love a guy who's essentially your best friend. I kept trying to tell him how I felt, but I couldn't, and then he went out with my friend Shauna. Which wasn't fair at all, because I had known him a lot longer than she had, and all of a sudden we weren't allowed to hang out as much as we used to.

Anyway, the whole Terence and Shauna situation was over now— they'd broken up after only two months together—but I still have a heart scar from that.

Items are due on the   dates listed below:

Title: Eleven Things I Promised
Author: Clark, Catherine
Item ID: 00005206885587
Date due: 4/26/2017,23:59

Title: Summer of Everything
Author: Clark, Catherine
Item ID: 00005206858513
Date due: 4/26/2017,23:59

Renew Your Items
we247.org
Willowick Public Library
(440)943-4151

Maybe a fling *was* the answer. A fling in which nobody got deeply involved and, therefore, nobody got hurt. And one in which I never had to tell a guy how I felt or how long I'd felt that way or hear him say sorry, but he didn't have the same feelings for me.

I hated the word "feelings," come to think of it.

"Define 'fling,'" I said to Heather as we walked up the steps onto the deck at the back of the house. "Because 'fling' is 'feeling' without the two *e*'s."

"Actually any good fling should have a couple *e*'s in it. Like, 'ee, this is fun, ee, he's kidding me—'"

"*Kidding* me? That doesn't sound fun," I commented, laughing.

"*Kissing* me, I meant to say. Give me a break, I have jet lag," Heather said. "You know, it's a romantic evening. You hold hands. You gaze at each other." She shrugged. "You act and feel goofy. You kiss. Dance, maybe."

"That's it?" I asked, climbing into a chair beside the pool.

"The rest is optional." She sat down beside me in a chaise longue chair. "Fun, but optional."

We both laughed.

"*Have* you . . . ? I mean, would you . . . ?" I whispered.

"No. I've had the chance, but you know, the person—the timing—it wasn't right. And I definitely don't think it's something you should do on, like, vacation. With some guy you don't really know all that well."

"Agreed," I said.

"But you could make out."

I leaned back and looked up at the sky. "Right."

"And if you got carried away . . ."

"No." I shook my head. "Still not. Too risky." The whole thing sounded too risky, if you asked me. If I didn't do well with guys I already knew, how would I handle things any better with strangers?

But I'd try to follow Heather's lead, the way I did every time we were on vacation together. When we were about eight, she dared me to eat ten red-hot fireball candies in a row, so I did. That same trip, she dared me to jump off a tire swing into a lake, and I did that, too.

I ended up with a burning-hot mouth and a red stomach from belly-flopping. That was when I decided that maybe Heather wasn't the best role model for me.

But maybe there were events worth following her in. And if Heather could find a guy to have an innocent—or fairly innocent— summer fling with, why couldn't I?

Besides, I'd already met someone. For once, I was a step ahead of *her*.

"What are you guys so busy talking about?" Mrs. Olsen had walked out onto the deck, followed by my mom.

"You could have told us the bad news, Mom," Heather said.

Mrs. Olsen looked a bit panicked for a second. "What bad news?"

"That Spencer's following us to Linden."

My mother laughed. "What? I, for one, think it's wonderful news," she said. "Don't you think so, Emily?"

I thought that it was strange. Weird. Potentially nice, because it never hurts to know lots of people. And potentially very embarrassing, because sometimes it's the wrong kind of people, the ones you'll never, ever turn to because they'd mock you for it.

"Sure, Mom. It's wonderful," I murmured, glancing over at Spencer. Absolutely, positively, wonderfully *bizarre*.

Heather suddenly jumped up and grabbed hold of my hands. "Come on, Em, let's go."

"What?"

"We need to talk some more—in private," she said under her

breath as she pulled me by the wrist. "We need a plan of attack, don't you think? We're just going down to the beach, stick our toes in the water!" she announced over her shoulder to everyone.

"If you're not back in fifteen minutes, I'm sending someone after you!" my mother called.

"Fine. Just send someone cute from next door," Heather added and we laughed as we ran down the steps toward the ocean.

Chapter 4

"Emily! Emily!"

I turned my head and slid my sunglasses down my nose to see who was calling my name. I was lying in a bikini on the beach with an open book across my bare stomach—I guess I'd fallen asleep while I was reading.

When I could focus, I saw that it was the guy from next door. I couldn't believe it. The same guy who'd loaned me his UNC sweatshirt, and before that, nearly decapitated me with a Frisbee. He was jogging down the beach toward me, wearing shorts, no shirt, with a striped beach towel slung around his neck, calling my name. "Em-i-ly! Em-i-ly!"

I quickly sat up, then jumped up from my own striped beach towel and hurried toward him. I ran faster and faster, but my feet kept slipping in the sand. I looked down and realized I had my ballet slippers on, and then I realized I was late for a performance and not only that, I was wearing a bikini instead of my tutu. My trig teacher appeared out of nowhere, asking for my homework. I just ran past her and leaped into his arms.

"Hey." He wrapped his arms around my waist and I put my arms around his strong shoulders and he pulled me closer. He lifted me in the air and tried to twirl me around, but unfortunately, something kept getting in the way. Something was wrapped all around my legs and I suddenly couldn't move. Seaweed—monster-size seaweed—was about to strangle me.

I sat bolt upright.

I wasn't on the beach.

I was in bed.

Alone. Very, very alone. And I was tangled up in my bedsheets. There was a magazine on my stomach, which I'd been reading the night before.

Well, at least I hadn't failed trig or ended up onstage in a bikini.

It took me a second to figure out where I was. I don't know if it's because I'm a photographer or what, but it seems like I have the most vivid, visual—and unusual—dreams. Sometimes it can really freak me out because I can't tell what's real and what isn't.

Unfortunately, the dream about next-door guy wasn't real. The scene of me waking up wrapped like a mummy in my sheets—that was.

Shoot. No pun intended. I'd planned to get up early and photograph the sunrise. I glanced at the alarm clock and saw that I was about four hours late for that. What had happened? Then again, if I'd been having dreams like that, no wonder I stayed asleep.

I quickly got dressed, throwing on a pair of white shorts and a pink polka-dot bikini top. The temp outside seemed pretty hot when I opened a window to quickly check it. Besides, I wanted to meet guys, right? When in Rome, and when on the Outer Banks, and all that.

I left my room and walked out into the fourth-floor hall. The house was four stories, with two large kitchens on the first and third floors. Each family had at least one room, or suite, with an attached bathroom—and some had two, like ours. It was sort of like being inside a hotel that was inside of a house. I was so happy that I didn't have to share a room with my parents—I had a small bedroom with a miniature bathroom, sort of like a little attic afterthought. The only other person on the fourth floor, with a similar room, was Adam. His door was closed, and I wondered if he—and everyone else in the house—was already up, outside, and on my mom's latest adventure. *Why hadn't she woken me up?* I wondered. That wasn't like her. Normally she'd pound on my door until I was up. Besides, she had Big Plans for this trip. Things we absolutely had to see.

I went to the third-floor kitchen, located the coffeemaker, and poured myself a mugful. Then I wandered over to the window to look out at the ocean (my bedroom faced the other way, toward the parking lot) and saw Adam's little brothers playing in the pool below, with the Thompsons and my mom and dad nearby. I wondered if the guy next door was up yet. Probably—everyone else seemed to be.

"Sleep much?" A voice behind me nearly made me jump through the window.

I struggled to keep from spilling my coffee. I turned to find Spencer, who I hadn't noticed sitting on the sofa in the attached living room. "You scared me!"

He looked up from the book he was reading. "You scared *me*," he replied. "Have you seen your hair?"

"Shut up." I glanced at my reflection in the oven door and ruffled my hair a little to make it fall more neatly. I guess I hadn't really paid much attention to it. "Heather and I stayed up late last night talking," I explained.

"Really," he said. "She's already out playing volleyball."

"With who?" I asked.

"Some guys. I think they live next door," Spencer said. "Typical Neanderthals."

"Do we have something against Neanderthals?" I asked. "Do we have a complex or something?"

"Complex. Not usually a word I associate with Neanderthals," Spencer mused.

I opened the sliding glass door and walked out onto the upper deck for some fresh air—and a better view. Down on the beach, Adam, Heather, and a couple of guys were playing against my platinum-blond friend and some other people.

So it's true, I thought. *The early bird catches the hot boy*. Or something like that. What was I thinking, sleeping in, when this was waiting for me on the beach?

I closed the door and ran upstairs to get my camera, then hurried back down, and out onto the lower-level deck. Before they noticed me, I managed to get a few quick shots of everyone. When Heather saw me, she stopped to wave, and the volleyball nearly nailed her in the face. My photo captured her sprawling to the ground, to get out of the way, but grabbing one of the guy's arms as she fell. I didn't know whether it was intentional or not, but her move sure worked, and they laughed and fell onto the sand together.

"Hey! How's it going?" my sweatshirt-lending friend called over to me.

"Hi!" I waved back to him. "Great shot!" I said, but the wind caught my hair and whipped it into my mouth, so it came out as more like "GWMFPT!"

"Game's almost over!" he called back.

I wanted to take a picture of him. What could I tell him to get him to pose? *I'm taking pictures to make a calendar and I want you to be Mr. July?*

I kept the lens trained on him, catching a few good action shots before the game was over and they stopped for a break. He jogged over to me, with Heather right beside him.

"Emily, this is Blake," said Heather.

Was it me, or was it completely wrong that she was introducing me to the guy that *I'd* met?

Not that she wouldn't have met him on her own, without me. But still. Just because I hadn't been clever or suave enough to find out his name—and wake up before ten in the morning—that didn't mean they were supposed to be hanging around without me.

Blake introduced me to his friends, all of whom seemed to have Southern accents as well, from the hardly noticeable lilt to a heavy drawl.

"Oh, hold on a second—I have your sweatshirt." I raced up to the deck to retrieve it. Unfortunately, the sweatshirt had fallen off onto the ground below, plus it had rained overnight, so it was sopping-wet, dirty, and covered with sand.

I wasn't sure he'd want it back now, but I walked over to him, holding it out. "Here's your sweatshirt." I looked around, wondering where Heather had gone.

He frowned at me, then gradually his mouth turned upward into a smile. "Remind me never to give you my clothes again."

I smiled, feeling my face turn warm, then hot, then scorching. "You know what? Why don't I see if there's a washer and dryer here—I can clean it and get it dry and then bring it back to you," I offered.

Blake shook his head. "Don't worry about it. I'll just leave it here in the sun to dry. No problem."

"You sure?" I asked.

"I'm sure." He nodded with a nice smile. "Hey, before I forget—what are y'all doing tomorrow night?"

"Um, I—I don't know yet," I stammered. "Why?"

"We're having a party. You should come!"

"Really?" I asked. "I mean, that sounds great. Cool." There was a slight pause. "Uh, thanks. We'll look forward to it."

"Don't expect too much. Just a casual, you know, thing. What are you up to this morning?" he asked.

"I'm not sure. My mom—she tends to plan everything to the hilt, so I'm sure there's something," I said.

We stood side by side, toes in the wet sand, the incoming waves washing over our feet. Where in the world was Heather? Did she expect me to do this all by myself?

"So, where are you guys from?" asked Blake.

"All over, actually," I said. "I'm from Wisconsin—"

"No kidding? I went there once."

"Once?" I smiled. "Only once?"

"It was winter. I didn't want to go back," Blake said, and we both laughed. "I think it was a *high* of ten. I'm not cut out for that. I grew up in Savannah," he said in his devastatingly cute Southern accent. "Y'all should move. Like, before winter."

Another "y'all." I could kiss him just on the basis of how cute that sounded. Not that it was anything I'd ever done before, just randomly kiss someone, but hey—what was I waiting for?

"I've tried to convince them, believe me," I told Blake. "I once had an entire lobbying plan to get us all to move to California. Everyone loved the idea, except, well, my mom and dad. My cat loved the idea."

He smiled, picking up a shell and skipping it across the incoming wave. "So how do you survive and have fun?"

"You learn to wear layers. Sometimes you're wearing so many layers you can't move," I explained. "So, um. Have you been here before? To this place?"

"Once before, when I was a little kid. Maybe six. And then my buddy Trevor—he's the one with the long brown hair. His family has a house here—that house, I mean. We're friends from UNC."

"Cool," I commented, sounding uncool.

"So, are you going to school anywhere warm, at least? Like, I don't know. Alaska?" Blake teased me.

"Not quite. Northern Michigan," I said.

"Ouch. Y'all *are* crazy." He laughed. "Well, you can always transfer. You could be a Tarheel."

"A what?"

"That's what they call us at UNC. Tarheels."

I peered down at his foot and saw that his ankle had a light black, slightly faded tattoo around it. I couldn't see what shape it was, exactly. "I don't see any tar," I said. "Maybe you're more of a sand heel?"

"Yo, Blake! Let's move! Tee time in ten!"

"We're going golfing. Hey, see y'all for beach volleyball later, all right?"

"Sure—sure thing," I said, not that I played beach volleyball, or any kind of volleyball. But I'd try. "Sounds great!"

"Cool. Later, Em!" he called with a little wave over his shoulder.

Great. Sounds . . . great. Also? Looks *great*, I thought as I watched him jog up the steps to his house's deck, and that was the last I could see of him.

"Emily. Emily!" My mother suddenly appeared, waving a brochure in front of my face. "Earth to Emily! We're going on a lighthouse tour this morning. Well, what's left of the morning. Then we'll go out for lunch, so why don't you go get dressed?" she asked.

I glanced down at my clothes. "I am dressed."

She cleared her throat. "*More* dressed."

"Mom, it's the beach, it's vacation," I argued. "Everyone here dresses really casually."

"Yes, but where we're going they might have the AC on. You'd freeze." She flashed a tight-lipped smile at me, and then pointed to the house. "Go change, or at least find another layer."

As much as I loved my mom, I was really looking forward to *not* being told what to do all the time, come fall. I might be homesick, living away from home for the first time ever, but I could use a little freedom in my life. Plus, my mom had this image of me as a fourteen-year-old in her head that she could not seem to get out. I was perpetually fourteen, being driven to lessons or going to the city to watch performances or spending vacations at ballet camp, all arranged by her. Not that I had a problem with it at the time—but in retrospect? I'd have to say my life was a little one-sided back then. I'd missed junior prom to appear in a dance recital. Need I say more?

I was on the way to reconfigure my outfit when I saw Spencer staring out at the ocean from the upstairs deck, where he was standing, book in hand. "You going with us?" I called up to him.

"Going with you where?" he replied.

"Lighthouses," I said. "Or at least one. Then lunch, I guess."

"Do I have a choice?" Spencer asked.

"Not according to her." I pointed to my mother. "*Everyone's* going."

"Then I'd hate to be left behind," he said. "But, you know, if you've seen one lighthouse, you've seen 'em all. And I hate feeling like such a tourist."

"So . . . don't come, then," I suggested.

"Why wouldn't I come? I mean, just because I might hate every second, that's no reason not to come along."

I looked at him, wondering when he'd turned into such an anti-social being. "You're weird. You realize that, don't you?"

"Oh, sure. I'm very, very strange," he said.

"Well, as long as you can admit it." I hurried into the house. On the stairs, I ran into Heather, who had already changed out of her sand-covered clothes and was on her way down. "Did I see you talking to Blake out there?" she asked.

"Yeah. What happened to you?"

"I was too sticky—I had to change. So, how'd it go?"

"You know what? He's really nice," I said.

"Awesome. Did you get his number?"

"No," I admitted. "Anyway, why do we need his number? He's next door!"

"Emily. Are you completely clueless?" she asked. "You get a guy's phone number. It tells him you're interested."

"Oh. Well, I got his name," I said in self-defense, somewhat feebly, knowing she was right about the clueless aspect.

"No, I got his name," Heather corrected me with a playful swat on my arm.

"Right." I laughed. "Well, I did talk to him, and he invited me—us—to a party they're having tomorrow night."

"You're kidding!" Heather said.

"Like, oh, my God!" Spencer squealed, coming up the stairs behind me.

Heather turned and gave him a disparaging look. "Who invited you? This is a private conversation."

"Then don't have it on the stairs. Because other people have to use them," Spencer said. "I'm only getting ready because she told me to." He pointed at me. "But you're going to do it again, aren't you?"

"Do what?" I asked.

"Spend the trip being boy crazy," Spencer said. "Just like last time."

"No, not like last time," Heather said.

I coughed. "Definitely not."

"Unlike you, *we've* actually gotten more mature," Heather said. "So it's not the same thing as being what you call 'boy crazy,' because that was us when we were eleven."

"Fifteen," Spencer coughed.

"Plus, we go out more often. Unlike you, I'm betting," Heather said.

"We do?" I said. "Right. We do. All the time. Constantly going out."

Spencer laughed in my face. "Yeah. Right."

How was it he could always manage to see right through me?

And how was it that I didn't punch him?

Chapter 5

"Everybody say 'squeeze!'"

"Squeeze!" Heather and Adam yelled, while Spencer stood a little sullenly off to one side. I didn't mind. I was actually getting good shots of him being less posed. This way, I'd get his true, miffed, unpleasant expression.

"Whatever happened to saying cheese?" he complained.

"We're from Wisconsin," I reminded him. "People call us cheeseheads. It's a bad stereotype."

"Too cheesy," Heather said.

We were standing on the observation deck of Currituck Lighthouse, and so far I'd taken pictures of everything: the tall grasses below, the ocean sound between the strips of land, the light-house and its 214 spiral steps to the top, which had made us all break a sweat but had given me very cool photos.

Before the lighthouse tour, we'd gone on a short hike, looking for the wild mustangs that supposedly roamed the area. We only ended up seeing one horse, and it was so hot and buggy that we'd made a dash for the van after not too long. My dad wouldn't stop singing this old U2 song, "Who's Gonna Ride Your Wild Horses?", only changing the lyrics to "Who's gonna find those wild horses?"

My dad has to sing a lot. In public. It doesn't make sense, given the fact he's an accountant, and they're supposed to be stable, boring types. It's because he was in a band in college—I've seen the videos and he wasn't half bad (back then, anyway).

Still, despite my dad's occasional bursting into song, I'd gotten a sense of how beautiful the area was, and how amazing it must have been in the past, before people like us were tromping all over the place, scaring off the wild horses.

"*Take* it already," Spencer said to me. "How many group photos do we need?"

"I'm getting it. I want the shot to be perfect," I said. "We need the lighthouse in the background and—"

Spencer let out a loud and overly obvious sigh. "It's like I said. Seen one lighthouse, you've seen them all," he said.

"Your enthusiasm is so refreshing," Heather commented, shoving him so hard that he moved out of my view just as I pressed the button.

"Perfect," I said. I turned off my camera and put it into my bag. "So, what's next?"

"We have to meet at the van at one," Adam said. "According to your mom. Who told me that about six times."

"Why do I feel like we're on a school field trip?" Heather asked.

"I know," said Spencer. "We have to take off on our own tomorrow. It's not like we don't have enough vehicles—and do we really have to go everywhere together?"

"My mom would never let me leave the group," I began to explain.

"Mine either," Heather added.

Spencer stepped back, putting his hand on his chest. "Not even with a reliable older person like me?"

I shook my head.

He looked a little shocked. "What, I'm not good enough?"

"Please. You're only ten months older than us," I said.

"If that," added Heather.

"I think I know when my birthday is," Spencer said with a laugh.

"Look, who cares? We can always just ask if we can go somewhere together without parental supervision," Adam said. "We'll phrase it in a way that they'll have to say yes. We'll tell them we're going somewhere safe."

"And won't we be?" I asked, wondering what exactly he had in mind.

"Sure, of course. I just meant . . . they might not like the concept of us all going scuba diving or something like that."

"Great idea—I've always wanted to try that," said Spencer.

"Me too," added Heather. "Love those fins. Dead sexy."

"Oh, yeah, we'll go scuba diving. We'll *totally* do that," I said.

"Why not? It's a great idea," Spencer said.

"It's not a great idea. Trust me. You'll have a mysterious accident somewhere off the pier," I said. "You'll end up on *Dateline NBC*."

"No, you will," Spencer said. "As a . . . a *fun* predator. Someone who tries to find and then kill all the fun." He stared at me, and I felt very uncomfortable all of a sudden.

"Me? I'm no fun-killer," I said. "You're the one who hates lighthouses and refuses to get in the picture."

"I'm just thinking ahead. I can see you Photoshopping me into something really embarrassing."

I took out my camera and turned it back on. "I hadn't thought of that yet, but thanks for the suggestion." I started to focus on Spencer again, noticing the small scar near his left ear where he'd gotten cut when we had a winter reunion once and he sliced his face with an ice skate in a bad fall. This will probably sound weird, but I loved that scar. I could look at it forever. It reminded me of being kids together and how easy it was to just play all day long, without ever having to talk or delve into anything deeper than whether we wanted fries or onion rings with our lunch. (Me: fries; Spencer: onion rings; Heather: celery sticks; Adam: ketchup.) And in another way, something about it was sort of sexy, too.

"Quit it!" Spencer said, pushing my arm to try to get the camera, which I was still pointing at him, lost in memory—or something like it. "What about you, why don't you get in the picture?" We were suddenly wrestling for my little camera, and I was so worried it would fall to the ground and break that I wrapped my arms around his waist and tried to trap him by the edge of the lighthouse wall.

"Okay, you guys, lighten up. We don't need someone falling off the edge." Adam grabbed my arm and separated us.

"What is with you guys? Let's quit arguing and focus, here. Suppose we do get a car." Heather took a pack of gum out of her pocket and popped a square piece into her mouth. "Which is a great idea, but like it or not, we're going to be traveling as a pack. Where should we go?"

"I've studied the guidebook, and there are lots of possibilities," said Spencer.

I sighed. "I'm sure my mother's already planned group outings to all of them."

"That doesn't mean we can't go twice," Spencer argued. "We'd see things differently. You guys are too pessimistic."

"No, more like realistic." Heather offered the gum to the rest of us.

"I'm thinking of another *r* word, actually," Spencer said as he took a piece.

I looked over at Heather. "He must mean ravishing."

"Or else really, really, r—"

"Revolting?" suggested Adam.

"Rigid." Spencer stood ramrod straight, arms at his side.

"You guys fight like two old married couples," my dad commented as he passed by us.

The four of us looked at each other, and Spencer made an exaggerated shiver.

Oh, yeah, like it was such a horrible thought. He could be so arrogant. How could I even have cared about him or his stupid scar, once upon a time?

"Excuse us," said Heather. "We have to get back to our actual *life*." She dragged me toward the spiral staircase. "Everyone knows that if you want to find out where to go in a place, you ask the locals. So, let's find some."

I followed her down the winding stairs, noticing that there were some okay-looking guys on their way up, and wondering if we should turn around and follow *them*.

We stopped outside the lighthouse door and surveyed the parking lot.

All I saw was a steady stream of tourists, mostly of the middle-aged variety. Cars with Ohio, Illinois, and New York license plates cluttered the parking lot, and several people who passed us looked as if they hadn't seen the sun in months—or a lighthouse, judging from their excitement.

"Do they look local?" I asked, pointing to a couple of guys on bicycles coasting into the parking lot. We watched as they rode up to an ice-cream vendor parked in the lot.

"Who cares *where* they live?" said Heather, and she dragged me over to where they stood in line, casually slipping into place behind them. Before I could think of a way to meet them, of anything slightly witty or interesting to say, Heather tapped the taller one on the shoulder. He turned around, a confused look on his face.

"Yeah?"

"Hey." Heather smiled up at him—he was at least a foot and a half taller than her. "I was just wondering, um, where are you guys staying? Because we totally want to rent bikes, too, but we don't know where."

"They're not rented," he said. "They're ours. We live here."

"Oh, you live here? Really? How cool," Heather said.

"Really cool," I added before I could stop myself from saying something so ridiculously redundant. They both looked at me as if I were a bit short in the IQ department.

"We could give you the names of a couple of rental places," his friend suggested.

"That would be great. Thanks. So, where do people go here in Corolla?" Heather asked. "I mean, for fun."

"It's pronounced Cur-all-a. Not Corolla, like the car," the taller one said. "Not that anyone *cares*," he muttered to his friend.

Somehow I didn't think we would end up going anywhere with these guys. They already thought we were idiots.

"We care," Heather told him. "We're going to college in this town in Michigan that nobody can pronounce—Pishnachaumegon."

"Bless you," the taller guy teased, and we all laughed.

"See? We understand," Heather said. "So can you tell us—where should we go? I mean, where do people here go at night?" Heather pressed. "Or, I guess we're staying in Kill Devil Hills, a little south. So what's down there?"

They started rattling off names of places, clubs, and it struck me they were probably old enough to *go* to bars, whereas we weren't even close.

Heather must have had the same thought, because she stopped jotting down names on her arm, and said, "You know, I almost forgot. There's this party tomorrow night. Not at our house, but next door."

My eyes widened. What was she doing?

"Seriously?" asked the taller one.

She nodded. "We're staying on the beach—come find us, we'll hit the party." She quickly jotted down the address on the edge of a lighthouse brochure, then added her cell phone number and handed it to him. "My name's Heather, and this is Emily."

"Hey. I'm Dean," he said. "This is Chase."

"Nice to meet you," I said.

"Call us if you're in the neighborhood, okay?" Heather said, smiling up at Dean.

"Cool." He nodded, and sounded genuine when he said, "We will."

"See you later!" Chase held up his cone in a kind of toast motion to us, then they got back onto their bikes and rode off. They managed to hold their ice-cream treats in one hand and steer with the other, something I'm sure I could never accomplish, and definitely not with people watching me.

Heather and I laughed as she grabbed our ice creams and we walked over to where the guys were waiting for us, outside the van.

Spencer was leaning against the van, foot propped behind him. "Don't tell me you just tried to pick up a couple of guys at the ice-cream truck. That's so middle school of you."

"We didn't," Heather said.

"Good." Spencer nodded.

"We didn't *try*, I mean." Heather smiled, then we both burst out laughing again. "We succeeded," she said.

"Yeah, right," Adam scoffed. "That's why they rode away at top speed."

"You don't know anything," I said. "They're coming to the party tomorrow."

"What party?"

"The one next door at Blake's. I invited them," Heather announced.

"I hate to have to point this out, but . . . that's not your party," Spencer said. "How could you invite them?"

"Oh, come on. You know how these beach things are. Totally casual, laid back. Haven't you ever watched a surfer movie? So," Heather said, turning to me. "Which one do you want?"

"Which one? Um, how about the sherbet—"

"Not that, silly. The guys." Heather handed me the cup of rainbow sherbet. "Do you want the one with the blue shirt or the one with the orange shirt? Chase or Dean?"

"Wow, you guys are picky," Spencer commented drily. "I thought you only dated guys with red shirts."

I raised my eyebrows and looked at him wearing a Ben & Jerry's ice-cream T-shirt. "Well, I don't know, but green shirts are definitely out of the question."

"Ouch. Ouch!" Adam pretended to dab blood from Spencer's nose.

We were arguing about whether it was ethical to invite people to a party that wasn't yours when our parents marched up. My mother stared at me. "Ice cream? Honey, you'll ruin your lunch."

"It's not ice cream. It's sherbet," I said.

"But we're going to Awful Arthur's. Home of the Happy Oyster," she said.

"Well, then. Forget this," I said, tossing my nearly empty container into a trash can. "Not that I like oysters or have ever tried one or wanted to try one."

"Is it true what they say about oysters?" Spencer asked.

"What?" My mother put her hand on her throat. "I don't know what you're referring to."

"They're supposed to have an aphrodisiac effect," said Spencer. "Do they?"

Heather stared at him, then scrunched up her face. "You mean they make you afraid to leave the house?"

"No, that's agoraphobic," Spencer said as we all laughed.

"Let me get this straight. You got into Linden, and I didn't," Adam said to Heather. "Really?"

"You know how they want a very diverse student body," Heather said. "Well, I'm diverse."

"As diverse as they get," Spencer muttered.

"So what *does* it mean?" Heather asked.

"It means we should be going," my mother said as she opened the van's side door. "Quickly. Climb in, everyone!"

Spencer got into the van. "Heather, it means that eating oysters makes you have certain thoughts. About members of the opposite sex."

"*Really*. Interesting," she commented. "Maybe we should look into that."

I felt myself blushing at the very suggestion as I sat in the second row back.

"Maybe *you* don't need to, Heather," Adam said, laughing as he dropped into the spot beside her.

"Hey, I saw you checking out that girl in the gift shop—" Heather began.

"Me? I was not."

"Yeah, she was too busy asking for my number," said Spencer, tapping his cell phone in front of my face as if that proved anything.

"Oh, right. You?" I scoffed.

"Why not me?" he said. Our eyes met, and he—unlike me—didn't seem uncomfortable at all. On the one hand, I was glad he'd forgotten our encounter—on the other hand, I hated that he had. Was he so arrogant that he'd just brushed aside the incident as a harmless crush? And how had I ever had a crush on *him*?

"Check it out." Spencer started to show us a picture on his phone.

"Who's that?" I asked.

"Oh. That's my neighbor's dog at home. She just had puppies, so . . ."

We all laughed.

"I knew you were making up that gift-shop girl story," Adam said to him. "Since when has anyone ever asked for your number?"

"All the time," Spencer replied. "Constantly. Just like you're constantly going out," he said to me.

Touché, I thought. "Yeah, well, you take really bad pictures," I said, looking at his phone. "Of cute puppies."

"It's a phone," he said, shoving it into his pocket.

After lunch, the four of us gathered on the beach outside the house. Adam hadn't stopped trying to convince us to play a sport—any kind of sport, he pleaded desperately, as if he were suffering withdrawal being around us.

"Two-on-two, come on," he urged. "Just like beach volleyball in the Olympics."

"All right, fine," Heather sighed. "But you're being really obnoxious."

"And you're bound to be disappointed because I'm not very good at this, okay? And by 'not very good,' I mean, the last time I played I was probably a foot shorter," I said.

"Come on, just try for fifteen minutes," Adam said. "If you hate it, we'll stop and . . . I don't know. Play cards or something."

Spencer tossed the ball to me. "Look at it this way, Em. If the next-door Neanderthals can play it—"

"You haven't even talked to them," I said. "How can you insult them?"

"It's easy. They're a type."

"*You're* a type. A really judgmental and rude type." I tossed the ball into the air and took a whack with my fist. I ended up spiking the ball, and it slammed into the sand right beside Adam, who jumped.

"Did you see her vertical leap?" He stood back in amazement. "You should have been playing basketball all these years, not ballet."

Spencer stared at me. "Were you aiming at me? Because you missed."

"I call Emily for my team. In perpetuity," Adam said.

"Purple what?" asked Heather.

"He means forever. For all time," I explained.

"Adam. I didn't know you felt that way about Emily," Heather teased.

"Shut up. It's a game. I care about winning," Adam said. "Now get over there and play."

I found myself wishing that Blake and his friends would see us and come out, to prove Spencer wrong. Apparently Heather had the same thought, because she said, "Hold on a second, let's see if we can get some more players. Come on, Emily—come with me!"

"Great idea," I said, joining her. We ran up to the steps to their deck and looked around for Blake, Trevor, and the other guys. The place looked deserted. We went down to the pool on the bottom level, and even knocked on the back door.

"Not home. Too bad," she said.

"It was still a good idea. Except then they'd have to see me play," I said.

"You wouldn't have to actually play, just pretend while you made small talk," Heather said.

"Oh, is that how you do it?" I teased her, and we jumped off the bottom step back onto the beach.

"So? Are they coming?" asked Adam, looking impatient.

"Nope. Not home," Heather announced.

"Probably out riding dune buggies and Jet Skis and trampling the earth," Spencer commented.

"Yeah, okay, Al Gore. Or maybe they're on a walk," I said.

"I'm just saying—did you see how much trash they left on the deck?" Spencer asked.

"They're probably separating stuff for recycling," I said.

"Come on, you don't really think—"

"Quit stalling, Spence," Adam interrupted. "Are we here to argue or to play?" He launched the volleyball across the net, and his serve nearly popped Spencer in the face.

"Game *on!*" Spencer said as he managed to get it back across the net to me.

As I leaped for the ball, I thought, *Please don't let Blake come back right when I do something incredibly stupid. Please!*

Before getting into bed that night, I walked out onto the tiny balcony just outside my bedroom. I didn't see or hear much of anything from Blake's house, but the moon was amazing. It wasn't a full moon, but it was close—maybe a day or two away. I went back inside to get my camera and tried to get some shots of it.

I'd taken a few photos when I heard some guys talking. I looked down below and saw Blake, Trevor, and some other guys heading across the parking lot, in the direction of the main drag.

"There goes your friend," a voice suddenly said in the darkness.

"Ack!" I let out a little scream—or maybe it was a big scream—as I nearly toppled over the edge of the balcony's railing.

Blake and Trevor turned around and peered back at the house, trying to see where the dying-animal noise had come from. I stepped into the shadow as much as I could, but also gave a pathetic friendly wave, in case they could see me. Thankfully, they didn't seem to notice me, and they turned around and kept walking, heading toward town.

Spencer leaned over the balcony that was diagonally downstairs from mine and peered up at me. "Good evening," he said in a creepy, fake-Dracula voice.

"That was you? Don't do that."

"What?"

"Embarrass me like that," I said. "How did you know I was out here?"

"I heard your door slide open. Light emerged. Et cetera."

"Well, next time give me some warning or something!" I pleaded.

"Oh, sure. I'll just yell, 'Hi, Emily, what are you doing out here, are you looking for the guys next door, because they're right there!' Or, you know, something like that."

If I'd had anything to throw at him, besides my camera and a plastic deck chair, I would have. "What were you doing out here, anyway?" I asked as I sat down and propped my feet on the railing.

"Oh. Well, I was thinking of sleeping out here." He leaned on the railing, looking up at me.

"Really? Isn't it kind of hot?" A couple of motorcycles accelerated from a stop sign out on the road. "And occasionally loud?" I asked.

"I want some privacy," he said. "My parents and I have a suite. So even though I have my own room, I kind of don't have my own room. You know what I mean?"

I tried to picture the layout of the room. "Not exactly."

"I'll show you tomorrow," he said. "Let's just say that the concept of *suite* is not exactly *sweet*. How did you get so lucky to score your own room?"

"We got here before you?" I guessed.

"Remind me to change the rules for the next trip. We'll draw straws," he said. "And I'll cut the straws, and I'll go first."

"That's exactly what I'd expect from you," I said.

"What's that supposed to mean?"

"Nothing. So what are you doing, reading by the light of the moon?" I asked.

"That, and some streetlights and a booklight. Kurt Vonnegut. Ever read anything by him?"

"No, I don't think so," I said.

"Really?"

"Yes, really."

"I'm just surprised. I mean, you go to a fairly decent school, right?"

"It was a great school, one of the top ones in the district," I said, defending the place that I'd complained about for four years straight. You found yourself doing strange things when you were insulted, when your West Side Lions pride was at stake.

"So what are you planning to major in?"

"I don't know. I want to leave myself open and be flexible. Photography, maybe?" I said.

"Photography. Huh. Can you actually major in that?"

"Why not?"

"Seems kind of lightweight."

I didn't know if I could do some kind of Spider-Man move and swing down to his balcony and kick him in the teeth, but I was tempted to try. "Do you really need to put me down? You always have to get your digs in, like you're so much better than the rest of us."

"Sorry!" Spencer laughed.

"It's not funny."

"I didn't know you were so thin-skinned," Spencer said.

"I'm not. *You're* so rude and arrogant." I pushed back my chair and stood up, wondering if it was too late to follow Blake and his pals into town. That sounded like a lot more fun than hanging out here, getting insulted by Spencer.

"Come on, Em, I was only—"

"And I'm only going inside," I said, sliding the door closed behind me.

Some people had changed more over the years than you expected them to, and some people hadn't changed at all.

Chapter 6

The next morning I managed to get up very early and took some gorgeous photos of the sunrise over the ocean. I was hoping that Blake would wake up early, too, see me out on the beach, and feel compelled to come join me. It could be just like in my dream. Sure, why not? He'd run out, call my name . . . I'd run toward him and jump into his waiting arms, and he'd twirl me around, the way in-love couples were supposed to do.

But no, the only being that had approached me so far was a seagull—a very aggressive seagull, who'd nearly made off with my breakfast bar. He'd twirled around me for about five minutes before giving up. That was the only twirling going on this morning.

I lay down on my towel and stretched my arms above my head, then I rolled over onto my stomach and rested my cheek against my arms. I was so relaxed that I was nearly ready to go back to sleep. Maybe it was time for me to go get another cup of coffee, I thought. Or maybe I should just give in: After all, this *was* my vacation, and maybe Blake would see me sleeping out here and decide to . . . I don't know . . . snuggle up against me because—

Suddenly, I heard someone clearing their throat.

I looked up just in time to see Blake drop onto the sand beside me. "Morning," he said. "Did I wake you up?"

"N-no," I said as I turned over to sit beside him. He was wearing long, madras plaid shorts, a bright yellow polo shirt, a white cap, and no shoes. Something about his getup didn't quite add up, but I didn't say anything.

"Nice day," Blake commented. He held out a white bag. "Here. We stopped by the bakery on the way home last night. There were thirteen to start with. I think. Have one," he offered.

"Thanks," I said, gently pulling a powdered doughnut out of the bag. "I think I saw you guys leave last night, when I was out on my balcony."

Blake snapped his fingers against my bare leg. "Was that you who shrieked?"

Oops, forgot that part. "You heard me? Well, I kind of slipped and lost my balance—no big whoop."

"You almost plummeted to your death. No big whoop," he teased. "Y'all are crazy."

"Anyway, what did you guys do?"

"Oh, we went into town to see if we could find something to do. We didn't. But we did find out about a band coming in a couple days. They're great—I've seen them play before."

"Yeah?"

"Yeah. We'll have to go," he said.

Was he asking me out? I'd hardly ever been asked out before, so I wasn't sure. Did "we'll have to go" count as a date? "Definitely," I said.

"Look out, you've got some powdered sugar right there." He brushed at my arm, and I felt a shiver go up my spine. "You have a great body. You know that? I mean, you probably know that. Never mind."

I knew that by this point, my entire upper torso must be blushing. I was used to having ballet instructors comment on my line—not guys comment on my curves. "I do? I mean . . . thanks."

"You do sports? Work out?"

"I dance," I said.

He shot me a questioning look.

"Ballet," I explained.

"Isn't that kind of expensive? Don't you have to starve yourself?"

"Yes, and no." I held up the doughnut, and we both laughed.

"What did you guys do yesterday?" Blake asked. "I looked around for you a couple of times but you weren't around."

He'd looked around for me? Why did I have to be touring lighthouses? Mom and her plans. Her wicked plans. "We, uh, we saw lots of things. We were basically stuck in a van with our parents for the whole day," I admitted, hating to seem young. "Today we're going to see if we can, you know, do something without them." *Unless I get a better offer, that is.* "What are you up to?" I asked.

"Us? We're off to play golf again."

"Barefoot?" I asked. *Who do you think you are, Spencer?* I almost added. And was the fact they had something in common a bad thing?

"My golf spikes are in the car. You only wear them on the green."

"Right. Of course. Well, then that makes sense, I guess." Open mouth, insert sand-covered foot.

Blake glanced at his watch. "I should get going."

"Yeah, me too, probably."

We both got to our feet, and I was about to ask him if he maybe wanted to teach me how to golf when Heather and Spencer came outside. Heather grinned when she saw me standing with Blake— me in my bikini and long T-shirt, and Blake in his golfing clothes.

"Well. *Good* morning," she said, walking up to us.

"Hey, y'all," Blake said. "Doughnut?" He held out the bag to Spencer. "We got them late last night, but they're still really fresh."

Heather's smile widened. "You guys have been out here eating doughnuts all night?"

Spencer looked slightly horrified by the thought as he pulled a chocolate doughnut out of the bag, as if the idea of me and Blake eating a baker's dozen tainted his breakfast somehow.

"No, not *all* night." Blake laughed. "I just came out and found her here."

"Funny. It's almost like she was waiting for you," Spencer said.

"I was taking pictures," I said through gritted teeth. I wanted to get Blake's golf clubs from the car and whack Spencer in the head with them.

He was just happily munching on the chocolate doughnut, like he hadn't suggested a thing.

"Actually, more like sleeping, when I saw you," Blake said.

"She needs to rest between pictures. Very exhausting work, photography," Spencer said.

I glared at him. "You have no idea."

"Anyway, we've got great news, kiddo," Spencer said, after taking another big bite of doughnut and polishing off the whole thing.

"I'm not a k-kiddo," I managed to stammer, despite the fact I was feeling like a kid with a crush. On Blake. I couldn't believe I'd ever had a crush on Spencer.

"We found three bikes in the shed beside the house—we're planning a trip down the coast," Spencer said. "There's enough for all four of us—one of the bikes is a tandem."

I glanced at Heather. Did we necessarily want to spend the whole day with Adam and Spencer?

"You guys have fun," Blake said. "I have to get going or I'll miss tee-time. See you tonight?" he called over his shoulder as he headed off the beach toward the parking lot.

"I don't know," said Heather. "I'm not sure."

He stopped walking and faced us. "Oh, come on, you've got to be there."

She laughed. "I was just kidding. Of course we'll be there!" she said.

"Oh, yeah, you won't get rid of them," Spencer said. "You'll try, like we've tried, but still, no. They're like—"

"We're *going* now," Heather said, dragging Spencer away by force.

"Okay, so . . . how did you convince our parents to let us go exploring on our own?" I asked.

"They're going to play golf too, and they couldn't see any reason to drag us along when none of us actually play," he said.

Well, no, but, um . . . If we were to happen to go to the same golf course as Blake and everyone, wouldn't that be kind of a nice coincidence? "We could learn," I suggested.

"Run around hitting a tiny ball wearing plaid shorts?" Spencer shook his head. "I don't think so."

"What are you talking about? I love the plaid shorts," said Heather.

"Me too," I said. *Especially on certain people.*

Spencer stared at both of us and let out a long sigh. "Well, you guys can golf. I'm going to explore the Outer Banks and try to make something out of this vacation. Emily, what are you waiting for? Where's your camera?" he asked.

"Right here. Why?"

"Don't you want to get a picture of that?" he asked.

"Of what?" I replied.

Spencer held out his hands as if he were framing a picture. "Volleyball dude driving away. Car vanishing. Taillights. Turn signal. Et cetera."

I laughed and shook my head. "You have no artistic sense."

"Oh, sure. It's *me* without the artistic sense," he scoffed.

"What, are you saying I don't have any?" I could have smacked him with my camera for saying that, except I valued it more than I valued Spencer at the moment. It might break on his hard, stubborn head.

"I'm just saying that your subjects are kind of limited so far," he commented.

I glared at him. "So is your imagination. How would you know what I photograph and what I don't? Are you psychic now in addition to being older, smarter—"

"All right, kids. Do I have to separate you?" Heather asked.

"Let's just say we won't be the ones riding the tandem bike," Spencer said as he walked into the house.

"Works for me!" I called after him.

After a lot of discussion, we'd decided to head out on the bikes to find a different beach to hang out at. Heather and Adam were managing to stay well ahead of us on the tandem bike, while Spencer and I were riding in single file. I didn't know how—or why—he managed to ride barefoot, but he did.

We'd talked Heather out of riding bikes up to Corolla in search of the lighthouse guys, since we'd already sort of seen the area. We'd headed south.

Finally Adam and Heather stopped at the entrance to a beautiful, sandy beach. "You guys, let's stop here and hang out," Adam said when we caught up.

I took off my helmet and brushed a damp strand of hair off my forehead. "Sounds good to me."

"Then maybe we can find a place to go windsurfing," Spencer said as we locked our bikes to the rack in the parking lot.

"Oh, yeah, we'll do that, we'll totally do that," I said, grabbing the towel I'd fastened onto the back of the bike.

Heather laughed. "Can you picture me on a windsurfer? I'm too short. I'd get knocked down."

"Not necessarily," Adam said. "It's all about balance, which you're good at. But you need upper body strength, too."

"Can I have some of yours?" asked Heather as we traipsed onto the beach.

I watched Adam and Spencer strip off their shirts and dive into the ocean. Heather was wearing a bikini under her T-shirt and shorts, and she stripped down and followed them.

I took out my camera and took pictures of the long beach, the rolling surf, and the trail of clothes leading to the water. There were a few small children farther down the beach playing in the water and building sand castles, and I tried to get good photos of them, too. I put my camera away, stashing it inside my shorts pocket and covering those with a towel.

"What are you waiting for?" Spencer called to me from the surf.

I stood there, water up to my ankles. Then my lower shins. Then my mid-shins. Then my knees.

Spencer swam a little closer. "What's the matter? Are you scared?"

"No, I'm not scared," I said. "I like to think of it as smart, actually."

His arms cut through the water as he made his way toward shore. He didn't have the same gigantic biceps that Adam had, but he was definitely in good shape. Just not the same weight-lifter look. "How do you figure?"

I wrapped my arms around my waist. "It's freezing! Why would I want to go all the way in?"

"Because the water feels great once you're in. But hey, if you want to stand there and shiver, feel free." He stood up and pointed. "We'll head out past the break, float for a while."

He turned to swim back out. I didn't want to go in, but I didn't want to be the only one who didn't, either. "But I—I can't just leave my camera here, without anyone watching it."

"No one's going to take it. Do you even see anyone else around? That's not it. You're afraid of seaweed or jellyfish or something," he teased.

"No, I'm not!" Although, come to think of it, I didn't like slimy, gel-like stinging creatures floating past me in the ocean. "Well, maybe. Have you seen any?"

"Come on, live dangerously for once. Do something not on your mom's list."

I slowly tiptoed farther into the water until it came up to my waist. "Since when do I not live dangerously? I mean, I'm here with you, right?"

"You are *so* going under." Spencer struggled to get close enough to push me into the ocean, but before he could, someone else pulled my leg out from under me and I went straight down into the water.

I came to the surface and saw Heather standing behind me, laughing. "Sometimes you just have to give Emily a little push," she said to Spencer, who was laughing.

"Oh, my God, you should have seen your face," he said.

I glared at both of them, then dove under an approaching wave and escaped out to calmer water by myself. I floated for a minute or two, looking up at the deep blue sky. It was very peaceful, and I felt myself getting lost in my thoughts as I gently bobbed in the waves. I was so lucky to be here, lucky to have this vacation with my family and friends.

I didn't want to get too deep—either in thought or in the ocean—but I couldn't help thinking that this was some sort of turning point, between high school and college. It wasn't just that it was the last summer before college, and not that I was one to make swimming metaphors . . . but I felt like I was on a diving board, about to plunge into a new life. Sort of like how I'd stood in the water just five minutes ago. Wasn't I ready to take more risks than that? Did I have to stand there and wait? Couldn't I just jump right in, like everyone else?

Maybe it was time to start doing things first, and worrying about them later.

"So." Heather swam over to me while I was contemplating how I could change my life. "What time are we going to go over to Blake's tonight, and what are you going to wear?"

I appreciate friends who can keep things in perspective.

We got out of the water after swimming for about twenty minutes. I felt like a prune. A very cold prune.

"You might have given up ballet, but you still have ballet belly," Adam commented as we walked up toward where we'd left our outer layers.

I laughed. "What's ballet belly?"

"No belly. A complete lack of belly."

I felt myself turn red. "Oh. Thanks. I guess."

You know how sometimes when certain people make comments, you really aren't sure if it's a compliment or not? That's how it was with Spencer and Adam. They were so used to teasing me and Heather, making fun of us, that you couldn't take anything they said seriously. They'd always follow it up with a quip about something we were doing wrong.

Then again, we weren't exactly kind to them, either. Over the years we'd learned to give back as good as we got.

Adam spread out a large T-shirt on the sand and sat on it, while Heather unfolded a beach towel. I grabbed the towel from where I'd tossed it in the sand, being careful to take out my camera first and place it carefully on top of my tank top.

Spencer dropped right onto the sand, soaking wet. "You look almost blue." He reached out and touched my arm. "You know what it is? You've got that ballerina skin. Gets cold faster."

"I know, I'm pale and—look, would everyone quit with the ballerina comments already? I'm not a ballerina!" I laughed, but I was serious. You know the expression, beating a dead horse? This was the same thing. It hadn't even been all that funny—or true—the first time.

"Maybe you just have thin skin," Adam said.

"Ballerinas don't have thin skin and neither do I," I said.

"Could have fooled me," Spencer commented.

I turned over and buried my face in the towel, wishing that everyone would stop talking about me. I was so tired and sleepy from getting up early that morning, and the sun felt so warm and nice . . . I could almost fall asleep, right here. In fact, I should.

"Let's not just sit around," Adam said. "Let's do something. I know—I stashed a Wiffle Ball and bat in my bike bag—I'll go get it and we can play Wiffle Ball."

"How about playing the napping game?" I mumbled into my towel.

"How about the game where we find a beach with other people on it?" Heather asked. "I'll go with you, Adam. I left my bike bottle on the bike and I need some water."

Spencer sifted grains of sand onto the back of my feet while they were gone. "Come on, get up."

"Why?" I muttered, still facing the sand.

"You know Adam—you have to play Wiffle Ball whether you want to or not. Besides, if you just lie here, facedown, you'll miss something else. I'm not sure what, but something. And everyone at home will ask how your amazing Outer Banks vacation was, and you'll have to say, 'Um, I slept through it.' Then you'll get to Linden and everyone will have to sit around in a circle during orientation and talk about their summer. Everyone will be bragging about canoe trips and mountaineering and NBA basketball camp—"

"How do you know all this?"

"I've, you know. Talked to friends. I've heard that's what they do," Spencer said.

"Oh."

"You won't have anything meaningful to say. You'll start yawning, thinking about this trip."

I sat up and rubbed the side of my face. "Well, whose fault would *that* be?" I readjusted myself so I was comfortably facing the ocean, and leaned back on my elbows.

"Yours. Totally yours," Spencer said. "And if I have to sit near you at any point during fresh-person orientation, I will disavow any and all knowledge of this trip."

"Oh, me too. It'll be like we never met," I said.

Are we flirting? I wondered. *I think we're flirting. Why isn't*

Heather here to tell me? Or, better yet, to STOP me?

I'd never told her about how I'd pined for Spencer that last trip, how I was convinced we were meant for each other.

Thank goodness only two of us had to be embarrassed for me on that account: me and Spencer. This was almost the first time we'd been alone so far this trip (not counting our balcony argument), and I was expecting it to be dreadfully awkward. But so far, it wasn't bad.

We sat and watched the water for a minute. In the distance I could see a large freighter that appeared to be moving at a snail's pace. I watched as the waves rolled onto the sand, the water bubbles foaming and then popping. "Why is being near the ocean so relaxing? I could sit here all day," I mused. "Tide coming in—"

"Actually, it's going out," Spencer said. "See how the dark line where the water ends is going down?"

"Oh. Well, whatever," I said. He always had to be right.

"So, do you spend a lot of time at the ocean? I mean, did you, um, go anywhere on spring break this year?"

"No, my parents didn't want me to," I said.

"You've been sheltered. Overprotective 'rents."

"Exactly. I think we've already established that."

"You should have worked with Habitat," Spencer went on.

What did he mean? With him?

"Because," he continued, "it could use more volunteers. But most people our age are too busy watching TV—"

"I volunteer plenty," I said. "I teach beginning dance and stretching classes for seniors at a retirement home. I organized a dance marathon at school that raised money for Special Olympics. Plus, I'm in a troupe that performs for hospital fund-raisers. So don't assume so much about other people, okay?"

"Okay." Spencer looked momentarily at a loss for words. "Sorry, Mother Teresa."

I jumped up as Adam and Heather returned, carrying the long, skinny bat and white plastic ball.

"I want Mother Teresa on my side," Heather said as Adam started to create a diamond, using clumps of dried seaweed for the bases. "Girls versus boys."

"Really?" Spencer asked. "Don't you think . . . um . . ."

"No, I don't. Really, I want to be on Emily's team. She kicked your butt in volleyball, didn't she?" Heather reminded him.

"Did I mention I haven't played Wiffle Ball in about three years?" I said as I took position at home plate, the bat resting on my shoulder. This wasn't going to be pretty.

Adam lobbed the first pitch to me, and I took a swing at it and missed. I tossed the ball back toward him, but it only made it halfway. "You sure you want to play?" I asked as we went through the same routine three more times.

"Come on, you'll get it this time," Heather said. "Don't give up."

I concentrated as hard as I could, took a big swing, and knocked the ball over to the left, past Adam, just as Heather's cell rang and she answered it. I was so shocked by the fact I'd gotten a hit that I stood there for a second without moving. Then I bolted for first base. I hit the seaweed base and turned to keep going, but my foot sank into the sand at a weird angle, and I yelped. It felt like I'd twisted my ankle. I hopped up and down while Spencer ran over to tag me out.

"I know you don't know much about baseball, but you're supposed to keep going," he said. "What dance is that?" he asked.

"The leave me alone hop," I grunted. "This kills."

"Spencer, help her already!" Heather cried. She was talking on her cell phone.

"I think I sprained my ankle," I told him as he put his arm around my waist to steady me, and guided me to a sitting position.

"Is it really sprained?" Spencer asked. "Because I'd hate Wiffle Ball to be the cause of you giving up your dance career—oops." He snapped his fingers. "You already did that."

I laughed, despite the fact my ankle was throbbing uncomfortably. "It wasn't a dance career," I said. "Think of it as my sport. Like how you played . . . wait a second. What *did* you play?"

"Lacrosse," he said. "Badly. So. How does it feel now? You know, I could take a look. I've twisted my ankle a dozen times."

"Fine. I guess." I heard Heather shrieking and looked over to see her and Adam chasing after the Wiffle Ball, which was blowing away down the beach.

Spencer put his hand on my ankle and gently pressed all sides of it. I winced, but more from the fact he was touching me again and sort of giving me a massage than from the fact that it did sort of feel like my ankle was swelling. I'd had serious ankle injuries before, too, and this didn't feel like one of them. But I hadn't ever had a cute boy treat them before, either.

Cute boy? What am I saying? This is Spencer.

Anyway, even if he is sort of cute, I can't like Spencer again, I thought. I didn't get it. How could I still be physically attracted to someone so rude and arrogant? Didn't my brain try to screen out these things?

But I had a feeling my brain was on vacation, like me, when it came to that sort of thing. My brain was not involved.

"You know what? I'll be okay," I said. "It doesn't hurt as much anymore."

"You sure?"

I nodded. "I'll just rest it for a while before we pedal home. But maybe you should help them—they look clueless." I pointed at Heather and Adam, who were standing onshore helplessly watching the ball go out with the tide.

Spencer shrugged, slowly letting go of my foot. "It's only a Wiffle Ball. We can buy another."

"Spencer, do your Al Gore thing. Think of the environment. Birds could choke on that."

"You're right!" He jumped up, ran off, and dove into the water, leaving me sitting there to contemplate what had just happened.

Chapter 7

"No, don't worry, you look fantastic. Only, how about we do this?"
Heather made a last-minute adjustment to my hair, un-clipping the
barrette and letting my hair fan out over my shoulders.

"Really?" I asked.

"Really. God, I'd kill for your hair. Show it off," she said.

I ran my fingers through my hair, combing it a bit. "I guess I'm
just more used to having it held back."

"The ballet and gymnastics years. I know. It took me months to
stop doing that," she said.

"Do you miss it?" I asked.

"What? The hairstyle?"

"No, the gymnastics," I said.

"Sure. Of course, who wouldn't?"

"Do you think maybe you'll get back into it sometime? At Linden,
maybe?"

"There's a club, so I'll check it out—it wouldn't hurt to try. Plus, it's always a good way to meet people, make friends. But it sort of seems like—that was my former life. As a kid. You know? I couldn't go back even if I wanted to. In some ways, I do want to, but . . . anyway. What about you?"

"I guess I'll still dance. I'll just try other things, too," I said.

"Like partying," Heather said.

I laughed. "Well. I wasn't exactly thinking *that*."

"Come on, get with the program. You know what? Maybe those guys from Kur-ulla will call soon, too. We might end up staying out late. Are we ready for that?" asked Heather.

I shrugged, wondering what else I could do to prepare myself. "Ready as we'll ever be, I guess."

"Oh, come on, you can do better than that. How about some enthusiasm?"

I frowned. "You sound like my mother."

Heather clapped her hand over her mouth. "Forgive me," she whispered through her fingers. "That was definitely not my intention."

We headed outside without inviting Adam and Spencer to come along at the same time. If they decided to show up, too, that was fine, but we didn't want to walk in the door and appear to be "with" them. That would ruin everything.

"Do you think they'll think we're too young?" I asked as we walked around the back of our house to theirs.

"Does who think that?" Heather asked.

"Blake and Trevor," I said in a soft voice. "I mean, they could be twenty, or twenty-one, even." Somehow, the prospect of my first fling being with someone that much older than me seemed a little unlikely. Not to mention a bit off-putting, in some way.

We stopped outside the door, and I heard music coming from inside.

"Eighteen-year-olds go out with twenty-one-year-olds all the time," Heather said. "What are you talking about?"

I'm talking about a totally inexperienced eighteen-year-old, I thought. Except I wasn't talking. Just thinking. And maybe, sort of, worrying. The way I was acting around Blake, flirting and all—that really wasn't me. That was just a part I was playing, trying to keep up with Heather.

I don't know the first thing about actually hooking up with someone, I thought as we walked in and I saw Blake standing by the kitchen counter, talking to several other guys.

The house next door seemed to have the exact same layout as our rental. A couple dozen people were hanging out on the first floor, sitting at the kitchen's long, tall counter or playing pool or lounging on the comfy living room chairs. "How do they know so many people?" I asked Heather as we edged into the room.

"They're popular?" she suggested. "Which is never a bad quality. Or, you know, *almost* never."

"Hey! You guys came!" Blake greeted us with a big smile. He seemed genuinely happy to see us.

"Sure, of course we did," said Heather. "Nice place. Looks kind of familiar. How long are you guys staying here, anyway?"

"A few weeks. My family owns this," Trevor said. "My extended family, I should have said—my parents, aunts and uncles, grandparents. We split up the time between families—my folks and a couple of their friends will be here next week, so it's not going to be as much fun," Trevor explained. "That's why we need to have all the parties *now.*"

I nodded. "Good idea."

"Or, how about this: Maybe we could get *all* the sets of parents to share one house and we could share the other," Heather suggested.

"Oh, yeah. They'd go for that." Trevor shook his head and laughed. "How about if you suggest it? They might take it better, coming from you."

"Be careful. She can talk people into anything," I warned him.

"These guys are from Wisconsin. Staying next door," Blake told the rest of the group.

"Wisconsin, huh? Have you defrosted yet?" asked one of his friends.

"Actually, I was thinking that it's kind of hot in here," said Heather.

"Yeah. We're fine. It's not that cold. *All* the time," I said.

We made small talk with different people and played a bad game of pool with two other girls, which took us at least half an hour. I managed to sink a couple of striped balls by accident, which would have been good if Heather and I weren't supposed to knock in the solid ones.

At one point I spotted Adam across the room. Where was Spencer? I wondered. Was he that antisocial? And then I remembered that I didn't care about Spencer and he could take care of himself, anyway. If he wanted to sit inside and read all night, and be surrounded by parents greedy for every last detail of his personal life, then so be it.

"Hey, where've you been?" asked Blake.

"Losing. Badly."

"Billiards aren't your thing?"

"No. And pool's not, either." We both laughed.

"Beach volleyball?"

I wrinkled my nose. "Mmm . . . not so much."

"That's okay." He put his arm around my shoulder and squeezed. "You know what? I'm really glad you decided to spend your vacation here."

"Well, I don't know if I decided anything, but me too," I said. "I mean, same goes for me. And you."

Blake laughed. "I think I know what you mean."

"Well, that makes *one* of us." I rolled my eyes. I didn't know what I was saying, but I did realize that it didn't make much sense.

"It's such a coincidence that you'd be here," Blake went on.

I laughed. "You invited me!"

"No," he said, putting his hand on my arm. "Not *here*, tonight. I mean, here, next door."

"Oh. Right. Um, how so?"

"Well, because we wouldn't have met. Usually you end up at these places, and you could be staying next to anybody. Could be some old people. Some young brats. Or snobs, or people who tell you to turn down the music all the time. That ruins everything."

"Right." I nodded.

"So instead, you're here. It's so awesome."

There was an awkward pause. I tried to think of something to say. It wasn't easy. Then I remembered something. "You know what? I got the best pictures of you guys from earlier today."

"You did? When?"

"You were on your boogie boards, surfing. Hold on, I'll show you." I reached into my shorts pocket. Cell phone—check. Camera? No check. "I can't believe it. I forgot my camera."

"Oh, well, I'll see 'em another time."

"No, I mean, this is really weird for me. I take it *everywhere*," I said. "I think I'd better go check my room to make sure I didn't lose it." That would be a nightmare. Without my computer here, I hadn't had a chance to back things up.

"I'll come with you," Blake offered. "Sometimes it helps to have another person look."

"Oh? Right. But, um, do you really think you should leave your own party?" I asked, suddenly feeling nervous about the prospect of being alone with Blake.

"It's only for a few minutes. Right?"

"Right," I said.

"We'll get your camera and come right back," he said.

"We'd have to," I said. "Otherwise everyone would miss us."

"Well, I don't know about *that*." Blake laughed.

On our way outside, I saw Spencer and Adam talking to a couple of girls in the kitchen, while they helped themselves to chips and soda. So Spencer had made it after all. I waved at Heather, who was perched on a stool by the pool table, watching the latest game.

Blake followed me up the four flights of stairs. "You're way up here? Cool," he commented. "You have privacy."

"You'd think so," I said as I opened the door. "So, um, this is my room. Now, about that camera . . ."

"You get a balcony, too? Cool."

"Ah! Here it is." I picked up my camera from my bed, where I'd left it, and followed him out onto the balcony. In the dark, I clicked through photos, trying to locate the ones of Blake from that afternoon.

Blake leaned over my shoulder to look at the display screen. "Hold on, I can't see anything." He pushed back my hair so that it fell over my shoulder and wasn't in his way. Then he put his hands on my waist and pulled me back toward him so I was leaning against him, and vice versa. "Okay, start the slide show."

I'd never stood so close to a guy before, let alone someone as good-looking as Blake, let alone someone that good-looking who I was kind of interested in. It was all I could do to remember how the camera operated.

All of a sudden, I heard a door slide open. I wondered which room it belonged to, and tried to ignore it.

Blake laughed as we scrolled through a shot where he wiped out on a wave. "Okay, y'all are not allowed to take any more pictures of me falling on my face."

"The camera doesn't judge," I told him.

"Emily?"

I looked down and saw Spencer, who I had *just* seen at the party, leaning over his balcony railing, looking up at us.

"I didn't know you guys were out here," he said.

"Well, we are," I said as Blake slowly released my waist. Was Spencer trying to ruin this moment for me?

"You guys hear about the storm that's coming?" Spencer said.

"No," I said through gritted teeth.

"What storm?" asked Blake.

"Supposed to be major. Strong winds. Hurricane-like," Spencer said.

"When?" I asked.

"Not sure exactly. They're talking about it making landfall sometime tomorrow."

Are we really out here discussing the weather, when I could—and should—rightfully be kissing Blake? "I didn't hear anything about a big storm," I said.

"Oh, it's all over the news. Tropical storm Brittany."

"I thought only hurricanes had women's names," Blake commented.

"Anyway. Well, you guys, uh—see you back at the party! Oh, and Emily—your dad was looking for you. He might be on his way up, actually."

Blake coughed and took a step back into the room. "You know what? I should get back to the party."

"Really?"

He made a beeline for the door. "Really. Like I said, I probably shouldn't leave my own party."

You didn't say that! I wanted to call after him as he disappeared down the staircase. *I said that! And I take it back!*

I stood there at the top of the steps, half fuming and half relieved. Fuming was winning.

Two minutes later, Spencer's mother opened the door, with a mud mask covering her face. His dad was lying on the bed, his back propped on pillows, watching TV. He waved hello.

"Emily! What's up?" Mrs. Flanagan asked. "Everything okay?"

"Sure."

"Really? You look a little flushed," she commented.

I put my hand to my cheek. "It's the sun. Lots of time in the sun."

"Be careful with that. You could do a mud mask with me. Or would you like some moisturizer? I have some excellent organic tea tree oil and coconut—"

"Thanks, but no thanks. Excuse me. I need to see Spencer."

"Oh, okay. I should have known, right? Have we told you yet how happy we are that you'll be at school together?"

Only about a hundred times. "I'm happy, too," I told her with a smile. *Just absolutely thrilled to pieces.*

She smiled and gestured toward a side door. "He's right in there. Got back a few minutes ago."

"Emily, how's it going?" Mr. Flanagan asked as I walked past him.

"Just great," I said. *If it weren't for your annoying son, it might be . . . going. Somewhere.*

I knocked on the door, heard Spencer call "Enter!" and slipped inside. His bed took up most of the room. His clothes lying all over the floor took up the rest of it. He was sitting in a small wicker chair by the door to the balcony.

"I see what you mean."

"What?"

"About the suite thing." For a second, I forgot my mission. I looked at all the stuff in his room, making my way across the T-shirt-covered floor to where he sat—not that I needed to be any closer to talk to him. "I didn't even know you *brought* this many clothes."

"So, did the party, um, break up?" he asked without making eye contact.

"Right. That's why I came to see you. What was *that* all about?"

"What? It *is* windy. I just thought—"

"You just thought you'd interrupt my night with a fake storm, that's what. And just because you sacrificed your nonexistent social life to help out—which I totally admire by the way and I wish I didn't right now—we're supposed to believe you when you invent stories about tropical storms, which isn't even funny, and you should know it isn't funny, because after all you saw the damage firsthand—"

"Whoa, whoa! Take a breath, why don't you?" Spencer said, laughing, kicking back, looking completely relaxed, while I fumed on.

"It comes down to this," I said. "You pretty much ruined my night. You were at the party, then we left, then the next thing I know you're back here—*checking* on us?"

"I got bored at the party. There wasn't anyone to talk to."

I narrowed my eyes at him. "There were *dozens* of people to talk to."

"Yeah, but no one interesting."

"I bet you didn't even try. I bet you just stood there and decided they weren't interesting on your own."

"Unlike you and Heather, I'm not here to try and make new friends—or get dates."

"Well, maybe that's why you're doing everything you can to make sure *we* don't," I said.

"What? I was just making sure you were safe, that's all."

"I can take care of myself, Spencer."

"You don't know this guy very well. Should you really be up there alone with him?"

"Okay, so, what's your plan? Are you going to follow me around this entire trip? And what about when we both get to Linden, will you follow me around there, too?"

He looked absolutely appalled. "God, no."

"Because, for someone who acts like he doesn't care and claims he doesn't care—you sure seem to care."

"I don't . . . care. I just think you should be a little more choosy, that's all."

"Gee. Could you be any ruder?" I responded, then I stormed out of the room. Who was he to tell me to be more choosy? I'd chosen *him* once. Did he not see the irony there? Not that I'd do it again, because he'd obviously gotten even more conceited over the past two years.

I decided not to go back to the party—it had ended on a fairly decent note, considering, unless you counted Spencer's interruption, which I didn't. I'd ruin any magic Blake and I had if I went back now and sort of lamely stood there with a pop, waiting for something else to happen.

I changed into my pajamas and lay down on my bed, totally exhausted. I picked up my camera and started going through all the pictures I'd taken that day, deciding which ones to keep and which to delete so I could free up my memory card.

As I went through them, skipping all the ones with Spencer, I thought about how Blake had touched my hair, how he'd slipped his hands around my waist while we looked at pictures earlier, how we'd been semi-snuggled.

Blake had actually been here, in my room. Maybe that was moving things along too fast, but come on—would anything seriously happen with seven adults downstairs? I mean, I guess it could have, and maybe it would have . . . and was I actually ready for that? Me, the person who couldn't even manage one decent kiss with a guy?

What was I thinking, inviting him up here? Maybe Spencer was right.

No. Spencer can't be right. That would make him even more conceited.

Maybe he could be right without me telling him that he was. Maybe then it wouldn't count.

Chapter 8

"Don't forget the tomatoes!"

The next morning, I'd been dragged to the supermarket by my mom to help buy groceries. And I do mean dragged. Out of bed. Feet first.

It was our family's turn to cook dinner that night, and Mom insisted I give her some input, even though she'd already made all the decisions. She was calling the evening "Fiesta! Night" and had grand ideas about decorating, appetizers, and *flan*.

I wasn't sure what sort of input there was left for me to give her. She had the whole thing pretty much figured out, start to finish. My mom is a great hostess but she can really get carried away with her concepts. I definitely wasn't looking forward to spending half my afternoon in the kitchen with her, preparing things. (Not that burritos and tacos take that long to make—for anyone *else*, that is.)

We'd already decided to have fish tacos, chicken burritos, and cheese enchiladas. Now she was picking out the perfect limes to slice for decoration in the frozen margaritas for the adults, and then kiwis for kiwi-lime slushees for us "under twenty-ones."

Then we had to get cilantro, lettuce, tomatoes, and three different kinds of hot peppers.

Everyone else in our group, right now, was either buying a kite, or flying a kite at the beach. The entire van had headed to Kitty Hawk Kites, because it was a breezy morning and because they were all going to do something fun.

Me? I was standing in the produce section with a perfectionist.

"How about we just order in?" I suggested. "I bet there's a very good—"

"Em. Try to get into the spirit of things."

"Olé," I muttered.

She smiled briefly. "That's more like it."

We hit the dairy case and picked up sour cream, cheese, and eggs. We reviewed tortilla types, corn versus flour, large versus small. We got various types of chips. We got enough snacks and lunch things for our family of three to last us through the next millennium. Finally, the cart was full, and we were approaching the registers, looking for a line that wasn't five-deep, when I saw Blake come striding into the store.

My heart started to pound the way it used to before a ballet solo as I watched him disappear down an aisle. *Aisle 4*, I committed to memory.

"You know what, Mom? I just thought of something that we still need," I said, already starting to move away, before I lost track of which aisle Blake had entered. "Black olives."

"Oh?" My mother's face scrunched into a worried frown. "What do we need them for?" she asked as if I were suggesting we put them on breakfast cereal.

"Have you ever tasted a burrito without them?" I asked.

"Yes, plenty of times," she said calmly.

"Oh, I know—I was thinking of the enchiladas, then. They definitely call for black olives."

"You know, you're right. But is it green or black?"

"Black." I didn't have time to stand in line debating culinary choices. "You wait here in line," I told her. "I'll be right back."

"If you're getting them, make sure you get enough!" she called after me. "There's nothing worse than running out!"

I raced around the store, trying to figure out where Blake had gone. I ran past three aisles before I spotted him just at the end of the canned veggies, fruits, and "international condiments" area, putting a jar of salsa into the basket he carried on his arm.

"Hey! What are you doing here?" I said all in a rush, so maybe he didn't even hear how stupid it sounded.

"Hey, Emily. How's it going?" he asked. He flashed a broad smile at me, and I think that I actually sighed with pleasure—but thankfully not very loudly. "What are you up to?"

"Not much. Olives," I said.

"Really. Olives." He looked at me and nodded. "You came all the way down here for olives."

"You know. A girl gets a, um, craving." I laughed, embarrassed. Why did I just say that? I considered toppling the pyramid of canned peaches behind me just to distract him from my stupid babbling. "Actually, I'm here with my mom."

God. That was even worse.

"We're supposed to cook tonight," I went on. "So anyway, I—"

Before I could get another word out, Blake leaned down and kissed me. On the lips.

Eek! What is this? I wondered as I attempted to get over the shock and kiss him back.

"You know what? You're cute when you're flustered," he said.

"I wasn't," I said feebly. "Flustered." *However, now, I definitely am,* I thought as he kissed me a second time.

I closed my eyes and wondered when my mother would run up, shrieking, "Emily! You don't kiss in grocery stores! Emergency, Aisle Four!"

"Um . . ." I said as he broke off the kiss. What was I supposed to say? Thanks, that was nice? Got any more where that came from? What gum do you chew, because that was cinnamony? I think I love you?

"Y'all should come out with us tonight," he said, backing up. "There's a great band playing in town. It's an all-ages show."

"Oh, yeah?" Was he inviting me to go out with him? Or them, anyway? "Cool."

"The guys and I are going down to Ocracoke for the day, so I've got to run. Just grabbing some food for the trip."

I glanced at the basket over his arm, which was filled with chips and candy. I didn't see any okra, not that I'd recognize it. "Okrawhat?" I asked him.

"Ocracoke. The island?" He was walking backward, smiling.

"Oh, yeah. I saw that in the guidebook." I smiled, wondering if it was too late to suggest we all go there, too. Knowing my mom, it was planned for a specific day and time, down to the minute. An impromptu sprint to the ferry—on Fiesta! Night—wouldn't cut it.

"So, see you tonight? How about if we meet y'all on the beach at eight, like, at the bottom of the steps?" Blake suggested. "If anything changes, just drop by, okay? If we're not home, leave a note on the door. Hey, have a great day!" He smiled and waved good-bye.

I felt my life changing in that exact moment, right by the cans of black olives.

When I got back to the line, in a complete and utter daze, Mom was already through and standing with the cart full of grocery bags, looking around impatiently for me. I smiled when I saw her and waved. I sort of drifted into line. I had to pay for a couple of cans of black olives, but it was well worth the two dollars.

"You're in a good mood," Mom commented as I loaded all the paper bags into the trunk of the car.

When I closed it, the Rustbucket gave up a few pieces of rust, flaking off onto my hand. "Oh, you know. Just glad we got this done, so we can go enjoy the rest of the day," I said.

"Me too. Now I have two more errands before we head home. . . ."

I wanted to get back to the house and share the good news with Heather. "But Mom. The meat—shouldn't it go in the fridge?"

"Yes, but it should be fine for a little while."

"Really? Because it's like eighty-nine degrees out. And didn't you get some frozen stuff, too?" I couldn't believe I had to point that out to her. She was usually the queen of food safety.

"Well, true. Would you mind if maybe I stop by the house and drop off you and the groceries—then go back out on my own?"

"Sounds great," I said. "I'll get the guys to help unload stuff."

My mother snorted. "Yeah, right."

"What do you mean?"

She slid into the driver's seat. "You have a lot to learn about boys."

Well, whose fault is that, Mrs. Overprotective? I wanted to ask, but didn't. I needed to stay on her good side—on *all* her good sides.

As she turned out of the parking lot, the car made a high, squealing sound as if we'd just run over a piglet. "What was that?" I asked.

"Don't ask," she mumbled.

I sat back and thought about Blake's kisses in the canned

vegetables aisle. Who would have thought that I'd have the most romantic encounter of my life at a grocery store?

After I put all the food away, I went outside and found Heather on the beach, flying a colorful kite with Adam and the twins, Tim and Tyler. I managed to pull her away for a few minutes so we could dish in private.

"I saw Blake at the grocery store. I mean . . . I *saw* him, saw him." I quickly told her the story and how he'd mentioned going to the club together that night. "It was the weak-in-the-knees type kiss."

"Seriously?"

"Seriously. And also? Plural," I said. "Then again, I don't know. I could've been weak-kneed because I didn't have breakfast yet. But still, it was shocking. And nice."

"That's so awesome!" She squeezed my arm. "For me, last night's party was kind of a bust. Didn't you think? I kept trying to hang out with Trevor, but there were so many people. He's really popular."

"He definitely seems to be," I agreed. "What about some of the other guys?"

"I'm not sure any of them even noticed me—there were so many other girls around." She shrugged.

"Not notice *you*? Impossible."

"I'm short. And then I went outside onto the deck for some air, and I saw my mom sitting over here by herself," Heather explained. "I had to go see if she was all right. We went for a walk, got some ice cream."

"Did you guys . . . have an okay time? Good ice cream?"

She laughed. "We bond over ice cream. So, yeah. But I totally missed anything happening for me at the party. But you—wow! Last time I saw you, you took off with Blake. How did that go?"

"Fine, until Spencer butted in."

"He did what? Hold that thought." She glanced at her phone, which had started to ring. "Unknown caller. Great," she said. "Just what I need."

I shrugged. "You never know."

"Hello? Oh. Oh! Hi. This is Heather. Yeah, of course I remember you guys. God, you don't think I give out my number to *everyone*, do you?" She covered the end of the phone with her hand and whispered, "It's the guys from Currituck. Corolla. Whatever!"

"You're kidding!" I whispered.

"So you're wondering what we're doing tonight?" she said. "Well . . . I think we're going to this place. Can't remember the name of it, but there's a club and live music—Yes! That one. You can meet us? Oh, great. That sounds awesome. Okay, see you then, Dean."

She closed her phone and we both looked at it, and each other, and burst out laughing. "See, good things happen when you take a risk or two. You're with Blake, and now I might have a chance with one of them—"

"I'm not *with* Blake," I said. "I mean, not totally."

"You kissed him! I think that counts for something," Heather said. "Unless you're planning on going farther?"

"No, I'm not. Absolutely not," I said.

"Unless, of course . . . you change your mind." Heather wiggled her eyebrows. "Heat of the moment and all."

"Shut up," I said. "If that happens? I'll un-heat. Okay?"

That afternoon, we quickly ran the going-out plan past Heather's mother, just to let her know. Of course, she had her own idea, which involved getting chaperones. It took us a while to convince her that Adam and Spencer would make good chaperones—then we had to actually convince Adam and Spencer.

We walked over to where they were standing in the surf, talking while they watched a big freighter out at sea. Spencer was holding a book, and Adam was dressed to go for a run.

"Will you guys go out with us tonight to a club? My mom said you need to go with us, so we don't 'look vulnerable,'" Heather said, making air quotes with her fingers. "Whatever that means."

"I'm not sure I get this. Why should we tag along just so you can go out with a random guy?" Spencer asked.

"They're not random," I said.

"They?" repeated Adam.

"We met Dean and his friend—the lighthouse guys—already, and then there's Blake. We already know him," Heather said.

"Not well," Spencer reminded me.

Actually? Better and better all the time, I thought, remembering again how Blake and I had kissed in the canned veggies section. I *hadn't* forgotten how nice it felt and I hoped he hadn't, either. But it definitely wasn't something I'd share with Spencer, who suddenly cut into my thoughts with, "You know, it never works out with the girl next-door. That's a total myth."

"Speaking from experience?" I asked.

"No, I'm just saying it's a stereotype, the whole girl-next-door, boy-next-door thing. It's like what you wish would happen, that this person you've known for a long time ends up being wonderful and you're perfectly matched, and you live happily ever after because they realize how incredibly fantastic you are, too."

"Dude. You sound jaded." Heather grinned. "I am totally going to ask your parents what this is all about. I bet your mom could tell me stories."

"There's no story, it's just an observation," Spencer said.

"Right. It just came out of *nowhere*. I'm sure," Heather teased him. "Anyway, you don't even know these guys."

"Maybe not, but neither do you," said Spencer. "I'm not trying to be mean, but if you think you're going to end up anywhere near Bl—"

"Bitter, jaded, pessimistic. What *aren't* you?" I interrupted.

"Your personal chaperone," Spencer replied calmly, giving me a look that was very close to *You're annoying me, you children. Go away.*

"Look, I already said *I'd* go," said Adam. "What are you guys waiting for?"

"You're the best. Thanks." I hugged him, and as I did, I caught Spencer's eye. Why was he looking at me like that? Like everything I did bothered him? "Do you have a problem?" I asked.

"What kind of problem?" he replied.

"I don't know," I said. "With me? With us going out to this club tonight?"

"Going out?"

"Are you just going to repeat everything I say?" I asked.

"Am I repeating everything you say? I didn't realize," he said.

I sighed in exasperation as Heather, Adam, and Spencer all laughed at me. I grabbed Spencer's book out of his hands and tossed it into the ocean.

"Hey! Hey! You don't drown Homer!" he yelled, diving in after the book.

Chapter 9

"Y'all dance really well," Blake said.

Did he mean me? I wondered. Or did he mean everyone? This "y'all" thing was confusing.

"Oh, well . . . thanks." I could tell him how many years of lessons I'd taken, how I'd studied ballet but also modern, interpretive, hip-hop, and jazz dance. But the place was so loud, it was impossible to hear or say much. Besides, I couldn't help thinking that anything I said might sound like I was bragging, and that would definitely be an annoying quality. "Thanks," I repeated.

"Thanks for what?" he asked, having already forgotten the subject.

"Oh, um. The dance. The club. You know, what's funny is that, like, if everyone had access to a place like this, then people would probably dance better." I wished I hadn't said that. I was starting to sound like Miss Teen South Carolina.

"What?" Blake asked.

I heaved a sigh of relief that he hadn't heard me. "Nothing," I said. "Not important."

We'd gotten to the club around nine o'clock. We'd all walked there together, traveling in a pack. Me, Blake, Heather, Trevor, and Adam. Spencer refused to show up before ten, because he said it wasn't cool. As if he'd know.

The minute we walked through the door and got our hands stamped, Adam bumped into a guy he knew from going to a baseball training camp during spring break in Florida. They started talking baseball, and the rest of us moved on to hanging out by the dance floor, then actually dancing to a couple of songs.

When the band went on break, Blake and Trevor took off with a mission to talk to the band about doing a show near their college in the fall. Before Heather and I could even talk about how things were going, she grabbed my arm.

"Hey, look who's here!" she cried.

I scanned the club, expecting to see a celebrity from the tone of her voice. "Who?"

"Dean and Chase," she said. "The lighthouse boys."

"Formerly known as orange shirt and blue shirt." I checked them out as they stood at the top of the steps, near the entrance. "They're taller than I remembered. And cuter!" I said.

"No doubt," Heather agreed. "I wish I knew which one was which, but oh well, I'll find out. It's not like they know our names, either. I've got to run. See you—"

"What? You can't leave me!" I protested. "They live here, which means they probably know tons of people—"

"Maybe, but I invited them to meet *me*. I can't let them stand over there looking clueless by themselves," Heather said. "That wouldn't be nice."

"They don't look clueless," I said. "*I* look clueless."

Heather swatted my shoulder. "You do not. Just get to know Blake. Get him to talk about himself. That's all you have to do." She squeezed my arm before she walked off. "Wish me luck!"

"Wish *you* luck? What about me?" I called after her, but the music drowned out my voice. "Come back! Heather. Heath—Heather—" I was panting when Blake returned from talking to the band.

"Everything okay?" Blake asked.

"Sure . . . everything's . . . cool," I said, as slowly as possible, stalling for time, wishing I knew how I was supposed to go about this. I didn't know how to pick up a guy and just have a fling. I wasn't cut out for this stuff. What made me think that just because I was in another state, I could do it now?

We might have kissed, but we had nothing to talk about.

"You, um, come to this place . . . like, pretty often?" I said.

"Now and then." Blake shrugged.

We stood side by side, just sort of nodding to each other and looking around the crowd. I was watching Heather laugh and enjoy herself with Dean and Chase. I didn't see Adam anywhere. He'd probably left to play baseball outside or something, I decided. So much for sticking around and protecting me and Heather. I couldn't imagine he really wanted that job in the first place. Spencer sure didn't—he wasn't even here yet.

"Where's, uh, Trevor?" I asked.

"Ran into someone he knows," Blake said. "Heather?"

"Same. Pretty much. I mean, she doesn't know them well, but . . ." I found myself at a complete loss for words. I was just standing there, twirling my hair, like a complete ditz. It was like I needed a time-out to collect myself. That, or I needed to run out of the place without looking back. "You know what? I'm really thirsty—you want a pop?"

Blake looked confused. "A pop?"

"Something to drink. With fizz? That's what we call soda in the Midwest," I explained.

"Oh, a Coke. That's what we call it here," Blake said.

"Really? Right, a Coke. I've heard that. So, would you like a Coke? Or a Pepsi? Or a root beer?" I asked.

He shook his head. "Nah, I'm fine, thanks."

"Mountain Dew?" I offered.

He laughed. "No, it's just called Coke."

"What is?"

"Never mind."

"Right."

It took me forever just to get across the club, and then there was a long line at the bar, probably because the band was on break. I tried to edge closer and was making progress, until I felt a tap on my shoulder. I turned around, ready to apologize for stepping on someone's toe.

"Fancy seeing you here," Spencer said.

"Fancy? Okay, Grandpa," I replied, staring at his outfit of blue plaid madras shorts and a striped green shirt. It was almost cool. *Almost*. "What are you doing here? I thought you were staying home and reading the *Iliad* or something."

"It's the *Odyssey*. Which is kind of the way I'd describe waiting for this bartender to notice us."

"I know. I just want a pop—a Coke," I corrected myself.

"Poppa Coke? Who's that?" he joked.

I glared at him, then sidled up to the bar a little more, pushing my way between two girls who were both on their phones and didn't even notice me. Spencer made his way past some guys walking away, beers in hand, and the two of us were suddenly only a body or two away from the actual bar. Finally, I got a chance to order.

When we both had our drinks, we pushed our way back out of the crowd. I was actually hoping to lose Spencer in the crowd, but no such luck—he stepped in front of me as I tried to get past him. "Where's your partner in crime?" Spencer asked.

"Which one?"

"Heather."

"Oh, she's over there." I gestured vaguely in case Spencer was thinking of heading over and embarrassing her.

"What happened to Adam? Wasn't he supposed to be watching you?"

"Watching us? No. Hanging around at the same place as us in case we need him? Yeah, I guess. Something like that. Anyway, he's here somewhere. He ran into some guy he met at a baseball camp this spring. It's all baseball, all the time." I took a sip of my cold pop. "What's a ribbie?"

"RBI," Spencer said. "Stands for Runs Batted In. Like, if you're at bat and you get a hit and the runner on third scores. You get credited with a ribbie."

It was like listening to someone speak Russian. It sounded nice, mysterious, and completely foreign. Maybe I had been living in a ballet bubble for too long.

"You know, if you want to talk to random guys you're going to have to brush up on your sports," Spencer commented.

"I don't want to talk to random guys," I said.

"Don't you? Seems like that's all you and Heather have been trying to do," he said.

"Oh. Well, *here*, maybe. At home, not so much."

"Really," Spencer said.

"Really. At home I just try to talk to guys I already know." I paused, taking another sip of my pop. "That doesn't go so well, either."

Spencer looked at me, and we just started laughing. I was giggling, even. It was like I'd just confessed to a crime. We were laughing the way we did when we were little kids.

Then I straightened up and headed back over to Blake, who was sitting with Trevor at a small table, a level up from the main floor.

Blake smiled up at me and I sat down in the one empty chair. "So. How often do you guys come here?" I asked.

"Here? This place?"

"Well, sure, here, or the Outer Banks, or Kill Devil Hills . . ."

"Hey, isn't that guy staying with you?" Trevor pointed to Spencer, who was standing around vaguely near us, without coming over. "Tell him to come sit with us."

"No, that's okay," I said. "I mean, he's fine. He wants to be by himself."

"He does?" asked Blake, looking confused.

"He's strange. He, uh, reads a lot," I said, as if that were a crime. "Kind of an outsider, loner-type deal."

"Really? I talked to him a couple of times. Thought he was really cool," said Trevor. "Yo!" he called, waving to Spencer. "What's his name again?" he asked me.

"Spencer," I said with a sigh.

"Yo, Spencer!" Trevor called.

"Hey, what's up?" Spencer came over and gave the two guys brief, cool handshakes, the kind guys do that work, unlike their pretend-hugs.

"Pull up a chair," Blake offered.

"No, it's all right, he was just leaving. Weren't you?" I said.

"Thanks." Spencer ignored me and pulled a chair over from a

nearby table. "So. You guys both go to UNC, right? I think Emily said that."

Blake nodded. "Yeah, it's our last year. Well, unless I screw up."

"Why would you do that?" I asked.

"Who wants to graduate? Then you have to get a job and work the rest of your life," Blake explained.

"Good point."

"What about you guys?" said Trevor.

"We're only going to be freshmen next year," Spencer said. "Technically, I could be a sophomore, so I'm calling it my freshomore year."

Could you be any freshomore annoying? I wanted to say.

"Where are you going?" Blake asked.

"Linden College," I said.

"Never heard of it."

"No, you wouldn't—I mean, it's a small college in Michigan."

"I thought y'all were from Wisconsin." Blake looked confused. "You know, cheeseheads."

"And how do you guys know each other again?" Trevor asked.

"Our dads have been friends since college, so . . ."

"They set you up!" Trevor nodded. "I get it."

"No!" I coughed. "No, we just have these group reunions. In groups. It's a very big *group*."

"Emily's the youngest in the *group*," Spencer said, seemingly out of nowhere.

"I am not," I said. "The twins are only four. They're practically infants. So no, I'm not the youngest."

Trevor, Blake, and Spencer started laughing at how defensive I was being. "Well, as long as you're older than *four*," Spencer said. "Then I guess it's okay for you to be here."

I scooted over a little closer to Blake. Then I leaned over and suggested quietly, "Maybe we should go outside."

"Outside? Why would we go outside?"

"So we could have some privacy. You know." I gestured toward Spencer and Trevor. "Like last night. On the balcony?"

"Yeah. Well, I can't go anywhere. I'm supposed to be meeting someone."

"Meeting someone? Like, other friends?"

Suddenly, a tall girl with spiky red hair, wearing a short black dress and tall black boots, came up to our table and dropped herself into Blake's lap.

"Where have you been? Oh, my God, I thought I wasn't going to see you again!" She planted a big kiss on his lips. "I missed you so much!"

Blake grinned and kissed her back, nuzzling her neck. "I told you I'd be here tonight, didn't I? Where have you been? I thought y'all were going to be here at nine."

Y'all. Why had I ever thought that was a cute expression? It was annoying, especially when it meant "not you, Emily—*her.*"

Chapter 10

"You know, I was doing fine until *you* came along," I muttered to Spencer as the band took the stage again. Blake and Mystery Girl had run off to the dance floor together, while I'd moved to a darker, less conspicuous area, so I could feel like an idiot in private. Spencer had followed me, no doubt so I could hear him gloat over the loud music.

"I think you mean until she came along," Spencer said. "Because I'm not the one who jumped into his lap."

I sighed and leaned against the railing. I thought that when Blake and I had kissed it actually meant something. Not a lot, maybe, but something. Apparently, I was just one of the many girls around here he kissed. But I didn't want to talk about it with Spencer.

"Why don't you make yourself useful and go check on Heather or something?" I asked.

He pointed to Heather, who was dancing with one of the guys from Corolla. "She seems to be doing fine."

"What are you talking about? She's all over him! They're so close they could be arrested in some states," I said. "Go break them up, why don't you?"

"Relax. They're just dancing."

"You know, I think I know why you agreed to come tonight."

"I can't resist the pull of a bad cover band?"

I narrowed my eyes and glared at him. "You can't stand the idea of me, of us, having fun without you. Having fun, period. Being happy. You probably knew about Blake and what's-her-name."

"Look, I didn't want to upset you, but . . . I never thought you and Blake were on the same page."

"What are you talking about? We just met, we still have to get to know each other, and—anyway, I'm sure she's just an old friend, and there's nothing wrong with friends."

"No, unless you have, like, seven of them. And you kiss all of them."

"What are you saying?"

"Emily, come on. Look. Didn't you see him and that girl?"

"But he's nice. He loaned me his sweatshirt."

"A sweatshirt isn't a relationship."

I frowned at him. "Are you thinking of putting that saying on a T-shirt? Because don't."

"I'm sorry, Emily, but the guy seems like kind of a player. Come on, I'll walk you home," Spencer said.

"Why would I leave just because Blake is dancing with some-one . . . else?" I yanked my arm away from his. The last thing I wanted was his pity. "Just leave me alone, okay?" I narrowed my eyes at him. "What are you wearing, anyway? Plaid and stripes should only be worn by rock stars, like Gwen Stefani, or someone on *Project Runway*."

"I think I'm crushed. Hold on," he said. He waited a few seconds and checked his pulse. "Nope. Still fine."

"Well, as much as this night is starting to suck, we're still not leaving. We can't just go and leave Heather here on her own."

"I'll tell Adam we're going. He can be in charge of her."

I laughed. "Do you think anyone can be in charge of Heather? Do you know Heather at all? Besides, has anyone seen Adam? I bet he's off playing baseball somewhere, some all-night lighted playing . . . place."

"Field. Or diamond. Baseball diamond," Spencer said.

"Whatever."

"Your dad's really into sports. How do you not know all these basic things that any six-year-old would know?" Spencer asked, making me sound like the dumbest person on the planet, or at least in the room.

"And how do you not have better manners than a six-year-old? How do you go around just insulting people without even noticing?"

"What? I do not."

"You constantly do," I argued.

"Look. If this is about what happened, you know, in the Dells—"

"It isn't."

That was the second time he'd brought it up, but we hadn't actually talked about it. I definitely wasn't in the mood to now. A person can only take so much rejection in one night.

We sat silently, watching people dance. I sipped my pop, then tipped the cup back and chewed some ice. All I wanted was to get out of there, but at the same time, I wanted to hang around and see how Heather was doing, make sure she was all right—make sure *she* had a better night than I did.

Spencer was apparently watching her, too. "Hey, is that orange shirt or blue shirt with Heather?" he asked. "I thought you had dibs on blue shirt."

I laughed, despite the fact I sort of wanted to slug him. "Shut up. I don't have dibs on anyone," I said. "Isn't it obvious?"

"Hey. If we need to kill time, I could always tell you the girl-next-door story," Spencer offered.

"For real?"

"Sure."

"Should I get a tissue?" I asked.

"For me, yeah. A box." He cleared his throat. "Don't get your hopes up—it's not a very long or interesting—"

"Just tell it," I urged. I was dying for something else to think about.

"Okay. Like I said, it's not a very long story. There was this girl, next door. Well, three doors down. Her name was Morgan. Still is, actually. I wanted to ask her to prom," Spencer began. "But we were kind of friends, you know, so it had to be really creative, had to blow her away. I kept plotting how to do it. I had a hundred brilliant ideas. Romantic ones. Thoughtful ones. Funny ones. In the end? Someone else asked her before I even tried *one* of my ideas."

I started laughing. Harder and harder.

"You think that's funny?"

"No. No! Yes! See, that kind of sort of happened to me, too."

"Well, I'm glad I could *amuse* you. Now, don't go anywhere. I'll be right back," Spencer said.

I surveyed the dance floor, checking on Heather.

Did Blake have to dance right there? In plain sight? Why didn't he go somewhere private—say, back to Georgia?

And what was he thinking, anyway? That it was okay to have two girls interested in him at the same time? Maybe I should go over there right now and make out with him, the way she jumped on his lap when I was talking to him. It wasn't too late. I could fight for him.

Did I want to, though? Did it matter?

"Hey. Spencer got me. Dragged me away, actually," Heather said, glaring over at him.

"He's good at that."

"I told him to wait for us over there so we could talk." She gave me a little hug. "He told me what happened. Don't take this thing with Blake personally. He's an idiot, that's all. Anyway, you more than accomplished your goal. You had a summer fling!"

"That counts? We only kissed twice. At a Publix."

"It counts."

"Right. Then why do I feel so bad that it's over all of a sudden?"

"Flings are like that. You can't take them too seriously."

That was easy for her to say. It meant a lot to me when I kissed someone—or it was supposed to.

"You know what? Maybe that wasn't the perfect fling. Maybe you need to set your sights on someone else."

"No thanks."

"Yes," Heather insisted. "Because Dean and I—we're totally hitting it off. He's very cool. And you know what? Maybe you could go out with his friend, Chase. I'll set something up!" she said excitedly.

I shook my head. "No, don't bother—it's okay."

"Emily, this vacation is far from over. Do you want to mope around or do you want to show Blake you can find someone else, too?"

I didn't really care about showing up Blake—I probably wouldn't ever see him again. "Can't I just sit here feeling crushed for a little while?"

"Fine, but I think you're overreacting," Heather said.

"I'm not," I said. "I was really into him! And he invited us here, and now he's making out with another girl!"

Heather gave one last look across the club. "Hmm. I see your point. You want to get out of here?"

"Thought you'd never ask," I sighed.

"Only . . . do you think you can wait a second while I go tell Dean good-bye?" she asked.

"Of course! Take your time," I told her. *Only . . . not too much, because I really want to bolt and every second of this is killing me,* I thought as I smiled at her, trying to put my best face on a bad situation.

"Emily, get whatever you want," Heather said when she slid into a booth at an all-night breakfast place fifteen minutes later. "We're treating."

"We are?" Spencer asked.

"Duh. It's tradition," Heather said. "The person who has the worst night gets treated to breakfast afterward."

"That's not fair. You haven't asked about *my* night," Adam said, pouting.

"Or mine, either," Spencer added, taking a sip of ice water.

"Fine." Heather set down her menu and faced them. "Do tell."

"Yeah. And don't leave anything out, we want all the details," I said, leaning against the wall.

Adam glanced at Spencer. "You want to go first?"

"Sure. Well, I went to this club. The band was supposed to be great, but it was mostly bad cover songs. I ran into some friends. And there was this one girl who would *not* leave me alone."

"You don't mean *me*," I said.

"If the shoe fits . . ." Spencer said.

"Shut up! You should be so lucky. You're the one who wouldn't leave my side."

"As if," Spencer replied. "I tried to leave about a hundred times. You just wanted to stay, for some unknown reason." He turned to Adam. "What happened to you, anyway? I didn't see you all night."

"First I ran into this guy from baseball camp. Then we went to hang out with some guys he knew. We went for pizza, then we hit an arcade, then we ran into more people—"

"Was it fun?" Heather asked.

"Sure. I just felt bad because I ditched you guys," Adam said.

"We've been ditched much worse than that tonight," I muttered. "Don't worry about it."

"Why? What happened?" Adam looked confused.

"Never mind," I said. "Let's talk about something else."

"Okay. Do you guys want to hear about Dean?" Heather asked.

"You know, I'm not sure if I should get the pancakes or the waffles. Can we have a table vote?" asked Spencer, trying to change the subject.

When we got our food, I wasn't all that hungry, so I started taking pictures instead. I got Spencer checking his reflection in the stainless-steel napkin dispenser, Heather trying to keep her long hair out of the maple syrup, and Adam's hands shaking as he had his fourth cup of coffee.

For a while I was having so much fun that I almost completely forgot that I'd been blown off in a major way by the first guy I'd really, actually ever kissed.

Chapter 11

"So, are you guys ready for today's tour?" my mother asked, in an upbeat, chipper mood that couldn't have been more opposite of mine.

We were gathered out back of the house, by the minivan. I'd managed to haul myself out of bed and swallow a couple of sips of coffee before I'd been rounded up for the trip. Everyone was going, which meant I had to, even though I felt more like spending the day in bed, recovering. Not from partying, mind you—from *lack* of partying. From extreme heartbreak, or at least, disappointment.

"Have a bagel, honey," Heather's mother said, holding a paper plate out to me. "You'll feel better."

"Thanks." I took a half and nibbled a corner of it. *But I doubt it.* I leaned against the van and closed my eyes, wishing I were back in bed. I heard the sound of flip-flops snapping toward me and finally opened my eyes, expecting to see Adam or Heather.

"Good morning, y'all!" Blake had sauntered over to greet us. "Where you off to?"

Ugh. I nearly choked on the tiny bite of bagel I'd just swallowed.

He was the last person I wanted to see. And what was with his attitude? Was he so clueless that he didn't realize what had happened the night before—that he'd been a total jerk? His long, green, preppy Bermuda shorts and polo shirt didn't seem so cute anymore. Neither did his tattooed ankle, his spiky platinum hair, his cut body, and his habit of saying "y'all."

"We're going on a drive. See some things," I said. "Lots of things. Cape Hatteras, you know."

"That'll be fun," said Blake. "If only you could ditch the parents . . ." he said out of the corner of his mouth.

"Oh, they're not so bad," I said.

Heather came racing around the corner of the house as if someone had just summoned her. Spencer was right behind her, walking at a fast clip.

"Morning, y'all," Blake greeted them.

"Oh, hi," Spencer said casually. "Didn't see you."

"Wow. Are people still wearing those?" Heather asked, pointing at the obnoxious Bermuda shorts.

"I know my great-grandfather has some," Spencer said. "Drags 'em out every summer for the family reunion."

It wasn't much of a put-down, but I smiled just the same. Blake was glancing down at his outfit, confused. He brushed at some sand sticking on his ankle, by his tattoo.

"Hey, Blake, I've been meaning to ask—what's that tattoo of?"

"It's a chili pepper," Blake said. "Got it in Mexico."

"Really? Is it one of those stick-on ones? Because it looks like it's coming off," said Adam as he approached us from the backyard.

"So what's that supposed to mean? You're hot?" asked Heather.

"Looks like a banana," Spencer observed. "Maybe it's supposed to mean he's bananas?"

"Yeah. Well, it's a jalapeño," Blake said, sounding a little stung that we weren't impressed. "Anyway, I have to go."

"Us too. Have a great day. Y'all," I tacked on bitterly as Heather nearly dragged me into the minivan.

"Good riddance, y'all!" she added with a giggle.

"In the van again . . . I just can't wait to be in the van again."

I groaned at my father's reworking of "On the Road Again." He was almost ruining the beautiful scenery we were passing through on the long, narrow coastal road. There were sand dunes on both sides of us, and sand drifted across the road in places. "Dad, please," I begged.

He kept singing, though. His voice carried. And carried. And carried.

"Dad!" I urged again.

"What?"

"You sang that yesterday," I said. "And the day before. You are embarrassing the entire van."

"Someone's in a good mood," Adam commented.

"Do vans get embarrassed?" Spencer asked. "I'm not sure, I've never seen a van blush—"

"Shut up," I said over my shoulder.

"Emily!" my mother said. "That's not very nice."

"Sorry," I mumbled.

"Like I said: Mood. Not good. Don't provoke her," Adam told Spencer.

"Right. That intense inner ballerina comes out, and when she

113

does, take cover," Spencer teased. "She'll go ballistic in a *Swan Lake* kind of way."

Despite the fact he'd sort of come to my rescue the night before, I wasn't in the mood to be mocked by Spencer. Not that I ever was, but that day in particular, I felt very thin-skinned. But *not* in a ballet dancer way, whatever that was. They should check out a ballet dancer's feet sometime and see just how thick the skin could get when you danced on it every day for hours. Mine had gotten a little softer over the past year, but not much.

Anyway, I felt thin-skinned over the whole Blake episode. Everyone knew that I'd liked him; now they knew he was not into me. I was desperately hoping that we could put it behind us. Getting away from the house for the day was a great idea, even if it meant listening to my dad sing.

In the grand scheme of things, Blake didn't mean all that much to me. I'd remember his shoulders. The way he could wear board shorts and his rock-hard abs. I'd show his picture to my friends at home and tell them how he'd invited me to a party, how he'd loaned me his sweatshirt, how I'd kissed him a few times. That was all true.

It would sound good, in retrospect. Running into him over the rest of our stay would be awkward and embarrassing, but I could handle it.

We pulled into the parking lot of Bodie Island Lighthouse, and Spencer sighed. "Here we go again. Seen one lighthouse, you've seen 'em all," he complained.

"Not really," I said, scooting over to the door to get out of the van. "This one's got stripes."

"As opposed to what?" He climbed out of the backseat. "Polka dots?"

"Just be a good tourist for once in your life, okay?" I sort of snapped at him.

"Maybe you could stop by the gift shop for some chocolate," he suggested before walking away with Adam. "Like, a pound."

While Heather veered off from the group to use her cell phone, my mother slipped into place beside me. "What's wrong?" she asked.

I shook my head. "Nothing."

"Your shoulders always slump when something's wrong. Your posture goes south. So tell me, what is it?"

I tried to raise my shoulders back to their regular height, because I didn't want to talk about it with her, at least not right now.

"Did something happen last night?" Mom asked.

"It just wasn't that much fun," I said. "Loud music, rude people. You know how it is."

"Oh. Well, better luck next time, hon," she said, then she hurried to catch up with Heather's mom.

What, did she have something better to do?

I didn't know whether to feel insulted or elated as I meandered along around the lighthouse park grounds. I mean, it was great that Mom had friends and that the spotlight wasn't on me, for a change. But I could have at least used a hug.

By the time I reached the lighthouse, everyone was turning back.

"We can't tour this one," Mrs. Flanagan told me.

"What a shame," Spencer muttered.

"Look at it this way, kid." His dad slapped him on the back. "That's two hundred and fourteen steps you don't have to climb."

Spencer looked over at him. "Who said I was going to climb?"

"Aren't you working on being a good tourist today? That's what Emily said," his father replied. "Good tourist means participating—"

Spencer lifted his father's hand off his shoulder. "Dad, I'm not eight, okay?"

"Emily. We're waiting for you!" my mother called.

"I'm here. Present and accounted for." I looked at her, not getting it. "What?"

"Before we go, don't you want to get our picture? That's your job," she said.

"Oh. Right. I forgot." I took out my camera while everyone arranged themselves in front of the visitor center sign. Other tourists were streaming in and out of the frame, but I decided it didn't matter—maybe I'd catch something unusual.

"Ready? Everyone say squeeze!" Heather yelled.

"What? Why?" commented Mrs. Flanagan. "Who am I supposed to squeeze, anyway?"

"It's an expression, Mom," Spencer said. "Roll with it."

He looked at me and rolled his eyes, like we'd both had more than enough of our parents for the morning already. I managed a small smile. "Everybody. One-two-three, squeeze!" I called, snapping a picture just as a tall man walked right in front of me.

"Oh, no. Sorry, miss. Sorry," he said.

"It's okay," I told him. "Don't worry about it."

"Let's just go down to Cape Hatteras and have our picnic lunch," my mother declared, and we headed back to the van.

"How much farther is it?" I asked.

"Oh, only about an hour and a half." She opened her backpack and pulled out a box of saltwater taffy, which she handed to me. "Pass these around. It'll make the drive go faster."

"I'll sit next to you," Adam volunteered. "Just in case you need help opening the box."

"No way are you hogging the saltwater taffy," Spencer said, jostling for position beside me as we climbed into the van. "Remember what happened on that trip in Maine? You ate the whole box, then got sick on the Ferris wheel."

"I was eight," said Adam.

"Those who don't learn from history are condemned to repeat it," Spencer said, settling onto the bench seat beside me.

I handed him the box. "Help yourself. Go wild."

"Why are we the only ones doing this?" Spencer asked, halfway up the steps to the top of the Cape Hatteras Lighthouse.

"Adam's up there. Somewhere," I said. "So, we're not the only ones. We're the slow ones."

Heather had stayed behind and had been sipping an iced tea when we decided to take the tour. I was so jealous of her right then that I could spit. Or sweat, anyway. The back of my shirt was getting damp.

"I was only trying to be a good tourist. It's your fault. You're the one who coined the phrase and now my dad is addicted to it," Spencer said. "I didn't read the sign. How many steps is this?"

"Two hundred and sixty-eight," I said, out of breath. "The sign said that it's equivalent to climbing a twelve-story building. I thought, how hard could that be?"

Spencer coughed. "Obviously you've never lived in a twelve-story building. It's really hot in here."

"Not to mention humid," I added.

"Hey, slow down. You're going faster than I am. Maybe I shouldn't have had those twenty-five pieces of saltwater taffy in the van."

"Or that country farmer's breakfast last night," I added. "Was that eight pieces of bacon or ten?"

"I don't know why we have to see the view. I mean, if you've seen one . . . lighthouse . . ." Spencer panted. "You've seen 'em . . ."

Suddenly, he tripped, his foot hitting a step. He fell forward onto me and we both toppled awkwardly onto the stairs with a yelp.

"Oh, God. I'm sorry. I'm really sorry." Spencer stood up and brushed himself off.

"Maybe if you weren't barefoot—"

"I'm not barefoot!" Spencer protested.

"Then it's the fact you're not used to wearing shoes," I said as I got up and brushed some dirt off my arm. "You don't know how to walk in them."

"I tripped! I'm not a *cave*man," Spencer said.

We both walked a few steps farther, then stopped on a landing to rest. A white-haired elderly couple passed us.

"So that's who was breathing down my neck," Spencer whispered.

"They've got to be, like, sixty," I said. "This is getting embarrassing."

"Getting?"

"Hey guys, how's it going?" Adam asked, already on his way back down.

"Just great! Show-off," Spencer muttered under his breath.

"We paid seven dollars to abuse ourselves like this?" I asked. "Okay, so technically my dad paid, but . . ." No wonder Heather had stayed behind.

"I thought I was in shape," Spencer said. "I am so . . . not . . ."

"Sure you are. You're just not in as good shape as half the senior citizens here."

We both collapsed in out-of-breath, winded giggles.

"Come on, if we don't get going we'll get lapped by the next tour," I said, urging him to continue. "You go first this time."

"Fine, but Emily? And I mean this. No pictures," Spencer said. "Okay?"

"What are you thinking? That I wanted a picture of your butt?"

"Who doesn't?" he replied, posing with a little bump to the right.

Another pair of grandparents passed us on the way down and gave us a look that could have stopped—or at least slowed—stairs traffic.

"Do we have to walk all the way back down or can we just rappel?" Spencer asked.

We were standing at the edge of the top of the lighthouse, looking down at the ocean. We'd finally made it after all. "What do you think this is, *The Amazing Race*? I mean, if you want to try skydiving, go ahead, but I don't see anyone holding a mattress down there, and I don't think the ground is very soft."

"I've been skydiving before," Spencer said. "And rock climbing. The only thing I'm not so good at is walking down all those circular steps. It makes me dizzy."

"We don't have to rush back down," I said.

"Technically, we do. There's a time limit, because there's a limit to how many people can be up here at one time."

"So we'll recuperate really quickly."

"Okay, but I want to be a good tourist. Not a bad one who lurks on the side and messes things up for everyone else." He glared at me.

"Keep working at it, you have a ways to go," I said. "How about enjoying the view?" I walked around the top of the lighthouse gazing at the expanses of water and land below.

"Come on, you two—time to get going," our tour guide said. "Time to begin our descent."

"Okay, but first—can I please take a few photos?" I said.

"Sure, but make it quick." She nodded at me.

"Do you have a timer on that thing?" Spencer asked.

"Of course, but—why? We don't need a picture of us together," I said as I focused the camera on the light at the top.

"Sure we do," Spencer said. "We're the only ones who had the legs to climb this thing."

"And Adam," I reminded him.

"Oh. Right, I forgot."

"Did you want me to get your picture planting the flag or something? You know, like people do when they climb Everest?" I teased.

"Excuse me. Sir?" Spencer approached a man standing next to us. "Would you mind taking our picture?"

"Not at all." He took the camera from me, and I showed him which button to push and explained how he had to wait to hear the little click. "Okay, guys. Stand over there. Closer, closer . . ." he urged.

"Aw. You guys make a cute couple," his wife said as we posed with big smiles, standing about a foot apart, our hands awkwardly perched on each other's shoulders, as if we were teammates on a very unclose team.

"Oh, we're not," I said.

"Of course you're cute, in fact you're adorable—and how old are you? Sixteen, seventeen?" she went on.

Spencer frowned at her. "Nineteen. And we're not a couple," he quickly said.

"Got it!" the man said. He handed the camera to me. "I took five or six. You can delete the ones you don't want."

"Believe me, she will. She loves to delete. She *lives* to delete."

What's he talking about? I wondered, but I ignored his comment, thanked the couple, and headed for the stairs, Spencer following me. We nearly sprinted back down the spiral steps with our group. It wasn't half as much fun as the way up.

"So. We can check that off the must-see list," Spencer said as we exited. "It was definitely worth it."

"Yeah. My mom will be thrilled," I told him. "Let's eat!"

Heather jumped up as we walked over to her and said, "I finally got in touch with Dean, and it's all set."

"What's all set?" I asked.

"You meeting Chase, what else? Tonight."

"Ooh! The excitement!" Spencer said in a high-pitched voice as he waved his hands in the air.

Why was it that whenever I started to not detest him, he did something like this?

"Did I *say* that?" I asked. "Do I ever act like that?"

"Hmm. Let me think."

"You know what? Never mind. I don't *care* what you think. You're always going around telling us how you're older and how you know more and how we're so immature. Well, guess what? You're the one who's immature. And as far as going to college? I don't think you're ready, even if you are a—a so-called sopho-man."

"It's freshomore," he said in a quiet tone.

"It's annoying, is what it is." Heather headed for the van and I followed her, glad to have backup.

Chapter 12

"How's it going?" the young guy standing at the photo printer beside mine asked.

"Oh! Hi. Fine," I said. I'd been sitting here for an hour, editing pictures and organizing shots, before I went ahead and made prints of the ones I wanted. "How are you?" I asked.

"Good. Tired but good."

"Yeah." I'd walked to a pharmacy to use their photo printer the next morning. I knew that according to Heather, I should be making every attempt to hit it off with this guy, that I should see what we had in common, which was easy because obviously we were both the kind of people who get up early in order to take pictures, or at least to get those pictures printed.

I could ask him about his camera. We could talk about focus and zoom features and lenses, and the rule of thirds.

But I was starting to feel like there was no point in me trying, that I was slightly-to-very jinxed when it came to guys. If I talked to this one, I'd probably end up wiping out all of his digital images or shredding all my prints by mistake. Best to just focus on the task at hand.

After I'd finished making prints, I was walking up to the counter to pay for an orange juice when I saw Spencer looking at his reflection in a twirling sunglasses display. I stopped and stared at him. "What are you doing here? You weren't following me again, were you?"

"Are you serious? Get over yourself," he replied.

His dad's head popped up from the other side of the display. He had on large, white, square sunglasses that seemed more intended for Taylor Swift than him. "We're heading out in the kayak this morning. Got to have sunglasses for that. Bright sun out there on the water."

"Right. You sure do," I agreed.

"I need new sunglasses because mine fell off somewhere yesterday between the 175th and 176th steps," Spencer said.

"Really?" I checked out his reflection as he slid a pair of wire-rim glasses over his nose.

"What about these? Hmm. Well, what are you doing here?" he asked. "Did you need sunscreen or something?"

"It's personal," I said.

His face started to blush slightly. "Sorry . . . I . . ."

"It's this." I held up the brightly colored envelope with the giant word PHOTOS on the side.

Spencer looked up slowly, as if he was afraid of what he might see. "Oh! Pictures. Can I see?" he asked.

"Not yet. I mean, I'm putting them together for everyone. I want it to be a surprise."

"You are? You never said anything about that."

"You never asked. And it's a surprise, remember? So don't tell anyone," I said.

"Okay. I'll just say I saw you here . . . buying juice. They'll believe it," he said.

"I have such deep, dark secrets," I muttered.

"You want a ride back?" he asked, following me to the door.

"No, thanks. I'll walk. But maybe you should pay for those before you set off the security alarm?" I pointed to his glasses, then swept out the door.

When I got back to the house, I saw Heather lying on the beach. I quickly ran up to my room and stashed all the prints in my room's desk, changed into my bikini, then hurried outside with my hat and towel.

"Where *were* you last night?" I asked in a whisper as I dropped down to sit beside her.

"Nowhere. What do you mean?" Heather laughed. "With Dean, where else?"

"Yeah? So *tell*."

"Tell what?"

"What did you do?"

"We played mini golf. It was really cool." She smiled.

I laughed. "It was?"

"Yes. Why is that so funny?"

"I just never thought of putt-putt being . . . romantic," I said.

"Well, as a matter of fact . . . at night, with all the lights? It's actually almost cool. We had a nice time by the twirling windmill."

"Really?"

"Really. We were kissing and this older couple with their little kids was like, 'Ahem. Ahem!' They were coughing so loudly but we just pretended we didn't hear them."

"That sounds fun. So you guys are kind of an item," I said.

"We'll see. It might be a one-date thing, you never know. But I'm sorry it didn't work out to meet Chase last night."

"That's okay. I tried that whole vacation romance concept once. It didn't work out so well for me. Ahem. Exhibit A. Or should I say B."

She followed my gaze over to our next-door neighbors' deck, where Blake was standing, checking out the beach. He caught us looking his way and waved hello. I waved back, feeling kind of pathetic. "Cheers," I muttered.

I looked down at the water, where Spencer and his dad were either getting ready to go out in the double kayak, or maybe just coming back in. "Excuse me for a sec, Heather," I said, and got up and walked down to the water's edge.

"Emily! You want to try it?" Mr. Flanagan offered. "It's great fun. I'm sure Spencer would be glad to take you out."

I had this image in my head of being stranded with Spencer out on open water. He'd probably mock the way I paddled. "I don't know, I mean, you guys are all set up—"

"That's all right, I want to go get some breakfast," Mr. Flanagan said. "You ought to give it a try."

"Oh, no, Emily doesn't do any water sports." Spencer shook his head. "She hates sports. She hates water."

I laughed. "I do not! That's not true."

I looked up and saw Blake coming closer, beach volleyball gear in hand. His red-haired girlfriend was right behind him, wearing what looked like a black vinyl—or possibly leather—swimsuit. If I had to stick around and watch the two of them, I'd go insane, or at least, more insane.

"Sure, I'd love to go kayaking," I said. "Thanks, Mr. Flanagan."

Spencer nearly dropped the kayak paddle. "Really?"

"Sure, why not?"

"Um . . . I can think of lots of reasons, but if you're up for it, that's great."

"Here you go." Mr. Flanagan handed me his life jacket. "I'm off to score some muffins."

I pulled the life jacket over my head and connected the various snaps and straps.

Spencer started laughing at me.

"What's so funny?" I asked.

"That's a bit large on you." He walked over to help me adjust it from his dad's size to mine. He put his hand on my waist, cinching the nylon belt.

"Can't you make it any tighter?" I gasped.

"What?"

"I can't breathe!"

"Oh! Sorry." He stepped in closer to make a few adjustments, and I found myself standing eye to cheek-scar. "We just have to make sure it's on there properly in case something happens."

"What's going to happen?" I asked, feeling funny about standing so close with so few clothes on.

"Nothing. A little splash now and then from paddling." He shrugged as he stepped back and got the boat ready for us. "You've kayaked before, right?"

"Sure. Sure." I nodded. "We had a kayak class at camp."

He narrowed his eyes at me. "You went to ballet camp," he said. "Didn't you?"

"Yes, but you can't spend the entire day indoors," I said.

"You can't? Then how do you keep your skin so pale?"

"Through the careful application of sunscreen." I frowned at him. "Just get in," I said.

"You first," Spencer offered. I slid into the front seat of the two-person kayak and picked up the paddle. *So far, so good,* I thought. No major incidents, nothing to embarrass me—further—in front of Blake.

"Emily. Emily! Where are you going in that thing?" my mother shouted. "Don't you know this area is known as the Graveyard of the Atlantic?"

"Mom, that's for big boats running aground!" I called over my shoulder. "Not us!"

"Wow." Spencer was just staring at me, holding on to both sides of the kayak.

"What?"

He nodded. "Impressed that you knew that."

"I'm a good tourist. I read all the brochures and signs." I smiled.

"Right." Spencer climbed into the kayak, and, at the same time, pushed off with his back foot. "Now, the thing we have to do is attack the water to get past these first couple waves, okay? So when I say paddle, you really have to paddle."

"Gotcha." I settled into my seat and we took our first paddle. A wave was curling about fifteen feet off, but I knew it would break before it got to us. We paddled on, through its foamy bubbles after it broke, and headed farther out.

I saw another medium-size wave coming, but it was still a ways off. Suddenly, just to my right, I spotted something jump. I watched again. "Look! Over there! Dolphins!"

"Paddle!" Spencer shouted.

"Dolphins—did you see?" I pointed with my paddle.

"*Wave!* Did you see—"

The bow of the kayak went straight up—then the wave crashed right on top of us—and we tipped to the right, completely falling over, getting tumbled and thrown around by the water. The kayak was tilted on its side and I was instantly drenched with water. I half fell, half climbed out.

"Not one of your more graceful moves," Spencer said as he swam and walked back toward shore.

I couldn't stop laughing. "Oh, my God, imagine how dumb that must have looked!"

"Don't worry, I'm sure only about two hundred people were watching, including your boy Blake, and his latest flame—"

"Quiet!" I said, still laughing as a strap from Spencer's life jacket got tangled up in the boat, and he fell into me, knocking me to the sand in the shallow water.

"Okay, apparently you neglected to read the brochure on kayak safety," Spencer began as we clambered to our feet, brushing sand off our swimsuits and legs. "The thing is that you have to get beyond the waves in order to start sightseeing. And when I tell you to paddle—*paddle!*"

"I know, but they were dolphins, Spencer. Real, live dolphins!" I said.

"What's the big deal? Haven't you ever been to SeaWorld?"

"No, and besides, these are wild dolphins. Free range. Whatever," I said. "That makes them so much more interesting. Let's go back out—we have time, don't we, before today's tour of whatever?" I looked at my pink watch. The numbers didn't flash anymore. "My watch!"

"Does that thing actually tell time or does it just beep when the Hello Kitty trend is over, so you know when to throw it out?"

"What? I'd never throw it out, what are you saying?" I looked at it again. "You got your wish. Kitty seems to have drowned. Good-bye Hello Kitty," I said, and we both laughed. "Why is everyone standing on the deck?" I asked. "Are they laughing at us?"

"I would be."

"Why are they waving hysterically at us?"

"Maybe those aren't dolphins," Spencer suggested. "Maybe they're sharks."

"What? No." I shook my head. "Definitely dolphins. Should we try to go out on the water again now or should we ask them what's going on first?"

"My mom's waving at me. We'd better see what it's all about." Spencer pulled the kayak up on the beach, closer to the house, and we laid the paddles underneath it.

I took off my life jacket and draped it over the edge of the deck to dry out, and Spencer did the same.

"What's going on?" I asked as we walked up onto the deck to join the group.

"Linden just called. The admissions office," Adam said. A big grin spread across his face. "I got in!" He picked me up and swung me around. "Isn't that incredible?"

"Congratulations, man." Spencer reached for Adam's hand to shake it, and they did one of those guy-hugs where they pat each other's shoulder and hug without really touching.

"Of course, I'm not that surprised. I knew I was going to get in," Adam said.

"Right. Of course," Spencer teased him.

"Can you believe it? All four of us at the same time?"

"So, you've been saving up?" my dad was asking Mr. Thompson, and they started teasing each other about how much textbooks would cost and how we'd bankrupt them before junior year.

"Now isn't the time to be practical. Let's celebrate! Group hug!" Mrs. Thompson said, and they forced us all into this mob-scene hug.

Everyone was hugging and laughing and the twins were shrieking, and I just stood there with my cheek crushed against Spencer's chest, thinking, *Boy, this feels kind of nice. And oh, no, this college deal is going to be awkward. I am really starting to like Spencer. Again. Or, rather, still. Maybe even more than the last time I saw him. And we're all so close. If I try to say anything again, and I blow it, we'll all be at the same school. And I'll want to transfer.*

But if I don't say anything and he goes out with someone else, I'll be completely miserable and I'll want to transfer.

I was stuck.

Chapter 13

"You know what would be great? If you all ended up in the same dorm," Heather's mom said.

We were having a big dinner to celebrate the news that Adam had gotten into Linden. All the parents had prepared it together, and we had clams, shrimp, steak, three different salads, and enough veggies, chips, and dips to feed an army.

"If you were in the same dorm, then the guys would be right there to look after you, keep an eye on you for us," Mrs. Olsen continued.

"Oh, that would be nice," my mom agreed, nodding.

"I can look after Heather," I piped in, feeling completely full from the last stuffed shrimp I'd eaten.

"Yeah. And I don't want to burst your bubble, but Adam's going to be too busy doing sports, and Spencer wouldn't do that at all," Heather said.

"He wouldn't? What do you mean?" Her mom looked surprised.

"Well, he pretty much only cares about Spencer."

Spencer looked over at us with an exaggerated, clown-like sad face. *"Me?"*

"That's not true. He volunteered for months," my mother said, coming to his defense. "He's given up a year of the most exciting time in a young person's life to help others."

"Wait a minute, Mrs. Matthias. Are you saying I can't get it back?" Spencer asked, looking puzzled. "That year is like, gone?"

I wanted to laugh, but at the same time I didn't want him to think he was funny. Is that selfish?

"Spencer, tell me about your year off," my dad said. "I'd love to hear more about that. What was the coolest thing about volunteering?"

"Meeting all the people. Amazing people. A lot more interesting than us, you know? Different lives. Some of them have been through so much, lost everything, and they're still positive," he said. "Which is incredible to me."

"Okay, so we're impressed by the way he helps total strangers," Heather said to the group. "But he doesn't associate with us . . . unless he has to. He already told us he wasn't even going to talk to us at Linden."

"What?" Spencer cried. "I never said that—"

"You did." I nodded.

"I wasn't serious! I was just giving you a hard time," Spencer said. "Come on, guys."

"I heard him, too," Adam said. "Plus, he gave me a hard time about not getting in."

"My apologies. To all of you," Spencer said.

I glanced over at Heather's plate and saw she hadn't eaten much, even though everyone else was completely pigging out on the delicious food. I wondered if she was feeling okay. She hadn't said anything, but she had seemed a little down for most of the night.

"Maybe you can redeem yourself by clearing the table," suggested Spencer's dad.

"Fine." Spencer got up and started taking away empty plates, and I took another look at Heather while our parents continued to plot what would be best for us when we got to college. I was starting to think they all needed to go back to school for advanced degrees—for any kind of degree. Just not at Linden.

"Are you done?" Spencer asked Heather, gesturing to her plate.

"For now. I'll eat leftovers later," she said.

"What's great about Linden is that it's a small campus, but you still meet people from all over the world," Mr. Thompson was saying.

"Oh, sure, but you have to sign up for activities, clubs—" my dad chimed in. "In fact, tell you what. First thing you do when you hit campus is go to the Linden Leadership Office."

"Actually, I think I'll find my dorm room first," Adam said with a laugh, looking over at me and Heather, as if to say, *Help! I can't take any more advice!*

Heather poked my leg. "Are you with me?" she whispered.

"What?" I whispered back.

"Just follow me!" Heather gestured to Adam and Spencer, too.

As the adults continued to talk about their best moves in college, Heather grabbed cups and a half-full bottle of white wine from the table, and the four of us sprinted for the stairs.

"Hey! Where are you—" my mother sputtered.

"We need to plot our own strategy, have our own celebration," I told her. "We'll be back, don't worry!"

We hurried outside, across the deck, and down onto the beach. Adam took the bottle of wine from Heather and started filling our cups. Then he set the bottle in the sand, grinding the bottom down a little so it wouldn't fall over and spill.

"Look out, I think you just killed something," Spencer said, holding something up to the slim moonlight.

Adam stared at it. "It's a shell."

"A shell of its former self, that's what it is," Spencer said. "This is a sand crab, and this little sand crab is part of a community, and—"

Adam groaned. "Listen up, Al Gore. We're trying to have fun here." He took a sip from his cup. "Okay? So don't mention how the tide is too high and the beach is eroding and we're killing all the sand life."

"Fine. I won't. But we are." Spencer drained the rest of his cup of wine, then grabbed the bottle for a refill.

Heather sank onto the sand beside me and stretched her legs, then scrunched up into a ball, hugging her knees. She took a sip of wine. She didn't seem to be in that celebrating mood we were all supposed to be in, and I wondered if the big, special dinner was making the adults happier than it was making us—and her, in particular.

"Great night," I said. "I mean, weather."

"Hmm," Heather agreed.

"So. I'm totally not trying to pry, but . . . how are things?" I asked. "Besides Dean, because we know things are going great there." I smiled.

"Okay." She sighed. "I guess."

"Are you sure?" I asked.

"It's just . . . some days are hard. I mean, it's been an incredibly hard year. I think that's why I want to unwind so much while I'm here, with you and everyone," she said. "It just feels really good to get away from there. From home, I mean."

"I can imagine," I said. "Sort of. I'm sure I don't know anything, though."

"At home there are lots of memories. I've never been here before, so . . ." She shrugged. "Despite the fact I have to hang out with all of my dad's best friends, it's actually okay. Then I think about going home."

"You won't be there too long," I said.

"True. But then we'll go to Linden. And Dad was all about Linden. You know?" she asked.

I nodded. "He'd be really proud of you, knowing you're going."

She squeezed her cup, crumpling it a bit. "But he's supposed to *be* there at Homecoming."

"I know. Totally embarrassing you by wearing a giant Linden sweatshirt with a matching hat, and shouting through a megaphone—"

"Yeah," Heather said. "Exactly."

Spencer sat down on the other side of her. "Now you'll just have to listen to Emily's dad singing the leaf song."

"It's not the leaf song," I protested. "It's called 'Linden, My Linden.'"

"Listen to her. Trying to suck up already by knowing the school song," Spencer said.

"You guys. It's not funny. It's not fair," Heather said quietly. I looked at her and saw a tear sliding down her cheek.

"It isn't fair," I agreed, "you're right."

"Completely unfair," Spencer agreed.

"It sucks, is what," said Adam as the four of us gathered in a semicircle.

Heather sat there for a minute, just quietly crying, resting her chin on her arms. I had put my arm around her, and Spencer put his arm around her, too. I didn't know what I could say.

"You know what, Heather?" Spencer said. "I really wanted to be there, for the memorial service. I only saw your dad a couple times a year, but he made a big impression on me."

"He did?"

"Yeah." Spencer nodded. "You know how my dad can be hard on me sometimes? Like, he thinks I should be exactly like him, and I'm not. Well, your dad must have noticed that, and he'd always find a way to tell me it was cool, whatever I decided to be. 'Football isn't life,' he said once, when my dad was criticizing my passing technique."

"Which you have to admit, sucks," Adam noted.

"Anyway, I just thought you should know—we all miss him, too. And we're not going to forget him," Spencer said.

"Thanks." Heather sniffled.

"When that happened . . . the real reason I couldn't come to the funeral was I had this really close friend—from high school. He got hit by a car, riding his bike off campus. It was the day before we were supposed to fly out and he was in a coma. I couldn't just leave him."

"Did he die?" I finally asked.

"No, but he was unconscious for a week, then he couldn't walk for months. His memory's still not all there. He's just getting out of rehab now, and . . . anyway. It's not about him. I mean, it's about— you find yourself walking around wondering what's the point? Because it *isn't* fair."

"Exactly," Heather said.

"And you have no idea what's coming, but all of a sudden your whole life can change. That's not fair, either," Spencer went on. "I can't even begin to imagine how much worse it is for you. We all miss your dad, but that's not even—a millionth of it."

I watched him just holding Heather, letting her collapse against him.

Suddenly, he seemed like the best and nicest friend a person could have.

I didn't just want to be in the same dorm with him. I wanted to be *with* him, with him.

"You know what we'll have to do," Adam said. "We'll have to all take off together some weekend. Go camping. Just get away from campus."

"Camping?" Heather scoffed. "How about a hotel? In Detroit or someplace. Or Los Angeles, maybe. Ooh—what about Mexico?"

"Are you talking about spring break? Already?" teased Spencer.

"What's wrong with camping?" Adam asked.

I cleared my throat. "Remember the night we all slept outside? By that cabin in New Hampshire? And a porcupine decided to try and sneak into the tent?"

"*What* tent?" Spencer said.

"Oh, yeah. *That* was the problem." Adam started to laugh. "And you—Heather—you tried to fend him off with your hair dryer—you brought your hair dryer camping—"

"And you threw a book at it—and missed, thank God—"

"Remember, Emily?" Spencer was holding his stomach. "You said, 'p-p-p-p-p-' for like ten minutes before you could get the word *porcupine* out."

We were all laughing so hard, it was impossible to talk. *Must be the wine,* I thought. Heather seemed happier, which was really all I cared about.

◦ ◦ ◦

"Em?" Spencer knocked on my door. "You in there?"

I was half undressed, toweling off my hair. We'd all run into the ocean for a late-night swim after our little wine party, and then we'd headed inside to change into dry clothes. I quickly pulled on a clean T-shirt, a dry pair of jeans, and opened the door.

"I think I got your fleece jacket by mistake. It's a small-medium and I haven't worn a small-medium since eighth grade." He handed me my jacket and walked past me into the room.

"You were really short back then," I observed.

"Thank you. I remember it well."

"I didn't know you could climb four flights without passing out," I teased him.

"I've been training." Spencer wandered around the room. "So this is what it's like to have the best room in the house."

"It's not the best—look how small it is," I pointed out.

"Look how private it is," Spencer countered. "Look how your parents are not sleeping in the living room."

"That's only because there *is* no living room."

"But you're all alone. What if you wake up in the middle of the night, crying? Your parents won't be there."

"Shut up," I said, shoving him so that he fell onto my bed.

He put his hands behind his head and bounced a few times on the bed. "Your bed is more comfortable than mine," he complained. "You have way more room up here than I do." Then he jumped up and went out to the balcony. "So this is what I look like from up here."

"Like what?" I asked, walking out beside him. The last time I'd stood on this balcony with anyone, it had been Blake. The balcony had a sort of jinxed feeling, like maybe if we stood here too long, we'd plummet to the ground.

"Um . . . short. I guess." Spencer shrugged. "So . . . when we were all talking, earlier, on the beach? There was something I wanted to say. But I couldn't tell everyone, but maybe I can tell you."

"Okay," I said slowly. "Go ahead."

"I have a confession to make. And I'm only going to tell you. I mean, eventually I'll have to tell everyone, or everyone will find out, anyway, but maybe for now we could sort of keep it between us. Okay?"

"Sure," I said with a smile, but I was afraid to ask. Afraid to find out. What if it was something extremely private? What if it was "I'm gay"? What if it was "I'm in love with Heather"?

"What is it?" I finally asked, after running through all the worst-case scenarios in my mind.

"The reason I know so much about freshman orientation? I already went through it," he said.

"You what?"

"I went through it already," Spencer said. "I started college last year."

"You did? Where? But you said—"

"I didn't stay long enough to finish the semester, so it doesn't count. We don't talk about it much, because my folks were so mad at me, because they spent the money."

"Okay. Explain," I said.

"I didn't want to go to Linden, because I was so sick of being pressured to apply there by my dad. I mean, I applied and I got in, but I applied other places, too, and at the last minute I decided to start at UVM instead of Linden. It was a lot less expensive, closer to home, and most of all—it was the opposite of what my dad wanted. A bigger school, and *not* Linden. I don't know if you know this. But my dad and I have this history of me trying to live up to what he wants—and it isn't what I want."

"I know a little about that," I said. "So what happened?"

"I went to UVM, but I didn't really want to be there. Nothing against the school—it just wasn't the right fit for me. There was that thing with my good friend getting hurt, so I was home a lot visiting him, and I didn't know how to deal with living in a dorm, I didn't like my classes—everything was just wrong."

"Maybe because the guys talk up Linden so much—like college is supposed to be *so* amazing," I said. "Anything less than that and you probably feel like you're missing out, or doing something wrong."

"Exactly!"

Spencer's eyes were shining in the small amount of light that came from my room. I'd never seen him so animated—it was like we were really connecting over this. I hadn't even had time to process what he'd just told me—that his time off had ended up being for a good cause, but that he hadn't started out exactly with that noble plan in mind.

"So, you left? You just . . . up and left in the middle of the semester? Wow. That's . . . gutsy," I told him.

"Not really." He shook his head. "I didn't know what to do. I didn't want to sit around at home, I knew that. And our community center and church were organizing this trip. I went for the two weeks, and then I just stayed. And stayed. After a while I realized how lucky I was, how I had all these chances to make my life be whatever I wanted. So I called and talked to the admissions counselor at Linden, and they let me reapply. And that is the long, boring story of why I'll be a freshomore."

"It wasn't boring," I said.

"No?" he asked.

"Well. Not nearly as boring as your girl-next-door story, anyway," I said.

"What?" he cried. "Hey, I only *told* you that because I felt sorry for you—"

"Well, it worked, because afterward I felt sorry for *you*."

We were laughing when there was a loud knock and suddenly Heather barged into the room.

"Oh, my God, you have to see this. The guys are all competing to see who can make the biggest splash in the pool—and my mom's videotaping. They're making total idiots of themselves—Spencer, your dad is winning! Come on!"

Spencer and I bumped into each other on the way off the balcony. Then we both tried to squeeze through the door at the same time.

"After you," Spencer said, holding out his hand to show me the way.

"No, after you," I said.

I felt closer to Spencer tonight than I ever had before. The problem was, what was I going to do about it *this* time?

Something? Anything? Nothing?

When we got downstairs, Heather was greeting Dean with a hug at the door to the pool area. Spencer and I waited to say hi to him, and just before Dean closed the door behind him, Blake stepped up out of the shadows. "What's going on, y'all? Sounds fun."

"Actually, it's a private party," Spencer told him. "Sorry. No Neanderthals allowed."

"No what?" asked Blake.

"Exactly. 'Night, y'all. Safety first." Spencer closed the door in his face.

I laughed, feeling almost as satisfied as if I'd been the one to dis him. "Thanks."

"No prob. We've got enough Neanderthals in here already." He pointed to his dad, who was about to do a cannonball off the diving board. "Run for cover!"

Chapter 14

The next morning we toured Kitty Hawk, for our Mom-influenced group activity. After lunch, Heather and I took off on a shopping spree. Well, as much of a spree as a person can have with only $45 in her pocket. I also wanted to spend time with her and make sure she was doing okay after last night. She was so strong and resilient. I really admired her for that, in the midst of our silly vacation stuff.

"This is great. We can meet Chase and Dean tonight for a late swim, then go to dinner—"

"Actually, um, Heather? I appreciate everything you're doing. But I'm not interested in Chase."

"How do you know? You've barely talked to him."

"The thing is . . . I think I'm interested in someone else."

"Not Blake. Still."

I shook my head. "No, not Blake."

"Phew. Then who?"

"Don't laugh, okay?"

"Why would I laugh?"

"Because it's Spencer," I said.

Heather giggled, then put her hand over her mouth. "Sorry. Not laughing. Because you're apparently . . . serious. You like *Spencer*?" she cried.

"Shh! Do you have to tell the entire store? What if he's in here?"

"Why would he be in here?"

"He's been known to follow us. Remember?"

"True. But I doubt that he'd set foot in Brenda's Bikini World."

I giggled. "Well, no, unless he was trying to meet girls." Then that thought sort of made me feel sick.

"You know, he was really great last night when I got upset. That was like a whole other side of him."

"I know. I feel like I've been getting to know him pretty well. Despite the fact he has this whole layer of arrogance. And I just . . . I find that I want to get even closer to him. Does that sound dumb? That sounds dumb."

"It sounds kind of sexy, if you ask me. So, is that why we're here?"

"Why we're where?" I asked.

"At this shop! Because you plan to make your move wearing something sexy?"

"No! We're in this shop because you dragged me in here. Anyway, I don't even know how to make a so-called move. I don't make 'moves.' I make . . . mistakes," I said.

Heather laughed. "But see, that's where you're wrong. So you're not the type of person to just have a meaningless fling. That's great. I totally support that. You're more about the long-term relationship."

I held up a red, flowered, strapless top. "Then how come I've never *had* one?"

"You were waiting for the right person."

"No, I was waiting. Period."

"What do you mean?"

"Well, whenever I've liked a guy, I've always waited too long to tell them how I feel. And then before I say anything, they end up moving away, leaving town, or even worse, hooking up with someone else."

"So. That isn't going to happen with Spencer. But it could, when we get to college. So don't wait any longer. Tell him."

"It sounds so simple. You know? When you say it, I can picture doing it. But when it comes down to making it happen, I can't."

"You know what? This totally makes sense. He likes you, too. I mean, why did he butt in where Blake was concerned? Why does he constantly give you a hard time—"

"He gives everyone a hard time," I reminded her.

"Please. He doesn't want you to be with anyone else because he wants you."

As much as I loved the thought of that, I wondered if it was just wishful thinking. Friends did that a lot for each other.

"He's into you. Trust me," Heather said.

"Why? Did he say anything to you?" I asked, feeling hopeful, wishing there was some sort of evidence that I could cling to so I'd feel more confident if I ever did go to him.

"No, but I can tell by the way he was looking at you last night. When I came into your room? Wait. Did I interrupt something?"

"No. Not exactly." I felt my face turn red. "Maybe. I don't know! He's so hard to read. Which is funny, considering all he *does* is read. That should make him transparent, don't you think? The thing is, I find it totally impossible to talk to guys. To tell them how I feel. So, what I was thinking was, how about if I just write him a letter? Slip it under his door?"

"Emily." She gave me a very serious look. "I know it's very hard. And really intimidating. But one thing to remember is you don't ever write a letter telling them."

I knew I should probably trust Heather on this. She had the rules: You get a guy's name and number. You let him know you're interested. "No? Letters don't work?"

"By the time he gets and reads the letter he could be hooking up with someone else."

"Really? But what if we're, like, meant to be?" I asked.

"What if someone else reads it? Or what if he shows it to other people?" She shook her head. "Oh, no. Trust me on this. Never write anything down. Don't even send a text or e-mail. It'll be retrieved from his computer one day and you'll die of embarrassment," she said.

"Okay. Well. I could do a photo collage, then. A story in pictures," I said. "I could show this progression—hold on, I could make a *movie*—"

"Emily, how long is *that* going to take? Two weeks? You don't have two weeks."

"I know, but what about Linden? I mean, what about the fact we're both going there—isn't this a horrible, terrible idea?" I asked.

"You're looking for excuses. Who cares about Linden? Get him alone. And tell him. And go try that on." Heather pointed to the eensy-weensy bikini I'd been examining.

"Are you sure?"

"What's the point of staying in shape and doing all that dancing if you don't show it off?"

"Well, the thing is, once I put this on, I don't think I'll be able to *move*," I said. "Without it falling off."

"Hey, no problem—that could really speed things along," she joked.

I stuck out my tongue at her as I swept the changing-room curtain closed. I'd brought in some other suits, too. I wasn't the type to be sexy by revealing everything—I needed something a little more modest, or I'd be so self-conscious I wouldn't be able to talk to anyone—or even leave my room.

When we got home, I put on my new bikini, slipped into a pair of pink nylon board shorts and my flip-flops, and went to find Spencer. I was feeling very charged up from the two coffees I'd had during our shopping spree, like I could accomplish anything.

He was sitting in the third-floor living room, reading yet another classic novel, right where I'd left him earlier.

What do I do now? I wondered. *He's alone. We're alone. I could slide onto the sofa next to him and just . . . tell him.*

But then the image of the last time I tried this popped into my brain. Me, lying on the floor in a sleeping bag, at the condo we'd rented. Spencer, sitting on a fold-out sofa. Me, getting up and sitting next to him, telling him how I felt, how I thought he was cool, how I wished we could see each other more often. And other embarrassing, personal things like that.

Him, interrupting me, changing the subject, saying anything except, "Yeah, I feel the same way about *you.*" Saying something about "I have to get some sleep," and disappearing under a blanket, his back to me.

What was I doing this for? Did I *enjoy* torture?

"Hey, Spencer. You want to go out in the kayak?" I asked, perching on the edge of the chair opposite him.

He looked over at me. "Not really."

"Come on. Please?"

He stretched his arms over his head and yawned. "I thought you hated water sports, and sports of any kind."

"Yeah, but I had a good time kayaking. Remember?"

"You fell *out* of the kayak."

Oops. "True. But I'm an excellent swimmer," I said. "Plus, I want to take some pictures out there. Find some dolphins again."

"You can't just find them. It's not like a whale watch. I mean, they don't have schedules."

"They don't?" I gasped, putting my hand over my mouth.

He laughed. "Okay, so we'll look for dolphins, but no crying if we don't find any."

"Like I'd cry. Have you ever seen me cry?"

"Please. I was there when your dad had to tie a string to one of your front baby teeth and pull it out. You cried."

"Oh. Well. Hopefully none of my teeth are going to fall out."

"And how about the time we went to that amusement park—and your cotton candy fell off the stick? Major tears."

"Can you blame me?" I asked as I followed him down the stairs.

He stopped walking, and I crashed into him. "What do you mean, you want to go out there and take pictures? You're bringing your camera after what happened last time? Do you not remember getting soaked?"

"Give me some credit. Don't worry, I have a waterproof, disposable one. Ten bucks and it floats." I took it out of my shorts pocket to show him.

"Well. As long as *we* float, too, that should work."

We grabbed the life jackets from the first floor and pulled the kayak down from where it leaned against the deck stairs, toward the water.

When we got in, I wished we'd capsize. Sink. Anything to give me an easy opening like, *Please don't sink because I like you! I'm drowning! I need mouth-to-mouth resuscitation!*

I didn't know how to tell him, what I was supposed to say. The way we sat in the kayak, his back was already turned to me, because he'd insisted on switching around this time. That didn't bode well.

"Lovely weather, isn't it?" I commented.

"Sure," he said.

"Ooh! Is that a dolphin?" I pointed out into the ocean at something sort of gray.

"That's a bird, floating," Spencer said.

"Oh." I kept paddling, making sure we stayed parallel to the coastline and didn't go too far out. I could swim, but not in a triathlon sort of way. "You know what? Birds are cool. Coastal birds. The way they just hover and then dive for the kill." *Maybe I could strive to be more like them*, I thought with a smile.

Spencer didn't respond. I didn't blame him. He was paddling very weakly as if he didn't care whether we got anywhere or not.

"You know what else is cool? The Outer Banks," I said. "Talk about a gem."

"What are you, the Chamber of Commerce now? You're taking this good tourist–bad tourist thing to extremes."

"Fine. I'll stop talking," I said.

"Great," Spencer replied.

I kept my mouth closed for a minute or two. But that wasn't the point of this ocean journey. If Spencer didn't want to talk, that was too bad—I had to make him talk. "Don't mind me. I'll just be taking some underwater photos back here. Ooh, look, a coral reef. An octopus. Buried treasure!" I cried. "No *way!*"

Spencer's neck turned ever so slowly to the right and he lowered his new sunglasses to give me an aggravated look. "Do you mind? I'm trying to read."

"What? You're not *reading*," I said.

He held his book over his head to show me.

"I hate you sometimes," I said.

"I know."

I glared at his back. "I hope we're not in any of the same classes."

"I know."

Suddenly, I realized that drinking two large coffees before going out on the ocean in a kayak was not such a great idea. "Since you're not really into it, why don't we just turn back," I suggested. Strongly.

"I'm into it," he said. "I'm just trying to multitask."

"Well, uh, I actually need to get back. I forgot that I planned to meet Heather," I said.

"Heather can wait."

"No, um, she can't." I awkwardly tried to turn the kayak around. "Little help?"

Later that afternoon, I thought about asking Spencer out for dinner, but he had already gone out with his parents.

When he got back, I challenged him to a game of pool, but the adults were playing, involved in some major challenge, with men versus women.

By the time it was ten at night and I still hadn't managed to say a real, actual word to Spencer in private, I decided that I had no choice. I knew he'd gone to his room earlier to read, but I didn't want to go through his parents' room. Again. I didn't want to watch a game with his dad or apply a facial with his mom. Small talk was out of the question; this was all about the Big Talk.

I stood on my balcony in my bare feet. I peered down at the railing on his. It wasn't that far down. I couldn't calculate how many feet, exactly, but I was hoping no more than five feet and five inches—my body length.

This was the perfect assignment for me. I was limber. I knew how to leap. I could pirouette in midair. Sure, not all these skills were relevant to the task, but I thought about them, anyway, to build my confidence.

In my bare feet, black yoga pants, and T-shirt, I stepped out onto my balcony. I put one foot over the railing, making contact with the edging. I pulled my other leg over, so that I was gripping the edge of my balcony with my toes. I grabbed the bars on the balcony railing and pushed off with my feet, lowering myself and also trying to swing to the left toward Spencer's balcony.

It took me about six swinging attempts to get my feet anywhere near the railing of his balcony. Finally, I made contact and wrapped my left toes around the metal. My right foot was stretched out in the other direction. It was sort of like doing a split in midair—something Heather might do in gymnastics.

I kicked my foot at the railing, trying to get a better grip, trying to swing the rest of my body closer.

Naturally, there was a pop can on the railing I hadn't seen. It clattered onto the balcony floor.

Seconds later, the door to the balcony opened.

Spencer's eyes went from the can to my foot to my suspended body. My upper body was killing me by this point.

"Is there a fire in your room?" he asked.

"No."

"What are you doing out here?"

"Stretching?" I said. Then I coughed, racking my brain for an excuse. "Well, see, I was trying to get a certain shot. Of the moon."

Spencer looked up into the sky, beyond me. "It's cloudy tonight."

"Well, sure it is now, but earlier—anyway, I was trying to get a shot and I fell. Could you just help me down, or up, or something?"

Mr. Flanagan was inside watching a baseball game, and he and Spencer came over to rescue me, pulling me in by taking hold of my legs.

I didn't want to stick around and get teased. I didn't want to talk about it, period. I just took the muscle-relaxant foot cream Mrs. Flanagan gave me and traipsed upstairs to my room, feeling hopeless.

I'd tried—more than tried—all day. If he couldn't tell what I was trying to do and say, and if I could never manage to say anything meaningful, then I was never going to be able to communicate it to him. He didn't seem to be dying to say anything to *me*, so maybe he didn't feel the same way. But Heather thought he was into me. . . . Was he?

I'd have to rent one of those planes that flew over the beaches, pulling advertising signs behind them. I could manage to get him onto the deck at a certain time, spell it out for him:

SPENCER, YOU IDIOT. CAN'T YOU TELL THAT I LIKE YOU?

That would be too long.

SPENCER. U R THE 1.

No, too stupid.

How about: SPENCER, I'VE BEEN TRYING TO TELL YOU SOMETHING, BUT BEFORE I DO, COULD YOU TELL ME SOMETHING FIRST, BECAUSE THEN I WON'T STRESS SO MUCH? DEAL?

But what if he didn't want to tell me anything?

Chapter 15

"How much longer do we have to wait?"

My dad checked his watch and peered at the ferry schedule clutched in his hand. "Half an hour? They run every half hour, and I think we'll fit on the next one, don't you?"

"Hard to say, since we didn't fit on the last two," Adam complained. He was in charge of his twin brothers for the day while his parents enjoyed a day on their own, and he'd been having a hard time keeping them entertained while we waited for the ferry. The thing they found most entertaining was running around the van, then around the Rustbucket (we'd driven two cars so we could split up, if need be), then running to the water's edge and looking like they were about to dive in, and then knocking on other people's car windows. Adam more than had his hands full looking after them, and we'd all been helping out, rescuing them from various disasters in the making.

Our two cars were now only third and fourth in our line, but there were several lines that waited beside us to board the ferry. We'd definitely moved up to the front, but I wasn't sure we were close enough to catch the next boat to Ocracoke Island. Each ferry was only big enough for thirty cars. We'd been warned by my mom to leave early in the morning, but we hadn't—and now we were stuck waiting with the crowd. The ferry took about forty minutes according to my mom's travel book—and it was free, which might have explained why so many people were making the trip.

I thought about how much things had changed since the day I'd run into Blake in the supermarket and he'd told me he was coming to see the island. We'd shared a kiss by the canned peach pyramids. What might have happened if I'd ditched my mom and told Blake I was coming along? That I'd rather fiesta with him than cook a fiesta meal with my mom?

I'd probably be disinherited by now, but maybe things would have worked out with Blake.

No, probably not, I thought. We'd have gotten to the ferry, and then I'd have found out that the red-haired girl was meeting Blake on the island. And I'd have been stranded here on the street, which would have been much worse than being dissed in the middle of a loud club. Even if the music sucked.

Spencer tapped my shoulder. "What are you smiling about?"

"Nothing," I said. "I was actually thinking something really bad."

"Huh." He didn't inquire about the details, which was just as well. "I'm thinking of something bad, too. Like the fact the day is already half over. Do you think the long wait for the ferry is really worth it? We could kayak there faster."

"Did you *bring* the kayak?" I asked.

"Spence, it's worth the wait," Spencer's dad assured us. "Don't you want to get out on the water?"

"And see where Blackbeard met his fate?" my dad added.

"Yo-ho-ho and a bottle of rum," Heather said. She glanced at her watch. "Are we ever going to get there?"

I sighed. "I'm going to get a pop over there in the visitor center—anyone else want one?"

"I'll come with," Heather said, and we headed for the vending machines inside the building. "Why didn't your mom come? She's always got the cooler full of drinks for us. I was counting on her." She fed two dollar bills into the pop machine.

"She said she wasn't feeling all that well." I shrugged. "What about your mom?"

"She just wanted some time by herself to read and reflect, she said. Personally, I think they're hitting a day spa together," Heather said. "Your mom's the tourist extraordinaire. Why would she miss an item on her list?"

"I know, it's strange," I said. "Maybe she just felt like staying home and making a new list. We've got all next week to fill up with tours and events, remember?"

"We do, that's true." We walked over and stood by the door, looking outside, enjoying the cool air-conditioning. "So. You didn't tell him yet, did you?" Heather asked.

"Not exactly," I replied. *Not this year,* I thought, wondering if I should finally tell Heather how this had gone for me the last time I had attempted it. Badly.

"When are you going to do it?" she pressed.

"I saw you last night! Do you really think I had time between now and then?" I asked her, laughing.

"At least twelve hours," she said. "And it's only going to take you like five minutes. What are you waiting for? Look at him over there. He's pacing around waiting for you to get back."

"Is he? I think he's just impatient for the boat."

"The boat—and *you*." She pressed my arm with her finger. "Exactly."

I rolled my eyes. "I love the spin you put on things, but I can't do it. Just thinking about it makes me want to throw up."

"Nah, that's just worrying about being on the boat. Telling him will not be as hard as you think."

"I already have a bruised knee and a questionable hamstring muscle," I said, "from trying to be Catwoman last night."

"Well, I didn't tell you to scale *buildings*," she said, and we laughed. After my disastrous attempts, I'd called Heather—she was just on her way home from seeing a movie with Dean, and we'd gotten together for ice cream in my room to laugh about it.

"I thought it was a brilliant idea," I said. "And it could have worked."

"Could have," Heather agreed. "But why don't you just try sitting next to him on the ferry and telling him? Might be a little less risky."

"With everyone else around?" I scoffed. "No way. That would be so embarrassing."

"It isn't easy. I know. Okay, I'll give you a hint."

"It better be a big one," I said. "I need all the help I can get."

"Shut up. You're constantly saying that and putting yourself down. You did fine meeting Blake. It just didn't work out, that's all."

"Well, that's sort of the truth," I said with a laugh.

"Anyway. What I usually do? Is give myself a deadline."

"A deadline?" I asked. "What kind of deadline?"

"Tell yourself that you're not leaving the island, or ending today, without telling him how you feel, that he's the Spencerest of all the Spencers you know, or whatever."

"Whatever I say? It's going to be better than that," I assured her as we both cracked up. "Wait a second. Did you just say today?" I nearly dropped my pop can on my foot. "Are you insane?"

"No," she said. "Do you want to spend the rest of your vacation pining away for him or do you want to start hanging out? And making out?"

"But what if I bomb like last time?"

"What last time?"

As we waited, I finally told her the story of what had happened when I was fifteen, and how Spencer had completely blown off my attempt to get closer to him.

Although it had been horribly embarrassing for me, she didn't seem fazed in the slightest.

"You know what? I would not feel bad about that at all," Heather scoffed. "I bet he didn't even know you were making a move."

How I wished that were true. "Oh, he knew. He's referred to it once or twice on this trip."

"In a fun way?" she asked.

"Let's see. Is teasing and glaring considered fun? Maybe in *some* cultures."

"That's Spencer, though. I mean, hate to say it, but he's not exactly the warm-and-fuzzy type. He doesn't have a clue about how to talk to people—that's why I told him he'd have to brush up on his socials skills—or should I say *skill*, because he doesn't have more than one—before he goes off to Linden and immediately insults a bunch of people."

"He's not that bad," I said.

"Easy for you to say. You're falling for him. Or you already fell, actually," she said. "Off your balcony."

"Great. I'm going to be teased about this for life, aren't I?" I said. Outside, my dad was waving his arms in the air, trying to get our attention. He pointed at the ocean, then at the car, then at us. I waved to let him know we got the message.

"Pretty much," Heather said as we hurried over to the car. A ferry was just docking, and everyone was starting their engines again, preparing to board. "Don't worry. We'll find something else soon."

"That's so reassuring," I said as we climbed into the Rustbucket.

"What's reassuring?" Spencer asked, turning around in the front seat, where he sat beside my dad, who was driving.

"Hold on. Here we go, kids!" My dad started humming the tune to the very old TV show *Gilligan's Island*, where the characters were on a three-hour boat tour and got stranded on an island for a few seasons.

"Dad. We're not going out in some small fishing boat," I said.

"Neither was Gilligan, Em. Neither was Gilligan." And there he was, driving us onto the ferry, singing the theme song at the top of his lungs.

Somewhere, the world was missing a very strange accountant.

Maybe he needed to take more vacation days.

Four hours later, we'd had a delicious late lunch at a café right on the harbor, seen the Ocracoke Lighthouse, the pirate museum, the place where Blackbeard was said to have met his fate. We'd also seen houses, gift shops, art studios, and the tiniest cemetery I'd ever seen, which was for four British soldiers killed during World War II. We'd done almost everything as a tight-knit group, so I hadn't had a minute alone with Spencer—in fact, we'd both spent lots of time holding on to or chasing Tim and Tyler.

We'd gone back to the visitor center in the middle of town, where we'd parked, so Adam could get some snacks for the kids out of the van. "Hey, my dad just called—there's some bad weather coming in—thunderstorms—and he was thinking I really should get the boys home at a semi-decent hour, so we need to head back."

"That's probably a good idea," said my dad. "We don't want to be out here in the middle of a storm."

"It's a really good idea," Heather agreed.

"Okay. We'll all go, I guess." I looked at Heather and shrugged.

"Yes. But we have the two cars," my dad said. "So you don't need to rush off."

"Yes. Really," Heather said. "You guys stay. Enjoy the local flavors. Go shopping!"

"No thanks, I'm done shopping," said Spencer. He turned to me. "You?"

"I'm broke," I said. "But maybe I should stay a little while and try to get some nighttime pictures."

"Well, you can't stay here by yourself. Who would like to stay and keep Emily company? How about you, Spencer?" my dad suggested.

"Yeah, sure. That's probably a good idea. What about you, Heather? You want to stay, too?" Spencer asked.

"Oh, I—I can't," she said. "I need to go check in with my mom and see how she's doing." Heather came closer and pulled me aside. "Listen, Emily. Don't you see—this is the perfect opportunity. I can't stay—I'm supposed to be meeting Dean tonight, so I've got to head back. But you and Spencer can stay, together."

"You're ditching me?" I asked.

"Did you tell him yet?" Heather asked.

"No . . ." I said slowly. "Do long looks at him count?"

She threw up her hands. "Then I'm definitely ditching you. What are you waiting for? Tell him."

"Give me a break! I haven't had a chance."

"Right. Sure you haven't," Heather said. "Well, you're definitely going to have a chance now."

"Okay. How should I—"

"Emily, you're smart. You'll think of something."

I raised my right eyebrow, daring her to leave me. What was this, tough love? She calmly walked over and climbed into the van, where Tim and Tyler were already buckled in and waiting. Adam got in beside her, then my dad got in, taking the driver's seat, looking like a chauffeur. Spencer's mom and dad were the last ones in.

"Call to check in!" Mr. Flanagan yelled over his shoulder, his voice mingling with my dad's, who was saying the same exact thing. Then the sliding doors dinged and closed, they pulled away, and Spencer and I were left standing in the parking lot.

"So where did you want to get those pictures?" Spencer asked.

"I was thinking some sunset pictures. By the lighthouse?" I suggested.

"If it weren't cloudy, that would be a great concept." Spencer looked up at the sky. "You didn't want to do that, anyway. Too clichéd."

"How about if I take some pictures of you, then?" I suggested.

"You must have enough to fill three albums and crash Instagram," he said drily. "You could photograph the storm. How do you feel about pictures of lightning strikes?"

I eyed the darkening sky. "I think they're the kind of weather photos other people should take. You know, maybe we should just go. If we leave now we could meet them at the ferry line."

"Yeah, but if we wait a little, maybe there won't be as much of a line," he argued. "We could grab a bite somewhere and wait out the storm?"

"Sure, okay. Except : . . I don't know. I—don't feel good." That wasn't far from the truth. I was feeling more nervously ill all the time.

He just stared at me, completely unsympathetic. "You were feeling fine ten minutes ago. When you ate that ice cream."

"Well, that's it, maybe it was something I ate, then."

"Are you going to get sick?"

Way to kill any romance, Emily, I thought. *By suggesting nausea.* "No, I just feel a little dizzy. You know, like when you try to read the newspaper in the car and all the lines start waving around and go blurry?"

"That doesn't happen to me."

"Oh."

"Maybe if you read more, you'd get used to reading in the car," Spencer said.

"Ha-ha. Do you really want to insult me when I feel sick?"

"Well, what do you want me to do?"

"Let's walk around some more. I'm sure I'll feel better in a little while."

"How about if we just sit down over there?" Spencer gestured to a picnic table by the water.

"Fine."

Spencer looked at his watch and then at the sky.

"You're contemplating leaving me here, aren't you?"

"No. I just wondered what we should do. We should probably go now, make a run for it, or wait until later. Unless you were thinking we'd spend the night here?" Spencer said.

Thought you'd never ask.

"Because that's absurd," Spencer said. "We don't have enough money to rent a room, even if there were any vacancies, which I seriously doubt."

"Right. Okay, well, we can go then, I guess." I wasn't very good at stalling. I consoled myself with thinking about the fact we still had the ferry ride back to Hatteras and then the long car trip from there to Kill Devil Hills. I had plenty of time to talk to him. Seriously.

We both got into the Rustbucket sedan and I turned the key. I waited for the inevitable roar, the bleating sound of old, worn-out engine belts, and the mild kicking sound from the exhaust pipe.

There was no sound. At all.

I turned the key again. Nothing.

"Let me try," said Spencer.

"Okay, but why would you be able to start it and I can't?" I asked as I opened the door and got out. Spencer slid into the driver's seat and tried to get it started, but nothing happened then, either.

"I think it's sea-logged," he said. "The rust has taken over."

"Now what?" I asked.

"We could leave the car here overnight and run to the ferry," Spencer suggested.

"It's a long way. And if it rains?"

He tapped his fingers against the steering wheel. "We'll hitch a ride, then," he said.

"People only do that in crime shows. And then they're the opening crime," I said.

"You watch a lot of TV, don't you?" he commented.

"Not really. It's more my mom's thing," I explained. "That's why she has this tendency to worry incessantly. Too many episodes of *Law & Order TDE.*"

"TDE?"

"Teen Daughter Edition," I said.

Spencer laughed and opened the driver's door. He got out and we both stood by the car, staring at it, willing it to work . . . wishing somebody would happen to drop by with a tow truck.

"I still say we have to give it a shot. We don't have to hitchhike exactly, we can just go over to the place where we had lunch and see if anyone's headed—"

There was a crack of thunder and it was as if a cloud directly over our heads opened up and dumped out all the moisture inside—right onto us. We both shrieked and jumped back into the car—me in the driver's seat, and Spencer right behind me.

We laughed as we tried to roll up the windows as water seemed to stream into the car from all directions.

Then we sat there, safe inside, and listened to the crashes and booms outside, watching water stream down the windows.

I peeked over the back of my headrest at Spencer. I could tell him how much I liked him right now, but then what? We were stuck in a car in the middle of a thunderstorm. Running away would not be fun—or easy. Or survivable.

The windows were starting to get steamed up, but not for any exciting reasons.

"I'd better, uh, call my dad," I said. "Tell him what happened, where we are. Or aren't."

Spencer nodded. "Good idea. I should check in with my folks, too."

I quickly told my dad what had happened, and while they were already heading home on the ferry, he said he'd call my mom to tell her what was going on and see what she could do to help. I think I interrupted him from singing everyone else in the van—or at least Tyler and Tim—to sleep.

"Okay. So we've checked in. Now what?" Spencer asked.

"Should we stay here, sleep in the car? It'd be cheap. Uncomfortable, but cheap," I said. "I think these seats recline."

Spencer eyed me and then the seats. "Let's look at that as our worst-case scenario."

I glanced over at him. *Thanks. Thanks a lot*, I thought. "It's not like I desperately wanted to spend the night with you, either," I said. "I mean, uh, spend the night in a car with my neck all bent funny and nowhere to brush my teeth and no pillow and—"

"It's cool. I know what you meant."

"You do?" I was about to say something like, *No, I don't think you do, actually.*

My phone rang—it was my mom. Saving me, thank goodness. "Emily, before you say anything, just tell me you're all right," she said, which is never a good start to a conversation, but which is fairly typical for her.

"Mom. I'm perfectly fine," I said.

"We called the Rustbucket Repair number, and unfortunately, they don't send out repair vehicles at night. But someone will be there in the morning. They said to leave the key in the car and leave the car unlocked. Nobody will take it."

"No doubt," I said. "Okay. Should we sleep here, or—"

"Goodness, no. We thought about Dad coming back in the van for you, but that didn't seem to make a lot of sense, not tonight. So instead, we've found a place for you to stay. Unfortunately, we were only able to locate one room."

"You found a hotel room for us?" I blurted. "Thanks, Mom!"

Of all the sentences I thought I'd say in my life? That wasn't one of them.

I felt like disappearing into my seat, falling through the

semi-rusted floor. "I mean, uh, a place to, uh, take shelter from the storm."

"It's a room at a bed-and-breakfast," Mom explained. There was a slight pause, and then she added, "I know I don't need to say this, because we're talking about Spencer, and you, and I know nothing *would* happen. But you might check and see in the lobby if there's a cot available or a sofa. The proprietor of the B-and-B said the bed was a double, which is not very big at all. But in case something did happen—"

I pressed the phone as tightly as I could to my ear. I did not want Spencer to hear what my mother was proposing. I couldn't get out of the car because it was still pouring. Occasional lightning flashes lit up our faces.

"You and I have talked and I know you're practically an adult—okay, maybe you are an adult—but you're still my baby, and I know you know to take precautions and be careful—"

"Mom? *Mom.*" What *else* was she going to say? I didn't want to know.

I appreciated her concern, but this really wasn't the time to go over things, when I didn't have even a yard of privacy.

"Well, honey, these things do happen," she said.

"Yes, but not to me," I said. "Anyway—thanks for setting us up. I mean, for setting up everything for us. We'll go find the B-and-B." Maybe I didn't want to go away to college, because sometimes her taking care of everything was nice. Maybe she does micromanage, but at least she's good at it.

"Call me if anything—if you need anything—we can come pick you up, if you like," she offered.

"Don't be silly, Mom. Spencer and I will be fine. The weather's rotten, and it's late—we'll just stay put."

"Are you sure?" Spencer whispered to me.

I nodded. "We'll call you in the morning, Mom, but just assume that we're okay. Because we are."

I'm also nervous. Dying of anticipation. And freaking out. But okay.

Chapter 16

When the rain let up, Spencer and I ran most of the way to the B&B. Mom had given us exact directions from the parking area. I put my camera under my shirt to keep it dry, just in case the skies opened again. I was glad our clothes didn't get drenched, since we'd likely be sleeping in them.

At the bed-and-breakfast, this supersweet older couple named Mildred and Curt let us in, served us iced tea, and showed us to our room at the top of the third-floor stairs.

"Now, it is only a double bed, but it's a generously sized double bed," Mildred explained.

Spencer stood in the doorway, just staring at the overly flowered comforter, with matching curtains, borders, and floral prints on the wall. "It looks like a single bed," Spencer said.

Curt nodded. "You're right. Sorry, I forgot. This is our mother-in-law room."

"That's okay. I was going to sleep on the floor, anyway," Spencer said. "Don't worry about it."

"I'll go get some extra comforters—you can build yourself a little nest."

"What am I, a bird?" Spencer whispered to me as Mildred gave us a brief tour, showing us the tiny pink bathroom, and how the pink rotary phone worked, and where to find extra pink towels. We were both trying not to laugh, because the room couldn't have been more *not* our style, even with effort.

"You poor kids." Mildred patted my shoulder as they prepared to leave us for the night. "Well, I hope you don't mind that our inn is very romantical. I know you're just friends and this is a dire situation—"

"It's not dire at all, actually," I said. "We're pleased to be here. Thanks so much for finding a place for us on such short notice."

We said good night and closed the door. Spencer pressed his ear to it and listened for a second, as if he wanted to hear them go back downstairs.

"They don't strike me as the eavesdropping type," I said, wondering if my mom in her insanity had asked them to keep close tabs on the two of us.

"You never know," he said. "Is everyone else here already in bed? I mean, is this an inn or a retirement home?"

"What are you saying?"

"I'm saying, I feel like there are more vacant rooms than just this one. And our parents wanted to save money, so they booked us in the smallest room."

"If this is about sleeping on the floor, I'll do it," I said. "Because I don't mind."

"No, but do you want a picture of my nest? It's very romantical."

We both laughed. I went into the bathroom and brushed my teeth with my index finger—it was a trick I'd learned on our various camping trips over the years. Spencer did the same thing, then settled onto his nest on the floor beside the bed. I climbed into the bed and looked over at him. "So."

"So."

"Here we are," I said.

"Right." He suddenly got to his feet. "You know what? I need a book. I always read before bed."

"Didn't you bring one?"

"No."

"Wow. That has to be the first time in your life," I said.

"Ha-ha. I'll go get one from the lobby—they said they had a library."

I lay there and waited, nearly holding my breath. Then I ran into the tiny bathroom and scrubbed my teeth one more time with my finger, using the guest toothpaste. Just in case.

I was back in bed, under the covers in my T-shirt, just as Spencer came back into the room.

"You won't believe this, but all they have is horror novels," he said. "Oh, and cookbooks."

"Horror novels? Them?"

"I borrowed the one with the best blurbs. It's about eight hundred pages long. Oh, and here. Mildred baked cookies." He held out a napkin with a large ginger cookie on it.

"Cookies? At this time of night? Um, I just brushed my teeth." *For the second time. Because apparently I have delusions that I'm going to get close to you.*

"Oh. Well, more for me—"

"But I'm starving. Gimme."

"I thought you felt sick," Spencer said.

"That was hours ago."

"Yum. Cookies and a bloodbath novel. I'm going to sleep like a baby." He snuggled back under the covers.

"What time should we try to leave?" I asked.

"As soon as the sun's up."

"Yeah. Well, I guess it depends when Rustbucket sends someone to get the car fixed."

"True."

Did we really have this little to talk about?

"Are you going to be able to sleep if I keep this light on?" he asked.

"Oh, sure." I was trying very hard to be agreeable. But the truth was that the longer I lay there, listening to him flip the flimsy pages, the brighter the light seemed to get. I covered my face with the light—pink—cotton blanket. It smelled vaguely like gingerbread cookies.

Or maybe that was me.

I peeked over the edge and made sure Spencer was lying down focused on reading, then I got up and scooted into the bathroom to brush my teeth for the third time, and wash my face. When I came out, Spencer was lying on his back, and he looked up at me. Our eyes met and I did this kind of awkward move, pulling down my T-shirt. What was I doing, walking around with hardly any clothes on in front of Spencer? I scurried back into bed and under the blanket.

"You know what? There's too much pink in here. There's like a *glow* to the room. I can't read a scary book in the middle of this environment."

"You're so sensitive," I teased him, getting comfy in bed again.

"And *you're* so obsessed about brushing your teeth."

"I was getting a drink of water," I said.

"Well. Um, you can turn the light off now," Spencer said.

"Okay." I reached over and switched off the lamp on the nightstand. I rested my head on the pillow, lay back, and tried to relax. I couldn't, though. I kept thinking about how disappointed I was in myself, that I hadn't yet had the guts to tell Spencer how I felt. And if I was disappointed, Heather was going to be even more so. She'd helped create this opportunity. We were *alone*. We were in the dark. If there was ever a good time to tell him, it was now.

"Spencer?" I said softly. "Spencer?"

"Yeah?"

"Are you comfortable enough? Do you want another pillow?"

"I'm fine. I'll just use this book for a pillow. It's big enough," he said.

I laughed. "Um, okay. Are you sure?"

"I'm sure."

"Won't it give you really bad dreams?" I asked.

"Nah. Don't worry about it, I'm fine. I've got this pillow from that chair over there, and it has a giant turkey on it. Very Thanksgiving. Wait a second. I'm hungry."

"Me too. Does the pillow smell like gingerbread, too? Because my blanket does," I said.

"Kind of. Do you think we're in a fairy tale? Like, which was the one with the creepy witch and the oven? That is so Mildred."

"'Hansel and Gretel.' Which one am I?" I asked. "I could never remember which was the girl."

"You're Rumpelstiltskin. No, wait—which was the one with the long hair? Rapunzel, Rapunzel, let down your hair."

I slid over to the edge of the bed and leaned back, letting my hair fall onto him.

"Ack!" he cried. "Don't scare me like that."

"Fine. I'll leave you alone. Quit reading horror novels and you won't be so on edge." I scooted back to the middle of the bed, put my head back on my pillow, and lay there for another five minutes. He might be sleepy, but I wasn't. At all. I was keenly aware of how close he was, of how we could be talking, but weren't. How we could be kissing, but weren't. How this whole night was slipping through my fingers like beach sand.

"Spencer? Are you asleep?" I asked.

"Yes."

"Good. I want to talk to you about something," I began.

"Uh-oh. Is this going to be about me getting you another cookie?"

"No," I said.

"If you need help falling asleep, I can go grab a cookbook for you to read," he offered. "They must have *Best Gingerbread Recipes of All Time*."

"*No*. I want to talk about what happened the last time we all got together," I finally said, as emphatically as I could.

"You mean . . . the pizza party? When they forgot to deliver our pizza, and my dad insisted they—"

"No!" I interrupted. "You know what? Forget it." I turned over. "Good night."

"Yeah, okay. Good night to you, too." Spencer sounded a little hurt. I couldn't believe how difficult he was being.

A few minutes later, he got up and crouched on the edge of the bed. I turned back over and held my breath, wondering what he was up to.

"You know, when you said that stuff. Way back. Our last trip," he stammered. "I was a real jerk about it. I'm sorry. That's the reason I didn't stay in touch. I just felt bad."

"Well, yeah, me too," I said. "Obviously."

"I didn't know how to react, so I didn't say anything. That's not a good excuse, it's just . . ." He shrugged.

"I guess it must have been kind of a shock."

"Not really. I mean, I . . . we did have a lot in common and we . . . well, anyway."

"Right," I said like an idiot.

"Right. So, um, good night."

"'Night." He slid off the bed, back into his nest of comforters on the floor.

A second later, I turned the light back on. Clearly, this could take me all night. "Sorry. But all the things I said back then. They're still true." I said. "I mean—"

"Can we talk about this tomorrow?" Spencer asked, shielding his eyes from the light.

"Oh. Tomorrow. Sure. Fine." I switched off the lamp on the bed-side table, turned over, and punched my pillow.

Then I sat up again. Cringing inside. It was like preparing to have one of my baby teeth pulled out, waiting for my dad to slam the door that was attached to the string that was attached to my tooth. But I couldn't cry, at least not yet.

"Actually, no. We can't. We have to talk now." *Oh, no. What am I doing? I'm going to be stuck out here—stranded—on an island that's haunted by a pirate's ghost, where I don't know a soul, unless of course Blackbeard had a soul, but actually I don't know him either, so . . .*

"Have to talk about what?" Spencer asked.

"Everything." I pulled off the cotton blanket, got out of bed, and sat beside Spencer, on the floor. "Would it maybe make more sense for us to both lie on the bed? It might be easier to sleep. And, uh, talk."

"No, I'm fine here," he insisted.

"Okay, but don't say I didn't ask." I hugged my knees to my chest. "Listen. I know this is weird. And we've known each other . . . forever. So it shouldn't be weird, but I actually think that's what makes it so weird."

He raised his eyebrows and sat up, leaning back against the bed. "Are you sure you shouldn't go to sleep?"

"Yes! Come on. You know how hard this is. It's like—you and that next-door girl. Megan. Magellan?"

"Morgan."

"Whatever. You couldn't tell her how you felt. And that's how it is with me. And with you, too, I think."

Spencer looked over at me. "You want to ask me to your prom?"

"Shut up. You are *not* making this easier."

"Should I?"

I stared at the little scar near his ear. I wanted to kiss it. I wanted to kiss him. "Yeah. You should."

"Okay, then." He reached for my hand, sending goose bumps up and down my arms. "How about if I say something for a change?"

"Sounds good," I said, scooting a little closer.

"Here. Turkey pillow," he offered, and I propped it behind my back, smiling.

"Well, the first thing I have to know is . . . are you done trying to meet other guys on this trip? And if you're not—could you be?"

"Hmm. I'm not sure."

His eyes widened. "You're not sure? What do you mean, you're not sure?"

"Give me a good reason," I said.

"I don't think they're worthy. Wait. I know they're not," he said. "Blake and his cheesy jalapeño tattoo."

I smiled, remembering how he'd insulted Blake for me. "So what are you saying?" I asked. "That you *are* worthy?"

"Well, yeah, of course, but that wasn't the point."

"It wasn't?"

"No."

"It's okay, you know." I squeezed his hand. "You don't have to be creative about this."

"What, do you think I can't do it?" he replied, sounding offended. "Because I can be very creative with this sort of thing. At least . . . in my head."

"How about if I start by telling you . . . how I feel about things?" I asked. "I think that, uh, you're the Spencerest of all the Spencers I know." I'd told Heather that I'd never use that line, and here I was—stealing it. And it sounded just as stupid now as it had when she'd said it earlier in the day.

"How many Spencers do you know?" His forehead creased with worry.

"One. You."

"And that's a good thing?"

"It's a great thing. Only . . . you tend not to talk. At least, not about anything important. You read too much—"

"Well, you take too many pictures," he replied. "You never leave home without a camera of some kind."

"Well, you never leave home without a book—"

"Ha! What about today?" he asked.

"That was a fluke, but okay. Fine. So I'm obsessed. Get over it."

"No." Spencer shook his head. "Get over *here*."

We both moved closer to each other, so we were sitting face to face. I felt like my tummy was doing somersaults. Spencer reached for my hair, which had gotten all mussed up from the trip on the ferry, the rain, the constant struggling to get comfy. . . . He ran his fingers from my ear, down my neck, to my shoulder. I think I literally shivered.

"You can't be the Emiliest of the Emilies, because that's just wrong," he said. "And it sounds like a French movie. But you're . . . my favorite person. And I can't believe how when I saw you, I nearly fell over, because it hit me that I'd been totally trying to avoid feeling this way about you for the past few years since you said that to me. And I'm such a chicken. I couldn't say anything. It was killing me, but I couldn't do it. You weren't interested in me. You were interested in . . . Blake. Of all people."

"I wasn't, really—I was just trying to, you know, have a fling, because Heather thought we should," I said. "I was upset when it didn't work out, but it didn't take me long to realize I wanted to be with you and not him, from the beginning. I was just trying to avoid it—and you. And this kind of, um, situation."

"What kind?"

I squirmed a little, feeling uncomfortable again, as if history was only bound to repeat itself here in a few seconds. "Where I tell you how I feel and you, uh, turn the other way."

"What? I didn't do anything as bad as *that*," Spencer said.

I nodded. "You did."

"Really? Wow. I don't remember it that way. I remember totally panicking, and thinking, we're leaving the next day and our parents are in the next room and what if something weird happens—"

"I thought all that stuff, too!" I said. "I just decided to take the chance."

"Yeah, well. You're young. You take chances when you're young."

"True. In fact, watch this." I moved closer and kissed him quickly on the cheek, right by his small scar. Then I kissed his mouth, and it was nothing like the fast kiss Blake had given me in the grocery store—it was soft and gentle and kind of distracting me from my point. Then I nuzzled his neck, brushing my lips against the slight stubble he had now whenever he didn't shave. He was so grown-up. What am I saying? *I* was so grown-up. I'd never done anything so bold in my life.

"Some risks . . . are . . . worth . . . taking. I guess," he murmured, and then he started kissing me back.

Chapter 17

"I've never had gingerbread pancakes before. Those were awesome," Spencer commented as we walked to the car the next morning. "I kept thinking, with their love of cookbooks and slasher novels, maybe they're trying to lure us into some evil plot, but I don't care. Pass the syrup."

"I hear you," I said, but the truth was, I'd been too happy and excited to eat much of anything. I just sipped orange juice and played footsie with Spencer under the table. I was absentmindedly eating a cookie as we walked along the road—Mildred had insisted I take one with me.

We'd spent the night talking, kissing, talking, kissing, occasionally snuggling—I think I probably slept about two hours. When I woke up with Spencer next to me, at first it seemed like just another one of my la-la-land dreams.

Then he said, "Nice bed head," and I knew it was the real Spencer.

I contemplated snapping a quick photo—you know, just for evidence's sake. That seemed a little odd, though, so I kept my camera put away.

We'd gotten up around 9:00 and eaten breakfast with Mildred, Curt, and a dozen other guests at the B&B before heading back to the parking lot at around 10:30 to check on our car. I hadn't checked in with anyone at home yet and I kind of didn't want to. I liked being secluded, on our own "romantical" island.

There was a large, red piece of paper slipped under the car's windshield wipers.

RUSTBUCKET READY! it said. RUSTBUCKET TO THE RESCUE! HAS BEEN HERE. YOUR CAR IS GOOD TO GO!

"Why do I have a hard time believing that?" asked Spencer.

When I opened up the car door, another slip of paper fell out, which turned out to be the repair bill. SPARK PLUG WIRES REPLACED. MINIMUM EMERGENCY CHARGE APPLIED TO YOUR CREDIT CARD AS PER CONTRACT: $300. HAVE A NICE DAY!

So much for saving money by using a cut-rate car rental place. Living dangerously—or rather, frugally—could sometimes catch up with my dad. "Okay, you can be in charge of handing this to my dad when we get back," I said to Spencer.

"Get back?" he said, leaning against the car. "What do you mean? We're going back?"

I stood beside him and leaned against the car. The morning sun felt great on my face. But it reminded me that I didn't have sunscreen—or a hair brush—or anything. I was in desperate need of a shower. "I need clothes that haven't been rained on, slept in, and worn again. How about you?"

Spencer shook his head. "I'm fine like this."

I rolled my eyes at him. "You would be."

He took my arm and sort of twirled me around to face him. "What? What's that supposed to mean?"

"You're so adaptable."

"Hey. I spent a lot of time the past six months sleeping on cots and other uncomfortable places, living out of a duffel of clothes and not always having a shower."

"I forgot. So, it's probably good I didn't see you then. Did you have a beard?"

"As a matter of fact—"

I held up my hand to stop him. "Don't tell me. I don't want to know."

"Well? Should we give the car a try?"

"I don't think we have a choice. Although now that it's daylight and not pouring, we at least have more choices than this," I said. I wasn't sure that was a good thing, after I said it. One great aspect to the previous night had been the fact that we were forced to share a space, unless one of us wanted to sleep in the car while the other slept in the B&B. . . . Well, *I* certainly wasn't about to volunteer for that. I wanted a room with a view. Of Spencer.

We got into the Rustbucket, where the key was waiting in the ignition. "One advantage of a cheap car is the fact you can almost always leave the key in it. That may be the only one, though." Spencer laughed. He rolled down the passenger window, and before he knew what I was up to, I took a quick picture of him.

"Hey! What are you doing? You know I don't get photographed before ten in the morning."

"It's eleven." I took another one of him grinning at me, then slipped my camera into the little compartment between the front seats, leaned over, and kissed him.

"Maybe we should just hang out here today," he suggested after a minute of sitting in the car, kissing. "Do we actually have to go back?"

"Mmm. Probably," I whispered into his ear.

It was nearly impossible to pull myself away from him, but somehow I managed. I gazed at Spencer for another second as I prepared to start the car. He looked sort of uncomfortable and I didn't know why. "Are you okay?" I asked. "You look like you're getting a headache or something."

He rubbed his temples. "I can't find my sunglasses. I think I lost them in our room. Maybe they're under the bed or in the bed or something," Spencer said.

I laughed. "Well, that's embarrassing. You could go back and ask Mildred."

"I'd never do that. I'd ask Curt. But no, thanks, I'll just squint. Who knows, maybe they're here in the car somewhere?" he said. He began rummaging around the seat, looking underneath it.

The car started easily, and soon we were headed away from the shops, down the road toward the tip of the island and the ferry. I looked over at Spencer and said, "Remember. We'll always have Ocracoke."

"We will?"

"It's a saying." I shrugged.

"Not a good one," Spencer said.

You could make out with someone all you wanted, but you can't change him from occasionally being rude and arrogant.

We snuggled close to each other on the ferry, and when we got close to the landing on Cape Hatteras Island, Spencer and I walked down to the first floor and stood looking at the shore. I saw a few people frantically waving at the ferry.

We got closer and I noticed my dad's trademark green Linden sweatshirt. I saw Spencer's dad standing beside him, and Spencer's mom, and *my* mom. Did we really need such a welcoming committee? When I called my dad this morning to let him know which ferry we'd be on, I didn't expect him to round up the whole gang! "Well. Back to reality and parents," I said over the noise of the churning water as the ferry pulled closer to the landing.

Spencer suddenly moved away from me. I grabbed his hand, but he held it loosely, our fingers intertwined where no one could see them. "Let's keep this between us," he said.

"Really?" I said.

He looked at me as if that were an idiotic thing to question. "Really."

"Why?"

"Because everyone will talk about it, and us—"

"I can't tell anyone? Not even Heather?"

"Especially not Heather. Can you imagine the grief they'd give us? All of them? Our parents would be over the moon. Over all of Saturn's moons, too. I don't want them to interfere."

"But they'd be happy for us."

"Too happy."

"What's that supposed to mean? And since when can anyone be *too* happy?" I asked.

"Come on, we have to get into the car." He started walking away from me, edging through the cars on the first level toward the Rustbucket, which was parked midway back. We got in and I closed the door.

I knew what Spencer was getting at, but I still thought he was being overly cautious. "Okay, so you're saying we have to be secretive. Do we have a password? Do we have code names and everything for each other? How about . . . you be 'Curt,' and I'll be 'Mildred.'" I made air quotes. "We'll only meet after midnight under the cover of darkness—"

Spencer shook his head. "Forget it. I knew you'd be too immature about this."

"*Me?* What about you?" I shot back as the ramp lowered and we followed the line of cars off the ferry. "What's your problem? Why shouldn't people know?"

I acknowledged my parents with a quick wave and looked for a place to pull over, so we could meet up with them.

"What's there to know?" Spencer said. "It's not like we're going to stay . . . together. You'll just find some other guy, another Blake or an even dumber Neanderthal, right?"

I parked the car and turned to him. "Why are you saying that? You know that's not true." As I was looking at him, looking at that same face that I'd kissed the night before, that was now steely and arrogant, my eyes quickly filled with tears. I was glad I hadn't lost my sunglasses. I needed them.

"Hey, kids!" My dad pounded the top of the car. "We thought we should follow you home, make sure the car's working and you don't get stranded."

I got out of the car, not wanting to spend any more time in it with Spencer. My mom ran up to give me a hug, and I have to admit that I hugged her a little harder than I normally would have. She gave me a curious look as we separated. "You okay?"

I nodded. "Just tired. Didn't sleep very well."

"Who would have, under those circumstances? Was it completely awful? I hated sending you to a place sight unseen."

"The B-and-B was fine. Very pink," Spencer said as he walked around from the passenger side.

"And how was the rest of the trip?" his mother asked him.

"Oh, you know. Seen one lighthouse, you've seen 'em all," Spencer said in a bored tone.

I glared at him, wanting to kick him. He wouldn't make eye contact.

"So, should we follow you guys?" Mr. Flanagan asked.

"Actually, if it's okay, I'd rather ride with you," I said to my mom.

She looked concerned, but thrilled at the same time. "Oh. Well, sure. Spencer? You want—"

"I'll stick with the Rustbucket," he said quickly. "It's gotten us this far, right?"

"How about if the guys go in one car, and the girls in the other?" Mrs. Flanagan said.

I nodded, not really able to talk just then.

"Good call," said my dad. "Spencer, I'll drive, and you can regale me with tales of Habitat for Humanity."

"Okay, but no singing," Spencer was saying as they got into the car.

Normally I would have laughed at that, but I didn't find anything funny about Spencer at the moment. What was going on with him? He was the one who mocked me for having a fling . . . but what was ditching someone after one day? A *fling*, right?

Or, quite possibly, the biggest mistake I'd ever made.

Chapter 18

When we got back, I walked into the house and ran right up to my room, telling my parents I needed a nap. I'd never gone from utter happiness to complete misery in such a short time. There had to be a world record for this sort of thing. I didn't want the distinction of having it, but I felt like I must be close.

I turned on the radio, lay down on my bed, and clutched the pillow to my chest. Seconds later there was a knock at the door. *Maybe it's Spencer*, I thought, getting up to answer it. *Maybe he wants to apolo—*

"Emily? Let me in!" Heather called from the other side.

I opened the door and she burst in, quickly giving me a little hug. "So? How did it go? I can't believe you were stuck there all night. How was it?"

"Horrible. And great. But then horrible," I said, and I started to cry.

"What happened? Oh, my God, don't cry. Please don't do that or

I'll cry," she said. She grabbed a tissue from the box on the nightstand and handed it to me.

"You don't even know what happened," I said.

"Not yet, but if it's something to make you that upset, I can't handle it," she said.

We sat down on the bed and I told her about the fun night we'd had—and about the not-so-fun morning afterward, how everything had been great until we saw our parents, and Spencer freaked out about everyone knowing about us. "He didn't even want me to tell you," I said. "Which is so ridiculous. Like, how could I not tell you? And why?"

"Is he one of those intensely private people?" Heather wondered.

"No, he's one of those intensely insensitive people. I mean, you don't have to tell the world, but you should be able to tell your best friend and your parents. You know? Then he called me immature because I made fun of him for wanting to be all secretive."

"But before all that—things were good? You told him how you felt . . . ?"

I nodded. "He said he felt the same way. I thought we really connected. I don't understand him. Why would he just—turn his back on me?"

"Because despite how cute and funny and great he can be, he can also be an arrogant idiot," said Heather. "Do you want me to talk to him for you? Or better yet, slug him for you? I have a mean right hook."

I smiled. "No. Not yet. Can I take a rain check, though?"

"You should just come out with me and Dean. Don't sit around here waiting for him to flip-flop again."

"Yeah. Maybe I will. How are things going with Dean?"

"You know what? I thought it was going to be a fling. But it turns out we kind of . . . we really click." She smiled and leaned back on the bed. "It's getting kind of embarrassing how much I like him, especially since we're only here for one more week."

"Maybe you could stick around here the rest of the summer—get a job down here," I suggested.

"I thought about that. In fact, I've been thinking about it all the time. But can you imagine suggesting that to my mom?" She cringed.

"I know. You talk to Spencer and I'll face your mom," I said. "And if neither works out, you and I can spend the summer together somewhere else. Like Alaska. And then we can *not* go to Linden in the fall, because Spencer's going to be there and I won't want to see him—"

"No way—if we ditch Linden, we're going to California," Heather said.

I laughed. "You have this all planned, don't you?"

"And if things don't work with Spencer, he can leave Linden, not you," Heather said. "There's no way I'm rooming with some total stranger."

Later in the afternoon, I was sitting on the beach, lazily clicking through pictures on my camera, when my mom came over to sit down next to me. "What's up?" she asked.

"Just looking. Deciding which ones to make prints of," I said.

"Can I see?" she asked.

"Not yet," I said. "I'll show you the good ones."

The reason I didn't really want her to see was that I was scrolling through all the photos of me, and Spencer, and me and Spencer. I'd gone from being so happy about having such great pictures, to wanting to delete all of them: Spencer and me on top of the Cape Hatteras Lighthouse, Spencer pointing to the B&B's sign, Spencer in the Rustbucket grinning at me. . . .

My mom turned out to be looking over my shoulder. "That Spencer, he's such a nice guy," she chimed in. "Always looking after Heather the way he does. How he stayed with you last night—"

I turned to look at her. "He had no choice, Mom."

"Sure he did. You both could have left or he could have left you there, the Rustbucket wasn't his car," she said. "He's a very responsible person."

I sighed. "Looks can be deceiving, Mom."

"What are you saying?" Now she was starting to look worried. "Nothing happened between you two. Right?"

"Right."

"But you're not hanging out," she observed. "I'd think you'd be hanging out together."

"Well. We're not," I said. "You know Spencer. He always wants to bury his nose in a book. Besides, everyone went their own way this afternoon. Heather's with Dean, Adam's at a batting cage with his dad and brothers—"

I stopped as I came to a photo of me and Spencer, one in which he had his arm draped around my shoulders, and we just looked right. I was about to delete it, when I stopped myself. I remembered Spencer teasing me that day at Cape Hatteras, saying how I loved to delete. It was so incredible that we'd managed, finally, to get together. Why did Spencer have to go and ruin it?

"You know, I think I'm going to take off, too," I said.

"Really? Where? Do you want some company?" she asked.

"No, thanks," I said. "It's, um, something I'm working on. A secret."

"Really?"

"Don't get excited—it's just a camera thing." I stood up and brushed sand off the backs of my legs. I dropped my camera into my pocket and picked up my flip-flops.

"*Just?*" Mom called after me. "Honey, anything to do with you and pictures, I'm interested in!"

I glanced up for some reason and spotted Spencer standing on the deck upstairs in his usual place, holding a book, looking out at the water and pretending he hadn't seen me.

I just walked past without saying anything.

As the prints came out of the photo printer, I contemplated cutting Spencer's picture out of the group shots. Fortunately, the drugstore didn't leave a pair of scissors around. Or unfortunately. I wasn't quite sure.

They had a table to work on and even stocked the kind of calendars I wanted to use to give each family as an end-of-trip present. I knew we still had a week left, but I wanted to start early to give myself plenty of time.

I laid out the prints on the table, trying to match each one to a particular month. I flipped through the open calendar and stopped when I saw September. It was coming up much too quickly. I'd be at Linden then. What would life be like? Would I be anywhere near talking to Spencer at that point or would we just not make eye contact when we walked past each other on campus? Was it too late to apply to UW? I'd always loved the Bucky Badger mascot. . . .

I was lost in thought when someone came over to the table. "Nice pictures," said a male voice.

I looked up and saw Spencer peering at all my work spread out on the table. "Nice? Don't you mean 'immature'?"

"No, you—you really have a gift for this. The way you caught the light there . . . and the water . . ." He seemed to be fumbling for words. "Anyway. They're great. Can we, uh, talk?"

"I'm pretty busy getting all this together." I started collecting all my prints, wondering how quickly I could bolt. I didn't want to be around him.

"Em, look. I'm sorry," he said, stepping closer. "I'm *really* sorry."

I stayed focused on my work, as hard as it was right then. I just couldn't look at him. "I *really* don't care."

"What I said this morning—I mean, I was just—that was me being stupid. You're not immature, Emily. You're the opposite of immature." He tried to touch my arm, but I pulled away and shifted to the other side of the table to collect more prints.

"Now you make me sound like I'm ready for a nursing home," I said. "Which is it?"

"Be quiet—I mean, don't joke around, I'm trying to say something and you're not listening," Spencer pleaded.

"Oh. Wow. I've never heard of that happening," I said drily.

"You had the guts to say what I was supposed to say—and do. You're brave enough to face everyone with this and just deal with it. But—what if—what if it didn't work out with us?" Spencer asked in a quiet voice. "I just felt embarrassed. I'd told you so much. About dropping out and how I felt, and I—what if you change your mind? What if it doesn't work out?"

I finally managed to look up at him. "It's not like I wasn't taking that risk, too. And Spencer, we've known each other for so long. I think we both knew it was a good idea."

"*Was?*" he blurted.

"What's a good idea?"

I looked up and saw Spencer's parents, who seemed to have materialized out of nowhere. They came over to the table.

"They dropped me off then went next door to shop," he explained under his breath. "Sorry. I didn't think they'd come back."

"Um." I coughed. "Making prints before my memory card gets full. Or erased. Or lost."

"Ah. What's taking you so long, Spencer?" Mr. Flanagan asked.

"I needed new sunglasses. I was, uh, asking Emily for her advice on picking out another pair, but then she started showing me her great photographs, and—"

"You lost *another* pair? That's two so far," commented Mr. Flanagan.

"I know, I know. I guess I, uh, dropped them," Spencer said. "On the ferry. I called, 'Shades overboard!' but nobody seemed to care."

"Emily, how are you after your overnight adventure?" asked Mrs. Flanagan, browsing the nearby shelves, while Spencer turned a rack of bumper stickers around and around.

"Fine. Just fine," I said, casting a glance at Spencer, wondering if visual death rays were just a myth.

"Can you believe how many bumper stickers there are?" he said. "I mean, look at this." He held one out to me that had the standard abbreviation for Outer Banks, OBX, only on this sticker the *O* was the shape of two lips giving a lipstick kiss.

I raised my eyebrow. Interesting choice.

"What are you doing over here, Emily?" Spencer's father asked as his mother grabbed some items and headed for the register to checkout.

"Nothing. I mean, it's a surprise. Or at least it was." I laughed nervously.

Spencer's mom returned from the counter, while his dad went up front to buy some candy and chips. "Here, Emily." Mrs. Flanagan handed me a travel kit filled with tiny bottles of shampoo, conditioner, lotion, and shower gel. "Happy early birthday. Or late birthday. Whatever." She smiled.

"For me? Am I going somewhere?" I asked.

Spencer laughed. "Good one."

I glared at him. *Great. Now he's probably convinced his parents to leave early, just in case something else happens between us and he can't deal with that, either. Or wait. Maybe they're kicking ME off the island.*

"It's for when you get to Linden. You need your little kit in case you don't always spend the night in your dorm room," Mrs. Flanagan said as if that were the most natural thing in the world.

"Mom!" Spencer exclaimed. "Jeez."

"Oh." She giggled. "I didn't mean *that*. Emily's not that kind of . . . Anyway, all I meant was that she's going to take road trips with her friends, her roommates. You can have this kit and think of this great vacation whenever you use it. One whiff of that saltwater ocean lotion and you'll come right back here."

"Really," I murmured. *The question is: Will I want to?*

"Mom. You're hopeless," Spencer said.

"What?" She put her hand to her throat, adjusting a patterned scarf she was wearing.

"You're not selling the product, okay? You're buying it. You don't need to convince other people to use it," he argued.

Wow. He's even that rude to his mom, I thought.

"Well, excuse me for caring. I wasn't forcing anyone to do anything," she said.

"It's okay, Mrs. Flanagan. I really appreciate the gift—your thinking of me. I love little mini products like this."

"You do?" Spencer looked like he'd just lost all faith in the human race, like I'd committed a felony. "You're into products?"

I finished packing up my s[...] [...]
out?"

"Fine." He headed for the [...]

"And don't get the same [...]
were hideous."

His forehead creased wit[...]
der. "I thought you liked the [...]

"Yeah. I thought I did, to[...]
so much." I turned and wal[...]
prints, calendars . . . and all-natural organic travel tote. That thing
come in handy when Heather and I left Linden for California.

Chapter 19

The next morning, I was sipping coffee and eating a piece of cinnamon toast in the third-floor kitchen, where everyone tended to gather. Almost everyone was already up and accounted for, before Spencer wandered in and sat at the table across from me. He silently shook out a bowl of cereal and kept looking up at me, as if he was waiting for something. As if I would talk first, but why would I talk to him? I'd been avoiding him ever since the drugstore incident. I'd gone out with Heather and Dean the night before, just so I'd be out of the house—we'd gone to dinner and a movie, but the whole time I hadn't been able to stop thinking about Spencer.

So this was what really falling for someone meant. It ruined your life.

I'd only bared my soul to him and what did I get in return? He told me I was immature.

Well, I wasn't.

Except that if he tried to say I was immature again, I'd say something in return like, "I know you are, but what am I?" which would only prove that I was in fact immature.

I had the potential to be immature, but I didn't exercise it. He did.

Adam came up the stairs in running shirt and shorts, carrying a bright red piece of something in his hand. "Excuse me, but what's this?" he asked the group.

"What is it?" his dad asked.

"I don't know—I just found it in the parking lot." He turned it over in his hand, and a piece of paper fell out onto the floor.

Spencer's eyebrows shot up. "I was trying to make a mini kite to sail, and that was the basket—" He leaped up from the table, nearly flattening Tyler, and tried to grab the paper off the floor.

Mr. Thompson got it first. He unrolled a note that was attached by a piece of tape and a string to the small piece of red fabric. He read out loud:

"E,
You were right. I was wrong.
I guess maybe I'm falling in love. I've never been in love before. So what do I know what we're supposed to do?
But I don't care if everyone knows. You're worth the embarrassment.
You're the Emiliest of the Emilies. (Sorry.)
OBX XOXO,
S."

I felt my face get warm. Then my neck. Then my arms.

"Woo-hoo! This is hot stuff!" Mr. Thompson said, fanning himself with the note.

"Wait a second. Did that say 'Emily'? As in, this Emily?" Heather's mom asked.

"Who's writing you notes?" asked Adam.

"What does OBXXOXO mean?" asked Spencer's dad. "Is that some sort of code?"

"Are you getting secret messages?" my father asked, peering at me as if he suddenly didn't know me anymore.

I wanted to hear the note again. And again. Spencer was falling in love? With me? Had he actually confessed that? To a *crowd*?

"Wow. Must be left over from some other people. Must have blown down the beach," Spencer began. "Whole message-in-a-bottle-type thing—"

"Wait a second," Adam said. "Wait a second. S? Are you S?"

"Yes, Sherlock Holmes. You figured it out," Spencer said in a grumpy voice.

"Ha!" Adam laughed.

Spencer came back over to the table and crouched down beside me, putting his hands on my legs. "I thought I threw that little parachute onto your balcony last night, but I guess it blew off. So, I apologize for the public reading of my note."

"I don't mind," I said.

"Well, I do," Spencer grumbled. Then he smiled. "Yes, it was corny. Still, I mean every word of it. Even the dumb words."

I smiled at him. "So . . . you're okay with this?" I asked, as around us, everyone was murmuring and then shouting things like, "*You? And her?*" And "*Her? And him?*" and "*THEM?*"

"Yeah. I am. I'm more than okay," Spencer said. "I guess I was just in shock and I kind of overreacted. Maybe I ate too many weird gingerbread pancakes. I don't know, but I'm sorry—I acted like a jerk. You're right—this is a great idea."

"You guys! I can't believe it." Adam shook his head as he looked at us hug. "Dude. That's awesome."

"Well, I, for one, am not surprised at all." My mother smiled and looked very pleased with herself, as if she'd predicted it, which was ridiculous because even I didn't predict it. "Didn't I tell you? These things have a way of happening."

"Say something," Spencer urged me.

"Um . . ." I had no idea what I should say at a moment like this. It's one thing to have your first boyfriend and have him say he's falling for you. It's a whole other thing to have everyone in the world find out about it the same time that you do. And still another to have it be your parents and their friends. I leaned closer to Spencer and whispered in his ear, "Do you think we could go somewhere a little more . . . private?"

He nodded. "But you forgive me, right? You still think I . . . we . . ."

"Me and you? Oh, yeah. As long as you keep saying that you were wrong and I was right," I said.

"Don't get used to it," he shot back. Then we both laughed and hugged.

"Aren't they so cute?" said Spencer's mom. "They're so right for each other. How could we not have noticed?"

"Got bad news for you, Em. If your dad pays for the wedding, it's going to be an outdoor event," Mr. Thompson teased. "Hot dogs, maybe. Generic chips and water. Not bottled water, either. Strictly from the tap."

"Give me a break, guys. What do you think I've been *saving* for all these years?" my dad cried. "Duh. She can have the wedding of her dreams. The in-laws, however, are going to be a major problem—"

"We're not getting married! Would everyone please shut up?" I said, getting to my feet.

But the guys were so busy arguing and laughing that they didn't even notice us slip away. Or so I thought.

"Hey! Where are you going?" Spencer's dad called after us as we headed for the deck outside.

"If you don't mind, we'd like to be alone," I said.

"Ooohhh, they want to be alone!" several of the guys repeated after me, in singsong voices.

My mother narrowed her eyes. "How alone?"

"See what I was saying? This is going to be awful," Spencer said as we closed the door behind us.

"Terrible," I agreed, taking his hand and squeezing it tightly.

We looked at each other and smiled.

"Somehow we'll just have to deal with it, I guess," he said, slipping his arms around my waist. "In the meantime, we have one week left here, and I don't intend to waste it."

"Hey! You guys!" Heather shouted from down below by the pool. Dean was sitting next to her and they were drinking coffee together, snuggled on a chaise together. "Knock it off already!"

I waved down to her. "See, it won't be that bad," I said to Spencer as we stood by the deck railing. "Just occasionally mortifying. Come on, let's go tell Heather the good news."

"What good news?" asked Spencer as we headed inside and past the still-talking-about-us group in the kitchen.

"Don't make me—" I threatened as I stopped halfway down the stairs.

"Kidding!" Spencer cried, colliding into me. "I was kidding!" He grabbed my hands and pulled me closer toward him, kissing me.

"You know, we have to stop meeting on stairs."

"Do we? I kind of like it," I said, kissing him back.

We ran outside and joined Dean and Heather by the pool.

"You guys did it, didn't you?" asked Heather as Spencer and I sat down on the pool deck beside their chair, and put our feet in the water.

"Did what?"

"Made up! And went public!" Heather cried. She looked really happy and I couldn't wait to tell her about the note I'd managed to shove in my pocket when no one was looking. No way was I leaving that around for someone else to read *again*.

"We heard everything. The windows are open," Dean said. "We thought there was a fire or something, from how loud everyone was yelling. 'You, and him? You, and her?'"

"The 'rents are a little overexcited," Spencer said, nodding. "It's sickening."

"Or it would be sickening, if it weren't so great. Right?" I corrected him.

"Exactly." Spencer put his arm around my waist and scooted closer.

"Hey, if you guys want to be alone . . ." Heather teased.

"We're fine right where we are," I told her.

A few nights later, our parents hosted yet another big party to celebrate all of us going to Linden. Mom had made a special cake, and a giant banner was strung across the deck that said: WELCOME LINDENITES!

"Do you feel like they had that banner made when we were two years old? And they've just been dying to use it?" Heather asked me.

"It does look a little dusty," I said. "And dated."

One afternoon, a large brown box had arrived, full of new Linden sweatshirts for all of us freshmen, plus two for the twins—Adam's stepmom had ordered them as soon as she found out Adam had gotten in. I took a group picture of everyone, including Dean, using the camera's self-timer and the TV stand as an impromptu tripod.

"Linden, my Linden . . . your tree is everlasting," my dad started to sing, in a deep—and deeply embarrassing—baritone.

"Sounds like 'O Christmas Tree' to me," Spencer said under his breath.

"I think it is," I agreed.

"You know, what they say. Heard one school song, you've heard 'em all." He grinned, but seconds later an empty can of pop flew across the room and hit him in the head. "Who threw that?" he asked. "No, seriously. Who threw that?"

"So. We haven't really discussed this yet," I began as I started putting away the camera. "But what do we do when we actually get to school? Is it going to be too weird?"

Spencer looked at me and lifted a strand of my hair that had come loose when I pulled on my sweatshirt, pushing it back behind my ear. "Why would it be weird? I think it's great."

"You, Mr. Let's Keep This to Ourselves?"

"I'm over that," said Spencer. "Can't you tell? I've practically had my arm around you all day."

"True. And I love it, by the way," I said. "But what do I know about going to college and having a boyfriend? Nothing."

"Well, if you're still feeling weird about it, why not take a year off and do whatever we want?"

I laughed. "Excuse me, but didn't you just *do* that?"

"Oh. Right." He smiled. "Yeah, but we could do it together."

As tempting as the offer was, I had goals I wasn't really ready to just toss aside. Plus, I could just imagine what my parents would have to say. "How about if we go be freshmen together, and sophomores and juniors and seniors, and graduate together? Then we can take a year off."

Spencer nodded. "Agreed. Except I'd like to skip the sophomore part, I hear that's a hard year."

"We'll go to Europe or something."

"Right. We'll do that, we'll *totally* do that."

I stepped back from him. "Are you mocking me? Again?"

"Would I ever mock you?" he asked. "Sorry. Okay, let's start small. What do you want to do tomorrow? Where should we go?"

"I don't know. Should we see what my mom has planned?" I asked.

"No, definitely not." Spencer laughed. "I've seen enough light-houses to last a lifetime."

"You're just afraid you'll have to climb all those steps again."

"Oh, *I'm* afraid? Really."

"Then again, if we ditch the group, like last time . . ."

"We're pretty good at not staying with the group, aren't we?" He held my hand, and I leaned against him.

"We can take off in the Rustbucket first thing in the morning."

Spencer kissed me. "If it starts, that is. Where should we go first?"

"I don't know, but we should probably avoid places with balco-nies," I said.

"And pink rooms—"

"And kayaks—"

"And family members," Spencer said as we spotted our moms sitting over on the corner of the deck, pretending to have a conver-sation, but spying on us.

"Okay, kids. Name the president of the college during the

tumultuous seventies!" Adam's dad cried.

Adam groaned. "You said this was a trivia test. Not an ancient history quiz."

"Oh! That's low! I think I need another beer," said his father, heading for the cooler. "Harsh."

"I thought they'd never end the quiz," I said. "Good job, Adam— way to appeal to their age."

"No problem. And by the way? Great cake."

"Thank you, Adam." My mother beamed at the compliment on her Linden leaf-shaped cake, which she'd worked on all afternoon. "You know, you can buy the pan at the campus bookstore."

Adam nodded at her with a serious expression. "I'll be sure to do that."

I covered my mouth, stifling a laugh.

Spencer turned to the parents. "So. Which one of you bribed the admissions office? I mean, what are the odds that we'd all get in? It's not as if Linden is easy to get into. Isn't the ratio something like six apps to one admission?"

"Eight, I think," said Mrs. Flanagan. "But the reason it worked here is because you're all very different, and you're all very interesting."

"Some more than others," I coughed, and Heather laughed.

"And that's what they want. Variety."

"So, maybe it helped that we were in your corner, and that we've given the school copious donations—" my dad added.

"And changed the world and brought glory to the Linden name along the way. Don't forget that," Spencer's dad chimed in.

"And instilled school spirit in our offspring," Adam's dad said.

"They could do this all night," said Spencer, scooting over closer to me.

"I know," I agreed.

"Do we have all night?" he asked.

I shook my head. "I don't think so. Actually, I think we're supposed to be somewhere. Right, Heather?"

She glanced at Dean and then back at me. "Yes, that's right. We're supposed to see, um, the beach. At night. You were going to get pictures."

"I was, wasn't I?" I took Spencer's hand and we edged toward the steps down to the beach.

"Come on, Adam!" Heather whispered, dragging him away from the Linden-fest.

We all ran down to the beach. As soon as we hit the hard sand, Heather turned and started doing back flips, springing down the beach doing one after another, just like she used to.

"Look out for the sand crabs!" Spencer called after her.

Heather stopped, waved at him, caught her breath, and then kept going, laughing and flying through the air. Dean followed along beside her, trying to walk on his hands, tipping over every other step.

"Hold on—wait for me!" I cried. I wasn't any good at back flips, but I knew how to do handsprings.

"Great. The tumbling twins are back," Spencer complained.

"I don't think they ever left. They were just in hiding," Adam said.

When I caught up with Heather, we hugged, laughing and out of breath. It was a nice feeling. So many things had changed, but so many hadn't, too.

I couldn't wait to head off to college with this group of friends.

And Spencer. Especially Spencer, I thought as he ran up to me and picked me up in an awkward hug, trying to twirl me over his head.

"What do you think? Is this ballet-like?" he asked.

"Not even close!" I shrieked as we both fell to the beach, arms and legs tangled.

"Sorry," he said, cleaning sand off of my arms, then my face. "You okay? Sorry." He brushed sand off of my mouth, his fingers lingering on my lips.

"Just kiss me already," I said, "and we'll call it good."

Wish You Were Here

Chapter One

I'm on my bike, bringing my semi-new, semi-boyfriend, Dylan, a bag
of Skittles, and the candies are rattling in my backpack like those little
fake rocks my mother has in her miniature Zen serenity desk fountain.

I picture getting to Dylan's house and spelling out his name, or
my name, with the Skittles, or encircling our initials in a heart shape
with a giant + in the middle. Then we'll frolic on his bedroom floor
in the Skittles as part of our long, romantic good-bye.

I have a very active fantasy life. Dylan's not the frolic-in-Skittles
type of person, and probably neither am I.

I am, however, addicted to eating Skittles, so I can't really see why
I'm giving away an entire bag. Maybe it's because now I'm addicted
to Dylan instead, or maybe it's because I had six bags stashed in my
desk drawer, so it was very handy and didn't require another trip to
Target, where I've already been five times in the last two days getting
stuff for our summer trip.

"Ariel, this isn't the only Target in the world," my mother keeps saying. "You realize there will be *stores* where we're going." But I don't trust her, because she won't even tell us where it is we're going. And besides, what does she know about being addicted to Skittles?

When I get to his house, Dylan opens the front door. He has sandy cinnamon-colored hair that's cut short, and he has sideburns that make him look older than seventeen.

His face lights up when he sees me, like it always used to when I walked into Spanish when we were in the ninth grade, back when we were friends, before we were whatever we are now. His light blue eyes have brown flecks, which makes them hard not to gaze into. I've tried. Like, all through ninth grade I tried.

I worry that he's only smiling because he sees me holding the Skittles, so I hand the bag to him, but he doesn't seem overly excited by them, and he keeps looking happy to see me. Which is sweet. Like Skittles-candy-sweet. Addictive, for sure.

"Hey, you," he says. "What's up?"

"Not much. Just packing. For the tenth time."

"Right. Me too," he says. "You want to come in? Come on in." He opens the door wide. When I walk past him, he does this cute little thing where he pinches my waist, only I don't have much waist, so he pinches hip bone instead. I still can't believe he actually does things like this to me.

I'm not saying that I'm an ultra-thin girl. I just don't seem to keep much weight on these days. I think partly it's because I'm a runner, and because my parents just had this ugly breakup, and because my mother plans to drag me all over the country this summer, and I'm worried how that's going to turn out. I mean, there are the normal worries, on that front, and then there are the new worries: like, what if Dylan has this amazingly exciting summer in Wyoming and meets someone new and falls in love with her? While I'm stuck on a road trip with my mom and sister? And did I mention that after our road trip, we're spending two weeks at my grandparents' house?

Of course, I could be home all summer, pathetically waiting for Dylan's return, which would not be any better, let's face it. If he's going to be gone for two months, then I might as well ditch too. I just wish we weren't going to be so far apart, for so long.

I'm barely over the shock of the fact that we hooked up at our school's Spring Fling. There I was, with two weeks left of school, just getting over the thrill of our track team coming in second in state, me coming in third in the 1600. (It was exciting, at least at the time, because nobody thought I was going to place that high, not even me.) Sarah and I were hanging out, wondering if there was much flinging to be done, really, when she left to talk to her physics teacher and I ran into Dylan, who throws the javelin. So we started talking about track, then about other stuff too, laughing and dancing.

We kept looking at each other and then we started holding hands. We even left the dance together, which was huge, and he was going to drive me home, because we live close to each other, but I had to go back inside because of course I forgot my cute little gold shoulder wrap thingie, and when I left again, there was Dylan, right where I left him, and I thought, *What is happening? Is he actually waiting for me? No one ever waits for me.*

I'm with Perfect Dylan now. It's the best thing that's happened to me during what has been a very imperfect year.

Now, two weeks later, it's the beginning of summer and he's leaving and I'm leaving and that is all so imperfect that I would promise to give up Skittles if it would change anything. But it won't, so what's the point in suffering? You don't go on hunger strikes, or ikes, for just *anything*.

k into Dylan's room and I flop onto his Green Bay Packers
hair by the door, which nearly swallows me. I struggle to
sit up.

"You know what?" I say. "I need your address at camp."

"I already gave it to you," Dylan says.

"I know, but I lost it," I say. Actually I didn't. In fact I have it, and
I've also already memorized it. Probably it's a bad sign to be lying
this early in our relationship.

"Oh. Well, okay," Dylan says, and he writes down the address
again on a scrap of paper that turns out to be a receipt from the
Hollister store at the mall, which I will cherish even though it's all
inventory numbers except for the words "s/s tee." I just want more
of his handwriting, more things to remind me that he exists when the
tires are rolling down the pavement and I'm staring at the back of my
little sister's head, because of course she'll insist on sitting up front
at least some of the time.

"Do you think you'll come home for a visit?" I ask.

"Nope. Not a chance." He slides into the beanbag chair beside
me and we snuggle, because there's no other option when two
people are in a beanbag chair, which is probably why they were
invented.

"Are you sure you're not going to have email all summer?" I lean
against his shoulder, the rock-hard javelin-pitching shoulder.

"Not unless they really changed things from last year," he says.

"My mom's insisting that we give up email and cell phones, too.
We're supposed to just enjoy each other." I laugh.

She says my cell phone has become a "crutch," and that she wants
some time alone for us as a family, so she doesn't want anyone to be
able to reach me. In other words, she doesn't want Dad to reach me.

He's not included anymore in the "time as a family" time.

It's ironic because my dad was the one who was into taking summer trips—my mom went along reluctantly, after my dad spent hours planning them. Now we're going, she has zero planned, and my dad will be at home, living with Grandma and Grandpa Flack, where he had to move after Mom kicked him out. All Grandma Flack could do was joke that at least she'd kept his room the same for the past twenty years.

"My mom wants me to focus on 'the now,' to experience the journey," I tell Dylan.

He raises his eyebrows. He's met my mom, and knows she's the type of person who can spend time canvassing the neighborhood to get everyone to vote to legalize hemp.

In other words, crazy, though she says that's not a nice word, because it's an illness, which she'd know because she's a counselor, and I should use the term "mentally ill" instead—but only when I'm talking about other people, and not her.

"So this sucks. You can't call, and I can't email you," Dylan says, as he keeps shooting a Nerf ball into the air and catching it again.

"Sometimes I might be able to, I guess," I say. "It depends on where we stop, you know?"

"You know what would be cool? If you ended up coming close to camp."

"That would be cool," I agree. "Impossible, but cool. It doesn't sound like we're going west, but you never know. Maybe I'll take over the driving. Carjack the Jetta."

Dylan laughs. "Is that possible when you're actually in the car already?"

"We'll see." I'm a little worried about Mom being able to pull off her so-called itinerary. She doesn't seem to have much planned at all. I've seen no maps, no GPS. She keeps saying how we'll let the winds take us and the stars can light our way and other feel-good, schmaltzy stuff like that.

I think it's because secretly she is a horrible navigator, and she's going to hand me that job—but no map—as soon as we hit the road. I'll have to look for stars to guide us, and I'll regret that I never paid attention to that astronomy mini class, and wish that the wind would quickly blow us home *Wizard of Oz* style.

I look at my watch and see that it's almost time for me to go home and see Grandma Flack, who's coming over to pick up my cat, Gloves. She's taking care of Gloves for the next few weeks while we're away.

But I don't want to leave Dylan, not yet. I want to stay here. I want to fold up into a suitcase with a big label that says, "Dylan Meander." Not as in "Property of," because that would be tacky and also it would set women's rights back a thousand years, but just so they know where to deliver me when the suitcase gets to his dude-ranch-style camp, which cabin they should drop me at.

Is that so wrong?

I guess.

I try to get up from the beanbag chair, but I keep slipping. Dylan tries to help me up, but then he sinks down beside me and puts his arms around my waist because I'm starting to sort of cry a little, which I hate.

I loathe saying good-bye at the end of the school year. I just do. Even to people who write in my yearbook when I don't even really know them all that well and they write really, really stupid things. I still feel myself getting choked up because it's so nice that they want to write *some*thing, and I love them.

Then they hand me their yearbooks and I hate them, because I don't know them well enough to write anything, and I, unlike them, can't come up with something on the spot. I'm the worst spontaneous writer in the world. I need Time, capital T, to think of what I want to say and how to say it best.

But then this year, now that I think about it, not as many people asked me to sign their yearbooks, which should have been a relief, but it wasn't. Because although I used to be fairly popular, ever since the thing with my dad being in trouble, some people dropped me. I'm not on the A list anymore. I'm somewhere between B and C, or maybe C and D. Unlike my bra size.

My mind is wandering. It's because I don't want to leave, because leaving is like stepping off a giant precipice into the scary canyon known as Summer. You don't abandon your first actual sort-of boyfriend. You just don't. Right? That's one of the rules. But I think about poor Gloves being taken away, without me there for comfort.

"I have to go," I say.

"Okay," Dylan says.

"So, bye."

"Bye."

We don't move.

"You first," he says.

"No, you," I say.

We look at each other and smile, and then he kisses me, and I kiss him. This should be such a romantic good-bye that I wait for that melting feeling, but it doesn't happen.

I tell myself that's because it's only June, which is not the melting season, and we've been dating only two weeks. In August, when we both get home from our summer thingies and look at each other, we'll melt like a couple of Skittles left in the car on a hot day with the windows up.

For now, Dylan is snuggling with me and doing these moves that I'm not really sure I understand. But okay, I'm new at this, and maybe he is, too. I don't feel anything except awkward, and sort of tense, and worried that his mom's going to walk in on us.

I contemplate fake-melting, until I realize that although I thought he was sort of ravishing me, he was actually trying to get his cell phone off the desk because it's buzzing to tell him he has a text message. I can't help feeling that although I kind of love him, right now I kind of hate him.

"Are you really going to read that now?" I ask.

"No, no, I just thought—maybe it was the camp," he says.

"Right. What's it called again?" I ask, hating that he's so excited about leaving for the place.

"Camp Far-a-Way," he says.

"Ha-ha."

"No, really. It is."

On the way home I drop my first perfectly written, preplanned postcard in the mailbox.

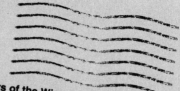

The cows are the real stars of the Wisconsin State Fair!

Hey—

I know we only saw each other like 10 minutes ago, but I wanted you to have something to read when you got to camp.

Me: preparing myself for life on the road with Mom and Zena.

You: getting ready for awesome summer on a ranch.

This is Not Fair.

Neither is it a state fair.

Miss you already.

Hurry back,

Ariel

Do not write below this line. Space reserved for U.S. Postal Service.

Chapter Two

I go home and Grandma Flack isn't there yet, so I review my mother's list of what I should pack, like the kind they give you when you go away to summer camp, which is where I should be going, with Dylan.

Camp Far-a-Way. Is he serious?

Shirts: 4
Pants: 3
Shorts: 4

I revised her list. Slightly. She doesn't seem to realize this road trip is two weeks long, and then we're going to Grandma and Grandpa Timmons's house, and even though I can do laundry there, do I really want to wear the same four shirts all summer?

Shirts: 23 (roughly)
Jeans: 7
Shorts: 10
Running shorts: 8
Running shirts: 8

Socks:	**Lots**
Shoes:	**16 (That's eight pairs, so it's really not as bad as it sounds. I have this sort of obsession with vintage running shoes, so in addition to my new favorites for running, of which I have two pairs, I also have five pairs for not running, and one pair of flip-flops.)**

Books: 7

Notebooks: 3

Large bags of Skittles: 5

My suitcase won't close without major amounts of sitting on it and smashing it.

Mom catches me jumping up and down on my suitcase and wants to know what's inside that's making it so hard to fasten and why I have an extra duffel on the side, like an order of French fries.

"It's all my running stuff," I say. "I have to bring clothes for every climate."

"Okay, whatever, Ariel," she says, looking frazzled. Her graying dirty blond hair is flying out in several directions, as if she's been caught in a hurricane—that's what happens to it when she doesn't use her blow-dryer and product. She and Zena have the same curly, wavy, unruly hair. Me, I have Dad's hair: dark brown, straight, ruly.

"But you definitely won't be able to buy anything new on our trip. We simply don't have room," she says.

"We don't? But it's only the three of us, and we always had room before," I argue.

"This isn't *before*," she says. "This is after." She pauses as if she wants to remember those lines for a chapter title for one of her new books. She forces a small smile. "Anyway, the road trip is only two weeks. How much could you possibly need to wear?"

"Maybe I like to change my clothes more often than you do." I check out her shirt, which looks as rumpled as her hair. "Didn't you work today?"

"Yes, but only in the morning," she says. "So, remember: no CDs, no DVDs, no cell phone—"

"Why is that exactly, again?" I ask.

"We're focusing on us. We're keeping it realsimple," my mother says. This is one of her buzzwords. "Realsimple." As if it's one word. She and everyone in her family have this thing for inventing words, mashing them together until they fit, the way you do with jigsaw puzzle pieces.

I'm surprised she didn't give us compound names when we were born.

Instead, it was Dad's idea to just close his eyes and flip to a page in the baby name book and point. Once a gambler, always a gambler, I guess.

The section they apparently kept landing on was called STRANGE NAMES, or NAMES TO EMBARRASS YOUR DAUGHTERS FOREVER.

Never mind that the movie *The Little Mermaid* was something everyone had memorized by the time I got to preschool, and I had to explain that no, I didn't have a tail. I got so many *Little Mermaid* gifts that for five years my room had an aquarium theme.

The only thing worse than being named after a cartoon character, in my opinion, is not being named after her, or anyone. Just being a random choice that your parents made with their eyes closed.

My twelve-year-old-sister, Zena, thinks having an unusual name is cool. But then, she also thinks that reading *Us* and *People* should count toward her Summer Literature List requirement. She loves signing things with her initials, because nobody else has them. ZIF. Zena Iris Flack.

She'd better hope that Mom doesn't want us to change our names back to her maiden name, which is Timmons, because her initials will then be ZIT. Monograms will be a problem. (My middle name is Frances, so I'll just go from AFF to AFT.)

Zena comes upon me and Mom arguing about the lack of email and phone, and says, "Just relax, A. So we won't have email, so what?"

We have this silly habit of calling each other "A" and "Z," because Dad always used to refer to us as "A to Z."

"Z, it's a big deal. I need to stay in touch with people."

"It won't be forever. What, are you worried Dylan's going to forget you or something?" she scoffs.

"No, of course not," I bluff.

But of course I am. So, the thing is, I'm going to write to him whenever I can. And send postcards of all the tacky places we go. My friend Sarah and I came up with the plan: she, because she doesn't want me to be out of touch for weeks; me, because I don't want anyone to forget me. Not Sarah, not Dylan, not even Gloves.

The doorbell chimes, and it's Grandma Flack. "Tamara. A pleasure," she says to Mom. "All set for the trip?"

"Almost." Without another word, Mom runs up the stairs to pack, leaving us to visit on our own. We always used to get along fine. Now it's weird and strained sometimes, like my grandma is guilty of something because she took in Dad, but it's not like I wouldn't want her to do that. Everything just feels extremely formal.

We shrug and look at each other as Mom thunders off. "She's busy," I say.

"Oh, sure." Our grandmother nods.

I wonder why my dad didn't come over with her to say good-bye, but then I remember that the last time he and Mom saw each other was not pretty. Nothing was hurled except insults, but still. It's not something you want to see twice in your lifetime, never mind thirty times.

My grandmother gives me an envelope. "This is from your dad," she says, and inside is a hundred-dollar bill, which I have to wonder how he could afford and if it's really from him, or really from her, trying to cover for him. "He wants you to have a great time on the trip, so here's some 'mad money,' I think he called it."

Mad money. Interesting choice of words. It's a good thing Mom isn't here, because she'd be furious at Dad for handing out money when he's supposedly bankrupt. "What about Zena?" I ask. "Is she getting some angry cash for the trip, too?"

Grandma Flack laughs. "No, she can share yours," she says. "She's not responsible enough yet."

Neither is Dad, I think. Not to sound pop-psycho like my mother, but I don't necessarily know if age has anything to do with how responsible a person is. Unlike my mom, I keep my opinion to myself. But I also get this weird feeling in the pit of my stomach when I wonder why my dad isn't on the scene to say good-bye.

"So . . . why didn't he come by to see us before we left, too?" I ask.

"I think we both know why," she replies. And although it's true, that the last bunch of visits have been weird, and I don't know how to feel around him now, and sometimes he just makes me nervous . . . I think he should keep attempting them.

"Um, I'll go try to find Gloves," I say.

I hunt around the house, in all of Gloves's favorite hiding places. Speaking of hiding, sometimes I think Mom's taking us on this trip just to keep us from staying in touch with Dad. In fact, maybe she's planning to stash us in some new town where he can't find us. Not that anything he did was so wrong, unless of course you prefer not having your life's savings, your college fund, and your house, even, stolen out from under you and used to bet on slots, cards, horses, and God knows what else.

The whole blackjack craze. Dad got swept up in it. Like, literally, off his chair and onto the floor and into the dustbin of history. From there it was an easy trip to the horse track, etc.

There aren't a lot of Flacks in town, so it wasn't something you could pretend was happening to someone else. At all.

Grandpa Flack told me that at his bar, there was a new game invented called "Flackjack," which was a version of blackjack that involved stealing from the kitty when the other players weren't looking. He didn't find it amusing and never went back to the place where he'd been a regular for twenty years.

Dad did things like this. He ruined things, kind of like when you throw a rock into a lake and it not only sends out ripples, it also lands on a fish and kills it.

That's us. The dead fish.

I spot Gloves lying under my comforter, on the corner of the bed near the window, basking in the sun. She shouldn't be a Wisconsin cat. She doesn't have thick enough fur. I scoop her overheated body up and give her a few kisses, right on the white patch over her eyes. "Don't worry, G. You'll be fine," I tell her. "Things are going to be weird, but I'll be home soon. If you get lonely, Dad will be there."

He's the one who helped me pick out Gloves seven years ago at the Humane Society. He was also the one who suggested we take her back after she cried nonstop on the way home.

I find Grandma in the kitchen, visiting with Zena and picking up the bags of cat food and other Gloves supplies that I packed that morning. "Hey, Dad's not in Las Vegas or something, is he?" I ask her.

"No, of course not. Why would he be in Vegas?" she asks, as if that's the most illogical thing I've ever said. "He's done with gambling," she says. "You know that."

"Right," I say. He's definitely promised to change, and I haven't noticed anything suspicious lately, but it hasn't been that long, either.

"So, I got you something, too." She gives me a thin plastic sleeve of stamps. Two books of regular first-class stamps, a few sheets of postcard stamps, plus some plain white postcards, already stamped.

We've always had this weird, slightly psychic connection. "How did you know?" I ask.

"Know what?" she says.

"That I need stamps," I say.

"Please. That bit about not bringing a computer along and springing for wireless, or giving you a phone? Ridiculous." She snorts. "Penny wise, pound foolish." She's always saying this about my mother, which probably isn't that cool a quality in a mother-in-law. Or an ex-mother-in-law, which I guess would be a mother outlaw.

I keep looking at her and wondering whether it was her who made Dad the way he is, or whether it was us, or whether it wouldn't have mattered who he was born or married to—maybe he was wired from the womb to be a gambling addict.

"I wouldn't last a day without emailing my friends," she says.

"Yeah. Maybe I won't, either," I say. A day sounds about right, give or take a few hours.

"Also, it wouldn't kill you to keep in touch with your father while you're away," she says. "Think about it."

It wouldn't kill me to keep in touch, but it might hurt, sort of like getting blood drawn. He lied about so many things that I still haven't really been able to forgive him for, even though at one point I really did decide that he was a good person at heart, a good person with a really big problem. And forgiveness is what we need here.

But so far the only one who seems really open to that idea is Zena, who says he can't help himself. I guess I understand that, but I don't really think it's an excuse.

Mom and I aren't budging, but for different reasons.

She's mad about the money, about his lying to her, about how he let everything spiral out of control before he told her what was going on.

And I'm angry about all that too, but I'm also mad about the reputation factor. First it hit the newspaper that he'd embezzled money from the motor vehicle department—which, face it, nobody loves anyway—to finance his gambling habit, after he'd spent all of our money. Then it was on the TV news, and they showed a picture of our house, which is pretty nice, I guess, which looks really bad if someone is stealing government money. Then the Fox News I-Team investigator came to the door and I opened it, not realizing who it was, and the reporter shoved a microphone in my face, and that night it was all over TV, with me saying, "No comment."

When I got to school the next day, it seemed like everyone stood back from me, or whispered, or walked by me saying, "No comment," and laughing.

A few days later, there was this big winter formal, and Sarah told me I had to still go, because I'd already bought a dress and because you can't just give in when people try to shun you. Mom told me to go, and for some reason I thought I might cut loose and have fun. At the dance I was trying to be brave, so I asked Tony Miller if he wanted to dance. He said, "No comment," and grinned at me, as if it were a hilarious and original thing to say. His friends started laughing, so I went into the bathroom to get away from them.

Unfortunately, I happened to be washing my hands at the same time a group of cheerleaders were fixing their hair and makeup.

Sherry Hansen said, "God, Ariel, that's so awful that now you're, like, bankrupt; that must be *so* hard," and another cheerleader tried to hand me a Kleenex, the whole time digging for sordid details, only being nice so they could get the scoop.

I went outside to get some fresh air after that, and Keith Johnson, who was standing there illicitly smoking, tried to commiserate with me by sharing stories of his brother in drug rehab. "Oh yeah, you have it so hard. That's *nothing*. It's *nothing* until he calls you from jail, or beat up in an alley."

"Well, thanks, Keith. I'll look forward to that," I told him. "Thanks *so* much."

Then after I stomped off in my heels, I felt really bad, because he really was worse off than me.

I spent winter break in hibernation. Going back to school afterward was one of the best and hardest things I've ever done. Fortunately there was a scandal involving a football coach and one of the previously mentioned cheerleaders, so everyone moved on to that and forgot about me and my problems. But not before I'd slipped down a few rungs on the cool ladder, rungs I've not managed to climb back up yet. I doubt I ever will. I've got zero upper-body strength. Zero upper body, actually.

I have these really angry thoughts and memories as I'm standing there smiling at my grandmother and clutching Gloves to me. I feel like such a hypocrite. How can I talk to her and make nice about this situation, but how can I not? It's so awkward that sometimes I'd rather jump out the window than feel it all over again. It's getting old and stale, like what happens to Gummi Bears if you open the bag and don't finish them.

I start crying while I say good-bye to Gloves. I've got my nose buried in her black fur, and the thought of abandoning her for four weeks is too much. I rub her white paws. I think about how Gloves will be at Grandma and Grandpa Flack's house, and how Dad will be there, too, and how we won't be, and I keep crying. I'm overreacting and I know it, but I can't stop.

"Pull it together already," Zena says to me. "It's only four weeks. And it's only a cat."

I glare at her through my tears as she hugs Grandma good-bye and then runs upstairs. "Thanks for the sympathy!" I yell after her. She should know that Gloves is not "only a cat." She's my confidante. Unlike my little sister.

"You can always write to her," my grandmother says as she hugs me. "While you're at it, write to me, too. It's going to be as boring as your mother's mac and cheese around here without you." My mother is notorious for her bland cooking, heavy on the dairy. She once made a soup that my dad called "cream of cream."

I laugh. "Okay, I will. I promise."

"Promise?"

"Right," I say, and she kisses my forehead, then gently lifts Gloves out of my arms.

As Gloves is being whisked away in a Pet Porter and plaintively meowing, the phone rings and it's Dylan. I'm glad for the interruption. He thanks me for the Skittles, which strikes me as weird. Of course, he is perfect, so knowing that it would mean a lot to me is probably why he felt compelled to, because we're in sync.

Then he says something not-so-perfect. "You know, whatever happens this summer . . . it's cool, right?" he asks.

"What do you mean?" I ask.

"We sort of have this thing, or we, like, had this thing at the end of the year, and that's cool," Dylan says, "but we won't see each other for ten weeks, and you never know, you might meet someone on your trip."

"Yeah," I say slowly, kind of like a dying breath. *What is he talking about?*

"All I'm saying is that it's going to be a long summer, so . . . don't sweat it if something else comes up," Dylan says.

I'm a little slow at this, but it dawns on me that he's giving me license to see someone else, which probably means that's what he wants to do. "Dylan, what are you saying?"

"Hey, lighten up. It's no big deal, I just want you to have a good time. You know what they say about road trips."

"No." *That they kill your relationship? Before you even leave town?*

"Like, whatever happens on the road stays on the road. Or whatever." He gives an embarrassed laugh.

"I thought that was Las Vegas." *Why does that city keep coming up?*

"Really? Huh."

"Dylan. I'm going on a road trip with my sister and my mom. Do you seriously think I'm going to do anything fun?" I ask. "I'll be in every night by, like, eight. Watching TV in some motel and fighting about what shows to watch."

We say good-bye and I hang up, and then I have that love him/hate him feeling again. I take that slip of paper with his address out of my pocket and stare at it. I have this urge to crumple it and throw it in the kitchen trash, but I don't.

Anyway, even if I did, I've already memorized it, so it would be all for show, and nobody else is around.

Riding the range in the San Juan Mountains of Colorado.
Fun for the whole family!

Hey Dylan,
Have fun becoming a cowboy.
   Hope this will spur you on.
   Okay, not funny.
   (I saved this from a trip 2 years ago.)
See you in 10 weeks!!!
Ariel

P.S. Why Why oming? Couldn't you pick
somewhere closer?

|..,||,.,||.,|.|||.,,.,|.,,.|.,||.,|.|..|.|,|.||.|.,|.|,,,.|.||

Chapter Three

We leave at five a.m. in our old diesel VW Jetta. My mother drives as if her hair is on fire. As if we are seeing all fifty states—today. Before lunch.

We hit a bird at about six a.m. and all she, birdwatcher in a former life with my dad the full-time gambler and part-time ornithologist, can say is, "What kind of bird *was* that?"

"Pigeon," I say, because I want to believe that only the ugly birds get hit by runaway middle-aged drivers.

Mom slams on the brakes and pulls into the emergency lane to stop completely; then she backs up, weaving a little. A giant truck lays onto the horn and veers into the left lane to avoid hitting us.

"You are going to kill us!" I say. "You realize that?"

"Just hold your horses," she says, and she climbs out, searching for the wounded bird.

Zena and I watch her wander up the side of the highway, in the dawn. "She has this urge to save helpless things," I comment.

"Helpless *dead* things," Zena corrects me.

"I didn't see anything," Mom says as she climbs back into the car. "Maybe I didn't kill it. Maybe the bird just bounced off the windshield and flew away."

"Mm," I say.

"Maybe," says Zena.

Highly doubtful, I think. This seems like a really bad start to our trip.

We all settle back into our seats and prepare for the next roadkill experience.

Sometimes Mom floors it up to eighty-five; then she'll get distracted and slow to sixty. I can't stand someone who's that inconsistent. If I can keep pace when I'm running and I don't even have a speedometer, then why can't she?

"Mother. There is such a thing as cruise control," I tell her.

She glares at me, then laughs at herself, then switches it on, then off, because she can't decide which she likes better: scaring others or saving gas money. She's seeming a little scattered and out of control this morning, and I wonder why, and want to suggest to her that it's because she's feeling cut off with this no email/no cell phone rule, which should immediately be retracted.

I'm supposed to be allowed to share the driving, but Mom isn't budging from the wheel, and we're not allowed to stop until we nearly run out of gas. This is very unlike my mom, who is always very safe and doesn't like to leave things to chance.

Mom's not the risk-taker; Dad is. She's changing on me, or something, right in the middle of I-94. Maybe she's been reading her own books, especially those chapters about reinventing yourself in *Change Your Wife, Change Your Life*?

Yes, I've read her three books. No, they haven't changed *me*.

I spend the first three hours of the drive doing some very significant highway dreaming.

I see: me and Dylan kissing good-bye in his room, which was very hot. Not the room, but the kiss. I wonder if he is thinking about it, too, if he's on the plane, staring out the window, thinking of me. Maybe the plane is overhead right now. At this second. I gaze up through the sunroof, but it's mottled because there was a light, spitting rain overnight that left lots of drecky polka dots.

I see: Dylan and me dancing at a party, but instead of us being on the edge of the dance floor, like we were at Spring Fling, we're in the middle or maybe toward the stage, because we've just been crowned fall Homecoming King and Queen, because everyone's forgotten my dad's a heel and I'm popular again, even more so because I'm with Dylan now, and there's a spotlight on us as we have this big, hot kiss.

Then the daydreaming stops because I actually fall asleep and do some very real dreaming, but unfortunately I can't control these and so it's not about Dylan; it's about showing up to take an exam and having forgotten to wear any clothes and everyone laughing at me as I try to shield myself with my driver's license.

Which is really, really small.

And also, not a great picture of me.

I wake up as we pull into a gas station. "Where are we?" I ask, rubbing my eyes. I hear the back car door slam and see Zena running into the convenience store.

"Get her!" my mother almost screams, and several other people pumping gas look around to see who the lunatic is.

"Mom, it's *okay*," I insist as I climb out of the car. As soon as everyone stops looking at us, I rearrange my shirt and shorts, which luckily I am wearing, unlike in my dream, and run off to follow my sister. I do a lot of this, or I used to. She's a bolter.

I find her browsing by the candy. Not that I can fault her for this. "You can't do that," I say.

"Do what? Buy M&M's?" she asks. "Why, because they're not Skittles?"

"Ha-ha. No, I meant take off, run into places by yourself," I say. "You're, you know. Vulnerable." I look around the store, where various people of various ages are buying various road foods. There's a giant case of knives over by the trucking supplies area that makes me wonder.

"I am not," Zena insists.

"Please. You're twelve. The 'v' in twelve is for vulnerable," I say. "You're twelvulnerable."

"Am not," she argues.

"Do you ever watch the news? Girls like you disappear every day." I look around for Skittles and see an empty display box, which just figures. This trip is off on the wrong foot in every way.

Zena edges a little closer to me. "I know what I'm doing."

"Fine."

"Mom is driving like a bat out of hell," Zena comments after we visit the restroom and buy some bottled water. "Why?"

"Um, because that's how she is? Because she's trying to be like Dad?" I suggest.

We sip our water and browse the postcard rack. Apparently we left Wisconsin while I was sleeping, and now we're in Minnesota. I'm flipping through postcards on the metal spinning racks and get bored and think if I spin the rack faster and faster we will go past those places faster and faster.

Suddenly the rack stops spinning and I hear this "Ow. Geez." And some other words I won't bother repeating.

There's a man standing on the other side of the postcard rack. He's tall, oldish, and has a strange mustache with twirly yet droopy ends, as if it can't make up its mind whether to stay on his face or not.

"Quit it," he says, glowering at me.

"You quit it," I say back.

We start wrestling with the postcard rack, which I can't believe I'm doing, except I was here first and I did have my eye on a goofy loon postcard and I don't think just anyone should be able to turn the rack when I'm already looking at it.

He sees Zena and all of a sudden he gets this gleam in his eyes. He smiles at her and says, "What's *your* name?"

She doesn't answer and I start to tell him it's none of his business, but he repeats, "What's your name? I want to buy you an ice cream." And he smiles his creepy smile with his creepy mouth and his droopy mustache and it's like I see his reflection in the knife case and suddenly know why it exists.

"Let's get out of here," I tell Zena. We run to the counter, I set down two quarters for the postcard, and we dash outside to meet Mom's waiting arms, or at least the open doors of the car. We're both laughing, and Mom wants to know why, because it's probably strange to see us having fun together.

"What happened?" she asks.

"Oh, nothing," Zena says.

Mom taps the top of the car. "Let's go, girls. We have a schedule to keep."

"We do? I thought we had a realoose itinerary," I say.

"Well, we do. But because of our motel reservation, we've got to get to Sioux Falls by five," Mom says.

"Sioux Falls. South Dakota. Why?" I ask.

She smiles as we all get into the car. "You'll see."

I hadn't really been paying attention until now, but I notice the road signs. We're heading west. Just like Dylan. "What do you mean, Mom? Where are we going?"

"To the starting point for our journey," she says.

"But we already started. In Milwaukee," Zena points out as she buckles her seat belt.

"Where we begin is not necessarily our starting point. Every journey has its mileposts," Mom says.

I roll my eyes at her psychobabble, then stare out the window at a mile marker as we get onto the highway again, and wonder what it is supposed to mean.

Dad used to take us on cross-country tours like this, but it was always rushed. We'd have to see this place and that place, and we'd do it all in one week.

We should have been suspicious last summer when we drove out east to Atlantic City, but we weren't. We enjoyed the ocean and the visit into New York City and we never once considered the reason he was so exhausted was because he didn't sleep at night; he sneaked out to the casinos. Which is why I'll be attending community college unless I can win a track scholarship.

"After South Dakota, then what?" Zena asks, leaning over the front seat.

"I have some surprises up my sleeve." Mom's sleeves being organic cotton and baggy, they're bound to fall out soon. But it reminds me of something Dad always said about cards up his sleeve, and it must remind Mom too, because her nose wrinkles as if she's just tasted the bottom of a bag of dill-pickle chips and gotten a mouthful of extra-sour pickle-chip powder.

The loon is the Minnesota state bird. Listen for its plaintive call.

Sarah,

Beware of strange men in truck stops offering free ice cream.

That's all I'm saying.

Also, my mom is crazy. But we knew that. Miss you and wish you were here instead. Zena has already run off once and doesn't believe she is a target.

Yours until I get abducted (not that it would happen because I'll outrun them),

AF

Chapter Four

For dinner we head to a diner across the street from the motel where we've checked in for the night in Sioux Falls.

Mom seems very excited about dinner, which is odd, since we're headed to a place called Matt's Turkey Diner. Clearly she's feeling the romance, the intrigue of being on the road. She hasn't seemed "up" like this very much lately, and now she's getting excited about turkey.

"Turkey dinner," Zena says out loud. "Yum."

"No, turkey diner," I correct.

"Who ever heard of a turkey diner?" Zena says.

Mom loops her arm through Zena's as we cross the street. "Isn't that what we're about to be, if we eat turkey?"

"You guys maybe," I say. "I'm not dining on any turkey."

"But it's the specialty," Mom insists. "The motel manager said it was the best food around."

"If they told you wolverines would make good house pets, would you believe them?" I say, quoting my favorite line from the movie *Planes, Trains and Automobiles*.

My mother's gullibility has been duly noted and recorded in county court transcripts. You'd think she'd become a little more suspicious with age.

Inside, the place reminds me of Luke's diner on *Gilmore Girls*, but without the witty banter and the cuteness.

I order blueberry pancakes. "Hold the turkey," I say. The waitress looks at me with narrowed eyes, as if the fact she has to serve breakfast all day is *my* fault.

Mom orders a piece of apple pie à la mode to start, which is her famous restaurant move, ordering dessert first and occasionally last as well, and then she has a turkey sandwich with potatoes, and a café mocha with whipped cream. The woman can put food away.

Zena puts ketchup on her open-face roast turkey sandwich. She covers everything with ketchup, as if she's still six. She has a milk shake (ketchup-free), while I sip iced tea and take a bite of my pancakes. The door opens and in walks this incredibly hot guy, Brad Pitt in his *Thelma and Louise/Seven* early years, pre-Brangelina. He looks like he's maybe eighteen or so. He has a very tan face and spiky blond hair and he looks like he's already been working outside all summer, though it's only June. Not only does he have muscles, they're tan muscles.

He gives me this long look before he sits down at the counter. Maple syrup drips down my arm because I've been holding my bite in midair for too long.

It's the sexiest moment of my life.

So far.

But I shouldn't be noticing him, even if he is staring at me. I shouldn't be looking at any other guys. Counter Boy looks nice, sure.

But he's probably not half as nice or interesting as Dylan.

But then I remember Dylan's phone call and him saying, "What happens on the road, stays on the road." And this is as "on the road" as it gets.

Just as I'm about to get up and go talk to Counter Boy, trying to think of some pretext, Zena announces that she needs more ketchup and walks up to the counter, right beside him.

She is such a horrible flirt and she's only twelve. It is really embarrassing—or impressive, depending on how you look at it. She has the body I'm supposed to have at sixteen, and vice versa.

Naturally, I drop my fork and jump up to follow her. It's my job to rein her in, according to my mother. When I get to the counter, Zena is laughing and telling the guy that yes, turkey and ketchup do go together. "Tastes great," she says.

"Less filling?" he replies with a sexy smile.

I wait for an opening, shuffling closer. "Excuse my crazy sister," I say, but as I reach for the ketchup in Zena's hand, I slip, and my syrup-covered hand ends up grabbing Brad Pitt Jr.'s arm. I try to pull it away, and there's a sucking sound, and I think some of his arm hair is coming off. "Sorry," I say, thinking it's very embarrassing to be literally stuck to someone.

"It's okay," he says as he dips a napkin in his water glass and brushes his arm with it. "You guys are *really* into ketchup, huh?" he asks. When he smiles at me, I notice he has these crystal-clean white teeth and is even cuter up close. I don't know how to make a move, but I know I should be making one. I could just kiss him right now and it would be totally random and exciting.

Before I can make a move of any kind, though, there's someone tapping on my shoulder. I turn, expecting my mom. But it's not her; it's a man.

It takes a second to register who this person is. No, he's not some random forty-year-old being too friendly in an invading-my-space kind of way.

It's my uncle Jeff.

In the flesh. Lots and lots of flesh.

"Uncle Jeff? What are you . . ." I start to say as he smiles at me. As Counter Boy gets set to eat his turkey burger, Zena screams, "Hey!" and hugs Uncle Jeff.

"You guys look fantasterrific," Uncle Jeff says as he smushes me in a group hug with Zena. It's like being hugged by a friendly grizzly, not that those exist.

Mom rushes over and slips her arm through Uncle Jeff's as he stands back to give us a breath. "Zena, Ariel? I have a surprise for you. We're not driving across the country," she says with a big grin.

"We're not? Yes!" Zena high-fives me, with my syrupy, sticky hand that was once destined for and connected to Counter Boy.

"Are we having a family reunion?" I ask. "In Sioux Falls?" Is there something about our family history I don't know, some unclaimed clan of cousins nearby?

"In a manner of speaking, it's a reunion, yes. We're not driving across the country, because we're traveling by bus," Mom says. "It's a ten-day tour, with Uncle Jeff and Grandma and Grandpa Timmons!"

I cough. My throat is suddenly closing up. Either I'm allergic to Matt's Turkey Diner's maple syrup, or I'm allergic to bus trips. Either way, I can't breathe. "What?" I gasp.

Grandma and Grandpa Timmons are already on their way over to us, big smiles on their faces.

I always used to call them "Tims-moms" when I was little, because I couldn't pronounce it right. "Cinnamon," Grandma T.

would say, over and over. "It's just like cinnamon." Which, honestly, I still don't get.

My grandmother kisses my cheek, and her silver-blond hair smells like permanent dye the way it always does, which makes my eyes water. It's cut short and sleek, and goes with her *velour du jour*, as I call them. She's famous for wearing the latest in trendy track-suits, hoodies, and loungewear. She's about a size four, tiny.

My grandfather, never a big hugger, stands back a little and claps me on the back, but seems as genuinely happy as anyone to be here. He retired recently, and although he isn't wearing a starched busi-ness suit right now, he still seems like he is.

I haven't seen them since Easter, when they came to help us move into our new, smaller house. It's definitely a shock.

"Can you believe this? Isn't this going to be fantasterrific?" Uncle Jeff, whom I call "Lord of the Necklaces," asks. He insists on wearing this gold cross, plus a necklace with a gold boat propeller charm, and a necklace with a little gold envelope.

He was a mailman until he was attacked by a family of squirrels, who dropped out of a tree onto his head, probably because he was talking too long to the house's resident and had bored the squirrels to death.

We had to drive up to St. Paul to visit him in the hospital where he was getting rabies shots. It was very traumatic, the whole squirrel attack and its aftermath, so now he's on disability, which was when he gained fifty pounds, which *is* kind of a disability.

Uncle Jeff hands me a box of Dots. "You still love these, right?"

"No," I say, "but thanks."

He looks a bit wounded. "I thought you loved chewy fruit candies and things of that nature."

"Skittles," I say. "Those are the ones."

"Oh. Well." He shrugs. "If I were you, I'd keep them anyway. We've got lots of travel days coming up. Need some road food." He smiles and sort of half punches my shoulder.

"Yes. We do." I smile at him. "We sure . . . do.

"Mother. What were you thinking?" I ask in a harsh whisper as we reshuffle our seats and make room, finally sitting down in a larger booth.

"You need a positive male influence in your lives," she says.

"Why do we need a male influence? We have Dad," I argue.

"I said *positive*."

I suppose Uncle Jeff is positive. In a very revolting, sickeningly sweet kind of way.

"That's why we could only let you bring the bare minimum luggage," my mother explains. "Because the bus has certain specifications; there are size restrictions for everyone's bags."

"You know, this sounds kind of exciting, if you ask me." Zena shrugs.

"We didn't." I glare at her. What would she know about exciting? "Where are we going?"

"We're going to see the Heartland," Uncle Jeff says proudly, as if he devised the tour. If he did, we're in more trouble than I thought. The man believes that birch trees are interesting. Birch. Trees.

"The Heartland," I repeat. What exactly does that mean, anyway? As if one part of the country is better than another, is more central and more vital to keeping it going. Where is the Liverland? The Kidneyland?

"We start here in South Dakota, and spend several days exploring it," Mom says. "Then we're off to—"

"North Dakota?" I suggest.

"Well, I don't know—that's one of the hallmarks of this tour company. They keep a few things a surprise."

"Up their sleeves," I mutter.

"What's the point of surprising us? You'd think they'd want us to know where we're going," my grandfather says.

"Exactly," I chime in.

"Don't be so rigid. This is going to be a totally new way to experience things," Mom says. "We can look around more and enjoy the scenery."

And I can enjoy the scenery of being trapped with fifty strangers, I think. "But, um, Mom?" I say, trying to be civil, trying not to scream about this.

"Yes, honey?"

"How am I going to keep up with my running?" I ask.

"Oh, we'll have plenty of pit stops. Same as if we were driving. Whenever we stop for a tour, or a hotel—you know, you can fit it in." She smiles.

I want to throttle her. She doesn't understand that I plan on winning the state cross-country championship this year. She has completely forgotten all about how I was third last year and how I want to move up. She acts as if this is an afterthought.

"I'll run with you, Ariel," my grandfather offers, and it's sweet, but ridiculous, because he's sixty-five, so I just pat his shoulder and smile like a good granddaughter.

"Can't we all just rent an RV or something?" I ask.

"Oh no," says Uncle Jeff. "This will be much, much better. We'll have a tour guide. We'll meet new people. It'll be great!" He stands up to snap our picture with a camera that looks decidedly undigital.

I slide out of the booth and go back over to the counter, where the cute guy is now eating an ice-cream sundae. "You're not by any chance going on a bus tour tomorrow, are you?" I ask.

"A what?" he says.

"A bus tour?" I repeat.

He shakes his head.

"Yeah. I didn't think so." I look back at our oversize booth, at my oversize mom and uncle.

Suddenly I notice the diner is full of retired-looking people, turkey diners here for the last meal before they hit the road.

The last supper.

Our final meal before execution.

And I want to sob.

I turn back to the guy. "You don't by any chance *drive* a bus?"

The Rainbow Lanes and Motor Lodge
Where every morning is a good morning! Sleep on our deluxe
full-size mattresses. Enjoy in-room shower and iron.

Hey Dylan—
We are at a really awful motel in South
Dakota tonight. Wish you were here.

And then I look at the postcard and realize I have to rip it up, because you can't tell a guy you want him to be in a motel room with you.

Not even if you sort of do.

The postcard is so old and outdated that after one rip, it crumbles onto the floor.

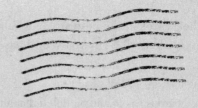

Matt's Turkey Diner: because you should never be too far from a hot turkey sandwich and some real mashed potatoes. Twenty-five years of talking turkey. Eat in or take out. Buses welcome.

Dylan,
You won't believe this. We're busing it.
    My uncle Jeff and grandparents are here, too.
    It's a Family Re-Union. On Wheels. The wheels on the bus go round and round. Etc.
    I regret that I have but one bus ride to give for my country.
    And this will be it.
    Your favorite patriot,
    Ariel
    P.S. Wish you were here, or I was there.

Chapter Five

The next morning we meet at the world headquarters of Leisure-Lee Tours, which is a sentence I never thought I'd write.

It's not exactly world headquarters; it's a small white stucco building with two buses parked out front—one old and one new.

There's a parking lot for everyone to leave their cars, and as we walk away from ours, I cast a longing glance over my shoulder at the old Jetta. What once seemed so horrible, those long family car trips, now seems like the Good Old Days. No, the Great Old Days.

The two buses bear the image of a guy wearing a leisure suit and lying sideways, and the name "Leisure-Lee" is written in script with big loopy Ls that kind of trail off like exhaust. "See the U.S. at *your* pace!" it says underneath him.

My pace? That would be really, really quickly. Let's pause in each state, see the highlights, then move on and get home. I like the sound of this. But I don't think that's what they mean. I think they mean that this is a bus for people who don't want to move all that quickly from place to place.

There are mostly senior citizens, but it isn't all older people. Just ninety-nine percent. There are one or two other families like us. There's a girl who looks like she could be Zena's age, and not-quite-identical-but-very-close twin boys who look like they're maybe in high school. They have short, bright blond hair and identical gold-frame glasses and Adidas soccer shirts.

I walk over to them to introduce myself, but then I hear them talking to their parents and realize they may be the only people my age on the bus, but English is not their first language. Poor, pitiful souls like me being dragged by their parents who are attempting to save gas money. In another country.

"Hi," I say, feeling really stupid and American.

"Hello," they say in unison, while their parents vigorously shake Mom's hand and say they are from Germany and can't wait to see more of our country.

Meanwhile, Zena and the other girl are chatting like they're long-lost sisters, instead of us.

That's it. The rest of the passengers are older people. Significantly older. I'm dying. Or I will die of boredom on this trip. And when I do, I'll probably have company.

We're standing there semi-cluelessly, wondering where to go next, when the newer bus's door opens, and two insanely cheerful people step down onto the pavement in front of us.

"Welcome, welcome, tourists!" the man says. He has pants and a shirt with many pockets, an Australian accent, and a hat with flaps. "My name's Lenny; I'm here to entertain you, tell you folks about the stops, keep things moving—"

"And I'm Jenny," the woman next to him says, no accent, but similar getup, as if she shops at REI and she's going hiking soon.

"I'll be keeping things moving because I'll be driving the bus! Hello, hello, everyone!" She raises her hands over her head as if she's just won a heavyweight bout, as if she's Million-Dollar Baby. "We were just doing a final safety inspection of the bus; you'll be glad to know it passed with flying colors."

"We've vacuumed every seat. We've dusted every armrest. If this is not the cleanest bus in America, you can call me a koala," Lenny says.

My grandfather frowns. "Koala?" he says.

"I thought that was New Zealand," my grandmother comments.

"Australia has the best stamps. Don't you think?" my uncle asks. "Especially the Sydney Olympics special edition. Those were keepers. I might have one on here." He takes off his floppy khaki hat, which is covered with pins he had made out of laminated stamps, and turns it around, searching.

Lenny and Jenny walk around to meet us personally. Jenny can't quite get over Zena's name, she loves it so much. "*Xena: Warrior Princess* was my favorite show!"

We have no idea who or what she's talking about, but we nod and smile and make nice, because this is what we've been trained to do, like circus seals.

"Well, how's everyone doing over here?" Lenny asks. He makes the rounds, introducing himself, and I can't help noticing his handshake is sort of an insincere clasp, a little on the dead-fish side.

"Pleased to meet you, Lenny. I have a question. Did you know Steve Irwin?" my uncle asks, referring to the famed crocodile hunter.

Lenny looks at Uncle Jeff as if he can't quite believe his ears. "No. I did not have the good fortune. Australia is a very large country, you know."

"I just thought, you're both in the media-slash-entertainment profession," Uncle Jeff says. "Maybe you'd met."

Lenny shakes his head. "No."

"Huh. Well, it's a small world sometimes, but then sometimes it's a big world. Take my postal route, for example." He starts telling people how much he loves delivering mail because it, and I quote, "brings sunshine to lonely people." He has this knack for engaging everyone in conversation. Whether they want him to or not. He likes to know his neighbors and his postees, as he calls them. "There's nothing like the feeling of delivering a birthday card. You just know you're making someone's day."

"You always say that, but what if it's a condolence card?" Grandpa Timmons asks. "A sympathy card? How can you tell what it is?"

"After a while you just know. It's the way people's handwriting looks. And, of course, glitter," Uncle Jeff says. "Sometimes it falls out."

"People put glitter in sympathy cards?" someone else wonders out loud, not quite getting it.

Jenny hands us luggage tags and "Hello My Name Is" tags. I fill out the first, but leave the name tag blank. I can't—and don't—see anyone else wearing the name badges, not even the older folks. Besides, do I really want to hear forty-five people ask me if I was named after the Little Mermaid?

A car pulls up in the little circular drive in front of the building, and an African American woman gets out of one side, while a tall guy who looks like her teenage son, maybe, gets out of the other. They're the last people to show up, so we all can't help noticing them, because we've been hanging around for a while, listening to the Lenny and Jenny Show.

The guy opens the trunk of the car and starts hauling out suitcases. He has light brown skin and cool rectangular glasses that make him look intellectual. He looks like he's my age, or maybe a little older. He's wearing a T-shirt with the message, WHOSE AUTHORITY?, long shorts, and low-cut sneakers with no socks.

He looks cool. I can't believe it. He's here to save me, to save this trip from being the death of me.

Then I think: Maybe he's not actually getting on the bus; maybe he's just dropping off his *mom*. That would not be cool. That would be one of the universe's many cruel jokes.

His mom stands there and supervises, lifting only a small bag out herself. She and my mom could wear the same size, somewhere around XL, except this woman is too well dressed to trade clothes with my mom. Let me put it this way: She has Outfits. Mom has Stay-In-fits.

"Excuse me, Jeffrey," Lenny says to my uncle as he walks past us and heads for the newly arrived passengers. "Hello, there! You must be the O'Neills. A pleasure to meet you. I'm Lenny."

My ears perk up. He said O'Neills. Plural.

"Hi, Lenny. Yes, I'm Lorraine, and this is my son, Andre."

"That's terrific. We're so glad you're here." Lenny clasps his hands together. "Now for the bad news. I'm sorry, but you'll have to scuttle a few of those bags."

"Scuttle?" she repeats.

"Compact. Compress. Discard," her son says.

"Oh no." She shakes her head. "I couldn't."

"I'm sorry, madam, but you'll have to. This trip is all about personal growth, except in this case, where it's about personal reduction."

"What are you implying?" she says, hands on her hips.

"Your luggage. That's all I meant." Lenny holds up four fingers, like he's used to dealing with people who don't speak English and has to use body language to communicate. "Because some people underpacked, I can give you room for four bags, maximum."

"That's not fair," someone else chimes in. "It was one per person."

"One large per person," someone else says.

"Not one per large person?" someone else adds, and everyone laughs.

This is bus humor. Or elder humor. Apparently.

"No, it's one large suitcase per traveler, one small," Jenny explains, again with the counting-on-fingers method.

"Define small," Mrs. O'Neill says, her eyes narrowed at Jenny.

"Forty-five linear inches." Lenny pulls a measuring tape out of his khaki pants pocket, which seems to carry a plethora of assorted supplies. They're the kind of pants with multiple pockets and zippers. So far I've seen him extract a Swiss Army knife, a screwdriver, a ball of twine, and a flashlight. "Let's have a look," he says, and starts to measure the suitcases.

"Well, this is just plain ridiculous," Mrs. O'Neill complains. "Are we supposed to dress like slobs just because we're on a bus?"

"Ma, I told you about the luggage limit, okay? So don't act surprised. Here, I'll get rid of one of my bags," her son offers. Then he smiles. "No, wait—I know. I won't go! Then you can use my seat for all *your* luggage."

I smile, biting my lip.

"Very funny, Andre," his mother says. "Just repack."

"Seriously, Ma. If there's not enough room—"

"Andre? Don't start with me."

"Fine." He starts randomly tearing clothes out of his large bag and jamming them into a smaller suitcase. He shows his mother an empty large suitcase. "I'll stick this back in the car, which means we can bring another bag of yours. My clothes are completely smashed and wrinkled, but as long as *you're* happy."

"I am. Thanks, sweetheart."

"Whatever," he says. After Lenny measures and approves the remaining bags, Andre carries them over to the bus, while his mom goes to park the car in the lot. I try to make eye contact, thinking I could introduce myself, let him know I feel his pain, but he's not looking at me—or at any of us.

"All right!" Lenny says once Mrs. O'Neill is back. "Everyone's here now; everyone's bagged and tagged. Wonderful. Come on now, gather 'round," he says, like we're not all standing beside the bus, waiting to get onto it. "Are you ready for the adventure of a lifetime?" Lenny asks. He waits for our response, but there isn't one. "I said, are you ready for the adventure of a lifetime?" He cocks his head to the side, holding his hand behind his ear.

"Yes!" everyone over sixty cries. Well, everyone except my grandparents.

"Great, that's great, but you're going to have to work on your cheers, all right? If you want Lee to come out here, he's going to need a big welcome. One, two, three, say it with me . . . are you ready for the adventure of a lifetime?"

"YES!" everyone screams, just as an elderly man totters out of the Leisure-Lee office. He looks frightened to death by our voices, and he walks a little unsteadily down a ramp to the parking lot. "Folks. Nice to see you," he says. He's wearing a cowboy hat and aviator sunglasses. I glance at the illustration on the bus, and then at him. Yes, it's the same guy.

"So you're retired now?" Uncle Jeff asks him.

"Oh no. Never retire!" Leisure-Lee says, waving his cane in the air. "Once you retire, you don't get vacation."

"Hm. An interesting perspective," Uncle Jeff comments.

Leisure-Lee starts to wobble a little, and Jenny quickly fetches a chair from inside the office. He sits down. The years on the road have clearly taken a toll.

"Now, our name Leisure-Lee Tours says it all. Most tour bus companies rush you from place to place." Lenny shakes his head. "Not us. Never have done, never will."

"Oh, great." I sigh.

"Shh," Zena says.

"You want to see something? We see it. We don't believe in rushing you through your vacation. Why? Because when life gives you a vacation, what do you do?" He waits for a second. "You take it! By the horns.

"Now, we'll see all the notable sites, but without the hustle, without the bustle. We want you to enjoy your vacation. Put your feet up. Relax. Have a little time for some introspection. In fact, we're the only bus tour out there committed to your personal growth."

My mother looks over at me and smiles, like a bit of a know-it-all. Of course, personal growth is one of her buzzwords, like "realsimple," and it's also "realconnected" to Mom's line of work, so of course she found a bus company that espouses it.

In reality, though, my mother the counselor, the expert on women's personal health and growth issues, was living with an addictive personality. For years. That chapter in her book called *Talk It Out, Work It Out* about healthy relationships? Pure fiction.

"Our founder, Lee, believes that life is all about seeing the small stuff," Lenny says.

Leisure-Lee nods. "Damn right."

Life is also all about eating the small stuff. I take out a handful of Skittles. If it would be possible for a meteor to hurtle from the sky right now and hit the bus as we head out on the open road? I'd be all for that. As long as it took out the bus, but missed the people. And our car.

Jenny then makes us introduce ourselves, and it starts to feel like a new season of *The Amazing Race*, and everyone will have little captions floating under them like:

GARY & BETTY, MARRIED

KRISTY & ROGER, RETIRED

LENNY & JENNY, MARRIED BUS HOSTS

and

THE FLACK FAMILY, SLIGHTLY INSANE

or

THE FLACKS, NO OUR DAD ISN'T HERE, DOING JUST FINE, THANKS

There may not be enough Skittles in South Dakota to get me through this trip.

"Find your own friend, A," Zena says when I get on the bus ten minutes later, expecting to sit with her.

Like I said, my little sister is not exactly supportive. "Z, there's nowhere else to sit," I say out of the corner of my mouth, feeling like I've landed in junior high all of a sudden and I should be holding a lunch tray. Mom is sitting with Uncle Jeff, while Grandma and Grandpa are sitting together. It's all in the family. Except for me.

"Right here, young lady!" Lenny points to a seat toward the front. "Right this way."

I pick up my backpack of Minimum Daily Requirements—pens, postcards, Skittles, lip balm, and a book—and head to the front of the bus. I see Mrs. O'Neill sitting with a gray-haired woman with a name tag that says "ETHEL" in giant letters, and across the aisle from them is an empty seat next to her son.

He glances up at Lenny and then over at me. "I have to sit up front. I get carsick," he explains. "Bus-sick, I mean."

"Great," I say, perching on the edge of the empty seat.

"Not *sick* sick, just kind of woozy. Hey, you want the window?" he offers.

"Sure," I say.

"That way if I do hurl, it'll be into the aisle," he says.

I wish he hadn't given me that image to worry about. "Thanks."

"Joking. Joshing. Not serious. Hey, have you heard the new Beck?" he asks, bobbing his head slightly and pulling out an iPod. He has a vintage baseball cap on, and the brim is starting to slide down over his face. "It's fantastic. Amazing. Incredible," he adds, I guess in case I don't know what "fantastic" means. He flips down the tray on the seat back, the kind they have on airplanes. He gets out this vocabulary book and a highlighter and starts reading, or skimming, or memorizing.

Highlighters make a very annoying sound if you're not the one wearing earbuds. Which I'm not. So it pretty much sucks. I stare out the window and wish I knew more about where we were going, so I could start counting down the mile markers, or counting them up, or something.

I excuse myself and go two rows up to Lenny, who's sitting in the seat right behind Jenny, who's driving. "Excuse me. Is there a bus postcard?" I ask Lenny.

"Please?" he replies.

I can't believe he's going to insist on manners. "Is there a bus postcard, please?" I ask.

"No, mate, I didn't hear you, that's all," Lenny says with a chuckle. "You want a postcard?"

I nod. "Something that's, you know, promotional or something. About the bus."

"No problem." Lenny reaches into a small compartment behind

the driver's seat and rummages around. Finally he pulls out a faded, dated postcard that looks as if it were made when color cameras were still new, when bus tours were still cool. It shows Lee, about fifty years ago, sitting in the driver's seat, beckoning people aboard a silver bus.

"I've only got the one," Lenny says as he hands it to me.

"One is perfect," I say. I go back to my seat and slide past iPod vocab guy. He gives me a questioning look and I hold up the postcard, as if to justify myself and my journey down the aisle and back.

In case he's wondering if I went up to ask for something embarrassing like a tampon. Not that I'd ask Lenny. Of course I'd ask Jenny.

I get out a pen and start to write. Already I have a lot to write home about.

"So." My neighbor takes off his headphones. "I'm Andre."

"Hi. I'm Ariel," I say.

"Like the mermaid."

I smile, but not happily.

"So, how did you get onto the bus?" he asks.

"Steps?" I suggest.

He laughs. "Really. Because I was dragged. Kicking and screaming."

"I didn't notice that," I say.

"You were probably too busy kicking and screaming yourself. Couldn't hear me."

"Exactly. What, you mean you're not thrilled to be spending ten days on a bus?" I ask him in a soft voice.

"I'm giving this trip two days, max," he says. "Then I'm ditching."

Just as he says that, music starts to blare out of the bus speakers. It's the soundtrack to the musical *Oklahoma!*

"Hey, you want to listen to this instead?" he asks, nudging my shoulder and pointing to his iPod.

I shrug. "No, it's okay," I say, wondering if he really means that part about ditching the bus. I hadn't thought seriously of that yet, except in my overactive fantasy life, as I lay awake the night before listening to my mother snore.

"Really. It's cool. You can have half." He takes out one earbud and hands it to me.

"My mom made me leave my iPod at home because she wanted us to *talk*," I explain as we shift positions and get comfortable. "Not that it's very good anyway; it was a bribe from my dad. Only he didn't buy a good one, so it wasn't much of a bribe."

"Parents." He smiles a little sadly. "Here." And we listen together. After Beck, some of the music I don't know but some of it I do, and it's nice even if it's only one ear's worth.

After a few minutes, when we're on the highway, he points out the window and I follow his gaze and see a gas station with a red flashing sign that alternates between:

EAT
GAS
EAT
GAS
EAT
GAS

I look at him.

"No comment," he says, and we both smile. It's the first time I've smiled hearing those two words together in a long time.

Leisure-Lee says, "Welcome aboard! Sit back and enjoy the ride in our new deluxe coach! See the U.S.A. at your pace!"

Dylan!
You won't believe this.
  I'm trapped on a tour bus with my relatives.
  And other crazy people.
  And two overly chipper tour guides.
  It's some crazy plan to get us to bond while seeing the USA.
  Wish u were here instead.
  Ariel

I₁.₁II₁₁₁.II₁₁I₁III₁₁₁₁.II₁₁₁.II₁₁.II₁₁₁I₁I₁III₁I₁.I₁I₁₁I.II

Chapter Six

We pull off the highway and stop at a rest area for lunch. Jenny slides out a giant tray of brown-bag lunches from a chilled compartment next to our luggage. Maybe that shouldn't gross me out, but it does.

We're spread out at various tables, eating bag lunches. Or at least some people are eating them. I had so many Skittles that I really can't think about eating much else, and besides, it doesn't look all that yummy. Something about our lunch being so close to the hot pavement that we were driving over is just wrong.

"Is every lunch going to be on the road?" I ask Jenny as she smiles and sets a brown bag in front of me. I'll go through it and pull out the stuff I want to eat later, just like I do for away track and cross-country meets. The apple and the cookie can be preserved. I'll drink the soda now. The sandwich can be tossed.

"Some will be, but others we'll eat out," Jenny says. "Any place with a sign up that says, 'Buses Welcome,' we're there." She winks at me.

I study her face, feeling like I can't trust her. They're keeping secrets for some reason. I'm sure of it. They're delivering us to some strange location, like that underground storage place in Nevada. We'll all be part of some bizarre genetic study involving nuclear waste, which might be less risky than eating this lunch. It looks slightly genetically modified, as if it were built to withstand two weeks on the road, though I don't know if this is possible with cold cuts. Or would they be warm cuts?

I turn the sandwich over in my hand. It has a sticker that says, HAM 'N' CHEEZ.

Just as I'm about to throw it out, I look up at my grandfather, who's watching me.

"Um, you want this?" I ask.

He just widens his eyes. "Hell, no," he says. "I have my health to think of." And he pulls out a PowerBar for lunch.

I'm sitting at a table with my family, but I cannot make eye contact with my mother. I refuse to. She's keeping secrets these days, too. Hoarding information. She's become a hoarder. One of those weird people with fifty-seven cats, only instead of cats, it's stuff I don't know but wish that I did.

"This is so much better than driving," she keeps saying.

"How is this better than driving? And why are we here? I don't mean to sound so existential, but really, what are we doing here?" I ask before I sip my soda.

"Would anyone be willing to trade?" Uncle Jeff is asking around. "I've got a nice ham sandwich here. I'm looking for turkey."

"Here," Andre says, offering up his Turkey 'n' Tomato.

"You sure now?" Uncle Jeff asks as he reaches for the sandwich trade, like this is elementary school and he's the big, yet polite, bully.

"I'm sure," he says.

"Fantasterrific!" my uncle says.

Andre looks at me and raises one eyebrow as he hands the sandwich to Uncle Jeff. As the sandwich travels past Andre's mom, a tiny dog's head pokes up over the top of her big purse and tries to eat the turkey sandwich right out of his hand.

Uncle Jeff, with his fear of small animals due to the Great Squirrel Incident, immediately drops his ham sandwich to the ground and leaps backward. "What the—"

"Cuddles. Cuddles! He's not usually so aggressive," Mrs. O'Neill explains, as if having a dog in her purse—on a bus trip—is perfectly normal. She tries to pull back the dog, who is barking and wrestling with the sandwich, trying to eat the whole thing even though his head is tiny and his mouth is smaller than a snake's.

"Ma!" Her son looks at her with disgust. "What were you thinking? How could you even think this would work, and you lied to me, and—"

"Anyone else have turkey?" Uncle Jeff is asking as everyone gathers around to see the dog. "Turkey, anyone?"

"I'll take a turkey," one of the older passengers says, clearly having misunderstood.

"Ma. I *told* you this would happen," Andre says.

"And I told you, I couldn't leave him at home in a kennel," she says. "He's just a baby." She makes embarrassing kissy noises, saying, "Who's my favorite boy?" as she snuggles the dog to her, kissing him on the mouth but getting mostly bread.

I try to picture smuggling Gloves onto the bus. She'd yowl so loudly that we wouldn't make it up the first step.

Lenny and Jenny march over, as if they're the police, which I guess they are in this case. "All right, people. Let's talk," Lenny says.

"We don't need to *talk* about it," Jenny says. "We've got a policy to deal with situations like this. It's called no pets!"

"But perhaps there's a reason for this. A medical emergency or something," my grandmother suggests.

"What kind of medical emergency can be helped by a Chihuahua?" my mother says. "And *is* that a Chihuahua, or a rat?"

"It's nothing more than a desire to look like one of those celebrities who carry little dogs in bags," my grandfather mutters to me. "Annoying. Cruel."

"Yet occasionally stylish, depending on the dog's outfit," I add.

Lenny climbs up on a picnic table and claps his hands to get everyone's attention, as if everyone's not already gathered around staring at the dog. "All right, everyone. Listen up. Now, the first thing we need to investigate is whether anyone in this group is allergic to dogs?"

He waits a second, but nobody claims to be.

"He's a very well-behaved dog," Andre's mom speaks up. "He's completely potty-trained, and you haven't heard him bark once, have you? He sleeps like an angel cuddled next to me. That's why I named him Cuddles."

Andre looks at me and rolls his eyes. I realize that maybe the two of us are going to get along, because I start thinking how much both our moms are annoying us right now. It isn't much to bond over, but it's something.

"I'll pay an extra fee, if need be," Mrs. O'Neill offers. "A pet deposit. Whatever you want. But please, please, don't ask me to leave him behind."

Andre adds, "Plus, she'll go insane if she has to leave the dog somewhere, and then we'll have an insane woman on the bus."

I glance at my mother. Two insane women on the bus.

"Nobody wants anybody to lose her mind on this trip, I can assure you," Lenny says. "That happened to us on a tour once. Middle of

Arizona. Woman went stark raving mad in the desert. Had to get her flown out by helicopter."

"That sounds promising. Do you think Mom did *any* research on this bus company?" I ask my grandfather.

He smiles at me. "Yes, she did, because she called us about a dozen times to ask if we thought this was a good idea."

"And you said . . . ?" I ask.

"Hey, we'll do anything to spend time with you guys," he replies with a shrug. "Well. Almost anything. We put the kibosh on a nature retreat with a bunch of life-coach seminars."

"Thank you." I sigh, turning my attention back to the dog debate.

"The issue is whether we let both of you stay on the bus," Jenny says. "This is a major infraction of the rules."

Mrs. O'Neill looks at her with narrowed eyes. "If I go, then my son goes," she says. "We'll demand a full refund. And that's two paid passengers you won't be able to replace at the last minute."

"Perhaps a surcharge, then," Lenny says nervously, "would be the best solution."

"No, we have to go by our published policy for situations like this," Jenny states with a meaningful glare at her hubby. "We're bringing it to a bus vote. Bus votes are what we do when we have conflicts. So. How many people are in favor of letting Cuddles stay on the bus?"

As I stand there watching some of the older passengers' hands shake as they hold them in the air, I realize that if the dog goes, Andre goes, and he is the only person on the bus I could remotely bond with, and he let me listen to his iPod.

I raise my hand as high as I can. "Let them stay on the bus," I say. "I bet half of us have pets at home that we miss." I look around the crowd and see everyone watching me. Why am I doing this, again?

"And unlike my cat, Gloves? Cuddles is transportable. He doesn't whine, or scratch, or demand to be let on and off the bus." Unlike me, too, I think. "So maybe Cuddles could be, like . . . our mascot. Every bus—every team—needs a mascot. Right? Like at my school, we're the mighty Panthers, and so it cheers us all up when the Panther's on the bus—"

"You have a live panther?"

"Oh, jeez, that'd worry me."

"Anyway," I say. "What's the harm in letting Cuddles stay? Maybe he could be like our, uh, therapy dog."

"Ooh!" my mother cries. "Great idea."

"But he's going to make it impossible for us to gain entrance to certain sites," someone complains.

"You'd be surprised. The policies on pets are changing everywhere," Mrs. O'Neill says. "He does have lots of cute outfits. He'll charm his way in."

"We can't hang out here any longer talking about this. Who's for Cuddles?" Jenny asks again. "Raise your hands."

Lenny counts the votes. "Thirty-three. That carries. The bus has spoken. Cuddles the Chihuahua . . . welcome to Leisure-Lee Country, where the miles and smiles aren't far apart." He reaches over to rub the dog's head, but Cuddles looks like he'd rather chew his hand.

As we meander back over to the bus, Andre comes up to me. "I don't know whether to kiss you or to kill you."

I feel my face turn red. "What?"

"That dog was my chance. To escape. And you blew it for me," he says as we stand in line to get back onto the bus.

"Sorry," I say. "I didn't think—"

He shrugs. "No, it's okay. I was joking. If we had to leave, I'd go home, and that's not where I want to spend the summer either," he admits.

"I hear you," I say. "Sort of."

"So is your mom as nuts as mine?"

"Probably," I say.

"My mom picked this tour because she wants us to bond," he says. "One, I get carsick on buses, which makes it hard to read; two, she brings the dog; three, we're, like, in the middle of nowhere, and could anyone stare at us more? All these old people want to kill us."

"What? No, they don't."

"Look at them." He subtly points to a couple of retirees who are regarding us with what can only be called skepticism. Or contempt. Or hatred.

"Probably they don't like anyone under the age of twenty," I say. "One of those ageist things."

"Teen hatred. Right. I'm sure."

"So, *are* you and your mom bonding yet?" I ask.

"Like rubber cement," he says. "Epoxy. Gorilla Glue."

"Really?"

"No. More like dry Scotch tape."

"I could go for a dry Scotch," my grandfather says with a sigh as he stands behind us in line to get back on the bus.

Look for the evasive jackalope—a legendary creature feared and respected by all who visit the American West. Able to run and hop at high speeds.

Dear Gloves,
I miss you. There is a dog on the bus. It's an outrage.
But you don't like riding in cars, so I doubt you'd like buses.
Because who does, really?
Go tell Grandma you're hungry for some chopped tuna. Starving, actually.
You've never been so hungry in your life.
XX OO
A

Chapter Seven

Here's another sentence I never thought I'd write: I think the Corn Palace is cool.

In case you haven't been there, it's this giant place covered in corn kernels. I don't think I can even describe it all that well, except to say that they have a theme every summer, and there are murals made out of different-colored corn kernels. Like, when you were little and didn't want to eat your vegetables, and you made a pattern on your plate of green beans and corn.

My grandmother has taken my mother and Zena to see the Enchanted World Doll Museum across the street. I bowed out and am killing time at the Corn Palace gift shop. Naturally I'm looking at the postcards, trying to find my next victim, when I try to spin the rack and it goes nowhere. I see a blue blur on the other side that looks like Zena's hoodie, so I say, "What's your name, what's your name, I want to buy you an ice cream," in a creepy, twangy voice, the way we've been doing whenever we talk to each other, which isn't often.

But the person on the other side doesn't respond and just keeps pushing at the postcard rack, trying to spin it, and my hand gets kind of wrenched.

"Oh my god, Zena, would you *stop* it?" I say, but then I see Andre step out on the other side.

"Don't call me Zena," he says. "I have enough problems without being called a girl."

"That's my sister," I say. "And you're right."

"Where is she? Where's your mother?"

"Across the street," I say.

"Same."

So far neither of us has asked about dads, and I like that.

He looks at the collection of postcards I'm holding, which are all fairly goofy. "You need a lot of postcards," he observes.

"I'm sending them to a bunch of people. Plus I want to save some for myself," I say. "Otherwise, who will ever believe I went on this amazing trip?" I roll my eyes to let him know I'm not serious.

"Your really long and boring testimony about it should scare them off. Somewhere, there has to be a recording of that dude's presentation." He mimics Lenny and his highway narrative. "The drought was absolutely devastating to the people."

"You have a pretty good Australian accent," I say. "Where are you from?"

"Chicago," he says.

"That explains it. Isn't there a neighborhood like Little Australia? Little Sydney or something?"

"No," he says, not looking all that amused. "Anyway, I'm from outside Chicago. You?"

"Way outside Chicago. Milwaukee," I tell him. "Actually, just outside Milwaukee."

He finally laughs. "So. What will you write on your postcards about the Corn Palace?" he asks.

"That it reminds me of Russia," I say.

"You've been to Russia?"

"No, I just meant those little thingies at the top." I point to a postcard in my hand, showing him what I mean.

"The spires? Minarets," he says.

"Right. Those."

"They're mostly used in mosque construction. Islamic mosques. So I don't know what they're doing on a corn palace in South Dakota."

"Are you, um, Islamic?" I ask. Oh no, I sound like an idiot. "Muslim, I mean. Is that why you didn't want that turkey sandwich?"

"No, I'm vegan," he says.

I smile. "Then the meat sandwiches aren't gonna come in handy, are they?"

"No, just kidding. I'm actually nothing," he says. He shrugs. "I mean, no restrictions. Food-wise, religion-wise—"

"Ariel." I feel a tug on my sleeve. "*Ariel.*"

I turn slowly and see Zena behind me. "Yes?"

"Give me ten dollars," she says.

I narrow my eyes at her. "For what?"

"This corn pen. Plus this snow globe with the falling corn."

When I look back around, Andre's gone.

When we get ready to leave, Mom has saved me the seat next to her. She has something to say, I can tell.

"Look, we got you something at the doll museum." I'm afraid she's going to hand me a doll, but Mom hands me a postcard. It's cool, but I don't want to tell her that, so I just nod. "Hm. Interesting," I say.

"How about 'thanks,' " she suggests.

"It's just a postcard," I say.

"Ariel."

"Thank you for the postcard, Mother," I say formally.

"What is bothering you?" she asks.

"Besides the fact you didn't tell us we were going on a bus tour with a bunch of senior citizens?"

"What's so wrong with that? I thought you'd be glad to see your grandparents," she says.

"I am, Mom. But weren't we going to visit them for a couple weeks, anyway?"

"Yes, but—"

"Where are we going, exactly? And what's the point?"

"Does there have to be a point? Don't be so rigid," she says. "Not everything in life is neat and tidy. You're so goal-oriented that sometimes you miss out on life."

Yes, I am missing out on life. Right this second, I think, as I look out the window and see an animal that could be a bison off in the distance. That's very cool, seeing a buffalo, and I almost tell her, but I don't want to make her happy by acting happy. Some wild animals that were once nearly extinct won't make up for the fact that we've been essentially kidnapped, all because she wants to get out of town and away from Dad and memories of Dad for a few weeks.

"I'm afraid you're not being open to the journey," she says.

"Mom, it's day two. Are you going to get on my case already?" I ask.

"Well, every day counts," she says, pulling her gray-brown hair back into an ear-of-corn-shaped barrette. It's curly and thick and the barrette barely contains it.

"How about the fact I didn't even know this was the journey we were going on? Does that count?" I ask.

She rummages in her oversize shoulder bag and pulls out a package of cheese sticks, offering me one. "What do you mean?"

"You didn't tell us what we'd be doing, or where we're going, or anything," I say. "Don't you think that was kind of misleading?"

"It was a surprise. A well-intentioned surprise," she says.

"Yeah, but did you think about us?"

"Of course."

"And you thought it'd be okay for me to spend day after day sitting on a bus and having to find time to run like it was an after-thought?" I say.

"Running's important to you. Yes. But it's June, and I thought it wouldn't affect you too much because the season doesn't start until the end of August," she says. "It's not like I planned this trip for August. I could have, I suppose."

"Well, who knows *what* you're planning for August. But you'll probably tell us in August."

There's a long, awkward silence, and then she says, "Speaking of August."

"What?" I ask.

She clears her throat. "We might be moving, actually. In August."

"*Moving?*"

"Sure, why not? Get a fresh start in a new house, a new neigh-borhood."

"But . . . we *love* our neighborhood. And—Mom. Dylan lives there," I say.

"Yes, well. We're not going to organize our lives around Dylan," she says.

She can be so heartless—and clueless that she's being that way. I'll be having the worst day ever, but instead of noticing, she'll work late helping some client of hers with a new life-coaching plan.

I can hardly believe she's saying this. "Moving. How far?" I ask.

"Maybe only a few miles," she says, sounding nervous. "Maybe more than that."

"I'm not changing schools," I declare. "No way. I'm not leaving Sarah and all my friends."

I can't handle this right now. I stand up and walk down the aisle a few seats. "Uncle Jeff?" I ask. "Could you switch with me? I want to visit with Grandma."

"Oh. Well," he says. He seems a little reluctant to budge.

"We need to talk about girl stuff. And things of that nature," I explain.

"Say no more." Uncle Jeff is up and moving, and I sit down next to Grandma Timmons.

"Hi, there. What's up?" she asks. "Did you want to talk?"

I wrinkle my nose. "Not really. I just needed a change of scenery. Is that okay?"

She nods. "Sometimes it's better just to think things through than to talk all the time about them. Let's play backgammon."

We used to play every summer at their cabin in northern Minnesota. As I set up the mini travel board and swing my checkers into place, I think about how we'd all crowd into that small cabin, and how my dad constantly wanted to play "double or nothing" when it came to backgammon, or gin rummy, or Parcheesi. Then it was quadruple or nothing, and pretty soon we'd be laughing at how many times he could double "double or nothing" without losing track. He'd start with the doubling cube that came with the backgammon set, but when he went past those numbers, he'd stack pennies on the counter, like towering poker chips, to remind him of the score between us on rainy days when we played for hours. One time when he was out of pennies, he used pieces of puffed rice cereal instead— Honey Bears, I think.

"So. How's it going?" Grandma asks as she rolls the dice.

"Fine. But we're not talking, right?" I ask.

"Not at all," she says. "But if you ever wanted to, you could."

"Right."

"But you don't have to."

"No."

"Agreed," she says.

I wonder if I could spell it out somehow in backgammon checkers. SOS.

Corn Palace, Mitchell, SD
The one and only corn palace in the world!*

Dylan,
I miss you.
    Corny enough for you?
    I think I just figured out what my next science/art project will be.
    Wish you were here.
    Is that corny also?
    This place is having an effect on me, what can I say.
    AF

***That *we* know of!**

|..ll...ll.ı.lll...ıl...ll..ıl..ı.ı.lll.ı.l.h....l.ll

Chapter Eight

We land at a place called the Horizon Inn for the night.

I don't see much on the horizon, except for days and days in the future spent sitting on a bus. The sun is nowhere near to setting yet, which is nice. We have free time until we all meet for dinner at the attached steakhouse at seven.

I want to go running, but when I look around the parking lot, it seems like there are no roads, just little streets connecting different parking lots.

When we walk into our room, the curtains seem to be made of old, sun-faded striped rugby shirts, and there is a generally musty smell, which reminds me of swampy places we've visited before. I wish I could crack a joke about the place, but I can't think of anything good, and it hits me that what this situation needs is a goofy dad.

One time we stayed at a motel where we lifted up the trash can and found a toad underneath it. My father immortalized it in a journal entry on our trip called "On the Toad, with apologies to Jack Kerouac."

Dad made a cage for the toad out of one of my running shoe boxes and we took it along with us for a day. When the toad died, we buried him at a rest area near Topeka and took a picture with the caption "On Golden Pond in the Sky" and labeled his grave HERE LIES TOAD.

We had a memorial service that a couple other people actually attended. Strange people who lurked on the edge. The kind who might frequent rest areas looking for, I don't know, companionship? The ones who might pull out those "Trucker Dating" flyers, looking for love on all the wrong interstates.

Anyway.

Dad might be completely irresponsible, unreliable, and shady, but he has this goofy side that can be fun, which is something Mom seems to have forgotten. He's not completely evil; he never was.

Now, I try to rifle through the drawers in the desk, but the drawers turn out to be fake. Then I spot a postcard on the bedside table, right above the shelf for the miniature Bible. The postcard features a picture of the hotel in its glory days. Before real beds and TVs with more than ten channels were invented, when nylon sheets were, I guess, okay.

I pick it up and write:

The Horizon Inn & Steak House. Convenient to I-90 and other attractions. HBO and phone in every room. Charges apply.

Hey Dad—
We haven't seen any dead toads (or frogs) (or Frog and Toad) yet, but if we do I will give them a proper burial.
   We did kill one bird so far, and I've seen more bugs die on the bus windshield than I ever knew existed.
   It would drive you nuts.
   So would the Leisure-Lee bus sing-alongs.
   So don't even wish you were here, because you wouldn't want to be.

   A

         ⚬ ⚬ ⚬

"You can't go running by yourself out here," my mother says to me five minutes later, but she doesn't offer to come along, which is fine by me. She makes some phone calls while I'm in the bathroom getting dressed, but I really don't pay attention to her.

However, when I step out of our room onto the cheap-looking rusted balcony, my uncle and grandfather are standing there.

My grandfather is wearing running shorts and a T-shirt that says, GRANDMA'S MARATHON 2002, and looks to be in pretty good shape. Why didn't I know this about him? Or did someone tell me and I forgot?

My uncle, on the other hand, is wearing he-capris, which are his extra-long khaki carpenter shorts, and a T-shirt that says, WE DELIVER FOR YOU. He has Greek fisherman–type leather sandals on his feet, with white tube socks.

It hurts to look at him, and it's not just the sun's reflection off the plate-glass motel window.

"I thought you were on disability," I say, trying to talk him out of it. "Are you supposed to be running? I don't think you're supposed to be running." I don't know CPR.

"I'm perfectly fine," Uncle Jeff says.

"It's not his legs; it's a mental disability," my grandfather chimes in. "Squirrelphobia," he whispers to me.

I notice that Uncle Jeff has a big scar on his shin. "Squirrel?" I point.

"No. Bike accident. Harley days."

I nod. You know how some people have what they call their "glory days" or "halcyon days"? My uncle Jeff has "Harley days."

"I just thought, since you're here, and we're all here, we could exercise together." Uncle Jeff smiles at me, and it's a sweet, honest smile, but is this really supposed to be the positive-male-influence stuff? "And if I can work off some of that weight I gained over the past six months, I'll be in better shape, come what may."

"True enough," Grandpa says.

As we're heading out of the parking lot, I see Andre coming back from a nearby store carrying what looks like a comic book. He waves at me, and I wave back. Then we stop near him, because already my uncle needs to make an adjustment to his sandals. This might be the longest, yet shortest, run I ever go on.

"Going to run to the next stop instead of taking the bus?" Andre asks.

"Hm. Good idea," I say.

He checks out my outfit, my legs, my school team T-shirt. I feel myself getting warm from the attention. "You probably could, couldn't you?" he asks.

"Sure, if they ever told us the next stops," I say.

"So, you run a lot," he comments. "Like . . ."

"Every day," I say. "Or at least six days a week."

"I always thought that people who ran were somehow mixed-up," he says.

I did like him, until now. "Mixed-up? As in . . ."

"Confused. Tortured. Disturbed," he says, but he's smiling at me. Why is he antagonizing me? What did I do? "Oh really? What makes you say that?"

"I don't know." He shrugs and curls the comic book in his hands. "Running, as a sport, I mean, how much fun can that be? You run and run and you never really *get* anywhere, just back to where you started."

"Runners are different," my grandfather steps up and says. "Runners have a certain inner drive that most ordinary people don't understand." He gives Andre a stare that would kind of make me start running, if I were him. "And they crave solitude."

"So . . . why are you running in a group?" Andre asks with a smile.

"Come on. Let's go," Grandpa says, exasperated with him.

"Well, I have to read this comic book and drink this grape soda. So whatever. I'm sure you'll have a much better time pounding the pavement." He lifts his can as if he's toasting us.

I glare at him. I can't believe my one and only ally just stood there and insulted me. Now what's left? I'm a hundred miles into this trip, and I've got nothing to look forward to.

We head for the streets, and it turns out that my grandfather is actually quite fast, which, again, I should have known, but somehow I didn't. He doesn't get out of breath; in fact I don't even hear him breathing much at all. For a second I wonder if he's still alive, but he must be, because he's still jogging and he has this completely comfortable gait.

My uncle, however, needs to lose about fifty pounds, and get some actual sneakers, and things of that nature. But he keeps chugging along, a few hundred yards behind us, and whenever I turn to check on him, he waves cheerfully back, as if this isn't completely killing him, which I know it must be.

When I run, I think. Usually I fantasize about things. Like things that happened in the past that I wish would have happened differently.

I think about the comment I should have had for the Fox News I-Team when I was unprepared. Instead of "No comment," I should have said, "This really isn't a good time for us, so we appreciate your understanding," or, "No, we didn't know anything about this."

When I stop rewriting the past in my head, I clue in to the fact that Uncle Jeff has caught up with us. He and Grandpa are talking about our possible destinations. Actually, Grandpa's doing most of the talking, while Uncle Jeff huffs and puffs to keep up.

"What do you think, Jeff? Montana? Colorado?"

"Unh," Uncle Jeff grunts.

"We're headed straight west at this point, so of course it's hard to say, and they're known for pulling a switch at the last minute. Or so they claim. They may be all talk, though. I don't trust either one of them," Grandpa says.

Have I been *sleeping* through this first day? Why didn't I realize or pay attention to the fact that we're heading west—farther and farther west, in fact? "Grandpa? If we kept going west from here, where would we end up?" I ask.

"The Pacific Ocean," he says.

I roll my eyes at him. "Before that."

"We'd hit Wyoming first, I guess," he says.

"Yes!" I throw both of my arms in the air.

"What's so exciting about Wyoming?"

"Oh. I, uh, have a friend there I could maybe visit. That's all," I say. "It'd be fun if we, you know, went anywhere close to where he—" I cough. "She lives."

"Mm-hm," says Grandpa. "And how do you figure you'll do that?"

"Bribe Lenny?" I suggest.

Grandpa doesn't look amused, but I don't care. Thanks to him I've just realized that I can ditch this bus trip and find Dylan. I can tell him that no matter what happens, no matter what my mom says? We're not moving in August, or anytime soon.

Or at least, I'm not. Dylan's family can take me in, or I'll live with Sarah.

When I explain these plans to my mother, she'll have only one choice: to decide this moving idea is for the birds. The ugly birds. The pigeons.

When we get back to the motel, I go to the lobby and ask the desk clerk/steakhouse host for a map. I look at where we are, what direction we're headed. If we keep heading west—and why wouldn't we?—we'll hit the Badlands and Mount Rushmore.

It's funny, because my dad always talked about visiting Mount Rushmore—it was always "on the table" with his other trip plans every summer, but we never headed in this direction. He has this list of major things to see, and though we did the Grand Canyon, the Rockies, the Everglades, and New York City, we never made it to

Rushmore. Now I will, and he won't.

I'm walking out to go back to the room and take a shower when Jenny walks in. It's not that hard to corner her by the plate of free beef jerky and cookies on the check-in desk.

"Hey," I say, stopping beside her. "I have a question."

"Sure thing, Zena," she says.

I frown. "Ariel. Anyway. Is it possible you could tell me where we're going in the next couple of days? You know, for the rest of the trip, actually."

"Oh no. You know the Leisure-Lee rules. It's a surprise itinerary. We find that guests have a much better time that way. It gives you the opportunity to relax without being hung up on timetables."

Does she have any idea she's talking to a runner? I'm standing here drenched in sweat, with a sleek Nike sports watch on my wrist, and she's saying that timing yourself is a bad thing. I live for time.

"But does *anyone* know where we're going?" I ask her. "I mean . . . you guys have to know."

Jenny shrugs. "Yes."

"So can you tell me, anyway? Because I *am* hung up on schedules and that kind of stuff. What day would we be at, say, Mount Rushmore?"

Jenny shakes her head and grabs another stale oatmeal raisin cookie, crumbs falling as she lifts it off the paper plate. "Impossible to predict. If we see something we really want to see, we'll spend more time there. We don't have to be anywhere on any particular night."

"But what about hotels? Those must be booked already," I argue. "And our bag lunches? I mean, someone has to make those in advance." Poorly, I might add.

"Well . . . yes," Jenny admits.

"So it can't be totally spontaneous."

She has a tight smile as she looks at me, as if she's considering calling a bus vote to ask me to quit bothering her. "Why is it so important to know everything?"

"I'm just . . . well, see, my training. There's a 10K race at Mount Rushmore on the, uh, twentieth," I improvise.

"A race at the monument?" She laughs. "What do you do, scale the thing? Sounds more like rock climbing than running to me."

Her sense of humor is right up there with her narrating skills.

"It's a race in Rapid City, but it's called the Mount Rushmore Race. So if we're going to be there then, I could run it," I say. Only a real runner will dispute this, and already Jenny's spent time telling us that she's a snorkeler, a volleyball player, and a kayaker. Not a runner. "And I need to run a certain number of races this summer to be, uh, eligible," I tell her. "For a scholarship. Really big deal, this scholarship."

"Really. Well, we'll see. Find out a bit more about the race and we'll let you know."

"But eventually we are going more . . . west?" I ask. "We are going to continue going west?"

"Sure," Jenny says. "We'll see the big things and the small things. And that's all I can tell you right now." She winks at me as if this is amusing tour-guide humor, and then leaves the lobby.

Which is all right, because she was grating on my nerves, plus she ate all the cookies, and I've found out everything I need to. We're heading west.

Which means, theoretically, Wyoming.

Which means I can meet up with Dylan and have this really romantic getaway for a day or two in the middle of this heinous trip. Or maybe I'll get away and I won't go back.

That's what's going to happen on the road: me and Dylan.

Well, not *on* the road, on the road. You know what I mean.

That night after dinner I write Dylan to tell him the good news. I bring his postcard down to the front desk to mail it even though I am in my pajamas, but then I see there's a mailbox outside, on the edge of the parking lot. If I leave it at the front desk, they'll read it; then they'll tell my mom what's on it or something.

How many days on a bus before you become a total raving paranoiac?

When I turn around after slipping the postcard into the mailbox, I see Andre sitting on his balcony. He's listening to his iPod and drinking a soda, and waves to me. He slides off the headphones. "Hey."

"Hey." I wish I were wearing more than my PJs, which consist of a tank top and boxer shorts. "How's that grape soda?" I call up in a whisper.

"It's orange. Cheers," he says as he lifts the can to show it to me.

"Isn't it kind of late?"

"To drink orange soda? Oh gosh. Do you think it will keep me up? I'm sharing a room with my *mother*. Do you understand?"

I laugh. "So am I."

"Yeah, but that's different," he says.

"Oh." I think about it for a second. "I see what you're saying."

"Right."

"Well, at least you have the dog."

We stand there, me with one foot on the balcony steps, him leaning over the railing. I feel like we're in a play. Not *Romeo and Juliet*, something American and Western that's really, really tragic, but without gunplay.

Wait, maybe it would be an Alfred Hitchcock movie. *Strangers on a Bus*.

"I still have four quarters," Andre says. "You want something from the vending machine?"

I'm about to say no when I realize that saying no means going back to my room, where Zena and Grandma are dyeing Mom's hair to make her look younger. They won't miss me for a while yet, and I won't miss them.

"Sure." He goes down the balcony to the machine, while I climb the steps, thankful for flip-flops. There are a couple of white plastic chairs, so I sit in one.

Andre comes back and holds out a can. "This is what they had."

I get a Dr. Stepper, which is apparently a knockoff brand, with an image of someone doing aerobics.

"Hey, you could be drinking this. Scorange." He holds it up and I see a giant soccer ball image on the can. "It's like some sports drink gone berserk. Mad. Insane. Over the edge."

"Quietly, leisurely crazy," I add.

We sit there for a while. "So, you have other plans for the summer?" he asks.

"Oh yeah. Lots." I sip the black-cherry soda, which is pretty far from being a sports drink.

"Me too."

We stare at the steady line of eighteen-wheelers pulling into the truck stop across the road.

"I was thinking. We're heading west, right?"

I smile. "Right."

"Well, my dad lives in California. I'm going to go there instead."

"Instead? How?"

He points across the divided highway at the truck stop. "They'd drive all night. Straight through, probably. Get us there in the morning."

Us? I think. Does he mean me, or the trucker? "You wouldn't actually do that. Would you?" Never mind the fact that I think his sense of time and distance is off.

"Catch a ride with a truck that's headed there? Why not?"

"Because bad things happen in trucks. You're too young."

"Am not."

"Only people who are too young say things like 'am not,' " I point out.

He laughs. "So what about you? You going to stay on the bus?"

"I guess it depends where we go."

"Yeah, I guess so. So why don't we find out?" He gets to his feet and starts walking away toward the stairs.

"How?" I ask, getting up to follow him.

"The bus, how else?"

"We can't break into the bus," I say.

"Why not?" Andre glances over his shoulder as we walk around to where the bus is parked.

"Because!" I reach out and grab his arm. "Lenny and Jenny. They probably sleep on the bus."

"Why would they do that?"

"I don't know. They're devoted to Leisure-Lee?"

"You're crazy."

"Not as crazy as you, obviously."

Andre tries to pull open the bus door, but it doesn't even give an inch. He grabs a stick from the ground and wedges it into the tiny opening, pushing and maneuvering until the stick breaks in two, flies off, and hits a nearby car.

Just then I see Lenny walking across the parking lot toward us. "Oops," I whisper.

"Does he have a bus-cam hooked up to his room or something?" Andre asks under his breath.

"What's going on, mates?" Lenny asks.

"Oh! I, uh, left something on the bus," Andre says.

"What's that then? Your ee-pod." Lenny chuckles.

"Right. My ee-pod," Andre says. "No, actually it's a book. It must have slipped out of my backpack, and I need it in order to fall asleep, so I didn't want to disturb anyone—"

"Say no more. Not a problem." Lenny unlocks the door and Andre gets on, hunting around for something. I climb up the steps halfway and peer around the driver's seat, looking for a map or any kind of clue, but the area is so cluttered with papers that I wouldn't know where to start.

"How's Chuckles?" Lenny calls from behind me.

"Cuddles, you mean?" Andre asks as he roots around underneath his seat.

"Fine. Sleeping soundly."

"Did he like the steak scraps we sent up?" asks Lenny.

"Loved 'em," Andre says, his voice muffled as he crawls around. "You know what? I can't find it. It must be in my mom's bag somewhere—she's got so much stuff in there, you need a flashlight."

When we step off the bus, Mom is wandering around the parking lot, calling my name. I call to her and wave.

Her hair is under plastic wrap, coated in white liquid. "*There* you are. You had us worried sick!" she says, hurrying over.

"I'd worry more about those chemicals on your head," I say, backing up from the strong smell.

"I'm going Mysterious Auburn Brown. With blond highlights," she adds.

"Those might be the only highlights on this trip," I murmur as I follow her back to our room.

The Horizon Inn & Steak House.
Eat like a man, sleep like a baby. Convenient to interstate.
Early check-in; late checkout available. Charges apply.

Dylan—

You won't believe this, but I think we're heading to Wyoming, or at least really close! Not sure when we'll get there, but in a week or so maybe.

Can you believe it?

I'll let you know details when we're getting closer so we can hook up.

Can't wait to see u!!!

Ariel

I...II...II.I.III...II...III...II..I.I.I.II.I.I.I....I.II

Chapter Nine

"*You* are a sweetheart. I can tell just by looking at you," Andre's mother says the next morning. She gives me a little hug as we stand in line to board the bus.

"I am?" I wonder out loud.

"For sure." Mrs. O'Neill is wearing a sleek black wrap shirt and jeans, with stylish high-heeled black sandals. A large black-and-pink-striped handbag over her arm contains the infamous Cuddles, whose collar matches the bag. "Your hair looks great, Tamara. I can't get over it. You look ten years younger."

"Really? You think so, Lorraine?"

Mom's hair is dark brown, with a few gray and blond streaks. I'm not sure what's mysteriously auburn about it. She's wearing a pair of gold corn earrings and a bright gold Corn Palace sweatshirt. That doesn't help matters.

"Definitely. Isn't this a great trip?" Andre's mother asks me, and I smile.

"It's not horrible," I say, with a tight-lipped smile at my mother.

"Is that the best you can say, honey?" Mrs. O'Neill asks.

"For now. Pretty much." I nod.

"Mm-hm. You sound just like Andre. You two need to get into the traveling mood, get your traveling shoes on."

Andre glances down at my green-and-white-striped vintage running shoes. "I think she's ready, Ma. See you."

Mom puts her hand on my arm. "Actually—hold up. I was thinking we should sit together, Ariel."

"Nonsense. You and I have *lots* more in common, Tamara," says Lorraine. "I want to talk, not sit and listen to Andre's music."

Now I'm the one who wants to hug *her*.

Andre and I leave our moms to enjoy each other and sit down in the third row again, scrunching down in our seats together. I've decided to forgive his running insult. I can't afford to antagonize the only peer I have on the bus, even if he already antagonized me. I think about our escapade the night before, wonder if Lenny is suspicious of us at all. I stretch out, recline the seat back a little bit.

Lenny finishes taking roll and climbs onto the bus. Jenny follows him, and soon we're pulling out of the parking lot, back onto the highway. Lenny leads everyone in his so-called eye-opening routine, which is a goofy song. This morning it's "If You're Happy and You Know It."

"Do you think Lenny caught on last night?" I ask Andre while everyone's singing and clapping hands.

"No. Not at all," Andre says.

"So should we try again?" I ask. "I'd really like to know where we're going. I hate this crap about everything being a surprise. We do road trips like this every summer, but before now I always knew what the destination was, what the *plan* was," I say.

His eyebrows shoot up. "Wow. No wonder."

"No wonder what?"

"You don't seem as traumatized as I do because you've done this before."

I laugh. "No, but—see, I am. Because we usually do the traveling in our car, not on a bus, and usually our dad comes along, and it's a lot more fun." Of course, I didn't always think so at the time, but in retrospect those trips were probably the most fun we ever had together as a family.

"Still. You don't seem totally upset," he comments.

"I hide things really well," I say.

He nods. "So when you want to kill me, I won't see it coming."

"Not at all," I promise.

"Damn. That's going to be tough." He opens his vocabulary book and starts highlighting. "So. Where's your dad this summer?"

"He's . . . uh . . . home," I say with an awkward nod. I give a nervous laugh, feeling like I want to both tell him the entire sordid story and crawl under the seat and go sit with my grandmother for a while and not talk about it at all.

I've been going to a counselor ever since my dad developed this gambling "problem," plus family therapy, and it helps some things, but it doesn't help others. Like, I don't really want to talk to other people and tell them what happened, even if it's in the middle of nowhere and I'll never see this person again after we get off this bus.

"My mom and dad split up over the holidays," I explain. That's nice and vague.

"So did mine," Andre says.

"What a coincid—"

"Ten years ago," he adds.

"Oh." I give an embarrassed, shoot-me-now smile.

"It's okay, I'm sort of over it," he says. "He moved to California. He sends money, and I visit a couple times a year. It's a 'quality relationship.' " He makes quotation marks with his fingers.

"My mom's the queen of 'quality relationships,' " I say, echoing his quotes. "Not having one. Just talking about it." I lean closer and whisper, "My uncle and grandfather are here to be positive male influences for me. Okay, so. My grandpa is totally miserable to be here—he didn't want to come, he didn't even want to retire, but my grandma insisted, because she wanted to take trips together. And the other one, my uncle Jeff, is so upbeat I don't believe a word he says because it all sounds fake. You know?"

"Positive's overrated." He sighs. "But I'm pretty sure this positively sucks."

I laugh, while he goes back to his vocabulary book, and I take out my stack of postcards, a few other things, and some art supplies I've collected. Lenny is talking about the geology of the area, and how we're headed for a fascinating little corner of the world known as Wall and we'll be there for a Leisure-Lee lunch. And every time I glance out the window I see a billboard for a place called Wall Drug.

I've picked up scraps from brochures, tickets, and receipts. I bought rubber cement at the last drugstore of choice (being a bus full of senior citizens we stop at a lot of drugstores) and I start pasting words and photos on top of the plain white prestamped postcards my grandmother gave me.

After I've done a few, Andre asks, "What are you, scrapbooking?"

"I guess," I say. "But not exactly."

"My mom does that. Or used to, anyway. I called it crapbooking. Yours looks cooler, though. When did you start doing that?" he asks.

"I don't know," I admit. "I guess about six months ago."

Over Christmas break when everything came to light—that there were no presents, that Dad had spent everything in the bank and then some—Mom signed up me and Zena for about twelve thousand activities to keep us busy. Art classes like Painting and Creative Memories. Gymnastics. Swimming lessons. Diving lessons. At one point she even suggested synchronized swimming and diving as a way to get me and Zena to become better friends. Which was funny, because neither Zena nor I like to swim all that much, and we can't stand each other half the time, so why would we dive together?

Anyway, all these classes were supposed to take our minds off the fact that they were getting the fastest "trial separation" in the history of Milwaukee, that Dad was moving back home with his parents, that Dad might be going *on* trial.

Pretty much the only thing I got out of it was the idea of making stuff by using found objects.

"Huh. It's good. Who's Gloves?" Andre asks a minute later.

I frown at him, because I thought he was busy writing something of his own. "Not that you're reading what I'm writing or anything. But she's my cat."

He lowers his glasses and looks me in the eye. "You're writing to your cat. That's pathetic. Desperate."

"You forgot needy," I add.

"That too," he says. "Your cat is named Gloves?"

I shrug. "She was named Mittens until I found out that was really common, so I renamed her. She has white paws, but the rest of her is black, except for this white patch over her eyes."

"That must get in the way of her reading your postcards," Andre comments.

"Shut up," I say, laughing. "Okay, so I guess basically this is for my grandmother. My other grandmother. The one who's not in seat twelve-B."

He laughs. "You're funny. The thing is, uh, maybe we should get something out in the open. Being, you know, on the open road and all."

"Okay," I say slowly, wondering what this is about.

"I don't really want to like you. Is that okay?"

I don't know what to say to that, so I sit there waiting for him to make sense, to say it three different ways.

"I'm not looking for . . . you know. A girlfriend. A mate. A—"

"Okay, fine," I interrupt. "I get it. Neither am I. I'm not looking for a mate or whatever. I'm already seeing someone, anyway." Sort of.

"Oh, you are?"

"Well, yeah."

"How come he's not on the bus? Or wait. It's not Dieter, is it?" he asks as he looks back at the German twins.

I just glare at him.

"Okay, so it's not Dieter." He pauses. "Is it Wolfgang?"

"His name's Dylan," I say.

"How uncommon," he says dryly.

"Look, are you going to mock everything I say?"

"Probably," he admits. "So where's the infamous Dylan?"

"He's at camp in Wyoming. Here." I pull out our impromptu prom photo, the one Sarah took when she saw me and Dylan leaving prom together. I show it to Andre, feeling kind of stupid as I do, as if I have to offer up proof.

Andre narrows his eyes as he stares at the picture. "Isn't he a little old for summer camp?" he asks.

"He's a counselor. Obviously." I try not to laugh, but it's impossible. "Quit making fun of him, okay?" I say.

"Why? He's not here; it's not like he'll know."

"Yeah, but I will, and then I'll have to dislike you," I say.

He looks at me as if he's thinking of saying something. But he holds back. He goes back to his vocabulary book and highlighter pen. "These little seat-back tables are the perfect height; have you noticed?"

We sit there and I work on doctoring a postcard while he studies words. His highlighting is annoying. "Are you going for spelling champ or something?" I ask.

"Whatever they'll give me." He hunches over the book, screening me out. And over the CD soundtrack to *Oklahoma!*, which Lenny and Jenny love to play, I just hear the *screech, screech* of a smelly orange highlighter.

"If you ever finish any of those pages, like, don't need them? Can I have them?"

He flips through the book and rips out a page. "Here. I'm done with the As."

I look at the page.

aromatic

asymptomatic

axiomatic

"Thanks." Then I rip off the one I can define and paste it onto a postcard. "You know what's weird about postcards? When you're used to texts, postcards are long, slow, and totally unsatisfying. You get, like, *no* response."

"I'd write back to you," Andre says. "Immediately. Instantaneously. At once."

"You would?"

"I would."

"How?"

He thinks it over for a second. "Carrier pigeon?" he suggests. "The thing is . . . Ariel. Um, I already have a girlfriend," he says. "A skirt. Arm candy. You know."

I stare at him in horror. "You don't actually talk like that, do you?"

"What?"

"Calling her arm candy. That's disgusting," I say.

He laughs. "Yeah. Maybe that's why she moved to Denver."

"No wonder."

"We're still friends, though. So if we don't hit California, maybe we'll hit Denver, and I can call her. We could probably stay with her awhile."

"Sure," I say, wondering when I became part of his escape plan. Apparently I'm not the only one on the bus with a big fantasy life. "But if I go anywhere, it'll be to Wyoming." And then the bus suddenly makes this loud bang and lurches to the side of the road.

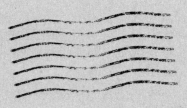

The tiny chipmunk is easy prey for a red-tailed hawk in the early-morning light.

Dear Gloves,

I ran into a friend of yours today. Okay, not a "friend." A "meal," once. Or did you just toy with it until it escaped? I can't remember.

Remember when Zena used to say "chickmunk" instead of "chipmunk"?

She has a gift for making up words, like the rest of our clan.

She's twelcreative.

Miss u.

P.S. Why do photographers just take pictures of these killings, and not stop them? Hello? ASPCA?

Sarah,

Met this guy on the bus.

I won't say much else about him because he'll read it over my shoulder.

In fact he's probably doing that now.

He actually referred to his ex as "arm candy." Is that disgusting or what?

Yes, you, Andre. You're disgusting.

Hope you're meeting better guys at your summer job.

At least you have more than one to choose from.

Xo

A

||..||....||.||.||.||...||...||..|||..|.|.|.||.|.|..|..|.||

Chapter Ten

Jenny manages to steer the bus onto an exit ramp, but from there things don't look promising. Whenever she tries to restart the engine, it kicks on for a minute, then dies again, so we just pathetically coast until we're in the parking lot of a place called the Wild Wilde West. Complete with wooden fence surrounding the Wild Wilde West Museum, the Wild Wilde West Gift Shoppe, and the Wild Wilde West Sculpture Garden.

Lenny gets to his feet, turns, and faces us, while Jenny scrambles out the door frantically.

"Well, this wasn't on the itinerary, now, was it?" Lenny smiles at all of us and coughs nervously. "And, uh, it's little gems like this place that you'll remember about the trip. Not the big stuff, mates." Lenny winks at us. "The small stuff."

"Like the bus maintenance record," my grandfather mutters, standing behind me in the aisle.

"We won't remember Mount Rushmore, but we'll remember this?" I turn around and ask him.

"In the way that bad memories often outlive good ones," he says, and we both smile—dejected smiles, but still.

"Everybody off, have a look around. This looks to be a fun spot. Right, then. We'll fix the bus and be back on the road pronto. And then we'll . . ." Lenny pauses.

"Hit Wall!" a few older tourists yell.

Lenny makes a clicking noise with his tongue. "Exactamundo." Then he shuts off his microphone and opens the door for all of us.

When I step outside, it's like walking into a wall of heat. "Wall" being the word of the day. "How did it get so hot? How is it possible?" I ask.

"Well, it's like this," Uncle Jeff says, and he starts to talk about weather, which I guess he knows a lot about, having to deliver the mail, no matter what.

"Mom, aren't you so hot in that sweatshirt?" I ask.

"Thank you." She takes a bow.

I look around for Andre, hoping for sympathy, but he's busy arguing with his mom about who's going to stay outside and watch Cuddles, because the dog's not allowed inside. I walk around the end of the bus and there are Lenny and Jenny in the middle of an argument.

"You should let me drive for a while," Lenny says.

"It's not the driver, you moron," Jenny says.

"Oh, isn't it just," Lenny replies. "And what did you call me?"

Maybe the heat is getting to them, I think. They have one of those relationships that you don't necessarily want to spend much time around, if you can help it.

I wander into the Wilde Museum and find out I'm the last person in, as the entire bus population presses into the small lobby. It turns out we're in time for the eleven a.m. tour of the Wild Wilde West, which is dedicated to the writer Oscar Wilde.

The tour consists of a bunch of stuff about Oscar Wilde, with hardly any connection to this place or to the West at all. Mom is laughing hysterically at all the Oscar Wilde puns and memorabilia, and the slightly-over-the-top-in-five-different-ways tour guide's attempt to claim that "Oscar Wilde Slept Here." If he did, does that really matter to us? And why would he? Did his tour bus break down, too?

"Poor Oscar Wilde," my grandfather mutters to me as the museum guide rambles on excitedly.

"No doubt," I agree. I don't know much about him, but my friend Sarah was in the play *The Importance of Being Earnest* in summer theater, so I saw it four or five times.

There's a wooden set piece here, a photo thing with a circle cut out for you to stick your head into, and you pose next to Oscar Wilde in chaps, and there's some line about if you have your photo taken here—for $19.95—you will not age, just like Dorian Gray in *The Picture of Dorian Gray*, which I unfortunately read last summer when I was bored and found it on my mother's bookshelf.

Andre comes up behind me, smuggling in Cuddles, who's tucked under his arm. "He was gay, right, but does that mean he wore chaps?" he asks.

"He also wore fur." I point at a photo of Oscar Wilde with a fur collar on his winter coat. "Does that make him Western?"

"No, but it makes him eligible to be hated by PETA," he says.

"Are these rhetorical questions? And if so, can anyone join in?" my mom asks.

We sort of edge away from her, without answering, toward the exit at the back, which leads out to the so-called sculptures. "Does wearing a dead animal make you a Western hero?" I ask.

"Do you think he actually slept here, or he just passed out here from the heat?" Andre says.

We stand in the doorway. There are five little cars sticking into the ground, their hoods buried in the sandy earth. Nose first, as if they fell from the sky.

Andre sets down Cuddles, who's on the world's smallest, shortest leash. Cuddles immediately runs over to one of the buried cars and pees on the tires.

"You've heard of Carhenge?" the museum guide asks us, stepping onto the back deck behind us.

"No," Andre says.

The guide points to Cuddles. "Is that your dog?"

"No," Andre says again.

"Totally cute," the guide comments. "I have a teacup poodle. Anyway, Carhenge is in Nebraska. It's made of vintage cars, and it's a replica of Stonehenge. You know, the mysterious, ancient circle of stones."

"We *know* what Stonehenge is," Andre says with a bored sigh.

"Well, this is Mini Carhenge. Because it's made of Mini Coopers. Get it?" He laughs.

We stand back and look at his miniature car circle. Only it's a semicircle, if that, and they're all the same height. "But that doesn't look like Stonehenge at all," Andre observes.

"I know. It's totally cuter," the guide says. "That's the point. It's a miniature version."

"Interesting. We should see if Lenny and Jenny will take us to Carhenge," Andre says. "I mean, we do have this loose itinerary and all."

"Oh, you really should go. It's magnificent," the guide says. "Breathtaking."

"Hm. Well, we'll just have a look around, take some photos," Andre tells him, and we step off.

"Don't forget your Wilde souvenir shopping," the guide says. "Plenty of mini mementos inside!"

"Right," Andre says. And he makes that little clicking noise that Lenny has started to make, with little gun gestures. "Exactamundo."

A tumbleweed blows across the half-dirt, half-grass surface, and Cuddles barks, charging at it in full-on Chihuahua attack mode.

Five minutes later Uncle Jeff comes outside and insists on taking our picture posing against the Mini cars, with Cuddles on top of one of them, except that the car is too hot and it slightly burns Cuddles's tender feet.

"A mini dog on a mini car," Uncle Jeff says. "Oh, this is fantaster-rific. The guys back home will love this. And when I say guys, I don't mean just guys; I mean people. Other letter carriers. We covered that in gender-sensitivity training."

"I have to get out of here," Andre says out of the side of his mouth as we pose for the tenth picture. "When do we mutiny, exactly?"

I look over my shoulder at him.

"Mutiny. A noun. Revolt. Coup," Andre says robotically.

"I know what it *means*," I say. Maybe he's not studying for tests, but if I stick around him long enough, I should be ready for anything. "Do you just assume you have to define every word with synonyms for the rest of the world?"

"Not the rest of the world. Just you," he says.

"Shut up."

"Seriously," he says.

"Yes. Seriously, shut up," I say.

We finish our photo shoot and walk around the side of the building, where we discover Jenny and Lenny arguing about what's wrong with the bus.

"We're not going to make Wall," Lenny is saying. "And this place, charming as it is, doesn't have a snack bar. Unless you consider Cadbury bars a lunch option."

"He said there's a pizza place in town. We'll have to get pizzas delivered," Jenny says.

Lenny shakes his head. "Lee told us no extra expenses."

"Lee? Why are you bringing up Lee? Are you trying to give me a heart attack?" Jenny asks. "The bus breaks down, that's bad enough. Lee's going to kill us."

"Exactamundo," Lenny says.

"Quit saying that already, or *I'm* going to kill you," Jenny threatens. "This is a disaster."

"Accidents happen, mate. We'll be fine."

"How can you be so relaxed? I hate that about you," Jenny says.

"And how can you be so uptight all the time?" Lenny replies.

Andre and I look at each other. "Things are taking an interesting turn," he comments. "Look at it this way. They fight some more, they turn against each other—they're vulnerable. Divide and conquer. Then we can make our move."

"What's our move?" I ask.

He shrugs and picks up Cuddles, who's whining a little bit. "Busjack? Is that even a word?"

To kill time while we wait, I go running. I'm already wearing clothes that'll work for a short run, but I go over to the bus to grab my real running shoes because I don't want to wreck my arches in my vintage suede Sauconys. As I tie the laces, I make sure Jenny sees me, so she'll buy into my plan of needing to be somewhere on a specific date for a specific run.

Grandpa comes with me, and so does Uncle Jeff, and to my surprise

Andre kicks into stride beside me. "What the hell?" he says. "What else am I going to do—buy and read an Oscar Wilde novel?" He starts breathing a little more heavily. "Wait a second. I think I will. See you."

He drops off, just like that. When I glance back at him, I see that behind me a trail of power-walking seniors, half wearing sun visors, has formed. We're going up and down the road as if we're on leave from a psychiatric hospital.

About half a mile down the road I hear a squeal behind us and turn to see my uncle sprinting at top speed in our direction.

"Squirrel—" he manages to get out. And he's moving so fast that I can't quite believe it's him running toward me.

"Jeff. Jeff, calm down. That was a prairie dog," my grandfather tells him.

"Oh." He's panting and panting, sounding sort of like a dog. And as soon as he reaches us he stops running. So we do, too. Then my grandfather lifts his water bottle and squirts cold water in his face.

"Snap out of it," he says. "A squirrel can't hurt you. Neither can a prairie dog."

"Well." Uncle Jeff clears his throat. "You never know how animals will act when they're threatened, and things of that nature."

"Prairie dogs don't bite," my grandfather argues.

"Have you ever had a rabies shot?" my uncle shoots back.

"Come on, Uncle Jeff, let's do a cool-down jog, so your muscles don't get tight," I say, and the three of us start moving again. "How are the, uh, shoes?"

"I think I'd better invest in some new ones," he says, glancing down at the leather sandals wearing a welt into the top of his foot.

When I get back from running, Mom is standing there cursing at the bus. "Damnit, damnit."

It's completely understandable, so I don't even know why I bother to ask, "What's wrong? Besides the obvious." I wipe my forehead with the bottom of my sleeveless T-shirt.

"I lost my ring, my wedding band," she says.

"What? How?"

"I bought this lotion inside. It was a joke gift for Marta; it's this Dorian Gray Forever Young Beauty Lotion, and I was trying it out, rubbing it on my hands, and it was so slick and greasy that my ring fell off and it rolled under the bus. Now I can't see it anywhere."

There's an awkward pause, and then she swears again. "Damnit, damnit, damnit," she keeps muttering, and then she starts crying.

"Don't worry, we'll find it," I tell her. "And, Mom, I'm not saying this to be mean, but . . . you're not married anymore," I say. "So, do you honestly still need the ring?"

"I know. I *know*," she says, anger in her voice. "But if you knew how many times I almost pawned that stupid thing when we were broke, and now it's lost, and I'm upset, and I don't *want* to be upset on my vacation."

"So why don't you let it go?" I ask. "That would be a realsimple way of looking at it. Leave it here."

"No. I couldn't leave it here—to get flattened in a parking lot when this bus finally moves again?" She's horrified by my suggestion.

"Why not? I mean, you're all about closure, right? What could be better than an abandoned ring getting crushed by a—"

"Ariel. Honestly. I don't want it to be ob-obliterated," she stammers. "The ring is part of my history, my life, and it's also about you guys. Your father and I made a commitment to be—to have—a family. We're still a family."

"Of course we're still a family," I say. As angry as she makes me sometimes, I don't enjoy seeing her this upset. "Of course we are.

Except that you keep trying to push Dad out of it, but—"

"He *is* out of it," she argues. "And it's entirely his fault that he is."

"He made a mistake. A big mistake. But he's . . . you know. Still the same guy. Still Dad."

"Would *you* trust him again?" she asks me with a sob, and I have to really think about it, not like I haven't thought about it before, but some days I say yes, and some days I say no. How do you balance someone's entire life against a yearlong streak of disasters?

Before I can say anything, my grandmother, who's just returned from a walk with Zena and Bethany, comes over to Mom and hugs her. "What's wrong?" she asks.

"My ring," she starts to explain.

I get on my belly and crawl partway underneath the bus looking for her stupid wedding ring. I run my hand over the pavement as far as it will go, but all I come up with is gravel. Suddenly there are purple sparkly flip-flops beside my head.

"*Why* were you yelling at Mom? Don't do that," Zena says.

"I wasn't yelling at her," I say, getting to my feet.

"You were," Zena argues. "And she was crying."

"You have no idea, okay?" I tell her. "You don't know everything that's going on."

"I don't? I think maybe *you* have no idea," she replies.

"Zena, please. You're twelve. You're naive. There's stuff you don't understand."

She looks at me as if I should crawl back under the bus and wait for it to drive off. "I understand everything. I've been there for Mom, while you're always running or out with Dylan or Sarah or whoever."

"Oh yeah? So she tells you everything."

Zena shrugs. "Enough, anyway."

"Well, did she tell you she's thinking about us moving?" I say.

And Zena's right eyebrow kind of twitches. "Moving? When?"

"August. She's not telling us where, just like she didn't tell us about this trip, okay? So if Dad kept secrets, he's not the only one."

Zena takes a beat to compose herself. "If we're moving, it's her business, it's her job and her house, and she'd consult us anyway before she did that." Then she turns away from me. "Mom? *Are* we moving?" she asks.

"Go ahead, tell her," I urge Mom.

My grandmother clears her throat and turns to me. "Honey, you look awful. You really ought to clean up. Come on, let's go inside."

She's right. I'm sweating from my run, my shirt is wet, and now it's covered in dirt, twigs, and gravel. I convince Jenny to let me get my duffel out of the luggage bay, and go inside to change.

"Please don't talk about it," I say to Grandma when she follows me into the restroom. "I'm so sick of talking about it."

"I wasn't going to," she says. "I told you, I don't believe in talking until you're blue in the face."

She watches while I rinse my face and arms off with cold water; then she hands me my clothes over the stall door to change into. When I come out, she insists on putting these cute doll barrettes in my hair. "I don't think so," I tell her.

"Just try it. Don't be such a stick-in-the-mud," she says.

"Me?"

"Yes, you."

"You know I'm sixteen, right?" I ask, looking at my reflection, which is kind of like someone trying to dress ten years younger than they are.

"Right, I know," she says. "But if you're sixteen, that means your mother is forty-four, which means I'm sixty-seven. I can't handle that. So let's just pretend for a second that you're not sixteen."

"Okay," I say. "Can I be eighteen?"

She laughs. "Definitely not. Ever."

When we come outside, there are feet sticking out from underneath the bus, and seconds later Wolfgang emerges, holding Mom's wedding ring. She hugs him and knocks off his glasses with her new Wilde cowboy hat.

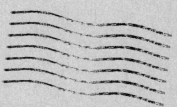

The Wild Wilde West: the only museum in South Dakota dedicated to Oscar Wilde, where you'll go Wilde discovering the Importance of Being Outwest.

Hi Dad,

How is your summer going?

It's really hot here in South Dakota.

I think we're going to Mount Rushmore. We always wanted to see Rushmore, remember?

But the bus is broken down, so at the rate we're going, we might be back home by September. Of next year.

Zena says hi.

Miss you. Wish you were here.

—A

Chapter Eleven

We sit outside the museum in the baking sun, eating hot pizza, while a mechanic works to repair the bus.

Lenny is playing a trivia game called Name the Presidents with some people, while others are playing bridge, and still others, finished with their lunches, are napping.

"Let's play Leisure-Lee Truth or Dare. South Dakota edition," Andre says.

"Is there any other?" I ask.

Zena and Bethany are doing karaoke, with no machine, using pop straws for mikes. Wolfgang and Dieter ask if they can have a turn, and Wolfgang starts singing a Daft Punk song, and Dieter does a kind of robotic dance.

"Dare," I say.

Andre points to a plastic container. "If you drink that garlic dipping sauce in one shot, I'll give you a hundred dollars."

It sounds like the kind of bet my dad would make, then lose. "You're not serious."

He shrugs. "Sure."

"A hundred dollars. Do you really have a hundred dollars to give me when I do it?" I ask.

"You're not going to do it. Because I have to get back on the bus with you, and I don't want you puking. But anyway, why wouldn't I?"

"Sorry. Just assuming your mom is as chintzy as mine," I say. "You say you have it, you have it." How do I know he's not carrying around forgive-me bribes from his father, too? I peel back the top and look inside the cup of dipping sauce. "No, I can't drink it. It's disgusting."

"Good, because I don't actually have the hundred. I have a ten. Want to sip it for ten?" he asks.

"God, no." I glance at the ingredients on the package, which all sound very nauseating. "I actually do have a hundred dollars. It's like . . . blood money, or whatever that phrase is."

"Blood money? You mean, like, tainted, illegal, wrongly gotten?"

He just described my dad and his finances in four words. "Maybe."

"So why not spend it right away?" Andre suggests. "Get rid of it."

"I don't know." I push a slice of pepperoni around on my plate. "I guess because I'm saving it, just in case."

"In case of what?" asks Andre.

I think: *In case he asks for it back when he's broke.* But that's too personal and weird for someone I just met. "Just in case," I say.

He nods. "Good plan." He leans back and looks around at the motley group of pizza eaters. "You know, everyone's pretty distracted right now. It wouldn't be hard to slip off."

I point out that we're in the middle of nowhere, that getting a ride out of here seems impossible, that it'd mean walking down a long, dusty highway. And dying of thirst. Nobody's been at this museum, except us, in the past couple hours. It's obviously not on the list of South Dakota must-sees.

"Okay, so maybe I'll dig out one of those Mini cars. Think they still run?"

"That depends. Did you take auto mechanics in school?"

Andre sighs. "Sometimes we don't know what courses to take until it's too late. You know?"

"Do I ever." When I look over at the road, there's a silvery shimmering wave coming off it. It's kind of the way my head feels. "Are you serious about this mutinous escape plan?" I ask.

"Yes. Up here, anyway." He taps his forehead. "Maybe it's just the garlic talking, but I can't see sticking around when life is actually happening somewhere else."

"Exactly," I say. "And nothing against this store—though it's a little weird—"

"A little?"

"Or these car sculptures—also weird—or the state. It's a fabulous state, and being from big Midwestern states ourselves, we can appreciate the bigness, and the stateness, and the fabulous tourist attractions."

"Definitely," says Andre. "Because we've gone on trips to see Paul Bunyan and Babe the Blue Ox before."

"You have?" I ask.

"Sure."

"Which one? Bemidji, Minnesota, Paul Bunyan, because I've seen that, or Brainerd—"

"How should I know? I was, like, seven," he says. "Anyway, it's not

South Dakota. Maybe I would have rather gone to New York or L.A., but whatever. It's the fact that we're on a bus and, like, nobody is on a bus anymore. And when I have to talk about my summer vacation, I'll have to say I took a trip on a bus. With forty senior cits."

"Is that so bad? The stigma or whatever?"

"When you go to a private school? Yeah. Pretty much."

"Oh."

"People take trips on yachts. Ocean journeys. They go see the Tour de France. And while they're at it, the rest of Europe," he explains. "We're not supposed to be here. I mean, look around. Everyone else here is at least sixty. Or German. Or your sister."

I laugh. "You know what I hate? They say the trip is all about *us*. But it's so not about us. You know?"

Lenny is making a tour of the captives and he stops in front of us. "How are you two enjoying our little detour?"

"Fine," I say.

"Great," says Andre. "What's next?"

"Well. I shouldn't tell you, but . . ." He looks to one side and then the other. "As soon as the bus is fixed, we're traveling up the road a bit. Heading north."

"I thought we were going to Wall," I say. "West. Can we keep going west, please?"

"Nonsense. There's a lovely little café where we've got dinner reservations. Best biscuits and gravy in the entire world, I'm telling you."

"We just had lunch."

"Well, we're not going straight there, of course not. This afternoon we'll be visiting one of the world's largest balls of twine. What is it, second-largest?" he asks Jenny, who's come up beside him.

"I can't believe you're telling them this," she says. "What happened to the element of surprise?"

"They can keep it to themselves. Can't you?" says Lenny.

"Definitely," I tell him.

Jenny eyes me suspiciously. "Anyway," she says. "Leonard, it's not a ball of twine. It's a ball of *yarn*. It's in the Knitting Hall of Fame."

"Twine, yarn, same thing."

"Not the same thing."

"Why do you always have to contradict me?"

"I don't!" says Jenny.

"There. See? You just did it again."

"I did not. Maybe you should ride in the back for a while. Visit with the passengers in the back rows."

"Maybe I will," he replies.

My mom should give them one of her books, or schedule an emergency session. Never mind the bus—I don't think their relationship is going to make it to Wall.

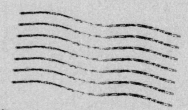

Yarn it all—come back! You've just missed the world's third-largest ball of yarn!

Gloves,
You could have a field day with this thing.
  Miss you,
  A

|...||...||..|.|||...|||...||..||..|.|.|.||.|.|.|,....|.|l

Chapter Twelve

The next day, we don't get to Wall until late afternoon. Our off-course adventure ended up taking a very long time because it turned out there had been a mistake (which made Lenny and Jenny argue even more) and we had no motel reservation. So we had to keep driving farther and farther off the beaten path to find a place with enough rooms for all of us. By that time we were practically in North Dakota, or perhaps Canada—I took a long nap and quit paying attention—but Lenny assures us that now we're back on track.

"You've seen the bumper stickers," Lenny says as we pull into a small town with old storefronts that could be real, or could be a movie set or one of those new shopping mall styles. It's really difficult to tell. "You've seen the billboards. Now, experience it for yourselves. Are you ready, guys? Are you ready? Then let's . . . hit Wall!" He pumps his fist in the air as half the people on the bus scream, "Hit Wall!" with him.

There's a story about how Wall Drug began as a place to stop on the older highway: They had a sign up that they offered free ice water to everyone passing by. Now they have a sign up that says their Western Art Gallery restaurant can seat 530 people.

"I want my free water," someone is muttering behind me as we drift into the massive store, as if water isn't free almost everywhere these days.

The clerks don't seem fazed at all when the big group filters into the store. They're friendly and smile and say hello. They must be used to bus tours. Either used to, or sick of. Then again, forty-five people could drop a serious amount of cash on souvenirs, so maybe they're excited, although we'd fill less than one-tenth of the restaurant.

Inside, it is postcard heaven. It's the hugest gift shop I've ever been in. Magnets. Jewelry. Black Hills gold, whatever that is. T-shirts, any kind of shirts, a giant wall of cowboy boots.

But there's also all the practical stuff, like shampoo and Advil. You could completely start your life over here with the contents of this store. You might not be exactly chic, but you could do it.

I stand there and fill my hand with postcards, skimming for new ones I haven't seen before, and grabbing as many as I can, as if this is a timed game show and I need to end up with the most prizes.

"I'm going to buy some sneakers for running," Uncle Jeff announces. "And maybe some cowboy boots."

"I'm buying cowgirl boots," Mom says, following him in her Corn Palace sweatshirt. "Keep track of Zena!" she calls over her shoulder, as if I could, as if Zena is even talking to me.

I wander around, considering mugs, glasses, sunglasses. Then I see the SEND AN EMAIL FROM WALL DRUG! sign. I can hardly move fast enough. I push aside some fellow bus-ees who are clogging the hat and bandanna aisle and rush to the computers. There are two of them, and only one is being used.

I check my email and it feels like months since I've done that, instead of only days. I'm expecting dozens, but since I told everyone I was going to be gone there are only a few random ones. But there's one from Dylan. So nothing else really matters.

AREIL,
Just in case you get email after all, 'cause it turns out
we do this year. Got a few of your postcards. Thanks.
Sounds like you're having fun.

It does? Really? Because I'm not, I Gchat him, but he's not online, which is probably a good thing, because that sounded weak. Again, I'm the kind of person who needs time to write something good. Rush into things and I come out sounding horrible.

Of course, I don't misspell someone's *name*; for instance I don't write DILLON, or DLYN.

Anyway. Wyoming is very cool, and camp's great, but
way too busy. My first day off isn't for another week.
I've met lots of people. Half the counselors are new, and
I was voted in charge of the sports activities. We have
a big competition in two weeks, all the cabins compete.
Areil, don't sweat it if things don't work out this
summer. I know I'm gone a long time and we really
aren't serious or anything. But you are cute.
CU, Dylan

My heart is pounding. I immediately start to type:

DYLAN, YOU WON'T BELIEVE THIS—WE ARE ALMOST IN WYOMING TOO!

And I sense someone looming over my shoulder and prepare my defense for Mom, but it won't be too hard because I didn't say anything bad about her yet, or anything too risqué, but it isn't Mom. And it isn't Zena, either, for a change.

It's Andre. It makes me feel weird to be writing even more to Dylan in front of him, like that's all I do or something. Which isn't true. Except maybe lately it is.

"Hey," he says. "You might want to turn off the caps lock."

"Not like you're reading over my shoulder *again*, or anything," I complain.

"Sorry. Just caught my eye." He slides into the now-empty seat at the counter next to me.

"Just caught your eye," I mutter. "Yeah. Right."

"It did! I'm sorry," he says, laughing as I turn my back toward him and resume attempting to write in all caps.

"Five minutes to a customer, okay?" The clerk behind the counter smiles and sets the electronic timer on top of each computer.

I start typing like crazy, but I do so much pausing and revising that I actually end up taking forever just to say a couple of things. Beside me, Andre has already written a novel or two, mailed to multiple addresses, created a trip blog, etc. I don't actually know this but I can hear how fast his fingers hit the keys, and it's entirely possible.

I lamely write:

I DON'T KNOW HOW YOU CAN CALL ME, WE'RE TOTALLY PHONELESS, BUT IF YOU SEND EMAILS I WILL TOO AT THE NEXT PLACE WE STOP. I THINK WE ARE GOING TO BE REALLY CLOSE TO YOUR CAMP. I JUST HAVE THIS FEELING.

Why did I use that phrase? Why didn't I think before I decided to tack that on at the last second? I want to hit delete because that sounded idiotic, but it's too late.

"So how's the boyfriend?" Andre asks as the timer rings, sounding like we've just completed a round in a prizefight. We both stand up, and immediately new emailers slide into our vacated seats.

"He's great." I smile, sincerely this time, because I am really happy about the turn of events.

"Where is he again?" Andre asks.

"Wyoming," I say. "It's a small town near Casper." We stand by a large wall of maps, and I point out where Camp Far-a-Way is located. It's not all that close to where we're going—yet—unless of course that *is* where we're going, because you never know with Leisure-Lee Tours.

"Come on, we have to check out the T. rex outside in the backyard."

"We do?" I ask.

"We do. That's what we do, remember? Investigate the backyard sculpture gardens of the Wild West." We stroll along past various displays. "A person could really get lost in here," Andre comments. "I mean, which room were we in?"

"I don't know."

We walk past photos of the Old West, of Wall Drug throughout history. We stop at the gigantic restaurant and I peek inside to see what kind of place can actually seat multiple bus tours, over five hundred people.

I spy Zena and Bethany sitting at the table, and go in to say hi and check on her. "Do you need some money?" I ask.

"No," she says, and then she slurps whatever's in her cup with a straw. "Bethany's treating."

"Because I have money," I insist. "And you could have some of it."

"No, thanks. We're good," says Bethany.

Zena stares over at Andre, who's standing in the doorway, leaning against the host stand. "Hey. I thought you liked Dylan," she says.

I shrug. "I do. I was just emailing him, actually."

"So why are you with *him* all the time?" She gestures toward the doorway.

"Why are you with Bethany all the time?" I counter. "I mean, who else am I supposed to hang out with?"

"But he's *weird*," says Zena. "He says everything in threes."

"You're weird." I grab one of her French fries and head over to Andre.

We're sitting in a photo booth having our picture taken as we pose like Western heroes when suddenly the curtain opens.

"*There* you are," Jenny says. "We've all been looking for you."

"You ruined the shot!" Andre complains. "You totally ruined the shot, and it was going to be the best one." He stands there and waits for the photo strip to print, then shows Jenny the last one, where we're both looking sideways and it's no good. He's right.

But Jenny's too wound up to care. "I just looked up an events schedule for the time we're around Mount Rushmore. There isn't a 10K like you thought."

"Oh." I feel the excitement sink out of me like a deflated balloon, without the embarrassing *pffft* sound, thank goodness. It's hard to ignore the fact that Jenny seems elated by this news, as if it's her life's mission to disappoint me.

"But there *is* a marathon." Jenny smiles so widely that I can see she is the type who flosses and whitens her teeth daily.

"Oh?" I squeak. A marathon. I've never run that far at one time. I might have run that far in one week.

"Isn't that great?" Jenny hands me a flyer about it and I see it's called the Keystone Key to the Black Hills Marathon, and there's also a fun run and various other activities, so I should be able to handle something. "You can enter the marathon," she says. "Isn't that great?"

What am I going to do, say no? "It's *so* great," I say, that is, if you consider major muscle damage and emergency ambulance rides to hospitals in strange towns great.

That gives me seven days to get in shape. Seven days to contact Dylan and see if he can meet me. And when he does meet me, I'll be absolutely exhausted.

But who cares?

"And we'll all be there to cheer you on," Jenny says. "There are so many of us that we can easily spread out on the course, so you'll never be too far from someone rooting for you."

"Because that's the way we run marathons," Andre says in an unnatural, syrupy voice. "Leisure-Lee style!"

Jenny glares at him. "Anyway, you two, it's time to go. Come on, everyone's waiting outside. We're all ready."

"I'm going to buy a soda first," Andre announces. "I'll grab one for you."

"Jenny, we just got here," I say. "We've been reading about this place forever and—"

"I know, but we got off schedule."

"Schedule?" I narrow my eyes at her. "I thought we didn't have a schedule."

"Don't be difficult. We need a place to sleep tonight, and we don't want a repeat of last night, driving around, calling for reservations. Come on, get your things and let's giddyap."

"I have my things. I don't even have . . . things that I take off the bus," I say. She looks at me as if I've just given her too much information, and I probably have. "But I just have one question. What about Wyoming?"

Jenny folds her arms in front of her and looks at me. "What about it?"

"Are we going there, too?" I ask.

"Interesting question. You should know by now that you never know with Leisure-Lee. Just enjoy the journey, Zena." She turns and walks away in a sort of huff.

"Ariel!" I call after her. "A-R-I-E-L!"

So I go out to the bus, but then I claim to need something personal from the pharmacy department, and so I'm off the bus again and sprinting into Wall Drug and there's a family using both computers, but I beg them to let me send just one short email, and they do.

Dylan
We will be near Mount Rushmore on June 21.
It's a Saturday.
Be there!

I quickly buy a few small bags of Skittles and dash outside. My uncle is rushing to the bus ahead of me. He has boxes balanced precariously in front of him as he speed-walks to the bus: boxes of cowboy boots, moccasins, sandals, and every other kind of shoe, it seems, but sneakers.

He can't see where he's going, of course, and when he trips on a small rock in the road, the boxes start to topple, then crash to the ground. I run to help him, catching what I can in midair and crouching down to the ground to help reassemble the rest.

Uncle Jeff shakes his head. "I'm so clumsy. I'm a complete klutz."

I stare at him, and there's a sadness on his face I've never seen before. "No, you're not," I say.

"I'm useless." He sighs. "Absolutely useless."

"You're not," I tell him. "You're the one who keeps us all sane."

He struggles to stack the boxes in his arms again. "Why did I just buy all these things, anyway? I don't even have my full income right now."

"Cheer up, Uncle Jeff," I say as we walk to the bus together, side by side.

That's definitely a sentence I never thought I'd write, let alone say. But I'm in a great mood because we're heading west again, and I'll see Dylan soon. This might be one of my last days on the bus, so why not try to have fun?

"Ariel, you are a niece and a half," Uncle Jeff says.

I smile, not sure what that means. "Thanks. I think."

Wall, South Dakota: a traveler's—and shopper's—dream come true.

D—

We just went to Wall Drug. It's HUGE. AWESOME. Everything the billboards say. Seriously.

The no-cent ice water and 5-cent coffee were both excellent.

Anyway, as you can see, still heading west. Next stop: Badlands.

See you soon. I hope I hope.

Love,

A

Chapter Thirteen

I barely have time to finish the postcard because The Badlands turn out to be only, like, ten miles away, and our motel is only fifteen. I could probably run back to Wall and email Dylan again—and pick up some more snacks—but apparently I won't need to, because this is the kind of travel stop that offers it all, which is nice because we're going to be here for a few days. Huge motel, huge lounge, huge restaurant, huge pool. But it's sort of dated, so they have everything except huge Internet access, which seems very bizarre, but there's some claim to be letting us experience history.

It's weird because the whole landscape is suddenly getting larger; everything's getting bigger—the sky, the land, and now even the motels.

It sort of feels, and looks, like we're on the moon. The mountains look like giant sand hills, but with a purplish tint. I've never seen anything like them before. They're sort of the color of the Grand

Canyon, but not exactly. They look like a giant made a series of sand castles, the kind where you pour water over sand until they clump into drips and shapes.

After a quick driving tour of Badlands National Park, we check into our motel and everyone stops to stare through the fence at the giant pool, clinging to the chain-link as if we're jailed and looking at freedom on the other side.

Before I hit the pool I go running with my grandfather, and with Uncle Jeff trailing us, speed-walking, wearing his new cross-training sandals. They're actually a cross between flip-flops and sneakers and look really uncomfortable. He keeps talking about the shock-absorbing soles, which must be something if they can absorb the shock of Uncle Jeff trying to run in them.

I shouldn't be so catty. He is really making an effort to be out here with me, and that does count for a lot, but I'm secretly worried he'll be in the background of my photo for the cover of *Runners World* someday. *She used to train with her uncle, who was a master of shoe trickery,* the magazine article will say. *It took years for her to recover from the thirteen-minute-mile pace and regain her strength, and by that time she was thirty. She missed qualifying at the Olympic Trials three times in a row. She was considered a never-been.*

"Ariel, you're really picking up the pace," my grandfather comments.

I must have been thinking too hard. "I have to pick up the pace," I tell him. "There's a marathon I have to run a week from Saturday."

"What? We can't do a marathon," he says. "That would be foolish. We haven't been training nearly enough."

"I know. Maybe there's a half marathon, though."

"Oh. All right, fine. That we could pull off."

"Seriously?" I ask.

"Sure. We could run that tonight," Grandpa says. "Well, except for not being able to see very well. When is it again?"

"The twenty-first. Jenny told me about it. It's outside Rapid City, I think a town called Keystone, and I'm not sure what altitude that is—"

I haven't even finished talking when it's as if little rockets appear on the backs of my grandfather's shoes and he's off, sprinting. We run intervals; then we time each other doing miles; then Uncle Jeff times us. We're a team in training. We can't be stopped. At the end of it, I'm out of breath, my uncle has a sunburned nose, and my grandfather has hardly broken a sweat.

"What are you made out of, exactly?" I ask him.

"Pardon?"

"You're like a man of steel. You have zero body fat. You never get tired," I comment.

"Experience, kid. And you don't have much on you, either." He squeezes my bicep. "Probably it's from being the head of this family. It makes you tough."

"Really?"

He looks to the sky and sighs. "You have no idea."

When we get back I change into my bikini and head out to the pool, which is mobbed, like no one has ever seen water before. My grandmother is sitting by the pool, giving Zena a pedicure while Zena "reads" the latest issue of *InStyle*. Mom is reading the new Dr. Phil book, because that's what she does for fun, keeps up on her "contemporaries," as she calls them. Sometimes I wish Dr. Phil would show up at her office and listen to her life story and ask, "And how's that working for you?"

Andre is sitting there in a T-shirt that says REALITY BITES, wearing long shorts and flip-flops. He's bopping his head to his iPod, the vocabulary book open on his lap to the Ks.

"Why aren't you in the pool?" I ask.

"Why isn't anybody? The water's chilled. Cold. Frigid," Andre says.

"But the air is extremely hot. Burning. Suffocating. Swim already," I tell him.

"Yeah, maybe." When he takes off his T-shirt and stretches his arms over his head, I can't help looking at his body. He has those cut muscles in his stomach, the ones runners and other athletes get when they're incredibly lean. I wonder how he gets them, because he doesn't run endlessly like me, and he seems not to care about being an athlete, though I guess I don't have much proof of anything. All I know is that I should probably stop looking at him and his cut body.

I sit on the pool's edge and stick my feet into the water. "Okay, so it's not warm." When I turn to look at him over my shoulder, I see him kind of staring at me. He coughs, embarrassed, and so I slide into the pool, even though it's cold enough to make me gulp.

"Come on, get in," I urge him.

He slides off his flip-flops and sits on the edge, near me, his feet in the water.

"You call that in?" I ask.

He flicks water in my face with his foot. "Give me a second."

I tug at his foot, and he gives up and jumps in. "Man. You think it'd be warmer," he says.

"You'd think," I agree.

We swim around for a while to warm up, then attempt to float, which is difficult now that people like my grandpa are swimming laps. We swim over to the edge and hold on, treading water in the deep end. It feels comfortable being with him, but sort of exciting, too. I'm not sure what's going on with him—or us.

Mom comes over to the edge near us and sits down. "So, Andre. Tell me about yourself," she says.

I look at her, my eyes narrowed. If she doesn't get into the pool soon, I will push her in. And possibly hold her down for a second or two, just to scare her.

"What would you like to know?" he asks, a lot more politely than I probably would.

"Well, what do you do for fun? Are you on any teams, in any clubs, do you read, do you only eat Skittles . . . ?"

"Don't give him the third degree, Mom," I warn.

"I play lacrosse," he says. "I have my library card, which is well-worn. And I vote. No, wait, I don't, because I'm only sixteen."

"So you'll be a junior in the fall, like Ariel?"

"A senior."

"How did you manage that?"

Andre pulls himself out of the water and heads for his towel. "I skipped a grade."

"That's impressive. I'm always telling Ariel to take AP classes as soon as she can. They're *such* an advantage."

I submerge and swim down to the bottom of the pool, staying there until I run out of breath. Then I get out, dry myself off a little, and flop onto a chair, facedown, my back to the sky. The sun starts to bake the water off my back. I love that feeling. This finally feels like vacation.

"See, if we went on a cruise, Mother, this would be our day. This would be so awesome," Zena is saying to Mom, who has finally stopped quizzing Andre.

"Boring," Mom says, pushing up her organic cotton sleeves. She refuses to take off her shirt, even though she has a bathing suit on underneath, and even though she made me look at the Lands' End site with her for about thirty-six hours picking out said swimsuit. "Pools are boring. And cruises are environmentally unsound."

Uncle Jeff does a cannonball off the diving board, completely splashing everyone.

Andre comes over to sit beside me in a webbed chair, and I turn to him. "That's my positive male influence. Him."

Andre unfolds the chair so he can lie down beside me, and it collapses with a crash, nearly tossing him onto the concrete deck. "Figures," he says. He unfolds it again and slides into it carefully. "Ariel, look."

I feel a tap on my shoulder and I turn over.

Andre gestures to Lenny, who's fast asleep in a lounge chair. Then he points to Jenny, who's busy playing water volleyball with some of the seniors. "This would be the perfect time to figure out our route. Or just find out some dirt about Lenny and Jenny. Or hide all the old people's travel pillows and watch them freak out when they get on the bus tomorrow."

I smile, picturing the chaotic scene. "Okay, but how are we going to get on it?"

"Come on," Andre urges. "Maybe we will, maybe we won't. But if we stay here, your mom's going to grill me some more."

I'm up for any nonfamily adventure, so I slide on my flip-flops, wrap a towel around me, and together we head out of the pool area. Why am I tiptoeing? I wonder.

"Ariel? Andre! Where are you going?" Mom calls to me.

Maybe that's why. "Just getting something to drink. We'll be right back," I say. "It figures that she sensed I was leaving. She's got Ariel radar," I comment to Andre.

"Don't take long!" she calls after us. "And bring me a coffee, okay?"

"I want an iced tea!" Mrs. O'Neill adds. "And not the green kind. And put some sugar in it!"

"How is this different from being at home, again?" Andre asks as we open the gate and head out to the parking lot. "Wait. Hold on." He grabs my arm midway to the bus. "The door's open. Why is the door open?"

"I don't know," I say. "Someone's cleaning it?"

"This is it. This is our chance. Maybe they left the keys, too," he says.

I find that I'm still tiptoeing, which isn't a good thing, because as I take my first step up onto the bus, I trip on my towel and nearly wipe out.

I grab Andre, who's ahead of me, to keep from doing a face-plant onto the steering wheel.

"Coordinated much?" he jokes, turning around to help me catch my balance. His hand's on my waist, and that's when I realize that my towel is now lying on the steps behind me. I'm not naked, but it's as close as I've ever been, standing this near to a guy.

"No, seriously. You're in really good shape. Really good," he says. "I'm sorry I made that crack about runners back in whatever town that was."

"It's okay. I mean, thanks." I feel this weird tension between us.

"Obviously it's something you take seriously and all, so . . ."

"Right."

"So."

"So."

Pool water drips off my hair and slides down the middle of my back, which is good because I'm getting seriously hot in here. I feel like Andre is about to kiss me, or maybe it's that I'm about to kiss him.

"Excuse me. Where are we?" Andre and I jump back from each other as a sleepy-looking old woman approaches us down the aisle. I'm pretty sure it's Ethel.

"Um . . . at the motel pool?" I say, unable to think of the name of the motel, still in shock over the fact that I almost made a move on Andre, which is ridiculous, because isn't going west and sneaking onto buses all about seeing Dylan?

"I must have been asleep when we got here, so they just let me be. Ha!" Ethel chuckles. "How funny. Haven't been able to sleep a wink since this trip started—blasted roommate snores like a freight train. So, what have I missed?"

"Honestly? Not too much," Andre tells her.

"Right." I struggle to retrieve my towel before Andre helps her down the steps. As we walk back into the pool area, I realize that I completely forgot my mom's coffee. Fortunately, we have Ethel to cover for us.

Big Badlands Motor Court—too big to fit on a small postcard!
All-inclusive resort. Try our famous chuck-wagon supper, sip
cocktails in the Pronghorn Lounge, or hit the pool with the
kids! AARP discount rates.

Sarah,
This bus can apparently time travel. Check
out the place on the front. We're back in the
sixties. Or seventies. Turn on the History
Channel and maybe you'll see us.
    Temperature is in the high eighties. "But
it's a dry heat," all the older people on the
bus keep saying.
    Help me, I'm writing about the weather.
    This place has a fantabulous pool.
    Have tons to tell you.
    XO
    Me

l..ll..ll..l.l.lll...ll...ll..ll..l.l.l.ll.l.l.l...l.ll

Chapter Fourteen

The next night, after hiking all day and being at a chuck-wagon supper for most of the night, we go to our motel room and Mom slides every single bar and lock on our door closed. As if Zena and I were both thinking of slipping out sometime during the night. And as if we couldn't unbolt all of the locks without waking her up, because she's a very sound sleeper.

I look over at Zena as I'm brushing my teeth. Is she thinking what I'm thinking—about escaping? But she's busy reading a fresh copy of *Entertainment Weekly* that she stole from the lobby earlier.

I go lie down beside her on the bed, which is fortunately a queen this time and big enough for both of us. I think about when we were little and Zena went through this stage on one trip when she couldn't sleep, and the four of us would crowd into one bed and all roll up together.

"So, Zena," I say, looking at her as I prop up on one elbow. "What's been your favorite part so far?"

"Hanging out with Bethany and the guys."

"The guys?"

"Dieter and Wolfgang," she says. "Who else?"

"But what *else*?" asks Mom. "You two cannot make this entire trip about boys. I forbid you."

Zena rolls her eyes at Mom and puts a pillow under her neck. "The antelopes, then." She tosses another pillow into the air and catches it with her feet.

"You're kidding," I say. "I didn't see them. You want to tell me about it?"

"Not really," she says.

"You would have noticed them too, Ariel, if you weren't spending so much time working on your postcards and hanging out with Andre," Mom says.

I ignore her postcard comment, because if she can't appreciate that I want to write them, then I can't explain it to her. "It's impossible not to spend so much time with anyone on the bus when you're *on a bus*. Captive audience and all," I point out.

"Yes, but this is a family trip," she says. "It's about the family. Spend time visiting with your grandparents, your uncle. In fact, starting tomorrow, you'll be sitting with one of us."

"Since when are you in charge of seating assignments?" I ask. "Did Jenny appoint you?"

"Ariel, don't take that tone with me. I'm in charge. Period."

"Oh, really. Were you in charge when Dad was taking our money and—"

"Why are you bringing this up now?"

I throw up my hands. "Why not?"

"We've gone over this. Your father always handled the bills, the banking, balancing the checking account, all of that. We never had a problem before, and there was no reason to suspect anything." She brushes and rebrushes her unruly hair.

I think about it. I know what she's saying is mostly true. It's only when I look back that I can see all the omens, or warning signs, and maybe it's the same for her.

"Anyway, back to tomorrow. You'll sit with family. Both of you should get to know your uncle and grandparents better. I mean, what if we end up living closer to them? Wouldn't that be nice?"

I feel like a trapdoor in the floor just opened and I'm about to fall into it. What is she talking about? "You want to move all the way to St. Paul? No," I say. "No, you can move, but I'm not."

"I didn't say we *would*; I just said that it would be nice."

Zena lifts her head from her pillow long enough to say, "That sounds sort of cool."

I glare at her closed eyes. I can't believe she's siding with Mom, even if she's half-asleep.

"Ariel? Forget your knee-jerk reaction and think about it. How would you really feel about that?" Mom asks.

"You know what? I don't want to talk about it. I want to stay where I am. It's junior year for me, Mom. It's not the time to just . . . start over."

"But can't you understand . . . maybe getting a fresh start would be a good idea for all of us?"

"Fresh start. That's like a breakfast cereal, right?" I turn off my light and snuggle under the covers, letting her know I am done for the night with this conversation.

"Ariel, Ariel, come on, let's talk," Mom urges as she slides into the other bed. "Nothing's ever solved by not talking."

"Maybe this will be the first time. Good night," I say.

I desperately want to fall asleep and forget this conversation, but

I don't drift off into dreamland the way I'd like to. Zena falls asleep, and then Mom falls asleep, while I lie there and think. I wait until my mother is snoring, then get up.

"I can't sit with you on the bus tomorrow."

Andre sits down across from me in the lobby. He's wearing shorts and a rumpled Marquette University T-shirt. "Is that why you called and woke me up? To tell me that?"

"No," I say, feeling kind of miserable. "Well, yeah."

"Okay." Andre rubs his eyes underneath his glasses. "Why can't you sit with me? Is it because your grandfather hates me?"

"What? No." I shake my head. "Why would he hate you?"

"Because I'm black?"

"Oh, really? You are? Huh."

"Shut up."

"No, he doesn't hate you, for that or anything else. He's just . . . protective. So if we spend time together, he's just . . . he wants to know you better. I guess. Anyway, my mom went on and on about how it's a family trip and I'm supposed to sit with my family. And now my mom is talking about us moving to Minnesota."

Andre yawns. "So what do you want to do? Should we sneak on the bus again?"

"I can't believe we'd want to spend *more* time there. I feel like that seat fabric pattern is becoming one with my skin. Everywhere I look, I see mauve diamonds."

"Stand up and let me see if it's coming off on you," Andre orders, nudging my leg with his foot.

"Shut up." I look over and see the desk clerk staring at us. "Come on, let's go outside."

* * *

We go out by the pool, which is open until midnight, although there isn't anyone actually in it. We pull two chairs close to each other and lie down.

Andre looks up at the stars and takes a deep breath. "This place is kind of awesome," he says. "I mean, it's *way* out here. I've never seen so many stars."

I gaze upward, too, looking for some kind of constellation I can point out, but I don't see anything. "Kind of awesome? That doesn't sound like you. Give me three words."

"Trance-inducing. Relaxing. Cool." He sighs. "I'm really tired. My vocabulary is lame right now. Lame as in pathetic, useless." He looks over at me. "So what's the deal with moving and not sitting together?"

I groan. "Thanks for reminding me," I say, but it's not as though I've had time to forget.

"Sorry. But what's going on?" he asks.

"It's . . . She wants me to get to know her side of the family better, because she's sick of my dad's, I guess, or just my dad. So she wants us to maybe move all the way to St. Paul to get away from him."

"Bad divorce?" Andre asks, adjusting the chair another notch so that he lies almost flat.

"You could say that. My dad . . . well, he kept going to work every morning, but it turned out he didn't actually have a job anymore; he was going to the racetrack. And the casino. Which is where he spent all our college money. After he ran through all the money he embezzled from his work. He didn't tell us any of this. We found out when he was arrested, and then it broke on TV, and it was all over school."

I didn't mean to say so much, but once I started I somehow couldn't stop. So there it is, out in the open. Like a bag lunch on a picnic table waiting for someone to pick it up or toss it. Or trade it for turkey.

"That's like . . . the longest sentence I've ever heard you say," Andre says.

"This stupid trip. It's getting to me," I mutter.

"Road rage?"

"Something like that. My mom's a counselor and she published some self-help books, but she's kind of clueless about people. She sits in her office listening to people pour out their relationship troubles, while her own marriage is going up in flames. And scratch cards. And horses." I pause. "Well, not that the horses are going up in flames; that sounds disgusting."

Andre laughs. "So. Are you and your dad still in touch?"

"Oh yeah. I'm just . . . Honestly? I'm still really blown away by what happened. He started acting really hyper and fidgety. Then he was never home. Then he was arrested. It's like . . . all these little funny traits he had were exaggerated and they weren't funny anymore. Like, we used to bet about things all the time, but I thought it was just a game to him. I guess whenever I'm around him, I feel nervous. Because I don't know who he is. He's a wild card. If he could do that to us once—over the course of, like, years—and he only stopped six months ago, when he *had* to . . ."

"Well, is he twelve-stepping it?" asks Andre.

I smile and nod in admiration. "That's a good one," I say.

"What?"

"Nothing. Zena and I just try to come up with new words and—"

"It's not a new word."

"Never mind." I sigh. "Yeah, he's making amends. Or claiming to."

"Hey, it's just your dad. You know?" Andre reaches over and puts his hand on my wrist, giving it a little squeeze. "It's not you."

"Right." It doesn't seem to matter that I know this, though. "So. What about you?" I ask, tired of telling and hearing my story.

"Everything seems pretty good for you. So why do you want to run away?"

"I'm sick of being good. Good is overrated," he says with a sigh.

"You tried to break into a tour bus. You call that being good?" I laugh.

"Living with my mom . . . She won't let me visit my dad. She thinks he's a bad influence, which he really isn't, and anyway, I'm old enough to decide things on my own. If I think he's a jerk, I'll be okay. Right?"

"When did they get divorced?"

"When I was six."

"Why?"

"Who knows?"

"You don't?"

"A hundred reasons, I guess. No, wait. A hundred other women, I think it was. Yeah. Anyway, I wanted to spend the summer with him in L.A. He wanted me to. Mom said no. She had no really good reason, and she's always urging us to get closer—but spend more than holidays together? No. Not an option."

I wonder about my future and how things like that will shake out. Will I see Dad on Thanksgiving or Christmas? Who will decide? Is Mom even allowed to take us that far away?

"Then she comes up with this trip idea. You don't know how many times we argued about this. 'We'll bond, Andre,' she said. 'No, *you'll* have a good time; I'll be bored to death,' I said. I mean, if you weren't here?" He pretends to hold a gun to his head.

"No way. You'd hang out with Ethel."

"Yeah. Dentures are *so* sexy."

"So that's why you'd head to L.A. if you could. You and Ethel, I mean," I say.

"I'm thinking about it," he replies. "Well, not the Ethel part."

"I'm thinking about meeting up with Dylan," I tell him. Like, that's pretty much all I think about—or did, until my encounter with Andre on the bus.

"You are? For real?"

"Sure. What's stopping me?" I ask.

"Well, um, a car. A bus. A bunch of relatives. A *plan*."

Not that he has a negative outlook or anything. "I have a plan," I say. I think it over. "Not a good plan. But, uh, Dylan could meet me and then I'd leave with him."

"And he's working at this camp. So what would you do? Go back there with him and get hired on, too? Or be a really old camper?"

"No, of course not. We'd travel together," I say.

"With no car," Andre says. "And like, how much money?"

I glare at him. I don't want to stay here. Or move to Dylan's camp. Or follow through on any of my options.

"My plan's better," Andre says confidently. "We somehow get to Denver. Whether it's on this bus or another bus."

"Okay. Then what?"

Suddenly a flashlight beam bounces across the deck, coming to rest on my face. "Excuse me, but the pool is closed," a man's voice announces.

"Grandpa?" I ask, shielding my eyes from the flashlight. "What are those, extra-strength batteries?"

He walks over to us and looks down at the way we're nearly sprawled on the concrete in our flat lounge chairs. "It's past your bedtime, isn't it?"

"We're too old to have bedtimes," I say.

"Hm. So am I," Grandpa says, "and yet I have one." He looks up at the sky and lets out a deep sigh. "On the other hand, it's nice out here. Our A/C unit is broken and the breeze has yet to find its way into our room."

He drags a chair over next to mine. Then he pulls his Nike headband out of his pocket. "Give me your hand," he says.

I don't know what's going on, but I do it, and Grandpa wraps the headband around both of our wrists, locking them together.

"You're cuffing me," I say.

"Call it what you like. This way if I'm asleep and you try to leave, I'll know about it."

"Do you want *me* to leave?" asks Andre.

"I don't care one way or the other, but if you do leave, don't take her with you."

"Yes, sir," Andre says, sounding intimidated.

Grandpa leans back in his chair next to mine, our arms propped on the armrest together. "Now. Don't let me interrupt. What were you two plotting just now when I walked in?" he asks.

"What else?" I say. "How to steal the *Oklahoma!* CD."

"I'm in," says Grandpa, and we all lie back, look up at the stars, and contemplate ways to get to Lenny and Jenny.

The Badlands: erosion in progress. Do not disturb.

Dylan,
Have you ever been to the Badlands?
 They are a lot more interesting than I
thought.
 Except that we had to attend a
chuckwagon supper, where they served
buffalo burgers, baked beans, and blond
brownies. And other things beginning with B,
like beer.
 I stuck to Skittles. Or actually, it was so
hot out that the Skittles stuck to me.
 Hope you're having a good time.
 XO
 A

Chapter Fifteen

The next morning, I nearly lose my breakfast when the bus goes roaring past the turnoff for Rapid City.

A detour? Again?

I don't just feel ill because I really wanted to go there, but also because Jenny takes this curve kind of too fast while I'm looking down at a postcard, and the fried-egg sandwich at the hot breakfast buffet seems like it wasn't such a great idea after all. Which is what I thought, but Grandma kept insisting I eat more, especially if I was planning on running as much as I have been, and Grandpa and I had just come back from a nine-mile run. (He covered for me not being in my room in the morning, saying I went to their room early that morning for a visit, which made my mother smile, and my grandmother look confused.) "Wasting away" is what she called it. "It's time for you to carb up," she kept saying, as if "carb" were a verb, as she carried over more wheat toast from the burn-it-yourself toaster. So I caved and carbed, and now the carbs are coming back up.

"But I thought . . . Excuse me, aren't we going to Rushmore?" I call up toward the front of the bus.

My voice is just one of the dozens asking the same question.

Lenny stands and faces us. "Yes, but if there's one thing I've learned over the years, it's this: You can't rush Mount Rushmore." He makes that annoying clicking noise with his tongue, and Jenny revs the engine, and I wonder if the two actions are connected, like she's ticked at him. I wonder how many times each summer they do this tour, how often she's had to listen to his presentations, how many times he's had to help her fix the bus.

"You can't?" someone asks.

"Nope. You cannot rush Mount Rushmore. You've got to anticipate. You've got to wait. Then you've absolutely got to see it from the right angle, from the right road. We'll see some other interesting sites first, and then we'll do a loop around and end up approaching from another direction, with breathtaking views. Rushmore is something you approach slowly, deliberately."

It sounds like a speech Lenny has crafted over the years, but that doesn't make it any less annoying.

"Well, I guess we just have to take his word for it," Uncle Jeff says to me.

We're sitting next to each other, as ordered by my mother. I don't even know if Uncle Jeff is happy about it. He's made lots of friends on the trip—maybe he'd rather sit with one of them.

"Guess so," I say.

"You know what, Ariel? All this running we've been doing over the past week?" He nods his head, and so do I. "It's really helping me. Every morning when I wake up I feel like my muscles are really alive."

"So you're getting over the, um, injury and stuff?" I ask.

He nods again. "I think so. I mean, it could be a while yet. But I feel stronger. I feel like I could conquer the world."

"That's cool," I comment. "I'm glad. But is it really the running?"

"You tell me," he says.

"Tell you what?" I ask.

"Is it the running?" he says. "Is that why you run so far, so often?"

"Sure. I guess."

"Because it makes sense I'd like it, genetically— Wait a second, hold on. There's Sturgis. Sturgis! I haven't been there in years. Why aren't we stopping? Lenny!" he calls. "Why aren't we getting off here?"

"Because this isn't one of our stops," Lenny replies.

"We're not stopping in Sturgis?" Uncle Jeff sounds stunned. "But we're going right through it."

"Exactamundo!" Lenny makes that clicking noise with his tongue. "We're going right past without stopping."

"But if you can't rush, uh, Mount Rushmore, then you can't, uh, leave Sturgis in the lurch-is," Uncle Jeff says.

"Work on it, mate, and get back to me," Lenny says, sounding like Simon Cowell.

Uncle Jeff slumps in his seat, looking sort of like a kid who was just told he wasn't getting his favorite toy for Christmas. I feel bad for him. This crazy bus trip might not have been *his* idea, either. "Do you want to ask for a bus vote?" I suggest. "Other people might want to see Sturgis."

His eyebrows shoot up, like that hadn't occurred to him. But then he shrugs and slumps down again. "I don't know, Ariel. Why tempt fate? Maybe it's a sign."

I look out the window, confused. "What's a sign?"

"My life. My Harley days. My motorcycle rally days. They're over," he says. "I have to move on."

"Just like that?"

"If I was still that person . . . well, I wouldn't be here on a bus, would I? I'd be meeting you in Sturgis because I rode there on my motorcycle." He taps the armrest between us. "I've changed; my methods of perambulation have changed."

I poke my head up over the seat back, where Andre's sitting with his mom and Cuddles behind us. Mrs. O'Neill has suddenly gotten interested in this "sitting with family" concept, too. She and Mom are conspiring, no doubt. "Perambulation?" I ask Andre.

"Technically it means tour of duty, but he probably means getting around," Andre replies instantly. Then he asks, "Your uncle gets around?"

"Not like that. On a motorcycle," I explain.

"Well, dudes on motorcycles sometimes *do* get around, you know."

"Shut up," I whisper. "You're talking about my uncle." I smile, then sit back down, while Uncle Jeff is explaining that Sturgis has a gigantic motorcycle rally every August, and how he used to go, how that was always his summer vacation week, how he'd arrange it far in advance, and how he met so many fellow carriers and even had a romance there once with a postal inspector named Sandra.

I look out the window at the signs, trying to miss some of the intimate details he's sharing. We're heading toward a town called Deadwood, which sounds familiar for some reason.

I feel a pen press on my ribs, and reach between the seats to grab it. Andre and I wrestle for it until a shadow looms over me.

"I'll be confiscating that highlighter now," Mrs. O'Neill says.

"That's the first thing they take away in jail. The pens," Andre comments.

◊ ◊ ◊

As everyone gets off the bus in Deadwood, I sit and wait until I'm the last one. "We are still *going* to Mount Rushmore, right?" I ask Jenny, who's sitting in the driver's seat. "Even though we're not rushing it."

She laughs. "Yes, of course we're going there."

"And I can still run that race on the twenty-first. The one in Keystone," I say, hoping to jog her memory, so to speak.

"Possibly, yes," says Jenny.

"Possibly?" I want to scream, but I hold it inside.

"I don't see why not, but on the other hand, you never know. The trip is ten days, and how we spend those ten days . . . well, it's not all set in stone." She shrugs and adjusts something in the little compartment above her seat.

"You know what? I don't know how you guys stay in business. This is the most wishy-washy trip I've ever been on in my entire life."

"Wishy-washy? What are you, twelve?" She snorts.

I glare at her. "No, that's my sister, Zena. The one whose name you keep calling me? My name is Ariel, okay?"

"Are you interested in achieving personal growth or not? Just relax," she says to me.

And what are you, my mother? I want to say. "Relax? How can I relax when I don't know where we're going? When one day you tell me I can do this race, and three days later suddenly you're not sure. Can I or can't I?" I demand.

"We'll see!" Jenny responds with a phony smile. "Now move along; I have to go park the bus."

When I stomp off the bus, my family is waiting at the bottom of the steps, looking concerned by my behavior.

"How can you get so riled up about running? God. It's just *running*," says Zena.

"Thanks for the support, as always," I tell her.

Fortunately, Grandma falls into step beside me. "Jenny's not exactly known for her people skills, is she?"

The first place we head to is Saloon No. 10, and Lenny tells us that this is where the famous Wild Bill Hickok, criminal at large in the 1800s, was killed in 1876. He was shot in the back of the head while playing cards. He had what is now known as the "dead man's hand," a pair of aces and a pair of eights. No news on the fifth card, but apparently also a dead man's card.

There are actors in historical costumes dressed up and walking around the streets, and it turns out we're only a day early for the town's Wild Bill Hickok Days, which is kind of annoying, because I bet those would be pretty fun.

I can't believe I wrote that sentence, either. But I'm serious.

We're also too early for the reenactment of the shooting, which happens every day at three p.m., which is okay because I don't like to think of poker players getting shot in the back of the head. Wild Bill's "dead man's chair," or a replica of it, hangs from the wall.

I start to get that nauseated feeling again. I try to hide it, but it really grips my gut like the way I can feel sick before a race.

Mom isn't doing much better. She's gone a bit pale. She's standing in the doorway, not committing to coming in, just staring at the chair plastered to the wall above the door, as if she's thinking of the title for her next self-help book: *Deadwood Dad, Deadbeat Dad*.

Come to think of it, I haven't asked her in a while if she's working on a new book, and if so, what it's about, but I have a feeling I'm on the right track with this. The Flackjack Track, that is.

Lenny goes over to her, looking concerned, and asks, "You feeling all right, mate?"

"Not exactly," she says.

"Why don't you come over here and sit down?" He tries to guide her to a seat at the bar.

"No—no, thanks," she says.

I watch her for a second, wondering if she's feeling the way I do. Dad isn't here, but yet he is. People are slumped at slots or bouncing on toes at card tables. He worked his way up—or down, depending how you look at it—and was proud of it, like he was really achieving something. Starting at nickel slots. Then quarters. Then dollars.

Then all the dollars.

He told me all about it the first time he apologized, trying to make amends when he started going to Gamblers Anonymous meetings. How once you got the adrenaline rush you couldn't stop. How every time you had the potential to win big, really big, and sometimes you did and it was exhilarating and you couldn't forget how on top of the world you felt, so you were always chasing that feeling again.

Then he told me how he started doing whatever he could to improve his luck, how one time he carried one of my cross-country race medals in his pocket and he won, so he kept carrying it. Which was sweet, I suppose, but also made my medal seem like a carnival token. If I ever win a real medal—gold or silver or bronze—he'd probably steal it and melt it down, or else just pawn it.

In some ways I'd like to cash in a couple dollars and go try my luck at the slots right now, but Mom has this piercingly sad look on her face, and I just can't walk away and ignore that, as much as I want to.

"Hey," I say, going over to her.

She sighs. "Hey."

"Are you thinking what I'm thinking?"

"I don't know." She frowns, more so than before. "That your father would love it here?"

"No. I was thinking we should go get ice cream," I say, trying to change the subject, because how many times can you beat a dead horse?

"Maybe we should. Or maybe we should stand here and try to understand." She gets this very serious look on her face, like she's channeling the ghost of Wild Bill Hickok, and it hurts her to do so.

"Or there's a realsimple solution," I offer. "We could just leave."

As I look around, not wanting to abandon Mom, but not really wanting to hug it out or hang out and talk either, I see a banner in the back of the room that says: SEND AN EMAIL FROM DEADWOOD! FROM WILD BILL HICKOK!

"Excuse me, Mom. Gotta go," I tell her. Family's one thing, but Dylan's another.

I start to type:

Dylan, we're in Deadwood, which is reallyreallyclose to Wyoming. I saw Devils Tower on the map and we're really close but probably not going. Any way you can get a day pass??? Or whatever they call it? After this we're going to Rushmore. Meet me online at 9 tomorrow night and we can Gchat.

Mom is behind me. "Come on, Ariel, we're leaving, I'm sorry." She tries to take my arm as if I'm six, and she pulls me over to where Lenny is leading the charge, chanting, "Lemon, lemon . . . cherry! Ah, mate, try it again!"

"Lenny, what were you thinking? This isn't appropriate for the kids," Mom is saying, and just as she does Dieter lets out a whoop because he has gotten three in a row and coins are spitting out of the machine like hail from the sky.

"This is supposed to be fun. Relax, Tammy, relax." Lenny puts his arm around my mother and tries to give her a shoulder rub, and she gives him a warning look, backing off.

"It's Tamara," she says. "Not Tammy."

Jenny, who's been off parking the bus at one of the lots reserved for tour buses, walks in just then and sees Lenny kind of accosting Mom, and she comes over and starts hitting him and accusing him of flirting with Mom. Which is extremely ridiculous, but I don't tell her that because she's been so unpleasant that I kind of enjoy watching her squirm with jealousy.

Lenny and Jenny start yelling at each other, and Mom's trying to counsel them about their marriage, and we've suddenly turned into the white-trash Jerry Springer bus tour.

Later in the afternoon, Andre and I skip the day's strange museum of choice in favor of people watching, and for some reason this is okay with our mothers. We have Cuddles with us, which is our excuse. We pick up a couple of coffees and park on a bench on historic Main Street.

Andre holds up Cuddles, checking out their reflected image in the coffee shop's window. "I'm like a glorified dog walker. I mean, how much does this ruin my image?"

I step back and look at him, at his semi-cut body, with his latest cool T-shirt, his great sneakers, his low-rise jeans, his stylish eyeglasses. Carrying a tiny Chihuahua.

"Are you trying to meet someone?" I ask. " 'Cause if so, here, I'll hold him," I offer.

He pushes my arm away. "No, it's okay."

"No, come on, let me," I insist. "Maybe *I'll* meet someone."

Andre rolls his eyes. "Yeah, lots of middle-aged women. Trust me on this."

"I didn't know so many people would be here," I say. "In Dead-wood."

"Why wouldn't they be?"

I shrug, then take a sip of my iced latte.

"I have a question. Does being here make you freak a little?"

"A little," I say. "Yeah. I mean, it looks fun. The thing is that I'd probably like it in the casinos. Or genetically I'd maybe love it."

"You think that kind of thing is inherited?"

I shrug. "I don't know. Does anyone know?"

"Well, are your grandparents gambling addicts?"

"No."

"It could be worse, you know. He could have been a drug addict."

"True, but there's a certain glamour to that," I say. I think about Keith Johnson telling me about his addicted brother, and how it didn't count until you got the call from jail.

"No. Not really. Haven't you ever seen those meth-addict post-ers? I mean, have you even looked at those *teeth*?" He shudders so violently that Cuddles barks, looking alarmed.

"Gambling's very smoky, and the coins and tokens make your hands stink. My dad used to have this weird lemon-lime smell, like he'd bathed in Sprite, and I couldn't figure it out, and we found out later it was from the little wet cloths they give you to clean your hands after handling all those metal tokens at the casino. But they didn't really work. In the end, it was just like my mom finding lip-stick on his collar, only it wasn't another woman. Well, unless you consider Lady Luck a woman, I guess."

"Again with the long sentences," he comments.

"Yeah, well." I take a crumpled bag of Skittles out of my pocket and offer him a handful.

"They're melting," he says as he looks at the clump that fell into his palm. "When you run out of Skittles, that's when we'll know it's time to leave." He reaches for the bag. "Getting close?"

He tries to pull the bag out of my hand, and Skittles clatter on the hot pavement. They start sticking to people's shoe and sandal soles as they walk past and make a sort of gooey tap-dance sound.

How hot is it? Hot enough to fry a Skittle on the sidewalk.

Later that afternoon, Lenny keeps glancing at his watch. He taps his pen against the clipboard. We've all reported to the bus. He's finished taking roll, and there's only one person missing: Jenny.

"Well. I guess we'd better go," he says.

"Do you know how to drive one of these?" asks Grandpa.

"Of course, I've got my commercial driver's license, just like my wife," he says. "We trade off all the time."

"Uh-huh," Mrs. O'Neill says, looking suspicious. "Then why haven't they traded off before now?" she comments to the rest of us.

We're trusting—or desperate, take your pick—so we climb back onto the bus. I sit with Grandpa, because so far I've sat with every family member but him. After a couple of misfires the engine purrs to life, and Lenny very, very slowly maneuvers out of the parking lot.

"So long, Deadwood," Grandpa says.

"So long, Jenny," I add.

"I can't say I'll miss her," Grandpa says to me quietly. "Or her musical selec—"

We look at each other as *Oklahoma!* booms out of the overhead speakers. Apparently Lenny can't drive and monitor volume at the same time.

Wild Bill Hickok says, "They don't call it Deadwood for nothing, now, do they?"

Dear Mars, Incorporated,
You should know that Skittles don't travel all that well.

On hot days, they will melt on sidewalks.

Also, the price could be lowered for those of us unable to get summer jobs because our mothers insist on dragging us all over the country.

Thank you for sustaining me and for your great product. My home address is below in case you'd like to send me a little something, like a five-pound bag.

Sincerely yours,
Ariel Frances Flack
Not the mermaid

Chapter Sixteen

"The bus has spoken, and the bus is dead," Andre announces as he steps off the bus and joins me and the crowd standing around the side of the road, looking less than pleased.

There's a gray-brown burro about ten yards off giving me the evil eye. I'm thinking it's time to move on. "I don't have any carrots or whatever," I tell it. "I really don't."

"I'll push that bus if I have to," someone behind me mutters.

"You might have to," says my grandfather. "We *all* might have to."

Several backseat drivers are telling Lenny that it's his fault the bus overheated. Now a tow truck's going to have to come out from the nearest garage and move the bus, and then it'll need to be repaired.

"You should have gone around that line of cars," Grandpa tells Lenny with some authority, as if he's done it before.

"We could have killed a burro if I went around. No. Absolutely not. God's creatures," says Lenny.

We were on our way through Custer State Park after seeing Crazy

Horse, which is an amazing mountain carving like Mount Rushmore, only it was started later, didn't get government funding, and is still in progress. The nose, the profile, is gigantic, and the people walking all over look like little gnats from afar.

We only saw it from afar, because Lenny said that our entrance fee wasn't covered by our Leisure-Lee fee, so we had a bus vote to decide if we'd see it, and it was narrowly defeated, 23–21. I'm still mad about that, because it looked very cool.

So we were driving along the Wildlife Loop Road, where there are burros along the way that stop cars to beg for food, and people feed them, so we ended up sitting and waiting behind a line of cars. Then the bus overheated, blew a gasket or something, and we coasted, again, into the nearest business parking lot, which in this case was Happyland RV Park.

"Well, folks, this wasn't exactly what we were planning, now, was it?" asks Lenny, rubbing his hands together and looking slightly on edge. "Time to break out that emergency gear. Time for a taste of the outback!"

"There's an Outback around here? Really?" Andre's mom asks, her voice thick with hope. "I'd kill for some mashed potatoes."

"Oh, I just love their Blooming Onion. It's amazing," adds another passenger.

"It's just a blooming onion," Andre jokes.

"That's not Outback. That's Texas Roadhouse," someone else says.

"Folks! Folks. Pardon the interruption, but I'm sorry. I wasn't referring to the Outback steakhouse. I was talking about the out-back, camping out–wise," Lenny explains. "We'll be staying the night here."

Mrs. O'Neill's eyes widen. "Camping out? Oh no," she says. "I'll sleep on the bus before I lie on the ground."

"You can't sleep on the bus." Lenny shakes his head. "Against safety regulations."

"Well, so are rattlesnakes. I've never slept on the ground and I don't intend to start now. This was most definitely *not* in the brochure," she says, and everyone laughs.

"That disclaimer part about being able to roll with the punches. Didn't you read that, mate?" Lenny asks her, a twinkle in his eye, as if he's hilarious.

Mrs. O'Neill doesn't look amused in the slightest. "I'll roll and punch *you*," she tells him.

"Ma, lighten up. It's only camping," Andre says. "You've camped before."

"No, I haven't, and you haven't either," she says, "so quit pretending. We're not Boy Scouts." She raises one very nicely plucked eyebrow. "I'm not camping out here. You're breaking our agreement," she says to Lenny.

"Not really, because we did tell you to be ready for anything," Lenny replies. "And you can consider it an even exchange. You broke *our* agreement when you brought your pooch along."

She takes a step back. "Cuddles? He's not a pooch."

"Thoroughbred. Purebred. Whatever," Lenny says. "He's not on the passenger list. Cuddles O'Neill." Lenny runs his finger down an imaginary clipboard. "Nope. Not on here."

With that, he begins to pull out equipment, tents, and sleeping bags that we were all instructed to bring, but we didn't know why—I just remember Mom telling me to bring mine "in case of emergency." Uncle Jeff goes over to help, and loses his stamp hat on a tree branch that nearly takes out his eye.

"Look at all this," Lenny says. "You think any other bus tour gives you this?" He sweeps his arm around, indicating the outdoors, the view, the Happyland RV Park sign. "Not on your life."

I desperately look for a place where I can email Dylan. I see the campground office and decide to head over there, cash in hand, like only an addict would.

That night Andre and I grab a couple of s'mores and escape the campfire ghost stories that Lenny is telling. It's not even dark yet, so the campfire and the ghosts don't really have the same effect they would in an hour. We find a kind of quiet place and sit on a rock.

I can hear the faint, tinny sound of Andre's iPod through his headphones amid the crickets and other night sounds. He reaches over and hands me one of the earbuds. We just sit there without talking, which is weird because we always talk. I don't know what's different, but something is.

When the iPod dies, I hand him the earbud and he puts it in his pocket and we just sit there. Now I can hear the wind in the trees, and it's a really hot night. Just sitting there next to him, not even touching him, for some reason it's way more melty a situation than anything I've ever felt for Dylan.

It's not because it's a hundred degrees, although that kind of contributes.

It might be because he's putting his hand over mine and we are about to hold hands.

And then as my wrist turns to either hold his hand or push it away, I see on my Nike watch that it's nine o'clock, which is the time Dylan and I planned to Gchat.

I jump up, and then am really embarrassed that I did. "Sorry. Sorry. It's just that I told Dylan I'd write him at nine, so—"

"No, it's okay, go ahead," he says.

"I wasn't, um . . . you know." I don't even know what I'm trying to say.

"Yeah, I know."

So I sprint to the Happyland office, where the manager told me earlier that I could get online on her computer with my Hotmail account if I paid her five dollars. So I do, even though that seems kind of like highway robbery. I'm getting used to that, buying stuff at souvenir shops.

Dylan? You there? We're in Happyland.

Ariel? Where r u?

My heart starts pounding, and I don't know whether it's from the excitement of Dylan or the fact I ran so fast to get here. *He's there he's there he's there!*

It's an RV park. We're camping.

Oh yeah?

So I might not have much time. But can you come meet us?

What? R u crazy? I don't think so.

Y not?

2 far

Oh. R u sure?

Yeah

Come on, D, it wouldn't be that hard. We could take off and

Come on airel, be realistic

You misspelled my name

Oh

Again

Sorry

I don't want to be realistic, I'm sick of being realistic

u could come here and visit, maybe

how

I don't know. Anyway I wouldn't have time to hang out with you.

It just seems stupid to be this close and not see u

Yeah

But that's life I guess

Yeah

Did he always just say things like "yeah"? This is the most boring IM ever.

So see u in august

Or not. Right

Ok gtg

Bye

CU

But think about it okay?

If there's any chance at all

Do it

Escape

right

but you're not going to, are you?

probably not

ok

great

fantasterrific

what?

I walk out of the office and the screen door slams shut behind me, bouncing against its frame. I feel vaguely crushed. I'd been putting so much into this idea.

Andre is standing there, leaning against a tree. I can't believe he's waiting for me. "So was he there?"

It takes me a second, but I finally nod. "Yeah. He actually was."

"What did he say?"

"Um . . . not much."

"You guys going to meet up? Reconnoiter? Rendezvous?" Andre asks.

I shake my head. "I don't think so." I feel like really crying, only that's silly because nothing bad happened. But nothing good happened, either, and right now that's reason enough.

"No? No. So . . . California, then?" he asks.

There's a rumble of thunder above us, and dogs in the campsites begin to howl, or maybe they're wolves. "I'm not going to take that as a sign," says Andre, with a dejected look at the sky, which has finally darkened, and I see lightning flashing across it.

"I should probably go to my tent. Who are you sleeping with?" I ask.

"Excuse me, that's personal," he says.

I punch him lightly on the arm. "I meant, sharing a tent with. Or whatever."

"Dieter and Wolfgang. But I'm not sure if I know the password because it's German, so they might not let me in."

"You're kidding, right?"

There's another, louder rumble of thunder, and I wave good-bye and take off for our tent. I'm bunking with Mom, Zena, and Grandma in a four-person tent, which barely gives us enough room. It starts to rain, and within seconds it's raining harder, then harder still, drops attacking the tent from all sides, pinging and rolling onto the nylon fabric.

Andre's mom calls through our tent door, and before we can answer she unzips the door and starts to climb in. "Room for one more?" she asks. "I don't feel safe over there by myself. I thought I wanted privacy, but this camping is for the birds. Can you believe they bring us out here without decent shelter?"

She comes in and settles herself in the middle of us like we've known one another for years. She's wearing silk PJs, and Cuddles is in her arms, as usual. He looks terrified.

"So," Mrs. O'Neill says as she scoots down in her sleeping bag and covers Cuddles to calm him. "Here we are. It's not exactly what I planned."

"Me neither," I say, and so do Zena and Grandma. The only person not surprised seems to be Mom.

We listen to the pouring rain and talk about our favorite and not-so-favorite things on the trip so far. While everyone talks, I lie there and think about my disappointing Gchat with Dylan. I have to wonder: Do I really like him, or do I just like the idea of him? Did he just save me from yet another horrible school party where I was feeling left out? Maybe I only like him so much because I had a crush on him for so long that it became part of my genetic sequence.

Andre is more my type. But what's the point of getting involved with him? We don't even live close by *now*, never mind in the future.

After a while, as I'm mulling all this over, Grandma asks softly, but loudly enough to be heard over the downpour, "Can anyone else sleep in this racket? Because I can't."

"I'm awake," I whisper, waving to her in case she can't hear me, but then I realize she can't see me, either.

"Do you want to play backgammon?" she asks.

"Sure." I scoot over to sit on her sleeping bag and hang a flashlight from the roof while she gets out the game. She looks good even at midnight in a tent, with a stylish scarf over her short hair, and pink-and-red polka-dot flannel pajamas.

Everyone else is fast asleep. Mom is snoring, Zena is laughing in her sleep, and Andre's mom looks peaceful and serene, even though she's never camped or slept on hard ground before.

"Double or nothing?" Grandma asks after I lose the first game.

"Why not?" I say. I'm up for taking chances these days.

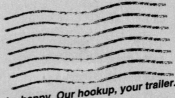

Sleep happy, stay happy, be happy. Our hookup, your trailer.

Happyland RV Park: "One Hookup for Life."

Gloves,

Tried sleeping with that infernal dog last night. Nowhere near as good as a cat. Didn't keep me as warm, plus slept on my head, plus does this annoying twitching thing in his sleep, like he's dreaming of chasing rabbits, which is silly because this dog is about ten times smaller than a rabbit.

How is your summer going? Have you caught many flies yet?

Wish you were here to share my pillow instead.

Your BFF,

Ariel

Chapter Seventeen

The next morning everything is wet, and we eat a breakfast of burned toast and leftover marshmallows and damp graham crackers. Or at least some people do. I opt for bottled water and an energy bar. Tents are hanging from trees to dry in the morning breeze. Sleeping bags are draped over bushes.

While we eat, we watch a tow truck hitching up the bus, which makes an awful groaning sound that must wake up every living thing in or near Happyland. Our luggage and all the stuff we had on the bus is sitting on the ground at our camp area.

Lenny comes by to pour "cowboy coffee," which tastes like burned cough syrup, and informs us that we'll all be going on a burro ride after breakfast. "We're going to be here a day or two, people. The bus can't be fixed, so we'll be getting a new one."

"And where's Jenny?" someone asks.

"Ah, yes, Jenny. She decided to take some R and R in Deadwood. Not to worry, we'll meet up with her later." Lenny tells us he's convinced a fellow Happyland camper to take him to town in his van so he can stock up on food and drink supplies. "It's all about going with the flow, people. Learning to adapt." He sounds extremely calm about our predicament.

Is it sick that I'm glad there's no bus, because then Mom can't tell me who to sit with?

"Lenny? I'll go to town with you," says Andre's mom. "I'll help buy the groceries."

"Lorraine, how sweet of you to help. Thank you, I'll take you up on that." Lenny bows to her.

"Help nothing, I need a day in civilization," she says as she goes to get her things ready.

"We could come help too," Andre offers. "Right, Ariel?" He nudges me, his elbow crashing against my ribs.

My mother chokes on her cowboy coffee. "I don't think that's a very good idea."

"Why not?"

"Well, uh—"

"We'll need the space for groceries. Sorry, kids, but thanks." Lenny surveys the crowd. "Now, who's going to volunteer for cleanup crew?"

My mother looks over at me and smiles, like she's achieved something.

"What did you think—we were going to run away?" Andre smiles and pinches my leg under the table.

"How fast do these things go, anyway?" my grandmother asks as she climbs onto her burro. He keeps sucking his teeth, like he just ate peanut butter, which makes him look a bit surly. He spits at the ground, then sucks his teeth again.

"Ma'am, have you ever been on a burro?" Mandy, one of the guides, asks her.

"I think I rode one about ten years ago in the Grand Canyon. At least my butt remembers," she says, and Zena, Mom, and I all laugh.

"Don't you have any jeans, or some thicker pants?" Mandy asks, surveying Grandma's pink *velour du jour* tracksuit.

"Sorry. This is how she rides," jokes Zena.

Grandma goes sort of cantering off, her surly burro slightly out of control. "What do I do?" she turns around to ask. "What do I do?"

"Hold on, woman; I'll be right there!" Grandpa calls, urging his burro to catch up to her.

"I usually travel by bike," Uncle Jeff tells Mandy as she helps him get onto one of the horses on the lot.

"Really?" Mandy asks politely.

"Harley," he says, puffing out his chest a little. He's trying to impress her, so he doesn't tell her that this was at least ten years ago. "Now, what's the difference between a burro and a burr-ee-toe?" he asks as he sets off, following Grandma and Grandpa across the field toward a trail.

"Should a person drink cowboy coffee and then go on a long ride?" an older woman riding behind me asks.

"How do you drive this thing?" her husband jokes.

"Where are my spurs?" Ethel adds. "Are spurs extra?"

After about twenty minutes, everyone who hadn't already left before me and Andre starts to pass us. We have the slow burros, the ones who've been ground down by the boredom, like us.

"Hey, guys!" Wolfgang says as he ambles by on the right.

"*Wiedersehen!*" Dieter calls over his shoulder as his horse goes galloping past on the left.

"How did he rate a horse?" I ask.

"He's tall? Or maybe he threatened to sing 'SexyBack' again," Andre says. *"Fee I pee . . ."*

"Don't," I say, laughing.

We let everyone pass us, because this isn't a race. We have all day to kill, even if the burros are only a three-hour rental. Andre suggests we take a detour. I point out that we'll lose the group if we do that.

"No, we won't," he says. "These animals are slow."

"Right. Especially *ours*. So how will we catch up?"

"We'll leave a trail of Skittles to find our way back."

"That's dumb," I say.

"But it'll work. Come on, try it."

I reach into my little backpack. But my burro leans to the opposite side and I wobble, and the Skittles bag slips from my hand. "Oh, shoot. I dropped the bag." I tell my burro to stop, which is easy for him because he didn't like moving much anyway. I get off carefully, holding the reins.

Andre stops beside me, but just sits up on his burro, watching me.

"Aren't you going to come down?" I ask.

"Sure. Of course. Definitely," he says. But he eyes the ground and then eyes the burro's neck, and looks around at its legs, its hooves. "How do you, uh, get off these things?"

"Just swing your leg over," I say.

"But what if he panics and throws me to the ground?"

"He's not Seabiscuit. He's a burro. Or she. Whatever," I say. "They're tame." I go and stand by his burro, and sort of put my hand on its flank to keep it from moving.

Andre slides off, into my arms, and we totally crash to the ground. Me cushioning his fall. In other words me, on the ground underneath Andre. Burros above us. Not running away. Not even caring.

Here's their moment of freedom and they don't budge.

I look away from them and up at Andre. He's not budging, either. *He's lying on top of me.*

"Here. I think you dropped this," he says, and he picks up a grape Skittle from the assortment on the ground and tries to put it into my mouth.

"That was on the ground. Ew." I look at him. This camping thing is making me desperate in more ways than one. That was my last bag of candy. My pulse is pounding in my ears, because Andre is *lying on top of me.* I can't breathe so well. It seems like everything that's happened between us so far is nothing compared to this.

"Are you going to eat it or not?" He pushes it against my lips.

"Quit it," I say, but it comes out sounding like "Mm-mm." I shake my head, and he pops the candy into his mouth, then kisses me, so I can taste the grape, too.

We start to make out right there, which is totally stupid and crazy and at the same time fun and exciting, and I'm melting as fast as that grape Skittle that is no more.

We stop for a second, and I look him in the eye. "This isn't cool. You don't want a girlfriend."

"No?"

"No, you don't. You said that. Really rudely, actually."

"Right." He kisses me again. "And then there's the matter of Dylan, who you're dying to see—"

I kiss him. "Right. I was. Which makes this—"

"Wrong." He kisses me. "Taboo." Kiss. "Not on the list of scheduled stops." Kiss.

"Actually they're . . ." Kiss. "Unscheduled . . ." I say. Kiss. "Stops."

Somewhere above me I hear a throat being cleared. Again. Louder. Still louder.

Then it's a cough and a hack, like someone choked on a piece of hard candy.

We unlock lips and I look up, and the sun nearly blinds me because of course my sunglasses fell off when I crashed to the ground.

"I think you two may have lost the trail," says Uncle Jeff, towering over us, looking sort of like a large knight on his steed.

He's holding a walking stick that could be taken as a sword, if you were far away and had poor eyesight. His floppy hat with a hundred laminated stamp buttons and pins on it is glinting in the bright sun and could be seen as a helmet.

It could also be seen as clashing with his three gold necklaces.

"Uh, oops!" I say, kind of too loudly.

We both stand up, brushing needles and dirt and bark from our clothes.

"You should have seen these crazy burros," Andre says.

"Oh yeah. They went totally wild," I add. "Threw us off."

Uncle Jeff looks at the burros, who are eating the dropped Skittles off the ground. More than tame, they're resigned.

"Why don't you try to handle them, and get back on?" Uncle Jeff suggests. He's not smiling.

Andre steps on a large rock to get onto his burro, while I climb up, dragging myself onto the poor animal. Once I'm back on I adjust my watch, which has gotten all twisted around.

"Let's go. I'll bring up the rear," Uncle Jeff says, and I try not to laugh, but then Andre snickers and I lose it.

We ride along the trail, Andre first, then me, then Uncle Jeff. When we catch up to the group on a scenic overlook, Zena ambles over to me. "Forget what I said, A."

"Which time?" I ask.

"About him being weird. He's not," Zena says, admiring Andre from behind. "He's totally cute."

I know, I think. "Great. Glad you think so. But we're just friends."

"Really? So I could ask him out?"

"No, Z, because you're twelve."

"Shut up," she says.

"You're twelve, as in twelvery young."

"And you're sixteen, as in sixtremelyannoyingteen."

"Well, so is he," I tell her. "He's going to be a senior, and no way are you asking out a high school senior."

"I've done it before," she says with a shrug. "It's no big deal."

"Where was this?" I ask.

"Wall Drug. Didn't you *see* us with those guys?"

"No." I lower my sunglasses and stare at her. "You almost picked up a guy at Wall Drug?"

She shrugs.

"That's dangerous, okay? Don't do that," I say. "Really, Z. Don't."

"But it's okay for you to make out with Andre," she says.

"Make out? I've . . . I've never—"

"No, but you thought about it," she says.

Of course, I *have* done it, and I've thought about it ever since. "You're twelvexing. You know that?"

"Oh yeah? Well, you're sixteeny-tiny."

I laugh. "I'm what?"

"I'll keep it realsimple from now on, so you won't get confused. But if you guys do make out, *tell* me." She nudges her burro with her heels and takes off to catch up with Bethany.

"Right. Like I would!" I call after her.

Actually, I wish I could tell somebody. But that's not exactly the kind of thing you put on a postcard—and definitely not to your cat back home.

When Lenny and Mrs. O'Neill get back with the groceries, there's a minor emergency—or actually, a big emergency about a small thing. Mrs. O'Neill thought Andre had Cuddles, while Andre thought *she* had Cuddles.

So nobody actually had Cuddles. And Cuddles probably thought . . . everyone had deserted him in the wilderness.

Everyone in the group splits up to look for him, even the ones who never wanted him along on the trip. We spend all afternoon calling his name, hunting for him.

When he hasn't been found by nightfall, Andre is pacing by the campfire. I'm trying to keep him company, but Andre is so stressed that he can't quite listen to me without getting upset.

Mrs. O'Neill is inside our tent, praying, with Mom and Grandma sitting by her side, consoling her in between random calls of "Cuddles! Come back, sweetheart!"

I tell Andre that his jeans are slipping down—he wears them low but these are too low, and his underwear is showing more than usual. I go over and try to playfully adjust them, and he bats my hand away.

"I'm dealing with a lot of stuff right now. My butt is the least of my problems."

"Okay, but I just thought—"

"What? In the missing-dog posters, my underwear might be showing?" he asks. "This is another thing my mom's going to hold against me. Just watch. I mean, someone stole him, obviously. And it's my fault because I was thinking about you, or maybe that makes this your fault. Instead of listening to her tell me to watch him, and— you know what?" Andre turns to me and takes a swig from a bottle of water. "The fact that he's missing. It's a sign."

"It is?" I ask.

"Yes. It's a sign that we're supposed to run off tonight too. We're supposed to follow his lead."

"Right," I say.

"What?"

I don't know what makes me say the next thing, probably stress, but it comes out meaner than I intend. "Andre, did you notice that you constantly talk about running away, but only Cuddles has the guts to do it?" It's supposed to be a joke, but it's one of those jokes that has too much truth in it.

Andre looks at me like he wishes there were two buses, one to put me on and one to put him on. Like he'd rather be anywhere else in the world.

"You know what? You were right," he says. "What you said earlier today. I don't want a girlfriend, and I don't want to like you."

"I don't want to like you either," I say. "You just happen to be here."

"Oh, really? I just 'happen' to be here. Well, no kidding. This wasn't my plan. And what, you'd rather be spending time with the infamous Dylan, who by the way left you for the entire summer, or haven't you noticed?"

Tears sting my eyes just as Uncle Jeff's voice pierces the darkness. "Found him!"

Everyone runs toward Uncle Jeff as he emerges from the woods, saying, "Got him! Call off the dogs! Sorry, didn't mean that." He nuzzles Cuddles's chin with his finger. "You're so little I could carry you in my postal satchel and nobody would be the wiser. Together we'd show those flying rodents a thing or two."

He hands Cuddles to Mrs. O'Neill, who starts weeping with happiness. It's embarrassing.

"I told you, Ma. I told you we'd find him," says Andre.

"Wh-where was he?" she asks.

"Found him over at that campsite, dragging a Pop-Tarts wrapper around, trying to dig a hole," Uncle Jeff says. "I thought it was a squirrel at first. So naturally I kept my distance." His face turns sort of red. "Anyway. Just glad I could help."

Mrs. O'Neill hugs Cuddles and offers him liver treats. "Who's my favorite boy?" she keeps saying. Then she looks up at Andre. "I can't believe you let this happen."

"Ma! It wasn't . . . he's not . . . You know what? Forget it," Andre says. "You should have bought Cuddles a seat on this trip—not me." He stalks off down the small road that winds through the campground. He's gone. I'm out of Skittles, and he's gone.

Why did I have to say that to him? Like he wasn't having a bad enough night already?

I feel horrible, so I decide to get ready for bed and try to forget this entire night. I grab my cosmetic bag from the tent and go over to the water pump to brush my teeth.

My mother comes over while I'm midrinse. I don't know where she comes from, but it's like an owl swooping out of a tree. "Ariel, we have to talk," she says. "And I'd prefer that we get it over with tonight."

I shake out my toothbrush and rinse my face with the cold water a few times, drying it on the bottom of my sweatshirt. "That sounds ominous." What else can go wrong tonight?

"It's not. But . . . look, Ariel. What I've been trying to say for the past few days . . . We are *going* to move," she says. "For sure. I'm sorry. I didn't know how to tell you. I've been trying and trying, but you don't want to listen to me."

"No," I say, twisting my bag in my hands, then shoving it underneath one arm and preparing to walk off. "We can't. I can't."

"We have to," she says.

"You want to leave Dad, fine. You did that already," I say.

"I want to leave that whole chapter of our lives behind," she says. "I don't want to see people pitying me, or us. I don't want to bump into them at the grocery store."

"So we'll leave our neighborhood a little," I suggest. "We'll move a few miles away, find a new store."

"I'm talking about leaving the state, Ariel. We need distance. My professional reputation is suffering. You can understand that."

"But, Mom, I'm not going to leave Sarah and all of my friends. And I've worked so hard to be part of the team. I've got people who totally believe in me," I say.

She shrugs. "You'll stay in touch with Sarah. And as far as running, if you're good there, you'll be even better somewhere else."

She doesn't understand. She's never understood. "What about Grandma and Grandpa Flack?"

"Yes, you'd miss them. So would I. But what about *my* parents? We've never lived close to them. We were going up there for two weeks, anyway, right? You'll help pick out the neighborhood, the house. We'll make sure it has everything you want. We'll get a location with a good school, great running team—there are coaches who would die to have you on their team."

"But I already have a coach," I say. "And where we're going . . . Dad won't be there. At all."

Mom shakes her head. "No. I can't see that he will be."

As uncomfortable as things are between us sometimes, do I really only want to see him on major holidays? "Are your parents behind all this?" I ask. I've loved spending this time with Grandma and Grandpa, but it's starting to feel like a conspiracy.

"Who do you think has been helping us out? Do you think I

just walked out into the backyard and found money growing on the trees? It's my parents. I need them right now—you need them, too. I mean, sure, I have a career and we'll build on that, but I can't do it on my own," Mom says.

"Well, I'm not moving," I say.

"Yes. You are," she replies. "We are."

"Jujyfruit?" Uncle Jeff offers, shaking the box as he walks up to us at the pump, completely clueless to the fact that Mom and I have just had this major blowout.

"No!" I say. Then I change my mind and take the entire box out of his hand.

As I do, there's a *putt-putt* sound getting closer and closer to our group site. Giant headlights turn into our parking area, and gradually I can make out that it's the old red-and-white Leisure-Lee bus pulling up.

Everyone climbs out of their tents, in pajamas, wearing curlers, or missing dentures.

We all stand in suspense as the door opens with a long, slow hiss.

"Welcome aboard!" Lee says, tipping his cowboy hat to us.

Buffalo of South Dakota

The bison is the biggest land animal in the U.S. Buffalo roam free by the hundreds in Custer State Park. Warning: Do not approach. Appreciate from a distance.

Dylan,

We're staying at Custer State Park, or as my uncle calls it, Custard State Park. Like it's Culver's and he's going to order a turtle sundae.

There is lots of wildlife—no turtles though.

I stop writing. This is pathetic. I've sent him a dozen postcards and none of them has been any good or said anything important.

He doesn't care, and the last thing he wrote that was interesting was probably my email address. He doesn't spell my name right. Ever.

I could even forgive that, because it's not a common name.

Only now that I've met Andre, I realize Dylan and I don't really have much. He's never asked about my dad. He's mostly only talked about himself.

Still, I can't bring myself to tell him that we're moving. He'll forget about me even more, and we're not even gone yet, but by the time he gets home from camp we probably will be. That good-bye grope, on the green-and-yellow Packers beanbag chair, that was it for us.

Life never gives you enough advance warning. On anything.

Chapter Eighteen

The next morning, Lee insists on driving, and it's frightening.

Not because he's older and slower. It's the opposite. He's done the route so many times that he bombs down the road without using the brakes. He takes the curves too quickly. Lenny drops his microphone twice before he gets a chance to say anything. He's flopping around the bus aisle like a passenger on a turbulent flight.

"This is known as the Pins and Needles Highway," Lenny says.

"No, it isn't. This is Iron Mountain Road," Lee corrects him, glancing over his shoulder as he takes a tight turn.

"Yes. Ahem." Lenny coughs. "Right, you're right, Lee, of course. Well, maybe I misspoke because I'm on pins and needles here," he says, "waiting for the exciting views of Mount Rushmore."

"Lenny, be quiet and let them enjoy the scenery for a change," Lee says.

Lenny falls into a seat and isn't heard from again.

The views through little stone arches over the road are truly incredible. It actually is breathtaking, the way Lenny said it would be. It's Mount Rushmore the way I've always seen it in photos, but in miniature. But to be fair, we are rushing it, or Lee is, anyway. I think the speed limit may have changed since the last time he drove this route. I expect him to send cars hurtling off the road in our wake.

There are oohs and aahs.

"This is just fantasterrific." Uncle Jeff sighs beside me. I kind of want to agree, except I still hate that made-up word. I glance up ahead to see where Andre's sitting, to see how many words he has for this view. He's staring straight ahead and frowning, as if he has something else on his mind. There's so much tension on the bus right now—between him and me, between him and his mom, and between me and my mom—that it could probably power the other bus's busted engine all on its own.

We get closer and closer. Finally we drive up a long and winding hill, past lots of cars and traffic, which takes forever because we didn't get an early start. And then we're there. The parking lot at Mount Rushmore. The granite faces loom above us and can't quite be believed.

"You have to experience it before you hit the gift shop," Andre says as we walk up onto the memorial's avenue of flags and I start to automatically peel off to the left when I see the gift shop.

We never made up, officially, after last night, but we're talking again. I have no idea how things stand between us. I love the fact that my last bag of Skittles was sacrificed to the ground, because of what it made us do. But when I think about it and him, I don't know how I'm supposed to feel now. Guilty? Happy? Like that was then, and this is now?

"No, I have to hit the gift shop and get postcards," I tell him. "Then I can write them while I sit outside and look at the faces."

He shakes his head. "Obsessed."

"Yeah, well. It'll only take me a second. You can wait out here and think of two more ways to insult me," I say.

"Hurry. It won't take me long," he promises.

I walk into the giant shop, overwhelmed by the choices. There isn't just one postcard rack; there are several. I don't know where to begin, so I go clockwise. Except that it's sort of an angular place.

I'm looking at the big cards first, comparing buffalo and state shapes and Rushmore trivia, when I hear someone say, "Ariel?"

That voice.

I nearly fall over.

It's my dad.

"Ha! I knew I'd see you first. Got here early just in case." He steps around the postcard rack and gives me a big hug. He's wearing an old tee and his faded Levi's and he looks thin and really relaxed, the way he always did on our road trips when he didn't have to shave and wear a tie every day and all that work stuff.

But he doesn't look exactly the same as the last time I saw him. He looks scruffier.

"So," he says. "How's things?"

How's things? Is that all he's going to say? What is he doing here? I shrug. "Okay, if you like bus tours."

"And things of that nature?" he says, and I know I'm supposed to laugh like I usually do because he's making fun of Uncle Jeff, but I can't make myself.

I start to feel nervous. I want to know why he's here, but I'm afraid to ask. "You want to go outside? You want to, um, explain why you're here?"

"What's to explain? We always wanted to see Rushmore, didn't we?" Dad puts his arm around my shoulder as we leave the store. I feel myself pulling him to the edge, not of the cliff but of the avenue of flags, because I'm hoping to shield him from Mom, and vice versa.

"So here we are," he says. "Is it like you pictured?"

"Not exactly," I say. See, in my vision, we all came here together, in a car. And my parents weren't divorced and my dad wasn't a pseudo-criminal who got off for lack of state's evidence.

"No?"

"No. It's, um, bigger." I look over at him. "How did you know we'd be here today? This morning?"

"I've actually been here since yesterday, trying to meet up with you guys. Where's your sister?"

"Oh, she's around, definitely. I wonder where," I say, scanning the dozens of people milling around, admiring the sculpted presidents' faces.

Andre somehow manages to find us in the crowd, and I'm thrilled, overjoyed, grateful to see him. "Funny. I don't see anyone I can relate to up there," he says, pointing up at Mount Rushmore. "Where's Martin Luther King?"

"I think they carved this in the forties," I point out.

"Figures. So, there's not *more* mountain up there to carve? There's room," he says, looking back at the monument. "If they can make Crazy Horse, then they can make Dr. King."

I smile at him, so glad he's here to defuse this really weird situation, even if he does it by creating one of his own. "Dad, this is my friend Andre."

"Hey, how's it going? Andre, like Agassi?"

Andre looks at me and we both roll our eyes. "Yes, that's it exactly, Dad."

Andre walks closer to the monument itself, and we follow him.

"You've been hanging out with Ariel, then you must be cool."

"Pretty much," Andre says.

"So is there anyone up there you *can* relate to?" I ask. "And let me tell you. There aren't any women up there, either, okay?"

"Maybe I can relate to Lincoln. But he was weird, right? He had psychological problems," Andre comments.

"No wonder you relate to him," I say.

"Oh! Oh! Prepare to be rushed at Rushmore." He wraps his arms around my waist and lifts me up to carry me and toss me over the edge while my dad looks at us, seeming a little left out. It's only going to get worse, I realize as Andre sets me down, because I see my mom headed in our direction.

"Richard," she says to him. "What on earth are you doing here?" She doesn't yell or curse, and I kind of admire her for that. I glance at her hand to see if she's wearing her ring that was rescued from under the bus, and she isn't, even after all that rescue effort. Which says something. And also makes her hand look smaller and kind of strangely naked.

"Hey, there! Sorry I couldn't let you know; you guys don't have any way of being contacted, so . . . anyway. Family summer road trip." He shrugs and shoves his hands into his pockets, kind of like a little kid would do. "Seemed like a good tradition we should keep up."

Mom doesn't look like she agrees with any part of what he's just said.

"Um . . . this might seem like an obvious question, but how did you know we'd be here today? At right this second?" Mom asks.

He shrugs. "I took a chance."

Mom looks like there can't possibly be enough miles between them. "I bet you did," she says.

Dad laughs. "No, actually I called the bus company. You told me what it was called in your postcards," he says to me.

"P-p-postcards?" Mom sputters. "Really."

I imagine the look on my grandfather's face when he sees Dad, and how he'll probably chase him all the way out of the state, how he and Uncle Jeff will devise a plot to trip up Dad, how my grandmother might put down a slick layer of nail polish and hair spray for him to wipe out on. They'll team up against him.

Where *are* they, anyway? I need help here. I try to signal to Andre, to say something like, "Save me!" with one look.

He appears frightened by my expression, but he gets it. "Mrs., um, Timmons. My mom wants to treat you to lunch," Andre says, and he somehow manages to drag my mother away, her fists clenched under her Custer State Park sweatshirt sleeves.

"Timmons?" my dad mutters, and I decide not to get into that conversation, not yet.

Dad starts goofing around, posing in front of the presidents' faces, as if I'm supposed to take pictures of him and we can laugh about them later. I wish I could laugh now, because this is really bizarre, but I just spent miles and miles getting away from him and the problems he created for us back home. And getting away wasn't a bad thing. As much as I love him, it was not a bad thing.

"Am I more a Lincoln or a Roosevelt?" he asks.

Not that I'm a presidential expert, but he's so unlike any of them. His pose reminds me more of a mug shot than anything else. There are these giant majestic faces of these great men, and then my dad.

So then I do take his picture, to make sure I'll remember. He looks a little disheveled, like perhaps he used his last dollar to get here, and slept in the car, or something like that. He has little cuts on his face, as if he shaved with an old razor at a rest stop. I wouldn't recognize this kind of stuff except I've seen some things in the past week, camping and roughing it and stopping at questionable rest areas, that I wouldn't have known about before.

"Well?" he prompts as all these things go through my head, and the wind won't stop blowing super hard, whipping my hair into my face, blowing the flags around us so it's almost hard to hear each other.

"You're more a Nixon," I say, and I only know this from one of Lenny's dumb games to pass the time while the bus was broken down, called Name the President.

"Ha-ha," Dad says.

"So, Dad. How did you get here, really, and why are you here?"

He looks taken aback, as if this is an absurd question, as if his being at Mount Rushmore isn't the thing that's absurd.

"Well, you have to admit it's a little strange. I mean, we'll be home in a few weeks," I tell him. "You could have talked to us then."

He shakes his head. "Not back there. Everything's . . . cloudy back there. I need to be on the road to sort things out. On the toad, rather."

He waits for me to laugh, but I don't. "And . . ." I prompt.

"You know how it is; you know how I'm always happier when I'm on an adventure."

I don't comment, because what I used to think of as his "adventures" maybe aren't so fun anymore.

"But, Dad," I say, thinking how strange it is that both he and Mom want to get away in order to make things work, but work in different ways. "What did you want to sort out?"

"Isn't it obvious?" He gazes up at the sun above, takes a deep breath. "I'm here to talk with your mother and see if I can work things out with her."

"Dad, you can't."

"What?"

"Talk with her," I tell him. "Or work things out."

"Why not?"

"It's too late."

"How can it be too late? We were together seventeen years, Ariel. That's not something you just toss away."

"Isn't it?" I say back. "I mean, isn't that what you did?"

Zena suddenly runs up and throws her arms around him, and I wish I could still do that, but I can't. Because I'm not twelve anymore. And not being twelve means knowing things that aren't necessarily things you want to know, that your dad's losing it a little bit, maybe more so now than he was before. That instead of pulling it together like you wish, he's headed in the other direction.

"But you don't have a car. So how did you get here?" asks Zena, curious in the same kind of way that I am.

"They have bus tours for everything, from everywhere. I got a cheap one to Deadwood, and then—"

"Of course you did," I say. "The gambling express, right?"

Dad looks shocked.

"We were there, Dad. Didn't see you at the casino, but then, there are lots to choose from."

"Ariel, I didn't go there to gamble," he says. "I couldn't get a decent flight to Rapid City, so Lee told me to fly to Scottsbluff and get a shuttle."

"Lee?" I ask.

"I called him. He also thought there could be an empty seat on the bus; maybe I could take it."

"No. There aren't any extra seats," I say quickly, because isn't this trip hard enough without adding Dad to the mix?

"Isn't there one?" says Zena. "The new bus has a few more rows of seats. We could bring it to a bus vote or something."

"That's what we do," I explain. "We have these bus votes. Really dumb, but, you know. Fair. Democratic. Majority rule and all."

"But hey, if there's no room on the bus, I want you all to come with me," says Dad earnestly. He puts his arm around me and squeezes.

That's when I smell it. That lemon-lime casino scent. The towelette. I smell it, and I want to punch him in the stomach.

I could ask, and he could tell me that it's restroom soap, but I know it isn't.

I could ask, and he could tell me it was something he got from a restaurant, the kind they give you after you eat a rack of ribs.

But that's not it.

I know where it's from.

And if I asked if it was from a casino, he'd have some story at the ready, about how he ran in just to use the phone.

The fact that he's still gambling doesn't make him an awful person. It just makes him . . . not reliable.

I need reliable.

"We'll rent a car, we'll get off the beaten path, we'll just see what happens, where we want to go," he's saying.

But we can't do that anymore—or maybe he still can, but I can't. If he's going to come all this way to find us, but still be hitting casinos, then I don't know what to say to him—at all.

No comment?

Mount Rushmore: You haven't seen America until you've seen it. Open 365 days a year. Your camera is waiting.

Sarah,

Everything is so screwed up right now.
Dad's here, at Mount Rushmore. And we're moving.

Not on the bus, mind you.
We're moving moving.
This sucks.
This postcard sucks.
Miss you.
Love,
AF

Before I mail it, I look at it again, and then I rip the postcard up and throw it out. One of the pieces misses the national monument trash can. I don't care. I watch it get blown away by the blustery wind, bouncing down the avenue of flags. The next thing you know it'll be sucked into the air and wind, and bounce off Roosevelt's glasses or Lincoln's nose.

Let someone else find it for once. Found objects are overrated, but let them discover that.

You know that expression, being at your wit's end?

I'm apparently there.

Chapter Nineteen

There's no bus vote to decide whether Dad can join us, but Mom brings it to a family vote. We've gotten a hall pass for the night, and we're at a "family restaurant." As a family. One big, weird, dysfunctional family. They should clear the restaurant when they see us coming.

Except Dad isn't with us. Mom asked him to "respect our space" and give us time to talk this over. I don't want to talk it over. I don't know what we should do.

"You should carb up for the race tomorrow," my grandmother says when she sees me picking at my side salad. "Have some of these rolls." She passes a basket to me and won't set it down until I take one and butter it.

My grandfather is having spaghetti with extra bread sticks, and my uncle, king of the strip steak, is eating a salad. "A salad?" I ask, pointing to it.

"Don't want to be bogged down." He pats his belly.

"Right," I say. "Good plan."

"So, Zena, Ariel. What do you think?" Mom asks after we've all had a few bites of dinner. Like she *wants* us to get indigestion.

"That my cheeseburger needs more ketchup," says Zena.

"That I don't actually like honey-mustard dressing after all," I say.

"Try ketchup," Zena offers.

"On a salad?"

Mom clears her throat after polishing off a hot fudge sundae and before digging into her main meal, fettuccine Alfredo. The blood in her arteries must be slower moving than the traffic on the road up to Mount Rushmore. "I meant, about your father."

"Oh," I say.

"Sure," says Zena.

"I will listen to you guys," Mom says. "If you tell me you want to go with him, then we will, or you will, and I'll stay here. Which will be really hard for me to do. But okay."

"I don't want to leave Bethany," Zena says.

And I *do* want to leave, I think, but not with Dad. "I, um, don't think it would be a great idea. You know how it is when you come into a theater or the living room and everyone else is in the middle of watching a movie? It'd be like that for him."

"So, is that a 'no' on inviting Dad onto the bus?" asks Mom, ready to wrap this up before we've even really discussed it.

"Yes. It's a no," I say.

"Right," Zena agrees, and I'm very relieved she agrees, but I can't help wondering why she does so quickly, when she seemed so thrilled to see him earlier.

"Well, then. How about going with him? On another trip?" Mom can barely choke the words out, I can tell. She's been twisting the same piece of fettuccine around her fork for the last three minutes.

"Does he even have a car?" Grandpa wants to know.

"Sure," says Zena.

"A *decent* car?" asks Uncle Jeff. "One that can get you from here to there?"

"He didn't drive here. That's all I know," I say. "So we'd have to rent a car."

"Rent a car." My mother coughs, that piece of fettuccine finally having gone down—the wrong way. "With his credit record, good luck."

"Mom? Not seeing any personal growth here," I comment. "You talked badly about him when we left home and you're still doing it."

She looks a bit taken aback by my comment, but she nods. "The purpose of this dinner is to give you guys a voice."

"So you're including us in *this* decision. But not in the moving one," I point out. "Zena? Listen. We're actually moving. I mean, aren't you furious? How can you just sit there?" I look over at my grandparents and uncle. "No offense, you guys. This is just . . . it's *news* to me. Brand-new news."

Zena turns to me, and her face for once looks older to me and slightly harsh, except she has a tiny drop of ketchup in the corner of her mouth that reminds me she's still Zena. "Ariel, I *can't* be furious. About anything. If I start being mad? It wouldn't stop. And it wouldn't help."

"But you're with me, right?" I ask. "You don't want to move. You'd have to leave your friends—"

"Half my friends ended up being jerks to me anyway," she says. "Do you know how many things I was suddenly not invited to this past spring?"

I think about it. "Yeah. I kind of know what you mean. But I just feel like we're running from our problems."

"Oh, really, and you don't do that? Anyway, making new friends isn't that hard. What about you and Andre?"

Uncle Jeff starts to cough. "A good guy. Andre. Good guy."

I hope they don't notice that my face is turning red, that I'm remembering him, and me, and him *on* me. I change the subject as quickly as I can. "Gloves. What about Gloves?" I ask. "She won't know where to come home to. She'll get lost, Z."

"She has that cat sense of smell. She'll figure it out," says Zena.

"She won't have her favorite window ledge anymore to lie on in the sun. That cat across the street. Oliver. They'll miss hissing at each other."

Zena just stares at me and raises her eyebrows. "I think she'll adjust, A."

Maybe she will, I think. *But what about me?* I could say that I wouldn't leave town, that I'd stay and live with Dad, only I can't. I know that. I guess I knew it before, but for some reason, now that I've seen him here, seen his road persona again, seen how he's a little nervous and unhinged, I know it even more than before.

"So. Have we voted?" Mom asks.

Grandma suddenly drops her spoon into her empty soup bowl with a clatter. Her face is bright red, like she's going to burst. I'm about to ask if she's okay when she says, "We? It's not up to us, Tamara. It's up to *them*." She points at me and Zena.

"Well, I'm sorry!" says Mom, tossing down her napkin.

"Here's what's going to happen, girls," Grandma goes on. "You'll come to visit us; you'll see what you think. Not everything has to be decided tonight, or on this trip. Give them a break! They've had enough to deal with. This is supposed to be their vacation, for goodness' sake!" She stands up, pushing her chair back, grabs her purse, and bolts for the ladies' room. Zena is right behind her.

Mom leaves, but doesn't head for the restroom—she goes straight outside. Uncle Jeff follows her.

That leaves me and Grandpa. I look awkwardly at him, but his face is stoic, even in the midst of this. Looking at him makes me think about my track coach, whether she really believes in me much or not, whether the team would care if I moved away. I think about all the offhand, rude comments from people, about how I feel like I have to prove myself over and over again. The newspaper article taped to my locker. *No comment.*

It doesn't take anything to become disliked. I mean, you can wear the wrong shirt one day and you're suddenly on the outs.

And this is so much more than that.

Whenever I see Dad now I just can't like being there, because I can't stop thinking about this stuff and how it's affecting me every day of my life. I make nice and talk to him, but the whole time I'm burning up inside.

I can't spend much time with him until he works on things long enough to get them right. I hate that I think this, because it sounds like something my mother would say, in fact, *has* said. I don't want to agree with her, on principle, because she can be awfully preachy and condescending about this stuff, but she's right.

It's not like the problem just started at Christmas. It started a long time before that, and just built until it reached a crisis point.

My grandfather looks like he wants to say something, but he can't. Maybe it's because Grandma told him to be quiet. Finally he says, "Would you mind going to check on them?"

"Sounds like a good idea." I stand up and walk to the back of the restaurant and into the restroom. Zena's blowing her nose, and Grandma is standing in front of the mirror, reapplying her eye makeup, because clearly they've both been crying.

"Maybe he is too old for you," Grandma is saying, "but are you at least learning any German?"

"My favorite word is *schlecht*," Zena replies.

"What's that?"

"Not good," Zena says as she opens the restroom door, striding out without even acknowledging me. "Crappy. Crummy."

We get back to the motel, where Dad was supposed to meet us at eight. He isn't there. We wait and wait. Finally our room phone rings.

"Dad?" I say as I answer it.

"No, Andre," he says. "You're out of Skittles, right?"

"Yes, actually," I tell him. "It's Andre," I whisper to Mom and Zena, though I wonder why I just admitted that to Mom.

"Can you meet me in the lobby?" he asks.

I look at Mom. "I don't know," I say.

"Come on, please. You've got to save me. My mom's talking about signing us up for the next Leisure-Lee trip—like, the one that starts the day after this one ends. I think it goes to Arizona. She and Lee spent a little too much time together at the cocktail lounge tonight. She just went down to the lobby to meet him and a bunch of other people for a nightcap."

"You're kidding," I say, sitting on the edge of the bed.

"No. I wish," he says. "Come on, Ariel. I know I was a jerk the other night, but you've got to come with me. It's the plan, you know? I won't make it to L.A. without you."

"You have a point," I say.

"So are you in?" he asks.

I look over at my mom, because she's making frantic signals at me and I don't understand them. "Ariel. Get off the phone! You've talked long enough. We need to keep the line clear."

"Why?" I ask her.

"Your father's probably trying to call, to explain why he's late," she says.

"Sure, Mom," I say. "I'm sure he is."

I sigh and flop back on the bed, looking up at the ceiling. Being on a real bed after camping for two nights feels so nice. Do I really want to trade it for a few questionable nights on the road?

Mom stands over me, holding out her hand for the phone. "Andre, I have to get going," I say. "But I'll see you for that early run we talked about."

"Early run?" he asks.

"Before the marathon—you know, the warm-up jog you're going on with me and the rest of the group. Meet me outside at six."

"Six?" He sounds as if he is nearly choking.

"Good night!" I say cheerfully.

"I didn't know Andre was a runner," my mom comments as I hand her the phone.

"Oh. Well, he is." I nod.

Black Hills Buffalo Barbecue & Co.
We kill it, you grill it.
Buses welcome.

Mom,

Don't worry about me. Andre and I will be together and I've got some money and we can take care of ourselves. I'll be safe. I'll be realsafe.

But I'm leaving because I just can't stand everything.

I don't want to stay where we are, and I don't want to move.

When I figure it out, I'll be back.

Love,

Ariel

Chapter Twenty

In the morning I get dressed to go running. I'll play it cool to my mom if she rolls over and wakes up, tell her I'm going out for a jog like every other morning. But of course she doesn't wake up, because she's not that kind of sleeper. She's the kind who needs three alarms just to get her attention.

I went down earlier this morning to stash my backpack in a bush on the edge of the parking lot, across from the lobby. I'm like that soccer-playing girl in *Bend It Like Beckham*. I've also left a note for Andre under his room door about where to meet me, for real.

I leave the postcard on the motel bathroom sink, but then I read it again and decide, no, I'm not leaving it. I'll figure out another way to get in touch. I throw it out, but then picture Mom searching the room and finding that, and it's not very good and doesn't really tell her anything. So I stuff the postcard under the waistband of my running shorts. As I do, the hundred-dollar bill from my dad falls out of my little key pocket. It seems like bad luck, so instead of putting it back in, I leave it as a bookmark in Zena's *Us* magazine.

Once outside, I crouch down to get my backpack from under the bush. When I stand up and glance back at the motel, I see my uncle peering out through the lobby window. Why do I have to see my uncle watching me leave? He's up early for the breakfast buffet, reading the newspaper, and I wave, and he looks at me like he's onto me. But I can outrun him, so it's okay.

He gives me a little wave and I hide the bag on my other shoulder, then start running.

I run under a banner that says KEYSTONE KEY TO THE BLACK HILLS MARATHON. A car goes by and some older guys leer out the window.

I run to the gas station where I told Andre to meet me—I'd scoped it out when my grandpa and I went running before dinner.

I think about that first day of our trip when I rushed into the gas station convenience store after Zena, and how that guy with the twirled mustache wanted to talk to her. Now here I am. Totally twelvulnerable, like her.

Tip: Never run away when you're wearing short shorts.

I pace around the parking lot nervously, feeling kind of stupid, but also determined.

Andre shows up to meet me, panting and out of breath. "I think Lee saw me," he says, and we both start laughing. "This should be a good place to catch a ride. Any prospects yet?"

"No. Did you make a sign?" I ask.

"A sign?" His forehead creases in confusion.

"You know, a sign. Like, 'L.A. or Bust,'" I explain. "Or whatever. We're hitching, right?"

"Yes, but subtly, so we don't get caught," Andre says. "Are you new at this?"

"Like you're not," I tell him. "You brought a big enough bag."

"I'm not planning to come back for a while," he says. "Hey, check it out. Here comes our ride."

A dated-looking avocado-colored RV with Ohio license plates pulls into the gas station. The RV is about as long as a football field and takes up two pump islands.

"Well, at least there would be room for your bag in there," I tease him.

"Shut up. Come on, let's ask them for a ride," Andre says.

"We'll have to see who's driving first," I say. "Check them out before they check *us* out."

"You think anyone dangerous gets around in *that* thing?" Andre asks.

We watch as a family with parents, a couple sets of grandparents, and six kids piles out of the RV.

"Told you," Andre says. "Come on, that's our ticket."

"We're here, kids! We did it!" The dad starts to high-five all the assorted kids as they all run around the RV, like some bizarre exercise/travel routine.

"Reginald. We're not *all* the way there," one of the grandparents says.

"Mother, please. This is as close as it gets without being able to actually touch Mount Rushmore. You said you needed to stretch your legs, so do it. I'll top off the tank."

"So we're actually doing this?" Andre asks as we walk over to the RV. Since the vehicle is so huge, it's not a long walk. "Ditching. Bolting. Abandoning ship."

I laugh. "I should have known not to worry. Your vocabulary can get us out of any dangerous situations."

Andre narrows his eyes. "What dangerous situations?"

"I don't know. Two teenagers with luggage. Doesn't exactly look, um . . ."

"Copacetic."

"Right."

"Or logical," says Andre. "But let's see if they'll give us a ride." We walk over and introduce ourselves, mention that we're headed back home to California, that our car broke down and we have no way to get there.

"Really," the dad, Reginald, says. "You two don't look old enough to be out here on your own."

"Oh, we're young, but we're in college," Andre says. "I'm eighteen and so is she."

"We took lots of AP courses," I add, which sounds really stupid.

"We actually were here on, uh, a class project," Andre says. "Extracredit summer course. Exploring the great back roads of America."

"And you're students at . . . ?" the wife asks.

"USC," Andre says quickly.

"Great school. Great football team. Nothing like Ohio State, of course." Reginald grins and half punches Andre's shoulder.

"Gotta love the Buckeyes," Andre says, nodding.

"Did we mention we'd give you some money for gas?" I add out of nowhere, smiling at the mom.

"We could take you as far as Denver," Reginald offers.

"Denver would be . . . incredible," Andre says, shaking his hand. "Thank you, sir. You have no idea how much this helps."

"A couple of road rules," his wife says after we meet the kids and grandparents, and we all step into the RV. "One, no smoking. Two, no anything else."

I nod. "Got it."

We try to find room to sit down and end up crammed onto a small bench together, facing the six kids on a sofa opposite us, grandparents on either side of us in seats. We pull out onto the road, but it's slow going. There's tons of traffic because of the marathon, which starts at eight. Streets are blocked off. We're moving so slowly that I glance out the window, wondering if I'll see my grandfather running—and passing us.

"This reminds me of a bus trip I took once," Andre says, smiling.

"Oh, I love bus trips," one of the grandfathers says.

One of the boys keeps sticking out his tongue at me, while another is making arm farts. The two girls are playing one of those clap-and-sing things that drive me crazy, and there's another boy in Spider-Man one-piece PJs, who's got his arms folded in front of him and is just staring at me. He looks about five years too old for Spider-Man PJs.

"Is this a great plan or what?" Andre asks out of the side of his mouth.

"No," I say as the camper struggles up its first hill. "Probably not."

"Well, you know what they say," the dad calls over his shoulder from the driver's seat. "You can't rush Mount Rushmore!"

Andre and I look at each other. It's like that movie *Groundhog Day*. We'll wake up every morning and go to Mount Rushmore until we change our ways.

One of the grandmothers falls asleep and, after a few minutes, rests her head on my shoulder. The other one is firing off questions at Andre, who's trying to answer them as best as he can, while he now has two of the boys in his face, attempting to arm-wrestle with him.

We go slower and slower. The engine groans. I glance out the window to see if we're actually moving at all, and I see black exhaust—or smoke—coming out from underneath the RV.

Finally Reginald pulls over, or attempts to. "Kids—folks—everybody off!" he says. "The Check Engine light is on. I'm going to refill the coolant, see if that takes care of the problem."

"Haven't we been on this bus before?" I ask Andre as we get out and stand by the side of the road—well, what's left of it, with the giant field-size vehicle pulled over. I don't know who looks or feels more pathetic—me, him, or the avocado RV.

Or maybe the boy in the Spider-Man PJs, who now has to watch dozens of cars and hundreds of people pass by, in his footed pajamas.

"Is it us, do you think? Are we a curse?" I ask Andre as Reginald works on the RV. People are honking their car horns because they have to go out into the oncoming lane to get around the giant beached whale of a camper. I think about Grandpa saying to Lenny, "You should have gone around," and if these cars don't go around, they'll probably overheat, too, and this town will grind to a halt, filled with broken-down automobiles.

"You want to kill time by writing some postcards?" Andre asks me.

"Not really," I say. I stretch my arms over my head and wonder if Mom and Zena are awake yet, if they've noticed that I'm gone and wondered where I am. "You want to learn some vocab?"

Andre shrugs. "Not particularly. And just so you know, you have ink on your stomach," he tells me.

"Really?"

"Yeah." He reaches out to show me where, and I flinch at his touch, then laugh, embarrassed.

"Oh yeah. I put a postcard there earlier," I say. "I forgot about it."

"You carry postcards on your lean little tummy. Okay." He leans forward to try to make out the words on my stomach. "Right. Okay, so, let's say this RV doesn't make it another foot. How much money do you have?"

"About forty bucks."

"What happened to the hundred?"

"I left it with my sister," I say.

Andre stares at me as if I'm the dumbest person on the planet. "Okay, who gives away a hundred bucks and then decides to run away? Who does that? Talk about a bad plan. You're undercutting yourself. Sabotaging. Derailing."

"Probably," I admit. "But I didn't want to use it. It seemed unlucky, since it came from my dad."

"For what it's worth," Andre says, "he seemed like a nice enough guy."

"He is. Or he was. He's just . . . pretty screwed up right now."

"Yeah. He seemed a little on edge. But not like terminal. Hopeless. A lost cause," says Andre.

"No? Really?" I ask.

Andre shakes his head. "You want a definition of that? You can check out *my* dad."

"But your dad's good to you."

"Sure, yeah. But he's also never going to be a big part of my life," Andre says. "I kind of realized that when I met his eighteenth girlfriend over the phone last week when I called. He spent about two minutes talking to me; then he had to go."

"Well, what did he say when you told him you were coming?" I ask.

"I didn't exactly tell him yet," Andre says. "If I called to tell him, he'd call my mom to alert her, and we'd never have gotten out the door."

"So . . . did you leave her a note?" I ask.

"Sure, of course. I put it in Cuddles's food dish. I know she'll look there," Andre says.

"What if Cuddles eats the note first?" I ask.

"Hm. I didn't think of that."

"He does like to eat paper. Pop-Tarts boxes, anyway," I remind him.

"Well, I wrote it on an actual Pop-Tart, so it should be safe," Andre jokes.

All this talk about Pop-Tarts makes me realize how hungry I am, so I reach into my bag, searching for an energy or granola bar. I usually take some extras from the continental breakfasts and stash them in my backpack. Instead of finding one, though, my fingers close around a plastic case I don't recognize, so I pull it out to see what it is.

I start smiling, then laughing. "Look." I hold up the *Oklahoma!* CD.

"Oh, man, you actually stole it?" Andre asks.

"I didn't. Didn't you?"

He shakes his head.

"Then . . . who?" But I think I know the answer to that already. The only other person we talked about this with was Grandpa. He didn't tell me that he'd taken it. He just left it for me to find. "When did he do that?" I wonder out loud.

I turn the case over in my hands, tracing the scratches in the case. The CD is so worn that it's amazing it still works. Did he want me to throw it out, I wonder, or keep it as a memento?

Either way, he's onto me, I can't help thinking. He knows I'm leaving and this is his attempt to get me back. And I hate him and I love him for it.

"You know what?" I turn to Andre and take his hands. "I think you're, like . . . the coolest person I've ever known. That I'll ever know, period."

"I feel the same about you. Otherwise I wouldn't be out here ⸢ ting carbon monoxide poisoning." He waves his hand in fr⸢ face as Reginald restarts the RV and a cloud of black s⸢

"But I still can't do this," I go on, as difficult as it is.

"You can't? Why not?"

"Because . . . this will sound really rude. Mean. Thoughtless."

"You're doing the three synonyms thing," he says.

"Oh. Sorry." I think of how much I'll miss that, how I'll probably keep doing that all year, and nobody will understand why, or that it's cool and in honor of Andre. "It's just . . . I really love spending time with you, and there's nothing more I want to do than get off that bus and away from my family for even one night. It's, like, *such* a great fantasy."

"So what's the problem?" he asks.

I think about our dysfunctional family dinner the night before. "The past year has been really hard. We've sort of had enough drama. If I take off, I'll be a little too much like my dad. He's never there anymore. Not even when he had the chance, the possibility, of taking off with me and Zena. He didn't show up. And even though my mom is not cool at all, I think I'd better not take off, too."

Andre looks at me and slides his sunglass visors up so he can get a better look. "You're serious. We've come this far. We've got a ride. And you want to go back."

"You know how nuts your mom went when Cuddles ran off? What do you think she'd do if you go missing?"

"I'm no Cuddles. I don't compete," he says.

"Shut up already. You're her favorite boy."

"No, I'm her *only* boy."

"...me thing," I say.

"...? Ariel? We're good to go," Reginald tells us. "Come on

...limbs back behind the driver's seat. His wife
...r seat, the kids and grandparents clamber
...there beside the road, not yet moving.

Reginald honks the horn, which sounds like an injured—or mating—moose must sound. The mom leans out the front window. "Kids, you coming?"

Andre narrows his eyes at her. "Did she just call us kids? Okay, I am definitely not going now." He picks up his backpack and waves at her. "We're good! Thanks!"

"You sure?"

"Yes, thanks anyway!" I call to her. "Have fun at Rushmore!"

"Good luck!" she calls back.

All the kids press their faces to the windows. One boy sticks his tongue out at me, and the two girls give us beauty-queen waves, while Spider-Man boy glares, and then gives us the finger.

"Well. We might have problems, but at least we're not in *that* family," Andre comments as they inch up the hill away from us. "Freaks."

"Totally," I agree. "So. You want to go out to breakfast or something?"

"Sure."

We walk and walk down the hill, into town, until we find a diner and sit down at a booth. I open the menu, wanting to order something big and hearty like an omelet and pancakes, except here they're called "flapjacks," which makes me laugh so hard that Andre nearly calls for a defibrillator.

"Flapjack," I explain. "It's like . . ." I find that I can't explain it, but I'll have to just buy a postcard of the place, so that I remember.

I meet Uncle Jeff at the fun run start line at noon, while Andre heads to the finish line.

"Ariel!" Uncle Jeff says when he sees me approaching. "You scared us half to death. Where on earth did you go?"

"Andre and I went on a, uh, hike. My dad's not around by any chance, is he?" I ask, eager to change the subject of Andre when Uncle Jeff is around, for obvious reasons. It's not every day your uncle sees you making out with a guy on the ground. And it shouldn't be.

Uncle Jeff shrugs. "Haven't seen him."

"Huh." I'm not surprised, but I wish the news were different. I stretch my muscles and look for a place to stash my backpack so it'll be safe. I decide to just wear it, so I don't lose anything. "Hey, Uncle Jeff. Do you ever read people's postcards?" I ask as we count down the last minute before the run.

"Oh no, of course not, that would be unethical," Uncle Jeff says, as if he's never done anything unethical, like, for instance, try to kill an innocent squirrel. "Anyway, I don't look at every individual piece of mail; it's in a presorted stack. On the other hand, if it looks interesting and I want to know what the picture is, I look at the back, and sometimes, well . . ."

"You can't help but read it," I say.

"Maybe. But usually I don't have time, and to be honest I don't care," he says. "Postcards are short and usually boring. Where it gets interesting is certified mail." He bends down, stretching his hamstrings. "So, how do you think I'll do?"

"You'll do great," I say. "You've trained and you're ready. Pretty much. Plus it's a fun run, so it's not exactly like a race, you know?"

"But I have one question. What's fun about running when it's a hundred degrees?"

I smile. "Feeling the accomplishment. The sweat. The journey." I shrug. "Things of that nature."

"Exactamundo," Uncle Jeff says. And he laughs. "Don't you hate it when Lenny says that all the time?"

"Hey, you got sneakers," I say, pointing at his feet. "When did you get those?"

"Last night. What do you think of them?"

"Well, the most important thing is, how do they feel?"

He twirls his right foot in a circle. "They feel fantastic, but what do I know?"

"Fantasterrific," I correct him.

Uncle Jeff looks at me like he's never heard that word before. As if I'm making it up or something.

"They look great," I say instead.

"I think so too," he says.

As we line up and start running along the course, I notice my grandmother in a bright lilac tracksuit holding up a big sign that says, GO, ARIEL!

We go a little farther and I see Mom in her new Mount Rushmore T-shirt, and I don't know if I should tell her that a woman as big as she is shouldn't wear a T-shirt with mountains printed over her breasts.

And if she does, she definitely shouldn't jump up and down and cheer.

Grandpa's at the finish line, waiting for us. He congratulates Uncle Jeff, but for once he doesn't look happy to see me. "Where were you? I had to run the half marathon alone." He glances over at Andre, who's nearby in the crowd, headed our way, and doesn't look thrilled to see him, either. Andre takes the hint and veers off toward the Gatorade tent.

"You survived okay?" I ask.

"Sure. But there was no one to talk to or help pace me. Just a bunch of young idiots obsessed with their splits," he complains.

"How'd you do?"

He frowns. "Second in my age group. Some ringer from Sioux Falls beat me. So. You still leaving?" he asks. "Or did you just come back to say good-bye?" He's hurt, and I'm surprised that he shows it.

I pull out the *Oklahoma!* CD. "How did you know that was my bag, and why it was outside?"

"As I think I've said before, being head of this family is a full-time job. I was out for an early-morning run, of course. A warm-up. I saw it sitting on the balcony. I figured you were up to something."

"So how did you get this?" I ask him.

He slips on his warm-up jacket. "I have ways."

He's not a hugger, but I hug him anyway. He doesn't seem to mind, but his body doesn't give, either; it's kind of like hugging a surfboard.

Grandpa pats my shoulder. "Here comes Lenny. For God's sake, put away that CD, or it'll be 'Oh, What a Beautiful Mornin'' all the way back to Sioux Falls. And by the way? You owe me a half marathon."

Mom's waiting for me when I get back to the motel to change. She's sitting on the bed with a notebook, writing.

"You probably have something to tell me," I say as I close the door behind me. I toss my backpack onto the bed and go over to my suitcase to get out some clean clothes. I can't wait to take a shower.

"Actually, that's what *I* was going to say. What happened to you?" Mom asks.

I turn to face her. "Should I tell you everything, or just the important stuff?"

"Tell me everything," she says sternly. "I'll decide what's important."

I sigh. "Would you settle for the Clairol highlights?"

"Okay." She closes the notebook and sets it on the bedside table.

I sink down on the bed beside her. "Andre and I went out for breakfast and a walk. I figured out some stuff. Here I am."

She watches me carefully, trying to interpret my condensed version of things. "That's it?"

I think about the last few hours. Someday I'll tell her all the details, and it'll be hilarious, but not now. "We also rode in an RV for about twelve feet. With a huge family and a bunch of obnoxious kids."

She nods, considering whether that's a felony or not. "Is *that* it?" she asks.

"Yup. Oh, and some guys in a car tried to hit on me. It was a drive-by type thing."

She lets out her breath and runs her hand through her brown-gray-blond hair. "I can't *wait* for this trip to be over."

I smile, amused by the turn of events. "So, what happened with Dad? Did he ever show up?"

"Not exactly," she says. "This was taped to our room door this morning when we headed out for the day." She reaches into the notebook and pulls out a postcard. "Go ahead; read it."

"We hold these truths to be self-evident, that all men are created equal, that they are endowed by their Creator with certain unalienable rights, that among these are Life, Liberty, and the Pursuit of Happiness."

—One of the granite giants of Mount Rushmore, Thomas Jefferson (second from left)

Tamara, Ariel, & Zena,

It was great to see you guys. Sorry I had to take off, but things weren't really working out.

I'm sorry I let you guys down. It seems like I can't stop doing that. I'm trying, you know? But not exactly succeeding. Yet.

I hope sometime, like next summer, I'll have things figured out for sure, and we can hit the road (but not the toad) together again.

See you when we all get home.

Love,
Dad

Chapter Twenty-one

Three days later, we stand outside in the Leisure-Lee world headquarters parking lot. Lenny keeps pulling suitcases and bags out of the bus, like a whale's belly being emptied.

Everyone looks sort of bereft, exhausted, disoriented, like they've lost something on the road somewhere and they don't know what it was or when it happened.

Jenny bursts out of the office and runs to Lenny, who hugs her and twirls her around in the air.

"I knew you'd be here. Happens every time," Lenny explains to the curious crowd. "Midsummer. We just can't make it."

"It's only June," Zena says out of the corner of her mouth.

Mom gives them her card. "Call me. I do phone sessions."

"Phone sex? You?" Ethel asks.

"*Therapy* sessions, over the phone," Mom explains.

"Oh. I didn't know you could do that."

"What's that?" someone else asks.

"Sex therapy. On the phone," Ethel says.

Mom throws up her hands. "Anyway. If you're interested in growing your relationship, sowing the seeds for future peace and happiness, call me. Heck, I'll send you some of my books for free."

Lenny, Jenny, and Lee say their good-byes and take off for the building to get ready for the next Leisure-Lee adventure. The rest of us are dealing with posttraumatic bus disorder.

My grandfather is sitting on his suitcase, rubbing his calves. "So what do you think? Are you ready for the season?" he asks me.

"Not yet. Not even close," I say. "For one thing, it's going to take another week for my legs to unfurl."

Unfurl? I have got to stop reading Andre's vocabulary book.

"But I've still got two months to be totally ready," I say. "What about you? Going to sign up for another marathon?"

"Maybe. But I think I'm probably going back to work," my grandfather says.

"I think that's probably a good idea," I say, nodding.

"You could tell, huh?"

"I think I'm going back to work too," Uncle Jeff announces. "The vacation days are gone. The holiday's been had. Party's over."

He's doing it too, saying things in threes. We probably all need to be moving on at this point, because we're turning cultish.

"It's like Lee said. If you don't work, you don't get vacation," Uncle Jeff says.

"How profound." Grandma rolls her eyes.

"Maybe you should get a driving route," my grandfather suggests. "You'd have a roof over your head."

Uncle Jeff laughs. "Right. That might be good. But I wouldn't get the exercise I need. Plus I enjoy talking with the people, being out in all kinds of weather, and things of that nature."

My grandmother comes over and stands beside me. "The nice thing is that we don't have to say good-bye. You'll be coming to our house tonight."

"But I really want to see Gloves," I say. "I'm sorry; I hate to admit that."

"She'll be okay. She'll be fine," Grandma says. "But I know what you mean. I really miss our cat, too."

"You do? But you never said anything."

"I don't believe in talking about everything, but it doesn't mean I don't have feelings."

"Right." I smile at her, thinking about her blowup at the restaurant the other night, when everyone melted down.

"Maybe you guys want to split up, ride with us," she suggests.

"Mm, okay," I say. "Well, I don't know. Is that okay with you guys?" I ask Mom and Zena.

"Yes, I get the front seat!" Zena cries, so I guess it's okay with her.

Mom and Zena are hugging Uncle Jeff good-bye, so I walk over to the Coke machine because my throat is parched. Andre comes over to say good-bye. I've been dreading this moment for the past couple of days, and even hoping the second bus would break down so we could spend more time together.

"You're the best person I've ever almost been a runaway with," he begins.

I slide two dollar bills into the pop machine, stand back, and look at my selections. "Is that all you can say?"

"This trip would have been nothing without you. I'd have taken off for sure. Day one. Rest area. Thumbed a ride."

"Been dead by now."

"Exactly," he says.

I choose an orange soda, but when I press the button, the

machine drops a bottle of strawberry milk instead. "What *is* this?"
I ask him, turning the bottle over in my hand. "Who even drinks
strawberry milk?"

"I haven't had that since I was two," he says. "Just open it and
drink it."

So I have a few sips and hand the bottle to him, and he has a few
sips.

"Do you have three words for this?" I ask.

He pauses for a second. "Sucky. Lousy. Pretty much undrinkable."

"Exactly." I stand there, not wanting to leave or say something
stupid that he'll remember as my last, stupid words.

"So, like. We should stay in touch," he says.

"We should," I agree.

"And I think I know how. You can send me bad postcards," says
Andre.

"Okay," I say, nodding, and then I'm crying. Because I always cry
at times like this. It's a yearbook-signing-type moment, saying good-
bye. I hate saying good-bye. I don't know what to say, what to write.

My whole life is up in the air, sort of, and unless we move to
Chicago instead of St. Paul, I probably won't see Andre much more
in my life. I hate thinking that.

"But I don't know about the whole romance thing," Andre says.

"Yeah. Me neither," I say. "I hate to say that. But I guess it seems
kind of unrealistic."

"Totally," he agrees.

"Absolutely. Definitely," I add. "Not realistic."

"But since when are we into 'realistic'?" Andre asks. "Anyway, we
could visit each other. I think there's this bus tour of Chicago you
could take."

"Very funny," I say.

"I thought so. And in the meantime, you know. We're going to have to live on, like, memories. So we'd better have a good Leisure-Lee one to remember." And he kisses me so I back up against the Coke machine and drop the strawberry milk. I hug Andre one last time.

"Come on, Ariel—time to go!" Grandma says, and we break apart, which takes some effort.

Andre and I hold hands until we can't any longer, and then he says, "See you," and wanders across the parking lot to his car.

I turn around to see Bethany and Zena hugging Dieter and Wolfgang, which almost sort of takes something away from my moment, but not quite, because they're never going to have the kind of devastatingly hot kiss Andre and I just had.

Or at least, I hope not, until Zena gets a little older.

When I go over to the car, Grandpa is still trying to fit everything into the trunk. "I can't fit all your shoe boxes into the car, Jeffrey. Did you have to buy so many shoes on the trip? Jeez."

"Did you see how many sweatshirts Tamara bought?" Uncle Jeff points out, as if they're still twelve and ten.

"Yes, but I'm not trying to fit them all in my car," says Grandpa.

"It's genetic. I brought eight pairs myself," I say to Uncle Jeff.

"Really?" Uncle Jeff's eyes light up.

We start to get into the car, but I suddenly remember something I've been meaning to do. "Wait—I almost forgot something. I'll be right back."

I run back to the bus and leave the *Oklahoma!* CD on the steps. I wouldn't want to deprive the next Leisure-Lee guests.

Leisure-Lee Tours: Weekly Departures from Sioux Falls.

When life gives you vacation, take it!

Because when you're driving, you miss the small stuff.

Because you can't rush Mount Rushmore.

Andre,

We're heading home now, or maybe to our new home. Anyway. Crossing Minnesota at the speed of light.

The sky is clear. Cloudless. Beautiful.

Azure.

Think of three more and write me back.

I miss you.

But I don't know how much that counts, because at this point, I even miss Lenny.

Pathetically perambulating,

Ariel

Turn the page for a peek at Catherine Clark's

Eleven Things
I Promised

CATHERINE CLARK

I was trying on a ridiculous prom dress when the call came.

I didn't even want to go to junior prom, but Stella was insisting. At the moment I was thinking of picking up a shift at McDonald's instead, just to *avoid* it, because I don't feel all that attractive in sequins and tight, fitted tube tops and flouncy things.

Those were the styles I was seeing at Flanberger's, my only retail option. If I planned on buying anything online, I'd need my mom's credit card and would have to explain why I wasn't going with Oscar and listen to her say, "It's such a shame you two aren't together anymore," for the thousandth time. (For the record, Oscar was a dirtbag, who I'd dumped after I found out he was cheating on me, like, a lot.) The concept of breaking up was somehow foreign to her, which was odd considering she'd been divorced eight years already.

Over the past week I'd become as determined as Stella to go to prom, no matter how uncomfortable it made me. Prom was a thing juniors did, whether they'd recently dumped dirtbags or not. Stella had decided she was going, that this was a thing we needed to do. Prom was the week after this big bike trip we'd signed up for—the Cure Childhood Cancer Ride—another event Stella had decided we'd do together. Of course, she was a real cyclist. I wasn't. She'd done the same ride spring of sophomore year. I hadn't.

But despite the challenges of riding so far, I couldn't wait to take off on a trip with Stella.

"We'll hit the road for a week, then we'll hit up prom. It's going to be a-mazing," she'd said as she laid out the plan in February. She was even planning to ride her bike to prom. She had it all mapped out.

She'd started outdoor training in March, as soon as the snow thawed. I hadn't. And I should have been out riding that late April afternoon with her, instead of trying to find a dress at Flanberger's. I guess I wasn't all that committed to the ride yet. I had three weeks before we left, and I knew it was time to get serious about it. Still, here I was, dress shopping. I guess I figured Stella would pull me through the ride, the way she did with most things.

Also? Sometimes I think I was put on this earth to procrastinate.

Stella had ordered her prom dress a month ago and it was hanging in her closet.

I needed to catch up on all fronts, which is typical for me. But I had to try, because did I really want to take orders from people when they waltzed in between prom and after-prom? Would you like fries with your date? What if Oscar came in with what's her name, or what're *their* names? He would, too. He'd be clueless like that because he had no actual feelings.

Meanwhile, I'd be like Cinderella.

Literally. Sometimes I do have to mop.

No, I wasn't working prom night. I'd get a dress if it killed me, and Stella and I would go together.

"That one won't go with a rose corsage," the salesclerk, Phyllis, told me, standing back to get a good luck at the short, flowered, sequined purple dress I was currently swathed in. "Trust me."

"I don't think I'm getting a rose corsage," I said. "Trust *me*."

"Boys don't think creatively about flowers." Phyllis sounded a bit world-weary all of a sudden. "You'll be getting a rose."

"No one's doing corsages this year. We're not allowed

to have the pins," I told her, not going into detail about the fact that I didn't have a guy for a date.

When Phyllis gave me a puzzled look, I added, "Potential weapons or something. They don't trust us."

"They're determined to kill prom. In my day, prom was important," Phyllis muttered. She pulled more dresses off the racks and skittered back to the dressing room with an armful. I followed her in a daze. It was like being on a Ferris wheel that you really, really wanted to get off of, but you couldn't get the attention of the ride operator to make it stop.

"Phyllis?" I murmured. "I think I need to take a break. Phyllis?"

She wasn't listening. I closed the door and prepared to change back into my own clothes.

No sooner had I started than Phyllis rapped on the door and gently threw *another* dress over the top. "Try the peach beauty on this instant," she commanded. "It will transform you."

The dress was an elaborate floor-length gown with layer upon layer of ruffles. Unfortunately, real ruffles, and not the potato chips.

No way was I wearing this, not even in a dressing room. What if there was a tornado that knocked down the entire store and I was discovered in a heap of debris with *this* thing on? Okay, so maybe tornadoes are rare in New Hampshire, but you couldn't be too careful. "No, I think I'm done," I told her. "I need to get going—"

"*Don't* walk away from this beauty," Phyllis insisted. "If you do, you'll regret it for the rest of your life. There's an old saying in women's wear. 'To peach her own.' It's a magical color."

So, now we were diving into the realm of magic. I was starting to think Phyllis needed to retire. But to humor her, I slipped out of my jeans again and pulled the dress on over my tee, not willing to commit to a full try-on. I looked at the angled neckline and how it framed my slightly round face. Something about the color did work—it wasn't one I usually wore, but it did look good against my skin.

Hold on a second. What was I thinking? The notoriously overheated Flanberger's was getting to me. *Get ahold of yourself. Those waves of fabric make you look like a curtain in a country-western furniture showroom.*

My phone rang, and I slipped it out of my purse. Stella's dad? Why was he calling? "Hello?" I said.

There was a cough, an awkward throat-clearing on the other end. "Frances, it's David Grant. Stella's been in an accident. A fairly serious accident. I wanted you to know right away."

"What—where? She . . . ?" I was already tucking my

purse under my arm, lifting the latch on the changing-room door.

"The ambulance is taking her to Mercy Regional," Stella's father said. "We'll meet you there."

I shoved the phone in my purse and started pulling the dress over my head. The zipper was stuck and I couldn't get the dress off. I heard a slight tear and stopped pulling. I just grabbed my shoes, jeans, and purse and ran out of the store, past Phyllis, past the checkout, straight out into the parking lot.

At the hospital I sat beside Stella's brother, Mason. He told me she'd been on Old Route 91, out by the dairy farms where the road dips and curves. "Roller Coaster Road" was what I used to call it when I was little, and I'd scream with delight as my dad floored it to go up a steep hill and then zoom down the other side.

"So . . . who was it? Or was it a hit-and-run?"

"A woman driving a minivan hit her," Mason said. "She had two kids in the back. She called nine-one-one right away, so that's good, but . . . I don't know. I have a pretty bad feeling. Car versus bike—it's never good. What if Stella . . . you know." His voice seemed to cut out, like a lawn mower that lost its choke. He ran his hands back and forth through his short dark-brown hair, which was sticking out in various directions.

"Don't think that," I said. "She's going to be okay." I had no reason to say that, nothing to base it on, but he needed to hear it. So did I.

We'd been sitting in the waiting room together for ten minutes, and we knew Stella was conscious and being treated for pain, and she had some leg and internal injuries. That was all we knew, and it was bad enough.

We'd made small talk about Stella, the ride, Mason's freshman year at Granite State College, my stupid peach dress. The minutes were wearing on us.

Mason kept bouncing his legs up and down in a very nervous way, like he wanted to run out. Maybe he did that all the time, but if he did, I'd forgotten. I felt just as jittery. I was tapping my fingers against the chair in almost exactly the same rhythm. We were a terrible ER mariachi group. The Jitterers.

Stella's parents had been in the exam room with her ever since I'd gotten here. I'd raced through the automatic double doors in the peach chiffon nightmare of a dress. I'd planned to change when I got here but somehow misplaced my jeans between Flanberger's and Mercy. I felt so self-conscious sitting next to Mason. If it was going to take another twenty minutes until I could see Stella, then I should go find the pants.

These were the dumb things I was thinking about while I sat there on that hard red plastic seat beside Mason. It was easier to think about that than about why we were here and what was happening . . . what might be happening.

All of a sudden Mason's expression tightened. I heard footsteps in the empty hallway, coming closer. I stood up, my stomach turning somersaults, my palms sweating. A female doctor in a white coat was walking toward us, beside Stella's parents. The doctor wasn't smiling. Nobody was smiling. I wasn't breathing.

"Mom?" asked Mason. "Say something, please. Somebody."

"Stella is resting now, and she's holding her own," said the doctor. "We've stopped the blood loss and we've made her comfortable."

It sounded like something I'd heard on my mom's favorite medical drama. To my mind, "making someone comfortable" meant giving up on them—it was the horrible thing the vet had said just before he put our dog to sleep six months ago.

"We're admitting her and moving her upstairs," the doctor continued. "There are still a lot of things to sort out. She'll need some surgeries right away. . . ."

Surgeries . . . plural? She kept talking, but I somehow stopped listening. It felt like I was standing under a shower that only sprayed bad news. *Bad news. Rinse. Repeat. Bad news.* The doctor was mentioning the broken bones, the stitches on Stella's arm, how her face was bruised but was really better than it looked.

"So, can we see her now?" I asked.

"Please. I wish you would." Stella's mom put her hand on Mason's arm, which was saying a lot. Their family didn't hug much. It was just the way they were. Stella and I weren't huggers, either. We knew we were close. We didn't have to make a show of it, the way other girls ran around hugging like they hadn't seen each other for weeks when actually it was forty-five minutes between trig and chemistry.

"Stella needs to rest right now," said the doctor. "So please keep your visits short. They'll be moving her upstairs, out of ER, as quickly as it can be arranged." She nodded at Stella's parents. "I'll check in with you shortly." She strode off back down the hallway.

Mr. Grant held Mason in his gaze for a second. "You two can go visit now. I know you won't say anything upsetting, Frances. But Mason . . . just don't tell her how bad she looks. She does look pretty bad, and I know you guys always tease each other. But don't this time. Just don't."

"Right. Got it." Mason nodded, and I followed him down the hall to the exam room. "Like I'd say something right now," he muttered to me. "I mean, seriously."

"I know. You—you wouldn't." He was a very decent guy, considering he'd once gotten a video of me falling off a trampoline and shared it with the entire world. "You want to go first?" I asked him. "Or you want to go in together?"

"Actually . . . I need a drink of water first. You go ahead on your own."

I wished he hadn't said that. I didn't feel brave enough to go in by myself. "I can wait for you," I said.

"No. You go ahead. I'll be there in a minute." He looked pale and slightly ill. He had a history of puking when his family was hurt—like when Stella cut her foot on a nail in the driveway when she was five, or when their older brother dislocated his ankle doing a skateboard trick. It was almost sort of cute, or would be if it didn't involve throwing up. I decided not to push him.

When I walked into Stella's hospital room, I felt a wave of anxiety nearly knock me over. The floor was wobbly. My legs were shaking. I wished Mason had come in beside me so I'd have someone to fall onto.

I surveyed the room, not wanting to look at Stella, which was crazy. I had to look, had to go comfort her. I was scared out of my mind. Her hands were wrapped in gauze, and her elbow was taped. She had one long, bright-red scrape on her chin, covered in ointment—it was stitches, I saw as I got closer. She had tons of small wounds on her face, probably gravel driven into her skin. Her blue eyes looked glassy, and at the same time, washed out.

I took a moment to compose myself. The last thing she needed was to see me freak out. She was going to be fine. She was banged up, sure, and she'd be on crutches for a while, but she was going to be okay.

"You look terrible," I suddenly blurted.

"Thanks," she muttered.

"I'm sorry, Stells. I'm really sorry I said that." Oh God. Why was I such an idiot at times? "I guess . . . it's a law for best friends to be honest, isn't it? Plus, I kind of panicked."

Stella took a long, slow breath and winced. "In that case," she said slowly, "that dress is hideous."

"I know, right? I was trying on prom dresses when your dad called and—anyway, how are you feeling?"

"I can't feel anything, actually," she said. "I guess I'm drugged up on painkillers."

"I'm sorry. I'm so sorry about what happened," I said.

"Quit saying sorry," she said. "It was fun while it lasted. We were going to prom. We were going to do the Cure Ride. And now nothing," she said in a flat voice.

"Don't say *nothing*! We can still go to prom, we can still . . ." My voice trailed off. "Do lots of things." I perched on a chair beside the bed. She looked exhausted, with dark lines under her eyes, as if she hadn't slept in a few days.

Bedsheets and white blankets covered her midsection, but tubes ran underneath the covers, connected to monitors, making clicking noises periodically with her vital signs.

She was pulling at a thread on the top blanket. "They gave me this stupid warming blanket," she said, "like it'll help." Tears trickled out the sides of her eyes. I grabbed a tissue and started to hand it to her, then realized she wasn't up to using her arms much. I'd need to do the work. I dabbed at the tears rolling down her cheeks. This was such a backward situation. She never cried. She was usually the one who handed *me* Kleenex. I fell apart at sad movies and pet stores and random other places.

Stella fiddled with the plastic hospital ID bracelet on her left wrist. When her fingers touched the IV tube in the back of her hand, she pulled her hand away. "I hate these things."

"I've never had one," I said. "Does it hurt?"

"Not exactly. More like it feels like you're trapped." We both contemplated that for a minute, me staring at her pinched skin, the heavy tape and plastic tube, and her looking anywhere but her hand. I looked up at the liquid dripping down the tube from a couple of plastic pouches, pulsing into her.

The door opened behind us, and I glanced over my shoulder to see Mrs. Grant walk in. Stella's mom walked over and laid her hand on my shoulder. "Franny, do you think you could go to our house and pack a bag for Stella? You'd know what she wants, and that way, we can stay here."

"Sure—sure, I'll do that. No problem." I knew they were probably trying to get rid of me for a while, and though it made me feel guilty to think this way, there was a part of me that was all right taking a break. Stella looked so unlike herself. It was almost as if I didn't know this Stella. I jumped up and started for the door, then turned back to take a last glance at Stella. "I'll be back later, okay?"

She didn't answer. I wasn't sure if she was asleep or if she just didn't hear me.

I headed out into the hallway and nearly bumped into Mason. He was holding a bundle of blue fabric.

"These jeans belong to you? I found them in the parking lot."

I couldn't respond.

"You said . . . you lost them? I went outside to get some fresh air by my truck and, well. I saw these crumpled on the pavement like someone dropped them."

The floor seemed to fall away underneath me, and I felt like I was losing my balance, plunging, arms outstretched, reaching for the ground as if I were in an elevator that was crashing.

"You don't look good." Mason grabbed onto my waist, forcing me to lean against him. "You feeling all right?"

"Not . . ." I couldn't find the words. I couldn't figure out what to do. I knew I should sit down, but I didn't know where to find a chair.

He took my arm and guided me to a chair by the nurses' station. "Sit down for a minute. Sit right here. Head down, Franny. Breathe slowly."

I leaned over, head between my legs, eyes facing the shiny hospital floor. I hugged the jeans as if they were my favorite blanket. My warming blanket.

"Come on, Frances. It's going to be okay." Mason crouched down beside me and rubbed my back once or twice.

Easy for him to say. He hadn't seen her yet.

How far would you go for a friend?

Frances has one week to complete the Fix-It List—a secret bucket list her best friend created. But as each item opens Frances up to new adventures and romance, it becomes more difficult for her to keep the most important promise of all.

The Summer That Changed Everything

How to Meet Boys

CATHERINE CLARK

For best friends Lucy and Mikayla, summer at the lake was
supposed to be perfect. But when Jackson, the boy who broke
Lucy's heart, meets Mikayla and sparks fly, the girls wonder
if this summer to remember is one they'd rather forget.

HARPER TEEN
An Imprint of HarperCollinsPublishers

www.epicreads.com